A PLUME BOOK

THE GENESIS SECRET

TOM KNOX is the pseudonym for the English journalist and writer Sean Thomas.

TOM KNOX

THE GENESIS SECRET

A PLUME BOOK

PLUME
Published by the Penguin Group
Penguin Group (USA) Inc., 375 Hudson Street, New York, New York 10014, U.S.A.
Penguin Group (Canada), 90 Eglinton Avenue East, Suite 700, Toronto, Ontario,
Canada M4P 2Y3 (a division of Pearson Penguin Canada Inc.)
Penguin Books Ltd., 80 Strand, London WC2R 0RL, England
Penguin Ireland, 25 St. Stephen's Green, Dublin 2, Ireland (a division of Penguin Books Ltd.)
Penguin Group (Australia), 250 Camberwell Road, Camberwell, Victoria 3124, Australia
(a division of Pearson Australia Group Pty. Ltd.)
Penguin Books India Pvt. Ltd., 11 Community Centre, Panchsheel Park,
New Delhi – 110 017, India
Penguin Group (NZ), 67 Apollo Drive, Rosedale, North Shore 0632, New Zealand
(a division of Pearson New Zealand Ltd.)
Penguin Books (South Africa) (Pty.) Ltd., 24 Sturdee Avenue, Rosebank, Johannesburg 2196,
South Africa
Penguin Books Ltd., Registered Offices: 80 Strand, London WC2R 0RL, England

Published by Plume, a member of Penguin Group (USA) Inc. Previously published in a Viking edition.

First Plume Printing, May 2010
10 9 8 7 6 5 4 3

 REGISTERED TRADEMARK—MARCA REGISTRADA

The Library of Congress has catalogued the Viking edition as follows:

Knox. Tom, 1963-
The Genesis secret: a novel / Tom Knox.
p. cm.
ISBN 978-0-670-02088-1 (hc.)
ISBN 978-0-452-29633-6 (pbk.)
1. Journalists—Fiction. 2. Excavations (Archaeology)—Turkey—Fiction. 3. Bible—History of contemporary events—Fiction. I. Title.
PR6070.H6555G46 2009
823'.914—dc22

Printed in the United States of America

PUBLISHER'S NOTE
This is a work of fiction. Names, characters, places, and incidents are either the product of the author's imagination or are used fictitiously, and any resemblance to actual persons, living or dead, business establishments, events, or locales is entirely coincidental.

Author's Note

The Genesis Secret is a work of fiction. However, most of the religious, historical, and archaeological references are entirely factual and accurate.

In particular:
Gobekli Tepe (pronounced *Go-beckly Tepp-ay*) is an archaeological site maybe twelve thousand years old presently being unearthed in southeast Turkey, near the city of Sanliurfa. The entire complex of stones, pillars and carvings was deliberately buried in 8000 BC. No one knows why.

In the region surrounding Gobekli Tepe, amongst the Kurds of southern Turkey and northern Iraq, there exists a group of ancient religions known as the Cult of Angels. Some of these cultists worship a god called Melek Taus.

Acknowledgements

I would like to thank Klaus Schmidt and the rest of the German Archaeological Institute at Gobekli Tepe; my editors and colleagues Ed Grenby, David Sutton, Andrew Collins and Bob Cowan; everyone at William Morris London – in particular my agent, Eugenie Furniss; and Jane Johnson from HarperCollins UK and Josh Kendall from Viking Penguin USA.

I would also like to thank my daughter Lucy – for still recognizing me, after I disappeared for several months to write this book.

And Abraham stretched forth his hand, and took the knife to slay his son.

—Genesis, 22:10

1

Alan Greening was drunk. He'd been boozing all night in Covent Garden: starting at the Punch, where he had three or four pints with his old friends from college. Then they'd gone to the Lamb and Flag, the pub down that dank alleyway near the Garrick Club.

How long had they lingered there, sinking beers? He couldn't remember. Because after that they'd gone to the Roundhouse, and they'd met a couple more guys from his office. And at some point the lads had moved from pints of lager to shorts: vodka shots, gin and tonics, whisky chasers.

And then they had made the fatal error. Tony had said, *let's go and look at some girls.* So they'd laughed and agreed and ambled halfway up St Martin's Lane and bribed their way into Stringfellows. The bouncer hadn't been keen on letting them in, not at first: he was wary of six young guys, obviously out on the lash, swearing and laughing, and way too boisterous.

Trouble.

But Tony had flashed some of his ample City bonus, a hundred quid or more, and the bouncer had smiled and said, *Of course, sir . . .* and then . . .

What had happened *then*?

It was all a blur. A blur of thongs and thighs and drinks. And smiling naked Latvian girls and ribald jokes about Russian furs and a Polish girl with unbelievable breasts and endless amounts of money spent on this and that and the other.

Alan groaned. His friends had departed at various times: collapsing out of the club and into taxis. In the end it was just him, the last punter in the joint, tucking multitudes of tenners into the G-string of the Latvian girl who gyrated her tiny little body as he stared at her helplessly, worshipfully, dumbly, idiotically.

And then at 4 a.m. the Latvian girl had stopped smiling and suddenly the lights were up and then the bouncers had him by the shoulders and they were firmly escorting him to the door. He wasn't quite thrown into the street like a bum in a saloon, in an old-fashioned western – but it was pretty close.

And now it was 5 a.m., and the first throb of the hangover was needling him behind the eyes; he had to get home. He was on the Strand and he needed to be in bed.

Did he have enough cash left for a taxi? He'd left his cards at home but, yes – Alan sorted groggily through his pockets – yes, he still had thirty quid left in his wallet; enough for a cab to Clapham.

Or rather, it should have been enough. But there were no taxis. It was the deadest hour of the night: 5 a.m. on the Strand. Too late for clubbers. Too early for office cleaners.

Alan scanned the streets. A mild April drizzle was falling on the shiny wide pavements of central London. A big red night bus was trundling the wrong way – towards St Paul's. Where could he go? He fought through the boozy fog in his head. There was one place you could always get a cab. He could try Embankment. Yes. There were always taxis there.

Collecting himself, he turned left: down a side road. The sign said Craven Street, and he'd never heard of it. But that didn't matter. The road headed downhill towards the river: it must take him directly onto Embankment.

Alan walked on. The street was old: lots of serene Georgian buildings. The drizzle was still falling. The first hint of a spring morning was bluing the sky above the ancient chimney tops. There wasn't a soul around.

And then he heard it.

A noise.

But not just a noise. It sounded like: a *groan*. A human groan: but somehow clogged, or distorted. Weird.

Had he imagined it? Alan checked the pavements, the doorways, the windows. The little side street was still deserted. All the buildings around here were offices. Or very old houses converted into offices. Who could be here at this time of night? A junkie? A homeless guy? Was it some old drunk, lying in a gutter, down there in the shadows?

Alan opted to ignore it. That's what you did if you were a Londoner. You *ignored*. Your life was hassled enough in this huge, frenetic, and bewildering city without adding to your daily stress by investigating odd groans at night. And besides, Alan was drunk: he was imagining it.

And then he heard it again: distinct. A terrible chilling moan of someone in pain. It almost sounded like someone saying 'help'. Except the word came out as '*eeeeelllbbbb*'.

What *the fuck* was *that*? Alan sweated. He was scared now. He didn't want to know what kind of person – what kind of *thing* – could make a sound like that. And yet he had to find out. All his moral reflexes were telling him to help.

As he stood in the gentle rain he thought of his mum. What she would say. She would tell him he had no choice. It was the moral imperative: Someone Is In Pain: Therefore You Help.

He looked left. The voice seemed to come from a row of old Georgian houses with dark purple bricks and elegant old windows. One of the houses had a sign up at the front, a wooden placard shining with rain in the lamplight. *The Benjamin Franklin Museum*. He had no proper idea who Benjamin Franklin was. Some Yank; a writer or something. But that didn't really matter. He was fairly sure the moan was coming from this house: *because the door was open.* At 5 a.m., on a Saturday morning.

Alan could see a dim light beyond the half-open door. He clenched his fists once, then twice. Then he went to the door, and pushed.

It swung wholly open. The hall beyond was quiet. There was a till in the corner, a table stacked with leaflets; and a sign that read: *Video Presentation This Way.* The hall was illuminated, barely, by some night-lights.

The museum seemed undisturbed. The door was open but the interior was perfectly still. It didn't look like the scene of a robbery.

'*Errrrlmmng . . .*'

There it was again. The curdling groan. And this time it was plainly apparent where it came from: the basement.

Alan felt the talons of fear grasp his heart. But he stifled his nerves, and walked determinedly to the end of the hall, where a side door led to some descending wooden stairs. Alan creaked his way down them, and stepped into a low cellar room.

A bare bulb hung from the ceiling. The light was soft, but bright enough. He gazed about. The room was unexceptional – apart from one thing. A corner of the floor had been recently and comprehensively dug up, the earth was turned over – to leave a big black hole going down a metre or more into the dark London soil.

It was then that Alan saw the blood.

He couldn't *not* notice it: the big sticky stain was vivid and scarlet, and spattered over something very white. A pile of whiteness.

What was this whiteness? Feathers? Swan feathers? *What?*

Alan walked over and prodded the whiteness with the toe of his shoe. It was *hair*: human hair maybe. A pile of shaved white human hair. And the blood was spattered luridly across the top, like cherry sauce on lemon sorbet. Like a sheep's miscarriage in the snow.

'*Errrllllbbbbb!*'

The groan was very close now. It was coming from the room next door. Alan fought back his fears one last time and went through the small, low-slung door that led to the next room.

Inside, it was very black, apart from the narrow slant of light thrown by the bulb behind him. The ominous moan reverberated around the room. Fumbling to the side of the door, Alan slapped at the switch and flooded the room with brightness.

In the centre of the room, on the floor, lay a naked old man. His head had been completely shaved. Brutally shaved – judging by the grazes and cuts. Alan realized that that was where the hair must have come from. They had shaved his hair. Whoever *they* were.

Then the old man moved. His face had been averted from the door, but when the lights came on he turned and looked at Alan. The sight was unnerving. Alan flinched. The terror in the old man's eyes was unspeakable. Wide and red, his eyes stared out, frenzied with pain.

The earlier drunkenness had gone: Alan now felt queasily sober. He could see why the man was in agony. His chest was cut with marks, slashed with a knife. A design had been carved into his soft, old, wrinkled white skin.

And why was he groaning so weirdly? So incoherently? The man moaned again. And Alan wobbled with faintness.

The man's mouth was abrim with blood. Blood oozed from his mouth, as if he had gorged himself on strawberries. Red blood was oiling down from his elderly lips, dripping onto the floor. When he moaned, more blood bubbled and gurgled, splattering his chin with gore.

And there was one final horror.

The man was holding something in his hand. Slowly, he opened the hand, and mutely extended it: as if he was kindly offering something. A gift.

Alan looked down at the extended fingers.

Clutched limply in the hand was a severed human tongue.

2

Carmel Market was busy. Full of Yemenite spice merchants arguing with Canadian Zionists, Israeli housewives examining lamb ribs, and Syrian Jews setting up racks of CDs by Lebanese torch-singers. The crowds were thronging between the tables of pungent red spices, stacked metal tins of green olive oil and the big liquor stall selling good Golan Heights wine.

Amongst them was Rob Luttrell, making his way to the far end of the market. He wanted a beer at the Bik Bik beer and sausage shop, his favourite spot in Tel Aviv. Rob liked to watch the Israeli celebrities in their paparazzi-fooling sunglasses. A few days back, one particularly cute starlet had actually smiled at him. Maybe she'd guessed he was a journalist.

Rob also liked the Czech beer at the Bik Bik sausage bar: served in plastic steins it went down a treat with those chunks of home-made salami and tiny pitas of spicy kebab.

'Shalom,' said Samson, the Turkish sausage man at the Bik Bik. Rob briskly ordered a beer. Then he remembered his manners and said Please and Thanks. He wondered if boredom was getting to him. He'd been back here for six weeks, kicking his heels after six months in Iraq. Was it too long?

Yes, he'd needed the break. Yes, he liked being back in Tel Aviv – he loved the city's vivacity and drama. And it was generous of his editor in London to give him the time off, to 'recover'. But now he was ready for action again. Another posting in Baghdad maybe. Or Gaza – things were kicking off there. Things were always kicking off in Gaza.

Rob drank from the plastic pint glass of beer, and then stepped to the front of the open air bar to look out across the corniche at the grey-blue Mediterranean beyond. The beer was cold, golden and good. Rob watched a surfer breasting the waves out to sea.

Would his editor ever call? Rob checked his mobile phone. The digital image of his little daughter stared back. Rob felt a serious pang of guilt. He hadn't seen her since . . . when? January, or February? When he was last in London. But what could he do? His ex-wife kept changing her plans, as if she wanted to deny Rob all access. Rob's yearning to see Lizzie was like a hunger, or a thirst. There was a constant sensation that something – someone – was missing from his life. Sometimes he'd find himself turning to smile at his daughter, and of course she wasn't there.

Rob returned his empty beercup to the bar. 'See you tomorrow, Sam. Don't eat all the kebabs!'

Samson laughed. Rob paid his shekels then headed for the seafront. He ran across the busy lanes of Thursday traffic, hoping not to get killed by the punchy Jewish drivers trying to run each other into the ocean.

The Tel Aviv beach was his favourite place to think. With the skyscrapers behind him and the waves and the warm, bracing wind in front. And now he wanted to think about his wife and child. His ex-wife and five-year-old child.

He had wanted to fly back to London immediately after the newspaper ordered him out of Baghdad. But Sally had suddenly got a new boyfriend and told him she needed 'space', so Rob had decided to stay put in Tel Aviv. He didn't want to be in England if he couldn't see Lizzie. It was too agonizing.

But whose fault was all this, really? Rob wondered how much of the divorce was his own doing. Yes, she'd had the affairs . . . but he had been away all that time. But this was his job! He was a foreign correspondent: it was what he'd spent ten years striving for back in London. This was how he earned his money. And now he'd made it in his mid-thirties and he was covering the whole Middle East – and there were more stories than he knew what to do with.

Rob wondered if he should go back to the Bik Bik for another beer. He looked left. The Dan Panorama hotel loomed against the blue sky – a great concrete lump of a hotel with a flashy glass atrium. Behind was the parking area, acres of car lots oddly situated in the middle of town. He remembered the story behind these car parks: when the Arab-Israeli war had broken out in 1948 this had been the main front in the urban conflict between Jewish Tel Aviv and Arab Jaffa. Then the Israelis had won and they'd levelled the shell-shocked slums that remained. And now it was just a big car park.

He made a decision. If he couldn't see Lizzie he could at least earn some money, to keep her fed and secure. So he decided to go straight back to his little flat in Jaffa and do some research. Find some more angles on that Lebanese story. Or trace those Hamas kids that hid out in that church.

Ideas fizzed in Rob's head as he headed to the curve of the beach, and the ancient harbourfront houses beyond: the port of old Jaffa.

His mobile rang. Rob checked the screen hopefully. It was a British number, but it wasn't Sally, or Lizzie, or his friends.

It was his editor, in London.

Rob felt the surge of adrenalin. This was it! This was the moment in his job he most loved: the unexpected call from his editor. Go to Baghdad, Go to Cairo, Go to Gaza, Go Risk Your Life. Rob adored this moment. The never knowing where he was going to be. The frightening sense of improvised theatre: as if he existed on live TV. No wonder he couldn't pin down a relationship. He clicked the phone.

'Robbie!'

'Steve?'

'Wotcher.'

The ultra-Cockney accent of his editor fazed Rob for a second, as it always did. He still had enough of the middle-American in him to presume that editors at *The Times* always spoke in pukka Oxford English. But his foreign editor spoke like a Tilbury docker – and swore even more. Sometimes Rob wondered if Steve put it on a bit – the Cockney accent – to mark himself out from his plummier Oxbridge peers. Everyone in journalism was so competitive.

'Robbie, mate. Whatya doing right now?'

'Standing on a beach, talking to you.'

'Fuck. Wish I had your job.'

'You did. But you got promoted.'

'Oh yeah.' Steve laughed. 'Anyway what I mean is, what you doing next? We got you on assignment?'

'Nope.'

'That's right, that's right. You're recovering from that fucking . . . bomb shit.'

'I'm OK now.'

Steve whistled. 'That was messy. Baghdad.'

Rob didn't want to think about the bombing. 'So . . . Steve . . . where . . .'

'Kurdistan.'

'What? Wow!'

He immediately felt excited, and a little scared. Iraqi Kurdistan. Mosul! He'd never been there and it was surely chock-full of stories. *Iraqi Kurdistan!*

But then Steve broke in: 'Cool your jets . . .'

Rob felt his excitement ebb. There was something in Steve's voice. This wasn't a war story. 'Steve?'

'Rob, mate. What do you know about archaeology?'

Rob looked out to sea. A paraglider was soaring over the waves. 'Archaeology? Nothing. Why?'

'Well there's this . . . dig . . . in south-east Turkey. Kurdish Turkey.'

'A dig?'

'Yep. Pretty interesting. These German archaeologists have . . .'

'Cave paintings? Old bones? Shit.' Rob felt a piercing disappointment.

Steve chuckled. 'Now now. C'mon.'

'What?'

'You can't always do Gaza. And I don't want you anywhere dangerous. Not at the mo.' He sounded solicitous, almost brotherly. Most unexpected. 'You're one of my best reporters. And that was a nasty spill in Baghdad. You've had enough bad shit, for a while. Don't ya think?'

Rob waited. He knew Steve hadn't finished. Sure enough, Steve explained: 'So I'm asking you, ever so politely, to go and look at this fucking dig in Turkey. If that's OK with you.'

Rob detected the sarcasm: it wasn't hard. He laughed. 'OK, Steve. You're the boss! I'll go and look at some stones. When do you need me to go?'

'Tomorra. I'll email the brief.'

Tomorrow? Not a lot of time. Rob started thinking about planes and packing. 'I'm on the case, Steve. Thanks.'

The editor paused, then came back on the line: 'But, Rob . . .'

'What?'

'I'm serious about this assignment. These aren't just . . . boring old stones.'

'Sorry?'

'It's been in the news here already. You must have missed it.'

'I don't read the archaeological press.'

'I do. It's highly fashionable.'

'So?'

The sea air was warm. Steve went on: 'What I mean is. This place in Turkey. What these Germans found . . .'

Rob waited for Steve to elaborate.

A long pause. Then at last his editor said, 'Well . . . it's not just bones and shit, Robbie. It's something really quite weird.'

3

On the plane to Istanbul Rob sipped at his watery gin and tonic in a little see-through plastic cup with a tiny swizzle stick. He read the printout of Steve's email, and some other stuff he had found on the Net about the Turkish dig.

The site being unearthed was called Gobekli Tepe. For an hour Rob thought this was pronounced Teep, but then he saw a phonetic spelling on one his printouts: Tepe was pronounced *Tepp-ay*. Gobekli . . . *Tepp-ay*. Rob said it himself – '*Gob-eckly Tepp-ay*' and then munched a mini pretzel.

He read on.

The site was apparently just one of a number of very old settlements presently being unearthed in Kurdish Turkey. Nevali Cori, Cayonu, Karahan Tepe. Some of them seemed incredibly ancient. Eight thousand years old or more. But was that *really* so ancient? Rob had no idea. How old was the Sphinx? Stonehenge? The pyramids?

His gin and tonic finished, he sat back and thought about his lack of general knowledge. Why didn't he know the answer to questions like this? Because, obviously, he didn't have a university education. Unlike his colleagues who had degrees from Oxford and London and UCLA, or Paris or Munich or Kyoto or Austin or wherever, Rob had nothing but his brain and an ability to speed-read – to digest information quickly. He had fled education at the age of eighteen. Despite his single mother's cries of despair, he had spurned the offers of several colleges and universities, and instead had gone straight into journalism. But who could blame him for this, really? Rob swallowed another mini-pretzel. He'd had no choice. His mum was on her own, his dad had stayed in America being a mean brutal bastard; Rob had grown up poor in the furthest reaches of dull suburban London. From an early age he'd wanted money and status as soon as they were available. He was never going to be like those rich kids he used to envy when he was a lad, able to take four years off to smoke dope and go to parties and drift into comfortable careers at a leisurely pace. He'd always felt a need to get a move on.

The same desire for swift progression had governed his emotional life. When Sally came along, smiling and bonny and clever, he'd grabbed at the happiness, and the stability, she offered. The birth of their daughter, soon after their precocious marriage, seemed like a signal that what he had done was a Very Good Thing. Only then had he realised, belatedly, that his kinetic career might be in conflict with settled domestic tranquillity.

The El Al economy seat was as uncomfortable as ever. Rob sat back, and rubbed his eyes. Then he asked the stewardess for another gin and tonic. A pick-me-up, and a help-me-forget.

Reaching in his bag beneath his feet Rob pulled out two books from Tel Aviv's best bookshop, one on Turkish archaeology, and one on ancient man. He had a three-hour stopover in Istanbul and then another flight to Sanliurfa, way out in the wild east of Anatolia. Half a day to do some speed-reading.

By the time they arrived in Istanbul, Rob was quite drunk – and fully apprised of the recent archaeological history of Anatolia. Particularly important, it seemed, was a place called Catalhoyuk. Pronounced *Chattal Hoy-ukk*. Discovered in the 1950s, it was one of the oldest villages in the world ever unearthed – maybe nine thousand years old. The walls of this ancient settlement were covered with pictures of bulls and leopards and buzzards. Lots of buzzards. Very old signs of religion. Very strange images.

Rob looked at the pictures of Catalhoyuk. He flicked through a few more pages. Then they landed at Istanbul airport and Rob carouselled his bags and threaded his way through the crowds of jowly Turkish businessmen, stopping at a little store where he bought an American newspaper with one of the latest reports from Gobekli Tepe, and then went straight to the gate to wait for his next flight. Sitting there in the departure lounge he read some more about the dig.

The modern history of Gobekli Tepe began, it said, in 1964, when a team of American archaeologists were combing a remote province of south-east Turkey. The archaeologists had found several odd-looking hills blanketed with thousands of broken flints: a sure sign of ancient human activity. Yet the US scientists did no excavating. As the newspaper phrased it: '*these guys must now feel like the publisher that turned down the first Harry Potter manuscript*'.

Ignoring the snoring Turkish lady asleep in the airport seating, right next to him, Rob read on.

Three decades after the Americans' near miss, a local shepherd had been tending his flock when he had spotted something odd: a number of strangely-shaped stones in the sunlit dust. They were the stones of Gobekli Tepe.

Tepp-ay, Rob said to himself, remindingly. Tepp-*ay*. He wandered over to a machine, bought a Diet Coke, then wandered back and went on reading.

The 'rediscovery' of the site reached the ears of the museum curators, in the city of Sanliurfa, fifty kilometres away. The museum authorities contacted the relevant government ministry, who in turn got in touch with the German Archaeological Institute in Istanbul. And so in 1994 'experienced German archaeologist Franz Breitner' was appointed by the Turkish authorities to excavate the site.

Rob scanned the rest of the article. He tilted the paper to have a better look. There was a picture of Breitner in the American newspaper. And underneath the photo was a direct quote from him: *'I was intrigued. The site already had emotional significance for the villagers. The solitary tree on the highest hill is sacred. I thought we might be onto something'.*

Armed with this insight Breitner had taken a closer look. *'Within the first minute I knew that if I didn't walk away immediately, I would be here the rest of my life.'*

Rob looked at Breitner's photo. He certainly looked like the cat that had got the double cream. His smile was the smile of a man with a lottery win.

'Turkish Airlines announce the departure of flight TA628 to Sanliurfa . . .'

Rob grabbed his passport and boarding card and filed onto the plane. It was half-empty. Obviously not that many people made it out to Sanliurfa. Way out in the savage east of Anatolia. Way out in dangerous, dusty, insurrectionist Kurdistan.

During the flight Rob read through the rest of the documents and books about Gobekli's archaeological history. The eerie stones unearthed by the shepherd turned out to be the flat oblong tops of megaliths, big ochre stones which were often carved with bizarre and delicate images – mainly of animals and birds. Buzzards and vultures, and weird insects. Sinuous serpents were another common motif. The stones themselves seemed to represent men, according to experts – the stones had stylized 'arms', which angled down the sides.

So far, forty-three stones had been unearthed. They were arranged in circles from five to ten metres across. Around the circles were benches of rock, smallish niches, and walls of mud brick.

Rob considered what he'd learned. All this was reasonably interesting. But it was the age of the site that had really got people truly excited. Gobekli Tepe was staggeringly ancient. According to Breitner, the complex was at least ten thousand, maybe eleven thousand years old. That was to say around 8000–9000 BC.

Eleven thousand years old? It sounded incredibly ancient. But was it? Rob went back to his history book to compare this age with other places. Stonehenge was built around 2000 BC. The Sphinx maybe 3000 BC. Prior to the discovery and dating of Gobekli Tepe, the 'most ancient' megalithic complex had been located in Malta – and that was dated around 3500 BC.

Gobekli Tepe was, therefore, five thousand years older than any comparable structure. Rob was headed to one of the oldest human constructions ever built. Maybe the oldest.

He felt his Story Antennae twitching. World's Oldest Building Found in Turkey? Hmmm. Maybe not front page, but quite possibly third page. A nice big splash. Moreover, despite these reports in the paper, it seemed as if no western journalist had actually made it out to Gobekli. All the articles in western media were second- or third-hand, via Turkish news agencies. Rob would be the first man on the ground.

At last his journey was over. The plane banked and dived and trundled to a halt in Sanliurfa airport. It was a dark clear night. So clear that through the windows of the plane the night actually looked cool. But when the door opened and the plane ladder descended Rob felt a blast of oppressively hot air. As if someone had just opened an enormous oven. This was a hot place. Very hot. They were on the edge of the great Syrian Desert, after all.

The airport was tiny. Rob liked tiny airports. They always had an idiosyncrasy lacking in huge, impersonal modern airports. And Sanliurfa airport was especially idiosyncratic. The bags were brought by hand to the Arrivals Lounge by a fat man with a beard and a stained vest, and Passport Control consisted of one guy half-asleep at a rickety desk.

In the airport car park a warm dusty breeze was knocking the fronds of some straggly palm trees. Several cab drivers eyed him from the taxi rank. Rob looked and chose. 'Sanliurfa,' he said to one of the younger guys.

The stubble-jawed man smiled. His denim shirt was torn, but clean. He seemed friendly. Friendlier than the other taxi guys, who were yawning and spitting. Even better, this young guy seemed to speak

English. After a quick chat about the fee and the whereabouts of Rob's hotel, the driver took Rob's bags and slung them manfully in the car boot, then climbed in the front and nodded and said, 'Urfa! Not Sanliurfa. Urfa!'

Rob sat back in the taxi seat. He was very tired now. It had been a long, long journey from Tel Aviv. Tomorrow he would go and see this weird dig. But now he had to sleep. Yet the taxi driver was keen to keep him talking.

'You want beer? I know good place.'

Rob groaned, inwardly. Flat dark fields were racing past. 'No thanks.'

'Woman? I know good woman!'

'Er, no, not really.'

'Carpet. You want carpet. I have brother . . . ?'

Rob sighed, and looked at the rear-view mirror. Then he saw the taxi driver staring back at him. The man was smiling. He was joking.

'Very funny.'

The taxi driver laughed. 'Fucking carpets!' Then, without taking his eye off the road, he turned and offered a hand. Rob shook it.

'My name Radevan,' the driver said. 'You?'

'Robert. Rob Luttrell.'

'Hello, Mr Robert Luttrell.'

Rob laughed and said hello. They were on the outskirts of town now. Lamplights and tyre shops lined the empty, litter-strewn street. A Conoco gas station sign glowed red through the sultry gloom. Concrete blocks of flats rose up on both sides. There was a sense of heat everywhere. Yet Rob could see women behind windows in distant kitchens: still in headscarves.

'You need driver? You here business?' asked Radevan.

Rob thought about this. Why not? The man was friendly, he had a sense of humour. 'Sure. I need a driver, and an interpreter. For tomorrow? Maybe more.'

Radevan happily banged the steering wheel with his palm, while he torched a cigarette with the other hand. Neither hand was actually on the steering wheel. Rob thought they were going to careen off the road into a small neon-lit mosque, but then Radevan cuffed the wheel and they were back on track. Between puffs on his pungent cigarette the driver chatted. 'I can help you. I good translator. Speak Kurdish English Turkish Japanese, German.'

'You speak German?'

'Nein.'

Rob laughed again. He was warming to Radevan big-time, not least because he had sped ten miles in ten minutes without crashing, and they were already in the middle of town. There were shuttered kebab stalls and late-night baklava shops everywhere. A man in a suit and a man in an Arabic cloak. Two kids sped past on mopeds. Some young women in jeans with brightly coloured headscarves were giggling at a joke. Traffic honked around a junction. Rob's hotel was right in the centre of town.

Radevan was looking at Rob in the mirror. 'Mr Rob, you Englishman?'

'Kinda . . .' Rob said. He didn't want to get into a long debate about his precise parentage; not now. He was too tired. 'Sort of.'

Radevan grinned. 'I like Englishman!' He rubbed his forefinger and thumb together as if asking for money. 'They are rich. Englishman very rich!'

Rob shrugged. 'Well . . . some of them.'

Radevan insisted, 'Dollars and euros! Dollars and pounds!' Another grin. 'OK, I take you tomorrow. Where you go?'

'Gobekli Tepe. You know it?'

Silence. Rob tried again. 'Gobekli Tepe?'

Radevan said nothing, and pulled the car up short. 'Your hotel,' the driver said, bluntly. His smile had suddenly gone.

'Er . . . you meet me tomorrow?' said Rob, lapsing into pidgin English. 'Radevan?'

Radevan nodded. He helped Rob carry his bags to the hotel steps, and then the driver turned back to the taxi. 'You say . . . you say you want Gobekli Tepe?'

'Yes.'

Radevan frowned. 'Gobekli Tepe bad place. Mr Rob.'

Rob stood at the door to his hotel, feeling as if he was in a film adaptation of Bram Stoker's *Dracula*. 'Hey. It's just a dig, Radevan. Can you take me or not?'

Radevan spat on the road. Then he climbed into his taxi and leaned out of the window. 'Nine o'clock tomorrow.'

The cab disappeared with a lusty wheel-spin into the fusty hubbub of the Sanliurfa streets.

Next morning after a breakfast of hard-boiled eggs, sheep's milk cheese and three dates, Rob got in the cab. They headed out of town. As they went, Rob asked Radevan why he had such an attitude towards Gobekli.

At first the driver was grumpy. He shrugged and muttered. But as the roads got emptier and the wide irrigated fields took over he opened up like the landscape. 'It is not good.'

'Tell me.'

'Gobekli Tepe could be rich. Could make Kurdish people rich.'

'But?'

Radevan puffed angrily on his third cigarette. 'Look at this place, this people?'

Rob glanced out of the window. They were heading past a little village of mud houses and open drains, grimy kids playing amongst the litter. The kids waved at the car. Beyond the village was a cotton field where women in lavender-coloured headscarves were bending to the crop in the dust and the dirt, and the searing heat. He looked back at his driver.

Radevan tutted loudly. 'Kurdish people poor. Me, I taxi driver. But I speak languages! Yet I taxi driver.'

Rob nodded. He knew about Kurdish unhappiness. The campaign for separation.

'Turkish government, they keep us poor . . .'

'OK, sure,' said Rob. 'But I don't understand what this has to do with Gobekli Tepe?'

Radevan threw his cigarette butt out of the window. They were back in open countryside, the battered Toyota rattling over a blurry dirt road. In the far distance blue mountains shimmered in the heat-haze.

'Gobekli Tepe could be like pyramids or like . . . Stonehenge. But they keep it quiet. It could be many many tourists here, pay money Kurdish people, but no. Turkish government say no. They not even put up signs or build road here. Like secret.' He coughed and spat out of the window, then wound it up to keep out the rising dust. 'Gobekli Tepe bad place,' he said again, then fell silent.

Rob didn't know what to say. Ahead of him the low, yellow-brown hills rolled endlessly towards Syria. He could see another tiny Kurdish village with a slender brown minaret rising above the corrugated iron roofs, like a watchtower in a prison camp. Rob wanted to say that if anything was holding the Kurds back it was possibly their traditions, their insularity, and their religion. But he didn't think Radevan was in the mood to listen.

They drove on in silence. The road got worse, and the semi desert more hostile. Finally Radevan scraped the car round another corner, and Rob looked up to see a solitary mulberry tree, stark against the cloudless sky. Radevan nodded and said *Gobekli* and then parked abruptly. He turned around in his seat, and smiled, his good mood apparently back. Then he got out of the car and opened the door for Rob like a chauffeur and Rob felt slightly embarrassed. He didn't want a chauffeur.

Radevan got back in the car and picked up a newspaper showing a big picture of a football player. He was evidently going to wait. Rob said goodbye and said *three hours?* Radevan smiled.

Turning, Rob walked up the hill and crested the rise. Behind him stretched thirty kilometres of dusty villages, empty desert and scorched cotton fields. In front of him was an astonishing scene. In the middle of the arid desolation there were seven sudden hillocks. And dozens of workers and archaeologists were scattered right across the biggest hillside. The diggers and workers were hefting buckets of rock, and tilling seriously at the soil. There were tents and bulldozers and theodolites.

Rob walked on, feeling like an intruder. Some of the diggers had stopped working and had turned to look at him. Just as he was getting really embarrassed, a genial, fifty-something European approached. Rob recognized Franz Breitner.

'*Wilkommen,*' said the German breezily, as if he knew Rob already. 'You are the journalist from England?'

'Yes.'

'You are a very lucky man.'

4

The lobby of St Thomas' Hospital was as busy as ever. Detective Chief Inspector Mark Forrester pushed through the bustling nurses and gossiping relatives and the wheelchaired old women with drips hanging from steel frames, and wondered, for the third time that morning, if he could hack what he was obliged to do.

He had to go and see a mutilated man. This was tough. He'd seen plenty of nasty sights – he was forty-two and he'd been a detective ten years – but something about this case was especially unsettling.

Seeing the sign for the ICU, Forrester briskly climbed a flight of stairs, went to ward reception, snapped his Met credentials at a sweet-faced girl – and was told to wait.

A few second later a Chinese-looking doctor came out, peeling rubber gloves from his hands.

'Dr Sing?'

'Inspector Forrester?'

Forrester nodded and reached out to shake the doctor's ungloved hand. The returning handshake was tentative, as if the doctor was about to impart bad news. Forrester felt a slight panic. 'He is still alive?'

'Yes. Just.'

'So what happened?'

The doctor looked somewhere over Forrester's shoulder. 'Total glossectomy.'

'Sorry?'

A doctorly sigh. 'They cut out *all* of his tongue. With some kind of shears . . .'

Forrester looked through the plastic doors to the wardroom proper. 'Jesus, I heard it was bad, but . . .' Somewhere in there, beyond the doors, was his only witness. Still alive. But without a tongue.

The doctor was shaking his head. 'The blood loss was tremendous. And not just from his . . . tongue. They also carved lines into his chest. And shaved his head.'

'So you think—?'

'I think if they hadn't been interrupted, it would have been worse.' The doctor eyed Forrester. 'What I mean is if that car alarm hadn't gone off, they would probably have killed him.'

Forrester exhaled. 'Attempted murder.'

'You're the policeman.' The doctor had adopted an impatient expression.

Forester nodded. 'Can I see him?'

'Room 37. But briefly, please.'

Forrester shook the doctor's hand again, though he wasn't sure why. Then he walked through the plastic doors, avoided a gurney stacked with urine gourds and knocked at the door to room 37. All he could hear was a groan inside. What should he do? Then he remembered: the man's tongue had been cut out. Sighing, the detective pushed open the door. It was a small, simple NHS room with a TV suspended on a steel armature at one end. The TV was switched off. The room smelled of flowers and something worse. In the bed was a fairly old man staring wildly at Forrester. His head had been entirely shaved leaving a mess of cuts and scars on the nude scalp. Forrester was reminded of a map of railway lines. The man's mouth was shut but blood was caked at the corners of his lips like dried brown sauce at the top of an old sauce bottle; bandages covered the patient's torso.

'David Lorimer?'

The man nodded. And stared. And stared.

It was this wild stare that gave Forrester pause. In his career he had seen plenty of frightened faces, but the sheer terror welling in this man's eyes was something else.

David Lorimer mumbled something. Then he started coughing and small flecks of blood spat from his mouth and Forrester felt an arching guilt. 'Please.' He held up a hand. 'I don't want to trouble you. I just . . . wanted to check something . . .'

The man's eyes were full of tears, like those of a troubled child.

'You have had a terrible ordeal, Mr Lorimer. We just . . . I just . . . want to say that we fully intend to catch these people.'

The words were pathetically inadequate. This man had been brutalized and terrorized. He'd had his tongue sliced out with shears. He'd had lines carved into his living skin. Forrester felt like an idiot. What he wanted to say was 'we're gonna nail these bastards', but this room didn't seem the right place for such absurd posturing, either. In the end he sat down on a plastic chair at the end of the bed and smiled warmly at the victim, trying to relax him.

It seemed to work. A minute or two passed and then the old man's eyes no longer looked quite so terrified. Instead Lorimer waved a shaking hand at some papers lying on his bedside table. Forrester got up and walked to the table and picked up the documents. It was a sheaf of handwritten notes.

'Yours?'

Lorimer nodded. Keeping his lips firmly shut.

'Descriptions of the attackers?'

He nodded again.

'Thank you very much, Mr Lorimer.' Forrester reached out and patted him on the shoulder, feeling self-conscious as he did so. The man really looked as if he was about to cry.

Pocketing the papers, Forrester left the room as quickly as he could. Out and down the steps and through the swing doors. When he reached the rainy late spring air of the leafy Embankment he breathed deeply, and in relief. The atmosphere of terror in the room, in the man's staring eyes, had been all too intense.

Walking briskly down and across the River Thames, with the Houses of Parliament yellow and Gothic on his left, Forrester read the scrawled notes.

David Lorimer was a caretaker. At the Benjamin Franklin Museum. He was sixty-four. Nearing retirement. He lived alone in a flat at the top of the museum. The previous night he had woken at about 4 a.m. to the muffled crash of broken glass downstairs. His flat was in a converted attic and he'd had to descend all the way to the cellar. There he'd found five or six unknown men, apparently young, and wearing ski-masks or balaclavas. The men had broken in, quite expertly, and they were digging up the basement floor. One of them had a 'posh voice'.

And that was pretty much all Lorimer's notes said. During the attack a car alarm had gone off, for some reason, probably sheer and miraculous coincidence – just as the men were carving Lorimer's neck and chest, and so the men had fled. The caretaker was lucky to be alive. If the young lad, Alan Greening, hadn't wandered in and found him he would have bled to death.

Forrester's mind was full of speculation. Turning right on the Strand, he headed down the quiet Georgian side street to the museum, the Benjamin Franklin House. The house was roped off with blue and white plastic tape. Two police cars were parked outside, a uniformed constable stood by the door, and a couple of obvious journalists with recorders were sheltering under a nearby office block awning, with cups of takeaway coffee.

One of them stepped forward as Forrester approached. 'Detective, is it true the victim had his tongue cut out?'

Forrester turned and smiled blandly and said nothing.

The journalist, young, female and pretty, tried again. 'Was it some kind of neo-Nazi thing?'

This made Forrester pause. He turned and looked at the girl. 'Press conference is tomorrow.' This was a lie, but it would do. Turning back to the house, he ducked under the tape and flashed his badge. The uniformed constable opened the door and Forrester immediately caught the piercing, chemical smell of Forensics at work. Fuming for fingerprints. Quasaring the place. Silicon gel and superglue. Stepping to the end of the noble Georgian hall with its portraits of Benjamin Franklin, Forrester took the narrow stairway to the basement.

The cellar was a scene of activity. Two Forensics girls in green paper nonce suits and masks were working at one end. The bloodstains on the floor were vivid, sticky and dark. Detective Sergeant Boijer waved from the other side of the room. Forrester smiled back.

'They were digging in here,' said DS Boijer. Forrester noted that Boijer's blond hair was newly cut, and expensively so.

'What were they digging for?'

DS Boijer shrugged. 'Search me, sir.' He waved a hand across the ripped-up flagstones. 'But they had a good old hunt. Must have taken them a couple of hours to shift all that shit, and get that deep.'

Forrester bent to assess the disturbed soil, the deep, damp hole in the earth.

Boijer chatted away behind him: 'Did you see the caretaker?'

'Yep. Poor bastard.'

'The doctor told me they were trying to kill him. Slowly.'

Forrester replied without looking around. 'I think they were bleeding him to death. If the car alarm hadn't gone off, and if he hadn't lucked out with that lad arriving he would have died of blood loss.'

Boijer nodded.

Forrester stood up. 'So it's attempted murder. Better speak to Aldridge. He'll want an SIO, and the rest. Set up an incident room.'

'And the scars on his chest?'

'Sorry?'

Forrester turned. Boijer was wincing, and holding a photo. 'You haven't seen this?' He handed the photo over. 'The doctor took a photo of the scars on the guy's chest. He emailed it to the station this morning, didn't get a chance to show you.'

Forrester looked. The caretaker's white chest was exposed to the camera, soft and vulnerable. Bloodily carved in the skin was a Star of David. Unmistakable. The flesh was crudely ripped, but the sign was clearly legible. Two juxtaposed triangles. A Jewish Star of David. Carved into living flesh and blood.

5

'So these are the carvings, the new ones they mentioned in the article?'

'*Ja*.'

Rob was in the middle of the dig, next to Breitner. The two of them were standing at the side of a pit, looking down at a circle of tall, T-shaped stones within the sunken enclosure. These were the megaliths. All around them the dig was proceeding with alacrity: Turkish workers were brushing and shovelling earth, shinning down ladders, trundling barrows of rubble along duckboards. The sun was hot.

The carvings were strange – and yet familiar, because Rob had seen them in the newspaper photos. There was a stone carved with lions, and a few weathered birds; maybe ducks. On the next stone was something that looked like a scorpion. About half the megaliths had similar carvings, many of them seriously eroded, others not. Rob took some shots with his cameraphone then scribbled a few impressions in his notebook, drawing the strange T-shape of the megaliths as best he could.

'But,' said Breitner, 'that of course is not everything. *Komm*.'

They walked along the side of the pit to another sunken area. Three more ochre pillars stood in this enclosure, surrounded by a mudbrick wall. Traces of what looked like tiling glinted on the floor between the pillars. A blonde German girl said *Guten Tag* to Rob as she pushed past carrying a small clear plastic bag full of tiny flints.

'We have many students here from Heidelberg.'

'And the other workers?'

'All Kurdish.' Breitner's twinkling eyes clouded for a moment behind his spectacles. 'I also have other experts here of course, paleobotanists and two or three other specialists.' He took out a handkerchief and wiped perspiration from his bald head. 'And this is Christine . . .'

Rob turned. Approaching him from the direction of the tented headquarters was a petite but determined figure in khaki trousers and a remarkably clean white shirt. Everybody else in the dig was smothered with the ubiquitous beige dust of Gobekli Tepe's exhausted-looking hillocks. But not this archaeologist. Rob felt himself go tense – as he always did when he was introduced to an attractive young woman.

'Christine Meyer. My skeleton woman!'

The small, dark-haired woman extended a hand: 'Osteoarchaeologist. I do the biological anthropology. The human remains and so forth. Not that we have found anything of that nature yet.'

Rob detected a French accent. As if he guessed Rob's thoughts, Breitner interrupted. 'Christine was at Cambridge under Isobel Previn, however she is from Paris so we are very international here . . .'

'I'm French, yes. But I lived in England for many years.'

Rob smiled: 'I'm Rob Luttrell – we share a background! I mean I'm American. But I've been living in London since I was ten.'

'He's here to write about Gobekli!' Breitner was chortling. 'So I am going to show him the wolf!'

'The crocodile,' said Christine.

Breitner laughed, then turned and walked on. Rob glanced between the two scientists, confused. Breitner waved a hand, beckoning him to follow. '*Komm*. I will show you.'

They took another circuitous walk around the various pits and spoil-heaps. Rob gazed about. There were megaliths everywhere. Some still half-buried. Others were tilted over at dangerous angles. He murmured: 'It's much bigger than I expected . . .'

The narrow path forced them to walk in single file. Behind Rob, Christine replied, 'GPR and magnetivity imply there may be two hundred and fifty more stones buried under the hills. Maybe more.'

'Wow.'

'It is an incredible place.'

'And of course incredibly old, right?'

'Right . . .'

Breitner was now racing ahead of them. To Rob he looked like a boy eager to show his parents his new den. Christine went on, 'In truth it has been very hard to date the site: there aren't any organic remains.'

They reached a steel ladder and Christine moved beside Rob. 'Here, like this.' She skimmed down it – vigorously. Evidently she didn't mind getting dirty, despite the shirt.

Rob followed rather less swiftly. They were now down at floor level in one of the pits. The megaliths loomed around them, like sombre guards. Rob wondered what it would be like here at night, and dismissed the fleeting notion. He took out his notebook. 'So you were saying, about the dating?'

'Yes,' Christine frowned. 'Until recently we couldn't be sure how old the place was. I mean, we knew it was very old . . . but whether it was late PP Neolithic A, or PPNB . . .'

'Sorry?'

'Last week we finally managed to carbon date some charcoal that we found on a megalith.'

Rob wrote this down. 'And it's ten or eleven thousand years old, right? That's what the *Trib* article said?'

'Actually that report was inaccurate. Even carbon dating is only an estimate. To get a truer date we compared the radiocarbon analysis with some of the flints we found, Nemrik points and Byblos points – types of arrowheads and so forth. Taking these together with other data we think that Gobekli is actually closer to *twelve* thousand years old.'

'Hence the excitement?'

Christine glanced at him, pushing dark hair back from her clear eyes. Then she laughed. 'I think Franz wants you to look at his lizard.'

'Wolf,' corrected Breitner, standing by another half buried T-shaped pillar. At the foot of this pillar, attached to the upright of a stone, was a sculpture of an animal about two foot long. It was delicately chiselled and looked strangely new. Its stone jaw was growling at the floor. Rob looked at Breitner and at the Turkish worker just beyond him. The Turkish man was glaring at Breitner with what appeared to be anger, or even hatred. It was a shocking expression. When the man saw Rob looking at him, he turned and abruptly climbed a ladder. Rob glanced back at Breitner, who was stoutly unaware of this little exchange.

'We only found this yesterday.'

'What is it?'

'I think it's a wolf, judging by the paws.'

'And I think it's a crocodile,' said Christine.

Breitner laughed. 'Do you see?' He put his spectacles back on and they glinted in the bright sun, and for a moment Rob felt a sudden admiration for this man: so delighted and enthused by his work.

Breitner went on, 'You and me and these workers, we are the first people to see this since . . . the end of the Ice Age.'

Rob blinked. That was a truly impressive thought.

'This carving is so new to us,' Christine added. 'No one knows what it is. You are seeing something very important for the first time. There's no one to interpret it for you. Your guess as to what this might be is as good as anyone's.'

Rob stared at the jaw of the stone creature. 'It looks like a cat to me. Or a mad rabbit.'

Rubbing his chin, Breitner replied: 'A feline? You know I hadn't thought of that. Some kind of wildcat . . .'

'Can I put all this in my article?'

'*Ja, natürlich*,' Breitner said. But he wasn't smiling as he said it. 'And now I think – some tea.'

Rob nodded: he was thirsty. Breitner led the way back through the maze of covered pits, open pits, tarpaulined enclosures and bucket-carrying workers. Over the last rise was a flatter area of open-sided tents laid with red carpets. A samovar in one corner produced three tulip-shaped glasses of sweet Turkish *cay*. The open tents afforded a spectacular view: beyond them were the endless yellow plains and shallow dusty hills undulating towards Syria and Iraq.

For several minutes they sat and chatted. Breitner was explaining how the area surrounding Gobekli used to be much more fertile – not the desert it had since become. 'Ten or twelve thousand years ago this area was much less arid. In fact it was beautiful – a pastoral landscape. Herds of game, orchards of wild fruit trees, rivers full of fish . . . That's why you see carvings on the stones of animals – creatures that don't live here now.'

Rob noted this down. He wanted to know more – but then a couple of Turkish workers approached and asked Breitner a question in German. Rob knew just enough of the language to glean the meaning: they wanted to dig a much deeper trench to access a new megalith. Breitner was evidently worried about the safety of such a serious excavation. Eventually Breitner sighed, shrugged at Rob, and went off to sort things out. As he went Rob saw that one of the workers was scowling: a strange, dark expression. There was definitely a tension here. Why? He wondered if he should mention his suspicions now that he and Christine were alone. The noise of the dig was muffled at this distance – all Rob could hear were little tinklings of trowels and spades, small noises occasionally carried over, on the hot desert wind. He was about to ask his question when Christine said, 'So what do you think of Gobekli?'

'It's incredible. Of course.'

'But do you know *how* incredible?'

'I think so. Don't I?'

She looked at him sceptically.

'Why don't *you* tell me, then?'

Christine sipped at her tulip-shaped glass of tea. 'Think about it this way, Rob. What you have to remember is . . . the age of the place. Twelve thousand years old.'

'And . . . ?'

'And recall what men were doing then.'

'What do you mean?

'The men who built this place were hunter-gatherers.'

'Cavemen?'

'In a way, yes.' She gave him a direct, earnest look. 'Before Gobekli Tepe, we had no idea that such early primitive men could build something like this, could create art and sophisticated architecture. And intricate religious rituals.'

'Because they were just cavemen?'

'Precisely. Gobekli Tepe represents a revolution in our perceptions. A total revolution.' Christine finished the last of her tea. 'It changes the way we must think about the entire history of mankind. It's more important than any other dig anywhere in the world in the last fifty years and one of the greatest archaeological discoveries in history.'

Rob was intrigued, and very impressed. He also felt a little like a schoolboy being lectured. 'How did they make it?'

'That is the question. Men with bows and arrows. Who didn't even have pottery. Or farming. How did they build this enormous temple?'

'Temple?'

'Oh, yes, most probably it's a temple. We've found no evidence of domestic habitation, no sign of the most rudimentary settlement, just stylized images of the hunt. Celebratory or ritualistic imagery. Possibly we have found niches for bones, for funeral rites. Breitner therefore thinks it is a temple, the world's first religious building, designed to celebrate the hunt, and to venerate the dead.' She smiled calmly. 'And I think he is right.'

Rob put down his pen, and thought about Breitner's twinkling and merry expression. 'He is certainly a cheery kind of guy, isn't he?'

'Wouldn't you be? He is the luckiest archaeologist in the world. He is uncovering the most spectacular site.'

Rob nodded, and took more notes. Christine's enthusiasm was nearly as infectious as Breitner's. And her explanations were more lucid. Rob still didn't quite share their wonderment at the 'total revolution in perceptions' Gobekli represented, but he was beginning to anticipate a very dramatic article. Page two of the main paper, easy. Better still – a big feature in a colour supplement with some vivid colour pictures of the carvings. Moody shots of the stones at night. Photos of the workers covered in grime . . .

Then he remembered Radevan's reaction to the mention of the place, and the worker's angry glare. And Breitner's slight change of mood when they talked about Rob's article. And the tension about the trench. Christine was over by the samovar, filling their glasses with more hot sweet black tea. He wondered whether to say anything. As she returned, he said, 'Funny thing is, though, Christine, I know this dig is amazing and all that. But does everyone feel the same way?'

'What do you mean?'

'Well . . . I just . . . got some vibe from the locals . . . some real attitude. Not so good. This place upsets some people. My driver for instance.'

Christine perceptibly stiffened. 'Go on?

'My cab driver.' Rob tapped his chin with his pen. 'Radevan. He got really angry about Gobekli when I mentioned it last night. And it's not just him. There's an atmosphere. And Breitner seems . . . ambivalent. Once or twice when I discussed my piece with him this morning he seemed less than keen on me being here . . . Even if he does laugh a lot.' He paused. 'You'd think he'd want the world to know, wouldn't you? What he's doing here? Yet he doesn't seem comfortable.'

Christine said nothing, so Rob stayed silent. An old journalistic trick.

It worked. Eventually, embarrassed by the silence, Christine leaned forward. 'OK. You are right. There is . . . there are . . .' She stopped, as if debating with herself. The breeze off the desert was even hotter, if anything. Rob waited and sipped his tea.

At last she sighed. 'You're here a week, yes? You're doing a serious story?'

'Yes.'

Christine nodded. 'OK. Let me drive you back to Sanliurfa. The dig stops at one o'clock because it's so hot, many people go home. I usually go home then. We can talk in my car. Privately.'

6

In the dusty square of car park that led to the dig, Rob gave Radevan a healthy tip, and told him he'd make his own way home. Radevan looked at Rob, then at the folding money in his hand, then at Christine, standing just behind Rob. He gave Rob a big knowing grin, and turned the car around. As the driver revved the engine he called out of the car window, 'Maybe tomorrow, Mr Rob?'

'Maybe tomorrow.'

Radevan sped off.

Christine's car was a rusty Land Rover. She opened the passenger door from the inside and hastily cleared lots of documents from the passenger seat – textbooks and academic magazines – chucking them haphazardly in the back. Then she gunned the engine and they set off at serious pace, for the main road – careering down the rubbly hillsides, out onto the burnt yellow plains.

'So . . . what's up?' Rob had to shout his question above the noise of the car tyres, popping over rocks.

'The main problem is politics. You have to remember this is Kurdistan. The Kurds think the Turks are stealing their heritage. Taking all the best stuff to museums in Ankara and Istanbul . . . I'm not sure it's totally untrue.'

Rob watched a flash of sunlight on an irrigation canal. He'd read that this area was the subject of a massive agricultural campaign: the Great Anatolia Project, using the waters of the Euphrates to bring the desert back to life. The project was controversial because it was flooding, and drowning, dozens of ancient and unique archaeological sites. Though luckily not Gobekli. He looked back at Christine, changing gear viciously.

'What is true is that the government won't allow the locals to make money out of Gobekli Tepe.'

'Because?'

'Because of perfectly valid archaeological reasons. The last thing Gobekli needs is thousands of tourists crawling all over. So the government don't build signs, they keep the roads like this. And that means we can work in peace.' She turned the steering wheel sharply, and accelerated. 'But I can also see the Kurdish point of view. You must have seen some of the villages on the way up here.'

Rob nodded. 'A couple.'

'They don't even have running water. Sanitation. They barely have schools. They are dirt poor. And Gobekli Tepe, if it were properly marketed, could be a huge money-spinner. Bringing a lot of money to the region.'

'And Franz is in the middle of this argument?'

'Smack bang. He has pressure from all sides. Pressure to do the dig properly, pressure to hurry up, pressure to employ lots of local people. Pressure to stay in charge even.'

'So that's why he is ambivalent about publicity?'

'Naturally he's proud of what he's discovered. He'd love the world to know. He's been working here since 1994.' Christine slowed to let a goat cross the road, then sped on again. 'Many archaeologists move around a lot. I've worked in Mexico, Israel, France since I left Cambridge six years back. But Franz has been here more than half his career. So yes he'd like to tell the world! But if he does that, and Gobekli becomes truly famous, as famous as it *should* be, well then some big chief in Ankara might decide that a Turk should be in charge. And get all the glory.'

Rob understood the situation better. But it still didn't quite explain the strange atmosphere at the dig. The workers' resentment. Or maybe he was imagining it?

They reached the main road, spun onto the level tarmac, and headed faster, through increasing traffic, for Sanliurfa. As they overtook fruit lorries and army trucks they talked about Christine's interest: human remains. How she used to work on human sacrifices at Teotihuacán. Her stint in Tel Gezer and Megiddo in Israel. The Neanderthal sites of France.

'Ancient hominids lived in southern France for hundreds of thousands of years, people like us, but not quite like us.'

'Neanderthals, you mean?'

'Yes, but also maybe *Homo erectus* and *Homo antecessor.* Even *Homo heidelbergensis.*'

'Er . . . OK . . .'

Christine laughed. 'Am I losing you again? Fair enough – let me show you something *really* cool. If this doesn't grab you nothing will.'

The car was headed for the centre of Sanliurfa. Concrete houses were jumbled on hills; big shops and offices stretched down dusty, sunlit boulevards. Other streets were more shaded and antique: as they clawed their way through the traffic Rob saw a section of Ottoman arcading, the entrance to a bustling, dark souk, mosques hidden behind crumbling stone walls. Sanliurfa was obviously divided into an old – very old – district, and new quarters sprawling out into the semi-desert.

Looking left, he saw a large park-like area, with glittering pools and canals, and bijou teahouses, a charming oasis in the grime and hubbub of the big Kurdish town.

'The Golbasi Gardens,' said Christine. 'And those are the fish pools of Abraham. Locals think the Prophet Abraham put the carp in himself. This city is amazing – if you like history. I love it here . . .'

The car had made it through the narrower streets of the old town.

Jerking the wheel left, Christine took a wide road up a hill and veered between the gates of a tree-shaded building. The sign said *Sanliurfa Museum*.

Just inside the museum were three unshaven men sipping black tea: they stood and greeted Christine warmly. In return she joshed with them in a familiar way, in Turkish, or Kurdish. It was certainly some language Rob didn't understand.

The pleasantries done, they passed through the inner doors into the small museum, where Christine led Rob to a statue. It was two metres high: a cream-coloured stone effigy of a man with black stone eyes.

'This was dug up in Sanliurfa ten years ago when they were laying foundations for a bank near the fishponds. It was found amid the remains of a Neolithic temple, maybe eleven thousand years old. So this is probably the oldest statue of a man ever found. Anywhere. It's the oldest self-portrait in stone in the history of the world. And it just sits here, by the fire extinguisher.'

Rob looked at it. The statue's expression was infinitely sad, or frighteningly regretful.

Christine gestured at the face. 'The eyes are obsidian.'

'You're right. It's amazing.'

'There,' Christine said. 'I persuaded you!'

'But what the hell is it doing here? I mean, if it's so famous, why isn't it in Istanbul and all over the press? I've never even heard of it!'

Christine shrugged and the movement made her silver crucifix glint against her suntanned skin. 'Maybe the Kurds are right. Maybe the Turks don't want them to be too proud of their heritage. Who knows?'

As they strolled out into the museum's leafy garden, he told her about the stare of the man, the apparent hatred. The odd atmosphere at the site.

Christine frowned. For a few minutes she paced around, showing Rob the various remains scattered in the garden, the Roman gravestones and Ottoman carvings. As they neared the car, she pointed to another statue: a representation of a bird-like man with wings outstretched. It had a narrow face with slanting eyes, cruel and menacing. 'That was found near Gobekli. It's a desert demon of the Assyrians, I think. Maybe the wind devil Pazuzu. The Assyrians and Mesopotamians had hundreds of demons, it's quite a scary theology. Lilith the maid of desolation, Adramalech, the demon of sacrifice. Many of them associated with the desert wind, and desert birds . . .'

Rob was sure she was stalling. He waited for her to respond to his question.

Suddenly, she turned to him. 'OK. You're right. There is . . . an atmosphere at the dig. It's funny. I've never experienced anything like it before, and I've been in digs all over the world. The workmen, they seem to resent us. We give them good money but still . . . they resent us.'

'Is it the Turkish-Kurdish thing?'

'No. Actually. I don't think it is. Or at least it's not just that,' Christine led them back to the car, parked under a fig tree. 'There's more to it than that. All these weird accidents keep happening. Ladders falling away. Stuff collapsing. Cars breaking down. It's more than coincidence. Sometimes I actually think they want us to stop, and go away. As if they are . . .'

'Hiding something?'

The Frenchwoman blushed. 'It's stupid. But yes. It's as if they are trying to hide something. And there's something else. I might as well tell you.'

Rob had the car door half open. 'What?'

Inside the car, Christine said, 'Franz. He does digs. At night. On his own, with a couple of workers.' She started the car, and shook her head. 'And I've absolutely no idea why.'

7

DCI Forrester sat at his messy desk in New Scotland Yard. He had in front of him more photos of the wounded man, David Lorimer. The images were hideous. Two viciously inscribed stars in the man's chest, blood trickling down the skin.

The Star of David.

Lorimer. Clearly Scottish, not Jewish. Did the raiders think he was Jewish? Were *they* Jewish? Or Nazis? Is that what the journalist was on about? The neo-Nazi angle? Forrester turned and looked again at the official scene-of-crime shots of the cellar floor: the treacle-black soil disturbed by the spades and shovels. The hole made by the raiders was deep. They were certainly looking for something. And looking hard. Had they found it? But if they were looking for something why had they bothered to mutilate the old man when he disturbed them? Why not just knock him out or tie him up, or kill him cleanly? Why the elaborate, ritualistic cruelty?

Forrester suddenly wanted a proper drink. Instead he sipped his black tea, from a chipped mug bearing the image of an England flag, then got up and walked to his tenth-storey window. From this vantage he had a good view across Westminster and central London. The big steel bicycle wheel of the London Eye, with its alien glass pods. The

Gothic pinnacles of the Houses of Parliament. He looked at a new building going up in Victoria and tried to work out what style it was. He's always had a hankering to be an architect; had even applied to an architectural school as a teenager, then beaten a retreat when he heard the training was seven years long. Seven years with no proper salary? His parents didn't like the sound of that – nor did Forrester. So he'd joined the police. But he still liked to think he had a well-informed layman's knowledge of the subject. He could tell Wrenaissance from Renaissance, post-modern from neo-classical. It was one of the reasons he liked working and living in London, despite all the hassle: the architectural richness of the urban tapestry.

He drained the rest of the tea, went back to his desk and sifted through the reports the SIO had distributed at morning prayers – the 9 a.m. meeting on the Craven Street incident. CCTV footage had failed to spot any suspicious characters on the streets around. There were no other eye witnesses, despite a day of appeals. The first twenty-four hours were the golden hours of any investigation: if you got no significant leads in that time you knew the case was going to be hard. And thus it had proved. Forensics were drawing blank after blank: the intruders had even erased, very carefully, their bootprints. The crime was cleverly and deftly executed. Yet they had taken time to maim and torture the old man, very precisely. Why?

At a loss, Forrester opened up Google, typed in *Benjamin Franklin House* and found that it was built in the 1730s and 40s. Making it, as Forrester had guessed, one of the older domestic houses in the area, featuring authentic panelling, box cornices, a first floor saloon 'with dentils'. There was a dog-leg stair, with carved ends and 'Doric column-newels'. He clicked open another window to find out what column newels were, and, for that matter, dentils.

Nothing of interest.

The rest of the description was more of the same. Craven Street was a survivor of early Georgian London. A snicket of the gin-drinking eighteenth century town tucked away between the Slovenian fire-eaters and Kiwi opera singers of modern Covent Garden, and the itinerant junkies and shouting cabbies of scruffy Charing Cross.

This info didn't help much. So, what about Franklin himself? Could there be some connection with *him* and the unknown men? Forrester Googled 'Benjamin Franklin'. He already had a vague idea about him being the guy who found electricity with a kite, or something. Google gave him the rest.

Benjamin Franklin, 1706–1790 was one of the best-known Founding Fathers of the United States. He was a leading author, political theorist, politician, printer, scientist, and inventor. As a scientist he was a major figure in the history of physics for his discoveries and theories regarding electricity.

Forrester clicked on, feeling slightly inadequate.

Born in Boston, Massachusetts, Franklin learned printing from his older brother and became a newspaper editor, printer, and merchant in Philadelphia. He spent many years in England and France, speaking five languages. He was a lifelong Freemason, including in his liberal circle Joseph Banks the botanist and Sir Francis Dashwood, the British Chancellor. He was also a secret agent for many years . . .

Forrester sighed, and clicked off. So the man was a polymath. So what? Why dig in his cellar? Why mutilate the caretaker of his museum centuries later? He checked the clock on his computer. He needed lunch, and he hadn't achieved much. He hated this feeling – a whole morning going by with nothing achieved. It was irritating at quite a deep and existential level.

OK, he thought. Maybe try something from a different angle. Something more oblique. He Googled 'Benjamin Franklin Museum cellar'.

And there, almost immediately. Yes! Forrester felt prickles of adrenalin. He scanned the screen urgently.

On the very first website was a verbatim newspaper report from *The Times*, dated February 11, 1998.

Bones Discovered in Founding Father's House

Excavators at the Craven Street home of Benjamin Franklin, the Founding Father of the USA, have made a macabre discovery: eight skeletons concealed beneath the flagstones of the wine cellar.

Initial estimates suggest that the bones are about 200 years old and were buried at the time Franklin was living in the house, which was his home from 1757 to 1762, and from 1764 to 1775. Most of the bones show signs of having been dissected, sawn or cut. One skull has been bizarrely drilled with several holes. Paul Knapman, the Westminster Coroner, said yesterday, 'I cannot totally discount the possibility of a crime. There is still a possibility that I may have to hold an inquest.'

The Friends of Benjamin Franklin Museum claim that the bones had no occult or criminal connection. They say the bones were probably placed there by William Hewson, who lived in the house for two years and who had built a small anatomy school at the back of the house. They note that while Franklin perhaps knew what Hewson was doing, he probably did not participate in any dissections because he was much more of a physicist than a medical man.

Forrester sat back. The cellar had been dug up before. With surprising results. Was this why the guys had returned? And what was this about 'occult or criminal connections'?

Occult . . .

The detective smiled. He was looking forward to lunch now. It was possible that he had the first sniff of a lead.

8

It was a soft, warm evening in Sanliurfa. In the lobby of his hotel Rob found Christine perched on a leather seat trying not to inhale the smoke from three cigar-puffing Turkish businessmen sitting nearby. She looked chic as ever – elegant jeans, sandals, a white sleeveless top under an aquamarine cardigan. When she saw Rob she smiled, but he could see stress in the corners of her eyes.

They were going to Franz Breitner's for a few drinks: a supper party to celebrate the great success of the latest digging season: the dating of Gobekli Tepe.

'Is it far?'

'Twenty minutes' walk,' Christine replied. 'And about thirty minutes' drive. It's right past the market.'

The restaurants and cafés were stirring after the torpor of the afternoon. The scent of roast lamb from turning spits wafted across the dust-whirled streets. Taxi drivers hooted; a crippled man in a wheelchair hawked yesterday's Ankara newspapers; the pistachio sellers were wheeling their glass-fronted barrows into position. Rob greedily inhaled the exoticism of the scene.

'Shall we buy some wine? To take to Franz's place?'

Christine laughed. 'In Sanliurfa?'

They walked past a clock-tower into the old town. Rob scanned the ancient colonnades, the kiosks selling garish plastic toys, the endless mobile phone outlets. Various open air cafés were full of heavy-set Kurdish men smoking hookahs, eating from plates of white Turkish delight, and staring hard at Christine. No one was drinking alcohol.

'They don't sell booze? Anywhere?' Rob felt his mood plummet. He hadn't had a beer or a glass of wine in three days. He drank too much, he knew that, but that was how he coped with the stress of his job. Especially after Baghdad. And three days without alcohol was quite long enough to reconfirm a fact he already knew: he wasn't suited to sobriety.

'Actually, I think there are a couple of liquor shops on the outskirts of town. But it's like scoring dope in England. All very furtive.'

'Jesus.'

'What do you expect? This is a Muslim city.'

'I've been to a few Muslim cities, Christine. But I thought Turkey was secular.'

'People think the Kurds are somehow westernized.' She smiled. 'They're not. Especially the ones around here. Some of them are exceptionally conservative.'

'Guess I'm used to Palestine and Lebanon. Even in Egypt you can get a fucking beer.'

Christine placed a comforting arm around his shoulder and hugged him. Her smile was sarcastic – but friendly. 'Good news is Franz has plenty of hooch. He brings it from Istanbul.'

'Thank God for that!'

'*Bien sur.* I know what journalists are like. Especially British journalists.'

'American, Christine.'

'Here – look – the fish pools!'

They'd reached the sweet green oasis at the heart of the town. The little tea houses twinkled in the twilight sun; Turkish bachelors were walking hand-in-hand along the tree-lined pathways. Across the waters of the pools, the beautiful stone arcades of a mosque were shining like ancient gold.

Christine and Rob watched a large family group: the men in baggy trousers and the women in full black veils. Rob considered how the women must have been sweltering through the day, and he felt an automatic resentment on their behalf. Christine, however, seemed unfazed. 'The Bible says Job was born here, as well as Abraham.'

'Sorry?'

'Urfa.' Christine pointed to the steep hill, beyond the fishponds and gardens, on top of which stood a crumbling castle – where a huge Turkish flag hung flaccid in the windless warmth, between two Corinthian columns. 'Some scholars think this is Ur, the original city in the Book of Genesis. The Akkadians, the Sumerians, the Hittites, they all lived here. The oldest city in the world.'

'I thought that was Jericho?'

'Pah!' Christine chortled. 'Jericho! A mere stripling. This place is much older. In the old town behind the bazaar there are people who still live in caves cut into the rock.' Christine glanced back at the fishponds. The shrouded women were feeding bread to the shoals of excited carp. 'The carp are black because they are meant to be ashes of Abraham. They say if you see a white fish in the pond you will go to heaven!'

'That's fantastic! Can we go and eat now?'

Christine laughed, again. Rob liked her good-natured laugh. In fact, he liked Christine a lot: her academic enthusiasm, her cleverness, her good humour. He felt an unexpected urge to share his inmost thoughts with her; show her a picture of little Lizzie. He suppressed the inclination.

The Frenchwoman was gesturing, enthusiastically.

'Breitner's house is just past the bazaar up this hill. We can take a look at the bazaar if you like: it's got an authentic caravanserai, sixteenth century, built by the Abbasids with some older elements and . . .' She glanced at him, then chuckled. 'Or we could go straight there and get a beer?'

The walk was short but steep, behind the back of the souk. Men ferrying silver trays of tea and olives came the other way, and all of them stared at Christine. An orange-coloured sofa sat inexplicably across the opposite pavement. The smell of hot unleavened bread filled the narrow alleys. In the middle of it all was a very old, very beautiful house, with balconies and Mediterranean shutters.

'Breitner's place. You'll like his wife.'

Christine was right. Rob did like Franz's wife, Derya: she was a vivacious, secular, smart, thirty-something woman from Istanbul, with no headscarf or veil, and excellent English. When she wasn't teasing Franz about his bald head or his obsession with 'menhirs' she served Rob and Christine, and the other archaeologists who had all gathered for the supper party. And the food was good: a splendid buffet of cold lamb sausages, rice in vine leaves, exquisite walnut pastries, thick gooey chunks of baklava and greeny-pink arcs of the freshest water melon. Even better, just as Christine had promised, there was plenty of icy cold Turkish beer – and some decent red wine from Cappadocia. Within a couple of hours Rob was feeling very relaxed, convivial and happy, content to listen to the archaeologists argue about Gobekli.

For his benefit, Rob guessed, they conducted the argument mainly in English, though three of the four men were German, and the other was Russian. And Christine kind-of French.

As he nibbled his third slice of baklava, chasing it with his Efes beer, Rob tried to follow the debate. One of the archaeologists, Hans, was questioning Franz about the lack of skeletal remains. 'If it's a funerary complex then where are the bones?'

Franz smiled. 'We will find them! I told you.'

'But you said that last season.'

'And the season before,' said a second man, standing nearby with a plate of green olives and white sheep's cheese.

'I know.' Franz shrugged, happily. 'I know!'

The director of the dig was sitting on the biggest leather chair in his sitting room. Behind him, the antique windows were open to the Sanliurfa streets. Rob could hear the evening town life beyond. A man was shouting at his kids in the house across the way. A television blared in the café down the road: probably showing Turkish football, judging by the cheers and jeers of the customers. Maybe Galatasaray versus the local team, Dyarbakir. Turks versus Kurds. Like the rivalry of Real Madrid and Barcelona, but way more venomous.

Derya provided them with more baklava straight from the patisserie's silver cardboard box. Rob wondered if he might expire through overeating. Franz was gesticulating at his juniors. 'But if it isn't a funerary shrine or complex, then what is it? *Ja?* There is no settlement, no signs of domestication, nothing. It has to be a temple, we all agree on that. But a temple to what, if not ancestors? Surely it honours the dead huntsmen? No?'

The other two experts shrugged.

Franz added, 'And what are the niches, if not for bones?'

'I agree with Franz,' said Christine, coming over. 'I think the corpses of the hunters were brought there and excarnated . . .'

Rob burped very politely. 'Sorry. Excarnated?'

Franz explained, 'It means picked clean. The Zoroastrians still do it. And some think Zoroastrianism came from here.'

'Practically *all* religions came from around here,' said Christine. 'Excarnation is a funeral process whereby you take the body to a special place then leave it to be eaten by wild animals, or vultures and raptors. As Franz says, you can still see this in Zoroastrian faiths, in India. They call them sky burials – the corpses are left to the sky gods. In fact, a lot of the early Mesopotamian religions worshipped gods, shaped like these buzzards and eagles. Like the Assyrian demon we saw in the museum.'

'It's very hygienic. As a form of burial. Excarnation.' The interruption came from Ivan, the youngest expert, the paleobotanist.

Franz nodded, briskly, and said: 'Anyway – who knows – maybe the bones were moved, afterwards. Or maybe they got shifted when Gobekli was buried itself. That could explain the lack of skeletons on site.'

Rob was confused. 'What do you mean? "Gobekli was buried itself"?'

Franz put his empty plate down on the polished parquet floor. When he looked up he wore the satisfied smile of someone about to reveal a delicious piece of gossip. 'This, my friend, is the biggest mystery of all! And they did not mention it in the article you read!'

Christine laughed. 'You got your exclusive, Rob!'

'In or around 8000 BC . . .' Franz paused for effect, 'the whole of Gobekli Tepe was buried. Entombed. *Completely covered in earth.*'

'But . . . how do you know?'

'The hillocks are artificial. The soil is not a random accretion. The whole temple complex was deliberately concealed with tons of earth and mud in around 8000 BC. It was hidden.'

'Wow. That's wild.'

'What makes it even more amazing is how much labour this must have taken. And therefore how pointless it was.'

'Because . . . ?'

'Think of the effort to put it all up in the first place! Erecting the stone circles of Gobekli, and covering them with carvings, friezes and sculptures, must have been a process that took decades, maybe even centuries. And this at a time when life expectancy was twenty years.' Franz wiped his mouth with a napkin. 'We imagine the hunter-gatherers must have lived in the area in tents, leather tents, as they constructed the site. Living off the local game for sustenance. Generation after generation. And all of it without pottery or agriculture, or any tools but flints . . .'

Christine stepped a little nearer. 'I think maybe I've already bored Rob with this?'

Rob raised a hand. 'No, really, it's not boring. Really!' He meant it: his article was expanding by the day. 'Go on Franz, please?'

'*Jawohl.* Well then you see we have the mystery, the deep deep mystery. If it took these barely human people hundreds of years to construct a temple, a shrine to the dead, a funerary complex, why the hell did they then go and hide it under tons of earth two thousand years later? Moving all that soil must have been almost as daunting as building Gobekli in the first place. Is it not so?'

'Yes. So why *did* they do it?'

Franz slapped both his hands on the tops of his thighs. 'That is it! We do not know! Nobody knows. We only confirmed it this month, so we haven't had a chance to think.' He grinned. 'Fantastic, *ja*?'

Derya offered Rob another bottle of Efes beer. He took it and thanked her. He was having fun. He'd never expected archaeology to be fun, he hadn't expected it to be puzzling either. He thought about the mystery of the buried temple. Then he watched Christine as she talked with her colleagues across the living room and felt a tiny and ludicrous pang of jealousy, which he immediately quashed.

He was here to write a story – not fall pathetically and fruitlessly in love. And the story was proving much more exciting than he'd hoped. The oldest temple in the world. Discovered next to the oldest city in the world. Built by men before the wheel: built by Stone Age cavemen with the curious gift of great artistry . . .

And then the great Neolithic cathedral, this Kurdish Carnac, this Turkish Stonehenge – Rob was imagining his piece now, writing the paragraphs in his head – then the whole damn temple was deliberately interred beneath tons of ancient dust, concealed for all time, like the most terrible secret. *And no one knows why.*

He looked up. He'd been in a journalistic reverie for maybe ten minutes. Carried away with his job. He liked his job. He *was* a lucky man.

The little supper party was coming to a head. Someone got out an old guitar and everyone sang a few songs. Then the raki flowed for a final round of nightcaps, and then it flowed again, and Rob knew he was getting too drunk. Before he disgraced himself and fell asleep on the wooden floor he decided he should head home – so he went to the window to inhale some fresh air and prepare himself to make his excuses.

Out there, the streets were much less noisy. Sanliurfa was a city that stayed up late, because it slept all the hot afternoon – but it was nearly 2 a.m. Even Sanliurfa was asleep. The only real sound came from directly below. Three men were standing in the street, just under Franz Breitner's elegant windows. They were singing a strange low-pitched song, almost like a chant. Quite peculiarly, they had a little trestle table erected in front of them: a table arrayed with three guttering candles.

For maybe half a minute Rob watched the men and the candle flames. Then he turned and saw Christine standing in the far corner of Franz's living room, talking to Derya. Rob beckoned her over.

Christine leaned out of the window, looked at the chanting men and said nothing.

'It's sweet isn't it?' Rob said quietly. 'Some kind of hymn or a religious thing?'

But when he turned to look at her he could see that her face was pale, and very tense.

She looked horrified.

9

Rob made his farewells and Christine accompanied him.

Outside, the three chanting men had blown out the candles, packed up the trestle table, and were now starting to walk down the street. One of them looked back at Christine. His expression was inscrutable.

Or maybe, Rob thought, it was just the lack of streetlight making it hard to see what the man was thinking. Somewhere in the distance a dog barked in its own lonely ritual. The moon was high above the nearest minaret. Rob could smell raw sewage.

Threading her arm through his, Christine guided them down the dark little road and out onto a broader, slightly better-lit street. Rob was waiting for her to explain but they continued in silence. Beyond the furthest apartment blocks Rob could just glimpse the desert. Dark and endless, and ancient and dead.

He thought of the pillars of Gobekli, standing naked in the moonlight, somewhere out there: exposed for the first time in ten thousand years; he felt cold for the first time since arriving in Sanliurfa.

The silence had gone on too long. 'OK,' he said, unthreading Christine's arm from his own. 'What was all that about? The chanting?' Rob knew he was being fierce, but he was feeling tired, irritable and a touch hungover. 'Christine. Tell me. You looked like . . . like you'd seen the Assyrian wind demon.'

It was meant as a joke, to lighten the mood. It didn't work. Christine frowned. 'Pulsa Dinura.'

'What?'

'That's what the men were chanting. A prayer.'

'Pulsa . . . di . . .'

'Nura. Lashes of fire. Aramaic.'

Rob was impressed, again. 'How do you know?'

'I speak a little Aramaic.'

They were down on the level of the fishponds. The old mosque was shadowy and unlit. No couples walked the paths. Rob and Christine turned left, heading for his hotel, and her flat just beyond.

'So they were singing an Aramaic hymn, that's nice. Busking!'

'It's not a hymn. And they weren't fucking busking.'

Her sudden vehemence surprised him.

'Sorry Christine . . .'

'Pulsa Dinura is an ancient curse. A hex of the desert. Of the Mesopotamian wastes. It's in some versions of the Talmud, the Jewish holy book, written at the time of the Babylonian Captivity. When the Jews were imprisoned in Iraq. Rob, it's very evil and it's very *old*.'

'OK . . .' He didn't know how to react. They were nearing his hotel. 'And what does it do? Pulsa di Nura.'

'It's meant to summon the angel of destruction. The whips of flame. They must have been aiming it at Franz. Otherwise why do it under his windows?'

Rob felt the irritation again. 'So they're hexing him. So what? Fair enough. Probably he's not paying them enough shekels. Who cares – it's just bloody mumbo jumbo! Right?' Then he remembered the cross around Christine's neck. Was he somehow insulting her? How religious was she? How superstitious? Rob was firmly atheist. He found religious belief and superstitious irrationality hard to accept and sometimes deeply annoying;

yet he loved the Middle East, birthplace of all those irrational faiths and desert creeds. And he rather liked the passions and debates stirred by these faiths. A strange paradox.

Christine was silent. Rob tried again: 'What does it matter?'

She turned to face him. 'It matters a lot to some people. In Israel for instance.'

'Go on.'

'Pulsa Dinura has been used a few times in recent years, by Jews.'

'Right . . .'

'Some ultra orthodox rabbis, for instance. They summoned the angel of death against Yitzhak Rabin, the Israeli leader, in October 1995.' She paused. Rob was working out the significance of the date. Christine got there before him: 'And Rabin was assassinated within the month.'

'K. An interesting coincidence.'

'Some more rabbis used Pulsa Dinura against Ariel Sharon, the next prime minister, in 2005. A few months later he fell into a coma, after a brain haemorrhage.'

'Sharon was seventy-seven. And he was fat.'

She looked directly into Rob's eyes. 'Sure. It's just . . . coincidence.'

'Yep. It is.'

They were at the lobby of his hotel. They were nearly arguing. Rob regretted this. He liked Christine. A lot. He didn't want to offend her. He offered – keenly – to walk the further half a kilometre with her to her apartment block, but she – gently – declined. They looked at each other. Then they hugged briefly. Before she left she said, 'As you say Robert, it's just coincidence. But the Kurds believe it works. Lots of people in the Middle East think Pulsa Dinura works. It is infamous. Check it on Google. So if they are using it . . . what that means is that some people really want Franz Breitner *dead*.'

With that she turned and walked away.

Rob watched her for a few minutes. Her disappearing figure. Then he shivered again. The night was getting colder as the wind blew in off the desert.

10

DCI Forrester sat back on the sofa. He was in a cosy sitting room just off Muswell Hill, in suburban north London. He was seeing his therapist.

It was kind of clichéd, he supposed. The policeman with the neuroses, the fucked-up cop. But he didn't mind. The sessions helped.

'So how was your week?' His therapist was sixty-something, Dr Janice Edwards. Posh in a nice way. Forrester liked the fact she was quite old. It meant he could just spill the beans, achieve catharsis, talk without any emotional distraction. And he needed to talk. Even if it cost fifty pounds an hour. Sometimes he talked about his job, sometimes about his wife, and sometimes about other stuff. Darker stuff. Serious stuff. Yet he never *really* got to the heart of it. His daughter. Maybe one day he would.

'So,' Dr Edwards said again, somewhere behind Forrester's head. 'Tell me your week . . .'

Staring at the window, blankly, his hands resting on his stomach, Forrester started telling his therapist about the Craven Street case. The caretaker, the mutilation, the weirdness. 'We've got no witnesses. They got out clean. They used leather gloves but Forensics can't find any DNA. The knife wound is useless. A standard blade. We didn't lift a single print.' He rubbed his head. The therapist murmured interest. He carried on. 'I did get excited when I found out the cellar they dug up was once . . . well they found some old bones there years back . . . but it wasn't really a lead, it was just a coincidence, I think. But I still have no idea what they were looking for. Maybe it was a prank, just a student prank that went wrong, maybe they were high on drugs . . .' Forrester realized he was meandering, but he didn't especially care. 'And that's where I am. I've got a guy with no tongue in hospital and the trail has gone cold and . . . well anyway that's been my week, a pretty shit week, and that's all really . . . you know . . .' He tailed off.

Sometimes in therapy this was what happened. You didn't say much of importance, and then you dried up. But then Forrester felt a surge of grief and anger – from nowhere. Maybe it was the darkness falling outside, maybe it was the quietness in the room. Maybe it was the thought of that poor man beaten and abused. But now he really did want to talk about something much deeper, something much darker. The real stuff. It was time. Maybe it was time to talk about Sarah.

But silence filled the room. Forrester thought about his daughter. He closed his eyes. He lay back. And he thought about Sarah. The trusting blue eyes. Her giddy laughter. Her first words. Apple. *App-ull.* Their first child. A beautiful daughter. And then . . .

And then. Sarah. Oh, *Sarah.*

He rubbed his eyes. He couldn't talk about it. Not yet. He could think about it: he thought about it all the time. But he couldn't talk about it. Yet.

She had been seven years old. She'd just gone wandering off in the dark, one winter night. She'd just gone wandering off, out of the door, no one was watching. And then they'd searched and they searched, and the police and the neighbours and everyone searched . . .

And they'd found her. In the middle of the road, under the motorway bridge. And no one knew if it was murder or if she had just fallen off the bridge. Because the body was so mashed. Run over by so many cars in the dark. The lorries and cars probably thought they were driving over a tyre.

Forrester was sweating. He hadn't thought about Sarah this deeply in months, maybe years. He knew he needed to release this. To get it out. But he couldn't. He half turned and said, 'I'm sorry, Doctor. I just can't. I still think about it every hour of every day, you know? But . . .' He gulped. The words wouldn't come. But the thoughts were racing. Every day he wondered, even now: did someone find her and rape her and then drop her off the bridge or did she just fall – but if she just fell how did it happen? Sometimes he thought he knew. Sometimes in his heart of hearts he suspected she must have been murdered. He was a cop. He knew this stuff. But there were no witnesses, no evidence. Maybe they would never know. He sighed and looked across at the therapist. She was serene. Serene and sixty-five years old and grey-haired and smiling quietly.

'It doesn't matter.' She said. 'One day . . .'

Forrester nodded. He smiled at their catchphrase. *Maybe one day.* 'I just find it hard sometimes. My wife gets depressed and she turns away at night. We never have sex from one month to the next, but at least we are alive.'

'And you have your son.'

'Yes. Yes we have him. I guess sometimes you have to be grateful for what is, rather than what isn't. I mean. What do alcoholics say in AA? You got to fake it to make it. All that bullshit. I guess that's what I've got to do. Just do that. Pretend I'm OK sometimes.' He stopped again and the silence echoed around the warm sitting room. At last he sat up. His hour was up. All he could hear was traffic, muffled by the windows and the curtains.

'Thanks, Dr Edwards.'

'Please. As I said, call me Janice. You've been coming here six months.'

'Thanks, Janice.'

She smiled. 'I'll see you next week?'

He stood. They shook hands, politely. Forrester felt cleansed and slightly lighter in spirit.

He drove back to Hendon in a calm and pleasantly pensive mood. Another day. He'd got through another day. Without drinking or shouting.

The house was full of his son's noise when he keyed the door. His wife was in the kitchen watching the news on TV. The smell of pasta and pesto wafted through. It was OK. Things were OK. In the kitchen his wife kissed him and he said he'd been to a session and she smiled and seemed relatively content.

Before supper Forrester went outside into the garden and rolled a tiny spliff of grass. He felt no guilt as he did it. He smoked the weed, standing on his patio, exhaling the blue smoke into the starry sky, and sensed his neck-muscles unknotting. Then he went back into the house and lay on the floor of the sitting room and helped his son with a puzzle. And then there was a phone call.

In the kitchen his wife was sieving the penne. Hot steam. The smell of pesto.

'Hello?'

'DCI?'

Forrester recognized his junior's slight Finnish accent immediately. 'Boijer, I'm just about to eat.'

'Sorry, sir, but I got this strange call . . .'

'Yeah?'

'That friend of mine – Skelding, you know, Niall.'

Forrester thought for a moment, then he remembered: the tall guy who worked on the Home Office murder database. They'd all had a drink once.

'Yeah, I remember. Skelding. Works on HOLMES.'

'That's right. Well he just called me and said they've got a new homicide, the Isle of Man.'

'And?'

'Some guy's been killed. Very nasty. In a big house.'

'Long way away, the Isle of Man . . .'

Boijer agreed. Forrester watched his wife sauce the penne with the vivid green pesto. It looked slightly like bile; but it smelled good. Forrester coughed impatiently. 'As I said, Boijer, my wife's just made a very nice dinner and I—'

'Yes, sorry, sir, but the thing is, before this guy was killed, the attackers cut a symbol into his chest.'

'You mean . . .'

'Yes, sir. That's right. A Star of David.'

11

The day after Franz's supper party Rob rang his ex-wife's home. His daughter Lizzie picked up. She still didn't really know how to use a phone. Rob called into it, 'Darling, use the other end.'

'Hello, Daddy. Hello.'

'Dar . . .'

Just hearing Lizzie talk gave Rob a stabbing sense of guilt. And also a sheer basic pleasure that he had a daughter. And an angry desire to protect her. And then an extra guilt that he wasn't there, in England, protecting her.

But protecting her from what? She was safe in suburban London. She was fine.

When Lizzie had worked out the right end of the phone, they talked for an hour and Rob promised to send her jpegs of where he was. Then he reluctantly put the phone down and decided it was time to get to work. Hearing his daughter often did this: it was like an instinct, something genetic. The reminder of his family duties energized his work reflex – go and earn some money to feed the offspring. It was time to write his article.

But Rob had a dilemma. Moving the phone from his hotel bed to the floor he lay back and thought. Hard. The story was so much more complex than he had envisaged. Complex and interesting. First there was the politics: the Kurdish/Turkish rivalry. Then the atmosphere at the dig, and amongst the locals: their resentment – and that death prayer . . . And what about Franz's clandestine late-night digging? What was all that about?

Rob got up and walked to his window. He was on the top floor of the hotel. He opened the window and listened to the sound of a muezzin calling from a mosque somewhere nearby. The song was harsh, barbarous even – yet somehow hypnotic. The inimitable sound of the Middle East. More voices joined the rising carol. The call for prayer echoed across the city.

So what was he going to write for the paper? A part of him strongly wanted to stay and investigate further. Get to the bottom of the story. But what was the point in that, really? Wasn't that just indulging himself? He didn't have forever. And if he included all this odd and perplexing stuff it altered and maybe even ruined his article. At the very least it complicated the narrative – and therefore compromised it. The reader would be left confused, and arguably unsatisfied.

So what should he write? The answer was obvious. If he just stuck to the simple and fairly astonishing historical stuff he would be fine. Man Discovers the World's Oldest Temple. *Mysteriously buried two thousand years later . . .*

That was enough. It was a cracking story. And with some striking pictures of the stones and the carvings and an angry Kurd and Franz in his spectacles and Christine in her elegant khakis it would look good, too.

Christine. Rob wondered if his barely suppressed desire to stay and investigate the story further was actually because of her. His barely suppressed desire for her. He wondered if she could tell what he felt. Probably. Women could always tell. Yet Rob never had a clue. Did she even like him? There was that hug . . . And the way she put her arm through his last night . . .

Enough. Picking up his rucksack and chucking in pens, notebooks and sunglasses, Rob left his hotel room. He wanted to visit the dig one last time, ask a few more questions, and then he'd have sufficient material. He'd already been here five days. Time to move on.

Outside the hotel Radevan was leaning against his taxi arguing about football or politics with the other cabbies, as ever. He looked up when Rob stepped out into the sunshine, and smiled. Rob nodded. They had a little rigmarole going now.

'I want to go to the bad place.'

Radevan laughed:

'The bad place? Yes, Mr Rob.'

Radevan did his chauffeur thing with the car door and Rob jumped in feeling energetic and determined. He'd made the right choice. Do the piece, invoice for exes – then head back to England and insist on some proper time with his daughter.

The drive to Gobekli was uneventful. Radevan picked his nose and complained loudly about the Turks. Rob stared out across the wastes, towards the Euphrates, the blue Taurus Mountains beyond. He'd come to like this desert, even if it unnerved him. So old, so weary, so malevolent, so stark. The desert of the wind demons. What else was hiding under its shallow hills? A weird thought. Rob stared across the wilderness.

They got there quickly. With a squeal of bald tyres, Radevan parked. He leaned out of the window as Rob walked to the dig. 'Three hours, Mr Rob?'

Rob laughed. 'Yep.'

The dig was frenetic today, busier than Rob had seen it. New trenches were being laid. Deep new gouges into the hills, showing ever more stones. Rob understood that the digging season was coming to an end and Franz was keen to crack on. The digging season was remarkably short – the site was simply too hot in high summer, and too exposed in winter. And anyway the scientists apparently needed nine months of exegesis and laboratory work to process what they had found in the three months of actual digging. That was the archaeological year:

three months of spadework, nine months of thinking. Quite relaxed, really.

Franz and Christine and the paleobotanist – Ivan – were having a debate in the tented area. They greeted Rob with a wave and he sat down and more tea was served. Rob liked the endless production line of Turkish tea, the ritual tinkling of spoons and tulip-shaped glasses, the taste of the sweet dark *cay*. And hot black tea was oddly refreshing in the dry desert sun.

Over his first glass of tea Rob told them his news. That he was finishing up, that this was his last visit. He checked Christine's face as he said this. Did he see a flicker of regret? Maybe. His mood sashayed a little. But then he remembered his job. He had to ask some more questions, his very last queries. That was why he was here. Nothing else.

His journalistic need was to put the dig in context. He'd been reading some more history books – prehistory books – and he wanted to place Gobekli Tepe somewhere within that history. See how it fitted in, how it gleamed in the mosaic of wider human history – the evolution of man and civilization.

Franz was happy to oblige. 'This area,' he waved his arm at the yellow hills beyond the open-sided tents, 'is where it all began. Human civilization. The first written language is cuneiform, that started not far away. Copper smelting is originally Mesopotamian. And the first true towns were built in Turkey. Isobel Previn could tell you all about that.'

Rob was mystified. Then he remembered the name – Christine's tutor at Cambridge. Isobel Previn. Rob had also read the name in various history books – Previn had worked with the great James Mellaert, the English archaeologist who excavated Catalhoyuk. Rob had enjoyed reading about Catalhoyuk – not least because they dug it up so quickly. Three years of lusty shovelling and it was nearly all revealed. That was the heroic, Hollywood age of archaeology. Nowadays, as far as Rob could tell, things had slowed down. Now there were so many experts in different fields – archaeometallurgists, zooarchaeologists, ethnohistorians, geomorphologists – it had all got very intricate. A complex site could take decades to unravel.

Gobekli Tepe was such a site. Franz had been digging in Gobekli since 1994; Christine had implied that he would spend the rest of his working life here. A whole working life on one site! But then again, it was the most amazing archaeological site in the world. Which was probably why Franz looked so chuffed most of the time. He was smiling right now – explaining to Rob about the early history of pottery and agriculture, both of which came after Gobekli Tepe was built. Both of which also started nearby.

'The first ever signs of farming can be found in Syria. Gordon Childe called it the Neolithic Revolution and it happened not far to the south. Abu Hureyra, Tell Aswad, places like that. So you see this really is the cradle. Metalwork, pottery, farming, smelting, writing all began near Gobekli. *Ja?*'

Christine added, 'Yes, though actually there is some evidence of rice farming in Korea in 13,000 BC, but it is enigmatic.'

Ivan, who had been silent until now, also joined in: 'And there is some strange evidence that pottery may have started and then stopped before that, in Siberia.'

Rob turned. 'Sorry?' Franz looked slightly irritated by his colleague's interruption, but Rob was intrigued. 'Go on?'

Ivan blushed. 'Erm . . . we have evidence from eastern Siberia, maybe Japan, of an even earlier civilization. A northern people. Possibly they died out, because the evidence disappears. We do not know. We have no idea where they went.'

Franz looked nettled. '*Ja, ja, ja*, Ivan. But still! This area is where it really happened. The Near East! Here.' He slapped his hand on the table for emphasis, making the teaspoons rattle. 'All of it. All of it started here. The first kilns for making pots. That was in Syria, and Iraq. The Hittites made the first iron. In Anatolia. The first domestic pigs were in Cayonu, the first villages were in Anatolia, and . . . and of course the first temple . . .'

'Gobekli Tepe!'

Everyone laughed. Peace had been restored, and the conversation evolved. Rob spent a diligent ten minutes copying out his notes, while the archaeologists chatted amongst themselves about domestication of early animals and the distribution of 'microliths'. The discussion was technical and obscure; Rob didn't mind. He had the final pieces to the jigsaw. It wasn't the whole picture – the mysteries remained – but it was a good picture and a compelling picture and it would have to do. Besides, he was a journalist, not a historian. He wasn't here to get everything right, he was here to get a vivid impression, quickly. What did they call journalism? 'The first draft of history'. That was all he was doing and all he was meant to do: he was writing the first rough draft.

He looked up. He'd been annotating for half an hour now. The scientists had left him to it; they had dispersed around the dig to do whatever it was they actually did when they weren't arguing. Examining dust and sieving old rocks. Sitting in their cabins having more arguments. Rob stood up, rubbed his stiff neck and decided to go for a wander about the place before making his exit. So he hoisted his rucksack and walked out around the nearest hillock, skirting the enclosures and the stones.

Beyond the main area of the dig was a vast bare field, scattered with flints. Christine had showed him this place on his previous visit. Rob had been amazed at the time to see so many twelve-thousand-year-old pieces of flint, knapped by Stone Age man, just lying around. Literally thousands of them. You could just kneel down and after a short search pick up an ancient axe, arrowhead or cutting tool.

Rob decided to do just that: he fancied a souvenir. The sun was hot on his back as he knelt in the dust. Within a few minutes he got lucky. He examined his find, turning it carefully between his fingers. It was an arrowhead, skilfully, even exquisitely knapped. Rob imagined the man who had made it twelve thousand years ago. Working away in the sun, in a loincloth. With a bow slung across his muscled back. A primitive man. Yet someone who had built a great temple, carved with serious artistry. It was a paradox. The cavemen who built a cathedral! It was also a good introduction to Rob's article. A nice vivid image.

He stood up and slipped the arrowhead into a zipped side pocket of his rucksack. He was probably breaking a hundred Turkish laws, stealing ancient artefacts, but it wasn't as if Gobekli Tepe was going to run short of Stone Age flint-pieces any time soon. Slinging the rucksack over his back, Rob took one last look at the undulating and treeless plains, burnt by the relentless sun. He thought of Iraq, somewhere out there. Not so far away. If he got in the car and told Radevan to drive he could be at the Iraqi border in a few hours.

And then an image of Baghdad flashed across his mind. The bomber's face. Rob swallowed dryly. Not a good feeling. He turned and headed back, and as he did he heard it. The most horrible scream.

It sounded like an animal being tortured. Like a monkey being knifed open. Hideous.

He quickened his pace. He heard more shouting. What was going on? Then someone yelled again. Rob ran, the rucksack banging on his back.

He'd come further than he realized. Where was the main part of the dig? The hills all looked the same. Voices carried a long way in the clear desert air. And not just voices: shouts and cries. Christ. Something really *was* happening. Rob turned left then right and ran over the crest of a hill. And there was the dig. A crowd of people had gathered around one of the enclosures: the new trench. Workers were jostling each other.

His desert boots slipping in the dust and scree, Rob scrambled his way down to the side of the crowd and he pushed his way through, smelling sweat and fear. Rudely shunting the last man aside, he got to the edge of the trench and stared down. Everyone was staring down.

At the end of the trench was a new steel spike, one of the lethal-looking poles they used to hold up the tarpaulins. Franz Breitner was skewered, face down, on the pole. Skewered straight through his upper left chest. Blood was guttering from his wound. Christine was standing next to him talking to him. Ivan was behind them frantically calling on his mobile phone. Two workers were desperately trying to prise the steel pole from the earth.

Rob stared at Franz. He seemed to be alive, but the wound was savage, maybe right through the lungs. A desperate impaling. Rob had seen a lot of wounds in Iraq. He'd seen wounds just like this – blasts that sent girders and poles flying into people, spearing into their chests and heads; piercing them cruelly.

Rob knew Franz wasn't going to make it. An ambulance would take a good hour to get here. There probably weren't any medical helicopters between here and Ankara. Franz Breitner was going to die, here, in a trench. Surrounded by the silent stones of Gobekli Tepe.

12

In the fishponds of Abraham, the carp were roiling excitedly, clamouring for the tiny bits of pita bread he was throwing into the water. Rob watched them, mesmerized. Their desperate frenzy was a repulsive sight.

He had come here to calm down – it was the only bit of tranquil green space he knew in the crowded city. But the tranquillity wasn't working. As he watched the thrashing fish, Rob kept twisting in his mind the events of the previous day. The hideous sight of Franz pinioned on the pole. The frantic mobile phone calls. The fateful decision, in the end, to saw the pole in half and drive Franz – still skewered – all the way to Sanliurfa in Christine's car.

Rob had followed with Radevan. The battered Toyota pursued the Land Rover down the hills and across the plains to the Haran University Hospital in the new quarter of town. There Rob waited in the slightly shabby corridors with Christine and Ivan and Franz's sobbing wife. He was still there when the doctors came out with the inevitable news: Franz Breitner had died.

The carp were now fighting for the very last bit of bread. Biting each other. Rob turned away. He saw a submachine-gun toting Turkish soldier lounging by a jeep parked at the edge of the greenery. The soldier scowled at him.

The city was on a special edge – and it had nothing to do with Breitner's death. A suicide bomb had gone off in Dyarbakir, the Kurdish-Turkish city two hundred dusty miles east, the centre of Kurdish separatism. No one had died but ten people had been injured, and it had notched up the tension of the area once more. The police and the army were visible and everywhere, this afternoon.

Rob sighed, wearily. Sometimes it felt as if violence was universal. Inescapable. And Rob wanted to escape it.

Crossing a small wooden bridge over a tiny canal he sat at a wooden table. The tea house waiter came over, wiping his hands on a towel hanging from his waistband, and Rob ordered water, tea and some olives. He really had to try and not think about Franz for a moment. About the sight of the blood in Christine's car. The pole sticking obscenely out of Franz's torso . . .

'Sir?'

The waiter had brought Rob's tea. The teaspoon clinked. The sugar lump dissolved in the dark red liquid. The sun was shining through the trees of the little park. A small boy wearing a Manchester United shirt was playing with a football across the lawns. His mother was shrouded in black.

Rob finished the tea. He had to get proactive. Checking the time in London, he picked up his mobile phone and dialled.

'Yup!' Steve's normal gruffness.

'Hi, it's . . .'

'Robbie! My archaeological correspondent. How are the stones?'

The cheery cockney accent lifted Rob's spirit a little. He wondered whether to ruin the mood by telling Steve what had happened. Before he could decide, Steve said, 'Liked the notes you sent. Looking forward to the piece. When's your deadline?'

'Well, it was tomorrow, but . . .'

'Good lad. File by five.'

'Yes, but . . .'

'And send me some jpegs! Nice shots of the—'

'Steve there's a problem.'

The end of the line went silent. Finally. Rob seized the opportunity and launched into it. He told Steve everything. The strange mysteries and difficulties surrounding the dig, the resentment of the workers, the weird death chant, the envenomed local politics, the odd nocturnal diggings. He explained to his editor that he hadn't mentioned all this stuff before, because he wasn't sure of the relevance. Steve snapped back, 'And it's relevant now?'

'Yes. Because . . .' Rob looked at the castle on the cliff with the big red Turkish flag. He took a deep breath. Then he told Steve the horrible story of Franz's death. At the end of which Steve simply said, 'Jesus. What are you like?'

'Sorry?'

'I sent you to this dig cause I thought you needed a break. Somewhere nice and quiet. A few fucking stones. No drama. No Luttrell in Trouble.'

'Yes, I guess . . . and . . .'

'And you end up in the middle of a civil war with a bunch of devil priests and then some Hun gets kebabbed.' Steve chuckled. 'Sorry, mate, shouldn't make light of it. Must have been shite. But what do you wanna do now?'

Rob thought hard. What did he wanna do? He didn't know. 'I'm not sure . . . I think I actually need some editorial guidance.' He stood up, his phone still pressed to his ear. 'Steve, you're the boss. I'm at a loss. Tell me what to do – and I'll do it.'

'Trust your instinct.'

'You mean?'

'Trust yourself. You've got a great nose for a story. You're like a fucking bloodhound.' Steve's voice was firm. 'So tell me. Is there a story here?'

Rob knew at once. He turned and looked at the waiter and motioned for the bill. 'Yes. I think there is.'

'There you are then. Do it. Dig around. Stay another two weeks, minimum.'

Rob nodded. He felt a professional excitement – but it was tainted with sadness. Breitner's death had been so sickening. And he was yearning to go home and see his daughter. He decided to confess. 'But Steve, I want to see Lizzie.'

'Your little girl?'

'Yeah.'

'Softboy.' Steve laughed. 'How old is she now?'

'Five.'

The editor went quiet. Rob glanced at the old mosque across the glittering fishpond. Christine had told him it was once a church – a Crusader church.

'All right, Rob. If you do this for me we'll fly you home straight afterwards. Business class, OK?'

'Thanks.'

'We like to encourage good parenting at *The Times*. But I'll need something from you in the meantime.'

'Like what?'

'Give me the basic stones story. Need copy for Thursday. But I'll put a little teaser in, hint that there's more. We can make it a series. From our man in the Stone Age. With the demons in the desert.'

Rob laughed, despite himself. Steve always had the ability to cheer him up with his naked Fleet Street cynicism, his ruthless humour. 'Cheers, Steve.'

He slipped the phone back into his pocket, feeling a lot better. He had a job to do, a story to write, a lead to investigate. And then he could go and see his daughter.

Exiting the quiet of the parks, Rob walked out into the Kurdish street. Where taxi drivers were shouting at each other. Where a man was tugging a donkey as it pulled a cart stacked high with watermelons. It was so busy and noisy Rob could barely hear his phone. He felt its vibration instead.

'Yes?'

'Robert?'

Christine. He stopped on the dusty pavement. Poor Christine. She'd had to drive Franz to the hospital. She wouldn't let anyone else do it. Rob had seen the blood all over her car, the blood of her friend. Gruesome and harrowing. 'Are you OK? Christine?'

'Yes, yes, thank you. I'm OK . . .'

She didn't sound OK. Rob tried to make sympathetic conversation; he didn't know what else to do. Christine wasn't interested. Her speech was clipped, as if she was holding in the emotion. 'Are you still flying out tonight?'

'No,' Rob said. 'I've got more to write. I'm staying on for a week or two, at least.'

'Good. Can you meet me? At the caravanserai?'

Rob was perplexed. 'OK, but . . .'

'Now?'

Still confused, Rob agreed. The phone went dead. Turning left, Rob strode back up the hill, right into the hubbub of the covered market.

The souk was a classic Arab market, the kind that was fast disappearing from the Middle East. Full of gloomy passages, grimy blacksmiths, beckoning carpet sellers, and entrances to tiny mosques. The brilliant sunlight came down in javelins through holes in the corrugated roof. In dark, ancient corners, knife grinders squirted golden sparks into the spice-scented air. And there, in the middle of it all, was a real old-fashioned caravanserai: a cool and spacious courtyard with café tables and beautiful stone arcades. A place for trade and gossip, a place where merchants had haggled for silk, and men had wived their sons, for maybe a thousand years.

Stepping into the busy open plaza, he scanned the many tables and groups of people. Christine wasn't hard to spot. She was the only woman.

Her face was drawn. Rob sat down opposite her. She looked deep into his eyes as if she was seeking something. Rob had no idea what. She was silent; awkwardly so.

'Look Christine I'm so . . . sorry about Franz I know you were close and . . .'

'Please. No.' Christine was looking down. Stifling tears, or anger, or something. 'Enough. It's very kind of you. But enough.' She looked up again, and Rob became uncomfortably aware of the topaz brown of her eyes. Deep and languishing. Beautiful, and brimming with tears. She coughed to clear her throat. Then she said, 'I think Franz was murdered.'

'What?'

'I was there, Rob. I saw. There was an argument.'

The clapping sound of pigeons, flying away, filled the caravanserai. Men were sipping Turkish coffee and sitting on vermillion rugs. Rob turned back to Christine. 'An argument doesn't mean murder.'

'I saw, Rob. They pushed him.'

'Jesus.'

'Exactly. And it wasn't an accident: they pushed him deliberately right onto that pole.'

Rob frowned. 'Have you been to the police?'

Christine waved the idea away, like an irritating fly. 'Yes. They don't want to know.'

'Are you certain?'

'I was practically marched out of the police station. A mere woman.'

'Wankers.'

'Maybe.' Christine forced a smile. 'But it is difficult for them, too. The workers are Kurds, the police are Turkish. The politics are impossible. And yesterday there was a bomb in Dyarbakir.'

'I saw the TV news.'

'So,' Christine said, 'just walking in and arresting a load of Kurds for a murder . . . that isn't so simple, right now. Oh God . . .' She leant her forehead on her folded arms.

Rob wondered if she was going to cry. Behind her a minaret rose above the arcading of the caravanserai. It had big black loudspeakers wired to the top, but they were silent for the moment.

Christine regained herself, sat back again. 'I want to know, I want to do some . . . investigating.'

'What do you mean?'

'I want to know everything. Why he was digging at night, why they wanted to kill him. Franz was my friend. So I want to know why he died. Will you come with me? I want to go to Gobekli and look at Franz's notes, his materials, the works . . .'

'But surely they have taken all that? The Turkish police?'

'He kept a lot of stuff secret,' Christine said. 'But I know where. In a little locker in his cabin at the site.' She leaned forward, as if she were confessing something. 'Rob, we need to break in. And steal it.'

13

The flight to the Isle of Man, across the Irish Sea, was bumpy but brief. At Ronaldsway airport Forrester and Boijer were greeted in the arrivals lounge by the Deputy Chief Constable, and a uniformed sergeant. Forrester smiled and shook hands. The four policemen swapped names: the DCC was called Hayden.

They walked out into the car park. Forrester and Boijer exchanged glances – and shared a brief, knowing nod at the Manx sergeant's rather odd white helmet. Very different to anything on the mainland.

Forrester already knew of the Isle of Man's special status. A Crown colony, with its own parliament, its own flag, a heritage of ancient Viking traditions, and its own unique police force, Man was not an official part of the United Kingdom at all. They'd abolished flogging only a few years ago. Forrester's SIO back in London had briefed Forrester carefully on the slightly unusual protocols involved in visiting the Isle.

The car park was cold, with a hint of rain in the air; the four men walked briskly to Hayden's big car. Silently they sped through farmland, down to the outskirts of the main town, Douglas, on the western coast. Forrester buzzed down his window and looked out, trying to get a feel for the place: a sense of where he was.

The lush green farmland, the rainy oak woods, the tiny grey chapels:

they looked very British and Celtic. Likewise, as they reached Douglas, the huddled houses along the beach, and the flashier office blocks, reminded Forrester of the Scottish Hebrides. The only indication they were outside the UK proper was the Manx flag; the symbol of a three-legged man on a bright red background, which rippled in the drizzly wind on several buildings.

The silence in the car was broken by occasional chit chat. At one point Hayden turned and looked at Forrester and said, 'Of course we've kept the body at the scene. We're not amateurs.'

It was a strange remark. Forrester guessed these policemen, from this tiny force – two hundred officers or fewer – might resent his presence. The big man from the Met. The interfering Londoner.

But Forrester had a serious task in hand; he was very keen to see the crime scene. He wanted to get to work straight away. Protocols or no protocols.

The car swerved out of the town and threaded down a narrower road with high woods to their right and the choppy Irish Sea to their left. Forrester noted a jetty, a lighthouse, some small boats bobbing on the grey waves, and another hill. And then the car dived between some rather grand gates and swept up to a very big, old, castellated white building.

'St Anne's Fort,' said Hayden. 'It's offices now.'

The place was roped off with police tape. Forrester saw that a tent had been erected on the front lawns and glimpsed a policeman carrying an old Kodak fingerprint camera into the building. Climbing out of the car Forrester wondered about the capabilities of the local force. When had their last homicide been? Five years back? Fifty? They probably spent most of their time busting dope smokers. And underage drinkers. And gays. Wasn't this the place where homosexuality was still illegal?

They went straight into the house, through the main doors. Two younger men wearing anti-putrefaction masks glanced at Forrester. One of them was holding a tin of aluminium powder. They stepped into another room. Forrester went to follow the forensic officers but Hayden touched him on the arm. 'No,' he said, 'the garden.'

The house was enormous, yet characterless inside. It had been brutally converted into offices: someone had ripped out the previous interiors and installed strip lighting and grey partitions, filing cabinets and computers. There were models of boats and ferries on some of the desks. A couple of nautical charts hung on a wall; the offices presumably belonged to a shipping corporation or marine design company.

Following the Deputy Chief, Forrester stepped into a hallway from which big glass doors opened on to a wide rear garden, closed in on all sides by high hedges, and a wooded rise right at the back. The garden had been rudely dug up in various places; in the middle of these chewed-up green lawns was a large, yellow, crime scene tent, the flap zipped shut, concealing whatever was inside.

Hayden opened the glass doors and they walked the few yards to the yellow tent. He turned to the two London officers. 'Are you ready?'

Forrester felt impatient. 'Yes, of course.'

Hayden pulled back the flap.

'Fuck,' said Forrester.

The corpse was of a man in his thirties, he guessed. It had its back to them; and it was stark naked. But it wasn't that which caused him to swear. The man's head had been buried head-down in the lawn – with the rest of his body sticking out. The position was at once comical and deeply unsettling. Forrester immediately guessed the victim must have asphyxiated. The murderers must have dug a hole, forced the man's head in, then packed the soil around, suffocating him. A nasty, weird, cold way to die. Why the hell would you do that?

Boijer was walking around the corpse, looking appalled. Even though the tent seemed to be colder than the windswept garden outside, a distinct smell came off the body. Forrester wished he had one of the SIRCHIE masks to block out the odour of decomposition.

'There's the Star,' said Boijer.

He was right. Forrester walked around and looked at the front of the corpse. A Star of David had been gouged into the man's chest; the wound looked even deeper and nastier than the torture inflicted on the janitor.

'Fuck,' Forrester said, again.

Standing next to him, Hayden smiled, for the first time this morning. 'Well,' he said, 'I'm glad you feel the same way. I thought it was just us.'

Three hours later Forrester and Boijer were sharing plastic cups of coffee in the big tent at the front of the mansion. The local cops were arranging a press conference, in the 'fort'. The two Met officers were alone. The corpse had finally been moved, after thirty-six hours, to the coroner's lab in town.

Boijer looked at Forrester. 'Not sure the natives are very friendly.'

Forrester chuckled. 'I think they had their own language until . . . last year.'

'And cats,' said Boijer, blowing cool air across his coffee. 'Isn't this the place where they have those cats without tails?'

'Manx cats. Yep.'

Boijer stared out through the flapping open doorway of the police tent, at the big white building. 'What would our gang be doing out here?'

'Christ knows. And why the same symbol?' Forrester knocked back some more coffee. 'What more do we know about the victim? You spoke to the scene of crime guy?'

'Yacht designer. Working upstairs.'

'On a Sunday?'

Boijer nodded. 'Yep. Usually the place is deserted, at weekends. But he was working his day off.'

'So he just got unlucky?'

Boijer swept his blonde Finnish hair back from his blue Finnish eyes. 'Like the guy in Craven Street. Probably heard a noise.'

'Then came downstairs. And our lovely killers decided to cut him up, then stick his head in the ground like a croquet hoop. Till he died.'

'Not very nice.'

'What about the CCTV?'

'Nothing.' Boijer shrugged. 'The woodentop told me they'd drawn a blank on the cameras, all of them. Zip.'

'Of course. And the prints and footwear marks. They'll get nothing. These guys are insane, but not stupid. They are the opposite of stupid.'

Forrester stepped outside the tent and gazed up at the house, blinking away the soft drizzle that was now falling. The building was dazzling white. Newly painted. Quite a landmark for local sailors. High and white and castellated, right above the jetty and the port. He scanned the battlements and scrutinized the sash windows. He was trying to work out what linked an eighteenth century house in London with what looked like an eighteenth century house in the Isle of Man. But then something struck him. Maybe it wasn't. He squinted. There was just something wrong with this building. It wasn't the real deal – Forrester knew enough about architecture to surmise that. The brickwork was too neat, the windows all recent – no more than ten or twenty years old. The building was evidently a pastiche, and not an especially good one. And, he decided, it was possible the killers knew this. The modern interior of the modern house was entirely undisturbed. Only the gardens had been dug up. The gang had obviously been looking for something, again. But they weren't looking in the house. Only the garden. Apparently, they knew where to look. Apparently, they knew where *not* to look.

Apparently, they knew quite a lot.

Forrester turned his collar up against the chilly drizzle.

14

It was just getting dark by the time they climbed into Christine's Land Rover. Rush hour. Within a few hundred metres the car had come to complete stop. Stuck in gridlock.

Christine leaned back, and sighed. She turned the radio on, and then off. Then looked at Rob. 'Tell me more about Robert Luttrell.'

'Such as?'

'Job. Life. You know . . .'

'It's not that interesting.'

'Try me.'

He gave her a brief résumé of the last decade. The way he and Sally had rushed into marriage and parenthood; the discovery she was having an affair; the ensuing and inevitable divorce.

Christine listened, keenly. 'Are you still angry about it?'

'No. It was me, as well. I mean – it was partly my fault. I was always away. And she got lonely . . . And I still admire her, kind of.'

'Sorry?'

'Sally,' he said. 'She's training to be a lawyer. That takes guts. As well as brains. To change your career in your thirties. I admire that. So it's not like I hate her or anything . . .' He shrugged. 'We just . . . diverged. And married too young.'

Christine nodded, then asked about his American family. He sketched in his Scots-Irish background, the emigration to Utah in the 1880s. The Mormonism.

The Land Rover at last moved forward. Rob looked across at her. 'And you?'

The traffic was really thinning out. She floored the pedal, accelerated. 'Jewish French.'

Rob had guessed this by the name. Meyer.

'Half my family died in the Holocaust. But half didn't. French Jews did OK, in the war, comparatively.'

'And your mum and dad?'

Christine explained that her mother was an academic in Paris, her dad a piano tuner. He had died fifteen years back. 'In fact,' she added, 'I'm not sure he did much piano tuning even when he was alive. He just sat around the flat in Paris. Arguing.'

'Sounds like my dad. Except my dad was a bastard, too.'

Christine glanced over at him. The sky behind her, framed by the car window, was purple and sapphire. A spectacular desert twilight. They were well outside Sanliurfa now. 'You said your father was a Mormon?'

'He is.'

'I went to Salt Lake City once.'

'Yeah?'

'When I was in Mexico, working at Teotihuacán, I took a holiday in the States.'

Rob laughed. 'In Salt Lake City?'

'Utah.' She smiled. 'You know. Canyonlands. Arches Park.'

'Ah.' He nodded. 'That makes more sense.'

'Marvellous scenery. Anyway we had to fly through SLC . . .'

'The most boring big town in America.'

An army truck overtook the Land Rover, with Turkish troops hanging casually out the back, shadowy in the dusk. One of them waved and grinned when he saw Christine, but she ignored him. 'It wasn't New York, but I quite liked it.'

Rob thought about Utah, and Salt Lake City. His only memories of SLC were of dreary Sundays, going to the big Mormon cathedral. The Tabernacle.

'It's funny,' Christine added. 'People laugh at the Mormons. But you know what?'

'What?'

'Salt Lake City is the only big town in America where I have felt perfectly safe. You can walk down the street at 5 a.m. and no one's going to mug you. Mormons don't mug people. I like that.'

'But they eat terrible food . . . and wear polyester slacks.'

'Yes, yes. And some towns in Utah you can't even buy coffee. The drink of the devil.' Christine quietly smiled. The desert air was warm through the open window of the Land Rover. 'But I'm serious. Mormons are nice. Friendly. Their religion makes them that way. Why do atheists sneer at people of faith, when faith makes you nicer?'

'You're a believer, right?'

'Yes.'

'I'm not.'

'I guessed.'

They laughed.

Rob leaned back, scanning the horizon. They were passing a concrete shack he'd seen before. Plastered with posters of Turkish politicians.

'Isn't this near the turning?'

'Yes. Just up ahead.'

The car slowed as they neared their junction. Rob was thinking about Christine's belief: Roman Catholicism, she had said. He was still confused by this. He was still confused by a lot of things about Christine Meyer: like her love for Sanliurfa, despite the local, very patriarchal attitude to women.

The Land Rover swerved off the asphalt. Now they were rattling along the rubbled track, in real darkness. The headlights picked out stray bushes, and bare rocks. Maybe a gazelle, skittering into the gloom.

A tiny village, illuminated by a few straggly lights, twinkled on the side of a hill. Rob could just make out the spear of a minaret in the shrouding twilight. The moon was just rising.

Rob asked Christine directly: about her attitude to Islam. She explained that she admired aspects of it. Especially the muezzin.

'Really?' Rob said. 'All that wailing? I sometimes find it intrusive. I mean, I don't hate it, but still . . . sometimes . . .'

'I think it's moving. The cry of the soul, imploring God. You should listen more closely!'

They took the second turning past a final, silent Kurdish village. A few more kilometres, and they would see the shallow hills of Gobekli, silhouetted in the moonlight. The Land Rover rumbled as Christine took the ultimate curve. Rob didn't know what to expect at the dig, following the 'accident'. Police cars? Barriers? Nothing?

There was indeed a new barrier, set across the track. It said *Police.* And *Keep Out.* In Turkish, and English. Rob got out of the car and pushed the blue barrier aside. Christine drove on and parked.

The site was deserted. Rob felt serious relief. The only indication that the dig was now the scene of a suspicious death was a new tarpaulin, erected over the trench where Franz had been pushed – that and a sense of emptiness in the tented area. Lots of things had been taken away. The big table had been moved, or dismantled. This season's dig was definitely over.

Rob glanced at the stones. He'd wondered before what it would be like, standing amongst them at night. Now, quite unexpectedly, here he was. They were shadowy in their enclosures. The moon had fully risen and was casting white darkness across the scene. Rob had an odd desire to go down into the enclosures. Touch the megaliths. Rest his cheek against the coolness of the ancient stones. Run his fingers along the carvings. He'd wanted to do that, in fact, the very first time he'd seen them.

Christine walked up behind him. 'Everything OK?'

'Yes!'

'Come on then. Let's be quick. This place . . . rather scares me at night.'

Rob noticed that she was averting her gaze from the trench. The trench where Franz had been killed. He sensed how difficult this visit must be for her.

They walked swiftly over the rise. To the left was a blue plastic cabin: Franz's personal office. The door was freshly padlocked.

Christine sighed. 'Damn.'

Rob thought for a second. Then he jogged back to the Land Rover, opened the car's back door, and fumbled in the darkness. He returned with a tyre jack. The desert breeze was warm and the moonlight glinted on the padlock. He shoved the jack in the lock, twisted, and the padlock snapped open.

Inside, the cabin was small and pretty empty. Christine shone a torch around. A spare set of spectacles sat on an empty shelf. Some textbooks were haphazardly scattered on a desktop thick with dust. The police had taken almost everything.

Christine knelt down, then sighed again. 'They took the bloody locker.'

'Really?'

'It was hidden down here. By the little fridge. It's gone.'

Rob felt a keen disappointment. 'So that's that?' It was a wasted journey.

Christine looked deeply sad. 'Come on', she said. 'Let's go before someone sees us. We've already broken into a murder scene.'

Rob picked up the tyre jack. Again, as he walked to the car, past the shadowy pits, he felt that strange urge to go and touch the stones. To lie down next to them.

Christine opened the driver's door of the Land Rover. The interior light came on. Simultaneously, Rob opened the back doors to stow the jack. And immediately he saw it: the light was glinting on a shiny little notebook. Nestling on the back seat; black but expensive looking.

He picked it up. Opening the cover, he saw the name Franz Breitner – in small, neat handwriting.

Rob paced around the car and leaned in through the passenger door to show Christine his find.

'Jesus!' she cried. 'That's it! That's Franz's notebook! That's what I was after. That's where he wrote . . . everything.'

Rob handed it over. Her face intent, Christine flicked through the pages, muttering: 'He wrote it all in here. I'd see him doing it. Secretly. This was his big secret. Well done!'

Rob climbed into the passenger seat. 'But what's it doing in your car?' As soon as he asked the question he felt a little stupid. The answer was obvious. It must have fallen out of Franz's pocket when Christine was driving him to hospital. Either that, or Franz knew he was dying, as he lay bleeding on the backseat, and took it out of his pocket and left it there. Deliberately. Knowing that Christine would find it.

Rob shook his head. He was turning into a conspiracy theorist. He had to get a grip. Reaching left, he slammed his door, making the car rattle.

'Whoops,' said Christine.

'Sorry.'

'Something fell.'

'What?'

'When you slammed the car door. Something fell out of the note-book.'

Christine was scrabbling on the floor of the foot well, running her hands this way and that beneath the pedals. Then she sat back, holding something in her fingers.

It was a dry stalk of grass. Rob stared at it. 'Why on earth would Franz preserve that?'

But Christine was gazing at the grass. Intently.

15

Christine drove even faster than usual back into town. On the outskirts, where the scruffy desert bumped into the first grey concrete apartment blocks, they saw a feeble attempt at a roadside café, with white plastic tables arrayed outside, and a few truck drivers drinking beer. The drivers were drinking with guilty expressions.

'Beer?' said Rob.

Christine glanced across. 'Good idea.'

She turned right and parked. The drivers stared over, as Christine climbed from the car and threaded her way to a table.

It was a warm evening; insects and flies were whirling around the bare bulbs strung outside the café. Rob ordered two Efes beers. They talked about Gobekli. Every so often a huge truck would thunder down the road, lights blazing, en route to Damascus or Riyadh or Beirut, drowning out their conversation and making the light bulbs shiver and kick. Christine flicked through the pages of the notebook. She was rapt, almost feverish. Rob sipped his warm beer from his scratchy glass and let her do her thing.

Now she was flicking this way and that. Unhappily. At length she chucked the book onto the table, and sighed. 'I don't know . . . It's a mess.'

Rob set down his beer. 'Sorry?'

'It's chaotic.' She tutted. 'Which is strange. Because Franz was not messy. He was scrupulous. "Teutonic efficiency" he would call it. He was rigorous and exact. Always. . . . always . . .' Her brown eyes clouded for a second. She reached firmly for her beer, drank a gulp and said, 'Take a look for yourself.'

Rob checked the early pages. 'Seems OK to me.'

'Here,' she said, pointing. 'Yes, it begins very neatly. Diagrams of the excavations. Microliths noted. But here . . . *look* . . .'

Rob flicked some more pages until she stopped him.

'See, from here it falls apart. The handwriting turns into a scrawl. And the drawings and little doodles . . . chaotic. And here. What are all these numbers?'

Rob looked closely. The writing was nearly all in German. The handwriting at first was very neat; but it did get scrawlier to the end. There was a list of numbers on the last page. Then a line about someone called Orra Keller. Rob remembered a girl he'd known in England called Orra. A Jewish girl. So who was this Orra Keller? He asked Christine; and she shrugged. He asked her about the numbers. She shrugged again – more emphatically. Rob noted there was also a drawing in the book: a scribbled sketch of a field, and some trees.

He handed the book back to Christine. 'What does the writing say? I don't know much German.'

'Well, most of it is illegible.' She opened the book towards the end. 'But he talks about wheat, here. And a river. Turning into more rivers. Here.'

'Wheat? But why?'

'God knows. And this drawing seems to be a map. I think. With mountains. It says mountains with a question mark. And rivers. Or maybe they are roads. It really is a mess.'

Rob finished his beer and motioned to the bar owner for two more. Another huge silver lorry thundered down the Damascus road. The sky over Sanliurfa was a dirty orange-black.

'And what about the grass?'

Christine nodded. 'Yes, that is weird. Why keep that?'

'Do you think he was frightened? Is that why the notes are so . . . messed up?'

'It is possible. Remember the Pulsa Dinura?'

Rob shuddered. 'Hard to forget. Do you think he knew about that?'

Christine picked an insect off the top of her beer. Then she looked hard at Rob. 'I think he knew. He must have heard the chanters outside the window. And he was an expert on Mesopotamian religions. The demons and the curses. It was one of his specialities.'

'So he was aware he was in danger?'

'Probably. Which might account for the chaotic state of his notes. Sheer fear. But still . . .' She held the book flat in her hands, as if assessing its weight. 'A lifetime's work . . . '

Rob could sense her sadness.

Christine dropped the book again. 'This place is horrible. I don't care if they do serve beer. Can we go?'

'Gladly.'

Dropping some coins in a saucer, they made for the Land Rover and barrelled off down the road. After a while Christine said, 'I don't believe it was just fear, it doesn't add up.' She swivelled the wheel so they could overtake a cyclist, an old man in an Arabic cloak. Sitting in front of the bicycling man, athwart the crossbar, was a small dark boy. The boy waved at the Land Rover, grinning at the white western woman.

Rob noticed that Christine was taking side streets. Not an obvious route back to the centre of town.

At last she said, 'Franz was diligent and thorough. I don't think a curse would have sent him over the edge. Nothing would have unsettled him like that.'

'So what was it?' Rob asked.

They were in a newer part of town now. Almost European looking. Nice clean apartment blocks. Women were walking the evening streets, not all of them in headscarves. Rob saw a brightly lit supermarket advertising cheese in German as well as Turkish. Next door was an internet café full of shining screens with dark heads silhouetted against them.

'I think he must have had some theory. He used to get excited by theories.'

'I saw.'

Christine smiled, staring ahead. 'I think he had some theory, about Gobekli. That's what the notes say to me.'

'A theory to do with what?'

'Perhaps he had worked out why Gobekli was buried. That is, after all, the big mystery. If he felt he was onto a solution that would get him pretty agitated.'

Rob wasn't satisfied by this. 'But why didn't he just write it down, or tell anyone?'

The car had stopped. Christine pulled the key from the ignition. 'Good point,' she said, looking at Rob. 'A very good point. Let's go and find out. Come on.'

'Where?'

'There's a friend here. Might be able to help.'

They were parked in front of a new apartment complex with a huge crimson poster advertising Turku Cola on the wall. Christine ran up the steps and pressed a numbered button. They waited, and then they were buzzed in. The lift took them to the tenth floor. They ascended in silence.

A door was already half-open across the landing. Rob followed Christine. He peered into the apartment – then jumped: just inside the door was Ivan the paleobotanist, from the party. Just lurking there.

Ivan nodded politely but his expression was notably unfriendly. Almost suspicious. He showed them into the main room of his flat. It was austere, just a lot of books and some pictures. On a desk a smart laptop computer was showing a screensaver of the Gobekli megaliths. There was one beautiful small stone object on the mantelpiece which looked like one of the Mesopotamian wind demons. Rob found himself wondering if Ivan had stolen it.

They sat down. Wordless. Ivan offered no tea or water but just sat down opposite them, looked hard at Christine and said, 'Yes?'

She took out the notebook and laid it on the table. Ivan stared at it. He glanced up at Christine. His young Slavic face was a picture of blankness. Like someone suppressing emotion. Or someone used to suppressing emotion.

Then Christine reached in her pocket and took out the grass stalk and laid it very gently on top of the book. All the time Rob watched Ivan's face. He had no idea what was going on here, but he felt that Ivan's reaction was crucial. Ivan flinched very slightly when he saw the stalk of grass. Rob couldn't stand the silence any longer. 'Guys? Please? What is it? What's going on?

Christine glanced at him as if to say *be patient.* But Rob didn't feel like being patient. He wanted to know what was going on. Why had they driven here, late at night? To sit in silence and stare at some piece of grass?

'Einkorn,' said Ivan.

Christine smiled. 'It is, isn't it? Einkorn wheat. Yes.'

Ivan shook his head. 'You needed me to tell you this, Christine?'

'Well . . . I wasn't sure. You're the expert.'

'So now you are sure. And I am very tired.'

Christine picked up the grass. 'Thank you, Ivan.'

'It is nothing.' He was already standing. 'Goodbye.'

They were escorted briskly to the door. At the threshold Ivan glanced left and right along the landing as if he was expecting to see someone he didn't want to see. Then he slammed the door shut.

'Well that was friendly,' said Rob.

'But we got what we came for.'

They buzzed the lift and descended. All the mystery was irritating Rob. 'OK,' he said as they breathed the warm, dieselly air of the street. 'Come on, Christine. Einkorn wheat. What the hell?'

Without turning to face him she said, 'It is the oldest form of wheat in the world. The original wheat, the first ever cereal if you like.'

'And?'

'It only grows around here. And it was crucial to the switch to agriculture. When man started farming.'

'And?'

Christine turned. Her brown eyes were shining. 'Franz thought it was a clue. I'm sure he thought it was a clue. In which case I think it's a clue.'

'A clue to what?'

'It might tell us why they buried the temple.'

'But how can a piece of grass do that?'

'Later. Come on. Let's go. You saw the way Ivan was watching at the door. Come on. Now.'

'You think we're being . . . followed?'

'Not followed exactly. Maybe watched. I don't know. Maybe it's paranoia.'

Rob remembered Franz, skewered on the pole. He jumped into the car.

16

Forrester woke in an almost feverish sweat. He blinked at the dingy curtains of his Douglas hotel room. For a moment the nightmare lingered: giving a palpable yet absurd savour of evil to the hotel fixtures: the wardrobe door had swung half-open, showing the blackness within; the television lurked, squat and ugly, in the corner.

What had he dreamed? He rubbed the sleep from his face and remembered: he'd dreamed the usual, of course. A small body. A bridge. Then the bump-bump-bump of cars, driving over a 'tyre'.

Bump bump bump.

Bump bump bump.

He got up, walked to the window and drew the curtains. To his surprise it was light: very light. The sky was white and blank and the streets were busy; *he was going to be late for the press conference.*

He made it just in time. The sizeable hall was already bustling. The local police had commandeered the biggest room in St Anne's Fort. A handful of local journalists had been joined by a dozen national hacks. Two news crews with digicams, big headphones and long grey microphones were loitering at the back. Forrester saw a familiar head of blonde hair: it was the London correspondent for CNN. He'd seen her at several media briefings before.

CNN? Someone had obviously tipped off the London media about the macabre nature of the murder. From the back of the hall, he surveyed the room. Three policemen were sitting at the front; Deputy Chief Hayden was in the middle, flanked by a couple of younger guys. A big blue screen above them said *Isle of Man Constabulary*.

The Deputy Chief Constable raised a hand. 'If we could begin . . .' He talked the journalists through the circumstances of the crime, citing the discovery of the body, and laconically describing the way the man's head had been buried in the soil.

One journalist gasped.

Hayden paused, allowing time for this gruesome detail to sink in. Then he appealed for witnesses to come forward. His presentation concluded, he scanned the room. 'Any questions?'

Several hands shot up.

'The young lady at the back?'

'Angela Darvill, CNN. Sir, do you think there is a link between this murder and the recent case in Covent Garden?'

This was unexpected. Hayden winced visibly, then flashed a glance at Forrester, who shrugged. The Scotland Yard officer didn't know what to advise. If the media knew about the link already there was nothing anyone could do about it. They would have to ask the media to keep it quiet so the murderers didn't know the police had linked the cases; but you couldn't unsay what someone had obviously said.

The DCC acknowledged Forrester's shrug then returned his gaze to the American journalist. 'Miss Darvill, there are certain shared peculiarities. But anything beyond that is mere speculation at the moment. I wouldn't like to comment further. We appreciate your discretion on this, as I am sure you realize.' With that, he looked around the room seeking a different questioner. But Angela Darvill raised her hand again.

'Do you think there is a religious element?'

'I'm sorry?'

'The Star of David. The carving in the chest. In both cases?'

The local journalists turned to stare at Angela Darvill. The question had thrown them; it had unsettled the whole room. Hayden hadn't mentioned the 'design' of the knife cuts.

The room was hushed as Hayden replied. 'Ms Darvill. We have a brutal and very serious crime to investigate. The clock is ticking. So. I think I should take a few more questions from . . . others. Yes?'

'Brian Deeley, *The Douglas Star.*' The local hack speculated about possible motive and Hayden said they had no motive at present. The two men batted some more questions and answers between them. Then a national newsman stood up and asked about the victim's circumstances. Hayden told them that the victim was a well-liked local man with a wife and children living in town. He was a keen sailor. The DCC gazed about the room, staring at each face in turn. 'Some of you might even know his boat, *The Manatee.* He used to go sailing with his son Jonny.' He smiled sadly. 'The lad is just ten years old.'

For a few seconds, no one spoke.

The Manx police, Forrester thought, were doing a good job. The blatant emotion was deft. That was how you got witnesses to come forward: appeal to the heart not the head. And they really needed witnesses. Because they had no evidence, no DNA, no prints. Nothing.

Hayden was gesturing at a balding man in an anorak. 'The chap in the corner? Mr . . . ?'

'Harnaby. Alisdair. Radio Triskel.'

'Yes?'

'Do you think the crime is linked to the unusual history of the building?'

Hayden's fingers drummed on the tabletop. 'I'm not aware of any unusual history.'

'I mean the way the castle was first built. Is it perhaps important? You know, all the legends . . . ?'

The policeman's fingers stopped drumming. 'As of this moment, Mr Harnaby, we are following all lines of investigation. But I hope we aren't pursuing legends. And that's all I can tell you. Now.' He stood up. 'I think we have some work to do, so if you would excuse us, I do believe there's coffee in the tent at the front.'

Forrester looked around. It had been a good, professional press conference: but he still felt unsettled. Something was bothering him. He looked at Harnaby. What was this guy talking about? The 'unusual history' of the building? It chimed with Forrester's thoughts. Something was wrong here. The architecture: the pastiche effect of the building: something was wrong.

Alisdair Harnaby was reaching under his chair for a blue plastic shopping bag. 'Mr Harnaby?'

The man turned, his thin-rimmed spectacles shiny in the striplight.

'My name is DCI Forrester. I'm with the Met.'

Harnaby looked nonplussed. Forrester added: 'Scotland Yard? Do you have a minute?'

The man put down his plastic bag and Forrester sat beside him. 'I'm interested in what you said. About the unusual history of the building. Can you elaborate?'

Harnaby nodded, his eyes twinkling. He gazed about the empty hall. 'What you see today is actually a rather crude copy of the previous building.'

'Right, so . . .'

'The original fort, St Anne's Fort, was demolished in 1979. It was also known as Whaley's Folly.'

'And it was built by?'

'Jerusalem Whaley. A rake.'

'A what?'

'A buck. A roisterer. An upper class thug. You know the kind of thing.'

'A kind of playboy?'

'Yes and no.' Harnaby smiled. 'We are talking real sadism here, through the generations.'

'For instance?'

'Whaley's father was Richard Chappell Whaley. But the Irish called him "Burnchapel" Whaley.'

'Because . . .'

'He was a member of the Anglo-Irish aristocracy. A Protestant. And he used to burn Irish Catholic churches. With the worshippers inside.'

'Ask a stupid question.'

'Well, yes.' Harnaby grinned. 'Quite unsavoury! And Burnchapel Whaley was also a member of the Irish Hellfire Club. They were an awful shower of hooligans, even by the standards of the time.'

'OK. And what about Jerusalem Whaley, his son?'

Harnaby frowned. The room was now so quiet that Forrester could hear the patter of drizzle on the long sash windows.

'Tom Whaley? He was another Georgian buck. As brutal and reckless as his father. But then something happened. He came back to Ireland after a long journey east to Jerusalem. Hence his nickname: Jerusalem Whaley. When he returned, it seemed that the journey had changed him. It broke him.'

Forrester frowned. 'How?'

'All we know is that Jerusalem Whaley returned a very different man. He built this strange castle: St Anne's Fort. He wrote his memoirs. A surprisingly remorseful book. And then he died. Leaving behind the castle and a lot of debts. But a fascinating life! Absolutely fascinating.' Harnaby paused. 'Forgive me, Mr Forrester, am I talking too much? I do get carried away sometimes. Bit of a passion of mine, local folklore. I have a radio programme, on local history you see.'

'Don't apologize. This is very interesting. I've actually only got one more question. Is there anything left of the old building?'

'Oh, no. No no no. It was all pulled down.' Harnaby sighed. 'This was the 1970s! They would have pulled down St Paul's Cathedral if they could. Really. Such a shame. A few years later and the building would have been conserved.'

'So nothing was left?'

'Yes. Although . . .' Harnaby's face clouded. 'There is something . . .'

'What?'

'I've often wondered . . . There is one more legend. Rather odd really.' Harnaby clutched his plastic bag. 'I'll show you!'

The older man waddled to the door and Forrester followed him into the front garden. In the breeze and the cold and the drizzle, Forrester looked left: he could see Boijer by the police tent. The CNN girl was walking past with her crew. Forrester mouthed to Boijer, and pointed at Angela Darvill: *talk to her: find out what she knows.* Boijer nodded.

Harnaby plodded across the soggy front lawns in front of the castellated house. Where the lawns gave way to hedges and walls, the older man knelt as if he was about to do some gardening. 'See!'

Forrester crouched alongside and scoped the wet dark earth.

Harnaby smiled. 'Look! Do you see? The soil is darker here than it is here.'

It was true. The soil seemed to change colour slightly. The soil of the castle lawn was definitely peatier and darker than the soil further from the house. 'I don't understand. What is it?'

Harnaby shook his head. 'It's Irish.'

'Sorry?'

'The soil. It's not from here. It's maybe from Ireland.'

Forester blinked. It was raining again, and harder this time. But he took no notice of it. The clockwork of the case was turning over in his mind. Turning over quite fast. 'Please explain?'

'Buck Whaley was an impulsive man. He once bet someone he could jump out of a second storey window on a horse and survive. He did it – but the horse died!' Harnaby chuckled. 'Anyhow. The story is that he fell in love with an Irish girl, just before he moved here. To Man. But this presented him with a problem.'

'Which was?'

'His bride's marriage contract said she was only ever allowed to live on Irish soil. Yet this was 1786, and Whaley had just bought this house.

He was determined to bring his wife here, despite the contract.' Harnaby's eyes were twinkling.

Forrester thought about it. 'What you mean is he shifted tons of Irish soil to live on? So she lived on Irish earth?'

'In a nutshell. Yes. He shifted a huge boatload of soil to the Isle of Man, and thereby fulfilled his vows. Or so they say . . .'

Forrester laid a palm on the damp dark earth, now spotted blackly with rain. 'So the whole building is built on that same Irish earth. This soil here now?'

'Very possibly.'

Forrester stood up. He wondered if the murderers knew this bizarre story. He had a firm sense they did know. Because they had ignored the building and instead had gone straight for the last possible authentic remnant of Whaley's Folly. The earth on which it was built.

Forrester had one more question. 'OK, Mr Harnaby, where would the soil have come from?'

'No one is entirely sure. However,' the journalist took off his spectacles to rub some rain from the lenses. 'However . . . I did once have a theory – that it came from Montpelier House.'

'Which is?'

Harnaby blinked. 'The headquarters of the Irish Hellfire Club.'

17

Rob and Christine retreated to her neighbourhood. They parked, with a jolt, at the corner of her street. As he climbed down from the Land Rover, Rob looked left and right. At the end of Christine's street was a mosque, its minarets were slender and lofty, bathed in lurid green floodlighting. Two moustached men in suits were arguing in the shadows down the way, right next to a big black BMW. The men briefly looked at Rob and Christine, then went back to their angry exchange.

Christine led Rob into a dusty hallway of a modern block. The lift was busy, or out of order, so they took three flights of stairs. The apartment was large, airy and bright – and almost devoid of furniture. Neat piles of books were simply stacked on the polished wooden floor, or shelved in their hundreds along one wall. A big steel desk and a leather sofa were set to one side of the living room. A wickerwork chair was in the opposite corner.

'I don't like clutter,' she said. 'A house is a machine for living in.'

'Le Corbusier.'

She smiled and nodded. Rob smiled too. He liked the flat. It was very . . . Christine. Simple, intellectual, elegant. He checked out a picture on the wall: it was a large and eerie photograph of a very strange tower. A tower of orange gold bricks surrounded by desultory ruins, with vast tracts of desert beyond.

The two of them sat side-by-side on the leather sofa and Christine got out the book again. As she leafed once more through Breitner's scrawled pages, Rob had to ask, 'So. Einkorn wheat?'

But Christine wasn't listening; she was holding the book very close to her face. 'This map?' she said to herself. 'These numbers . . . and these here . . . The woman Orra Keller . . . Maybe . . .'

Rob waited for his reply. There was no reply. He felt a breeze in the room: the windows were open to the street outside. Rob could hear voices – out there. He went to the window and stared down.

The moustached men were still hanging around, but now they were standing right beneath Christine's block of flats. Another man in a dark puffy anorak was lurking in the doorway of the shop opposite: a big Honda motorbike showroom. The two moustached men looked up as Rob leaned out of the window. They stared at him wordlessly. Just looking up at him. The anoraked man was also looking up. Three men were staring at Rob. How menacing was this? Then Rob decided he was being paranoid. The whole of Sanliurfa could not be following them; these men were just . . . just men. It was just coincidence. He pulled the window to, and looked around the room.

Maybe one of the many books on the shelves could help. He thumbed his way past a few titles. *The Syrian Epipaleolithic* . . . *Modern Electron Microanalysis* . . . *Pre-Columbian Anthropophagy* . . . Not exactly bestsellers. He saw a more general book. *Encyclopaedia of Archaeology.* Slipping it down from the shelf, he flicked straight to the index and found it right away. *Einkorn wheat, page 97.*

With Sanliurfa's night breezes filling the room, and Christine silently perusing the notebook, Rob scanned and digested the information.

Einkorn wheat, it turned out, was a kind of wild grass. According to the book it grew naturally in south-east Anatolia. He looked at a small map on the facing page of the encyclopaedia which showed that Einkorn was local to the area around Sanliurfa. In fact, it seemed to grow in very few other regions. Rob read on.

Einkorn was apparently a grass of the lower mountains and the foothills. It was crucial to the first agriculture, the move from hunter gathering to farming. Along with Emmer wheat it was probably 'the first ever life form domesticated by man'. And that first domestication had occurred in and around south-east Anatolia. Around Sanliurfa.

The page he was reading linked him to another article: on the origins of agriculture. Judging by the Einkorn, this subject was important to the whole Gobekli mystery – so Rob turned to this article, too. He speed-read the pages. *Pigs and chickens. Dogs and cattle. Emmer and einkorn.* But then the final paragraphs caught his eye.

'The great mystery of early agriculture is the Why, not the How. There is ample proof that the transition to early agriculture meant great hardship for the first farmers, certainly when compared to the relatively free and generous lifestyle of a hunter-gatherer. Skeletal remains show that these primal farmers were subject to more diseases than their hunting forebears, and had shorter and harder lives. Domesticated animals in the early stage of farming have, likewise, scrawnier physiques than their wild ancestors . . .'

Rob thought about the little stalk of wheat, then read on. 'Contemporary anthropologists further attest that hunter-gatherers lead a relatively leisured existence, toiling no more than two or three hours a day. Yet farmers need to work most of the hours of daylight, especially in spring and summer. Much of primitive farming is backbreaking and monotonous.' The article concluded: 'Such is the striking shift in conditions that some thinkers have seen a certain tragic decline in the onset of agriculture, from the Edenic freedom of the hunter, to the daily labour of the farmer. Such speculations are clearly beyond the remit of science, and this article, nonetheless . . .'

Rob shut the book. He could hear the breeze in the curtains. The cool, slightly mournful desert wind was really picking up now. Rob slotted the book back on the shelf, and momentarily closed his eyes. He was tired again. He wanted to go to sleep, lulled by this lovely wind. Its soft and gentle reproach.

'Robert!' Christine was scanning the last page of the notebook minutely.

'What?'

'These numbers. You are a journalist. You know a story. What do you think?'

Rob sat down beside Christine and looked at the last pages of the book. Again there was the 'map'. One waggly line which became four lines, which looked maybe like rivers. The bobbly lines seemed to be mountains. Or sea. Probably mountains. And then there was a crude symbol of a tree – indicating a forest perhaps? Besides that was some kind of animal. A horse or a pig. Breitner was definitely no Rembrandt. Rob leaned closer. The numbers were bizarre. On one page was a simple list of digits. But many of these same numbers were repeated on the page with the map. Above the map was a compass sign with the number 28 by the arrow for east. Then 211, next to one of the waggly lines. Twenty-nine was written by the tree symbol. And there were more: 61, 62 – and some much higher numbers: 1011, 1132. And then that last line about Orra Keller. There were no more numbers after that. No more of anything. The notebook ended poignantly – halfway down a page.

What did it mean? Rob started adding the numbers together. Then he stopped doing that because it seemed pointless. Maybe they were connected to the dig – maybe the numbers were a code for finds, and these marks showed places where the finds had been unearthed? Rob had already speculated that the map was a map of Gobekli. It was the obvious solution. But it didn't seem to fit. There was only one river near Gobekli – the Euphrates, and that was a good thirty miles off. The map moreover had no symbol for Gobekli itself – nothing indicating the megaliths.

Rob realized he had been in a reverie for several minutes. Christine was looking at him.

'Are you OK?'

He smiled. 'I'm intrigued. It's intriguing.'

'Isn't it? Like a puzzle.'

'I was wondering if the numbers mean finds? Things you have discovered in Gobekli? I remember seeing numbers written on some of those little bags you have . . . where you put arrowheads and stuff?'

'No. It's a nice idea, but no. The finds are numbered when they go to the vaults, in the museum. They have letters joined with numbers.'

Rob felt he had left her down. 'Ah well. Just a theory.'

'Theories are good. Even if they are wrong.'

Rob yawned again. He had done enough for one day. 'Do you have anything to drink?'

The simple question had a bracing effect on the Frenchwoman. 'My God.' She stood up. 'I am so sorry. I am not being very hospitable. Do you want a whisky?'

'That would be fantastic.'

'Single malt?'

'Even better.'

He watched as she disappeared into the kitchen. Moments later, she came back with a tray bearing a mug filled with ice, two chunky glass tumblers and a bottle of mineral water alongside a tall bottle of scotch. She set the glasses on the desk and unscrewed the bottle of Glenlivet, pouring out two serious inches of scotch. The dark, tigery liquor glittered in the light from the sidelamp.

'Ice?'

'Water.'

'*Commes les Brittaniques.*'

She splashed some water out of the plastic bottle, handed Rob the glass and sat down beside him. The glass was cold in Rob's grasp, as if it had been kept in the fridge. He could still hear the voices outside. They had been arguing for an hour. What about? He sighed and pressed the cold glass to his forehead, rolling it from side to side.

'You are tired?'

'Yeah. Aren't you?'

'Yes.' She paused. 'So. Do you want to sleep here? The sofa is very nice.'

Rob thought about this: about the moustached men outside. About the dark loitering figure in the doorway. He suddenly felt a very strong urge not to be alone, and he really didn't want to walk the half a mile to his hotel. 'Yeah, if it's OK.'

'Of course it is.' She quickly swallowed the rest of her scotch, then went about the flat, finding him a duvet and some pillows.

Rob was so tired he fell asleep the moment Christine turned off the lamp. And as soon as he slept, he dreamed. He dreamed of numbers, he dreamed of Breitner and a dog. A black dog streaking along a path and a hot sun. A dog. A face.

A dog.

And then his dreams were interrupted by a bang. He was woken by a very loud *bang.*

He jumped up from the sofa. It was light. How long had he been asleep? What was that noise? Groggily, he checked his watch. It was nine in the morning. The flat itself was quiet. But that repeated banging, what was it?

He rushed to the window.

18

Rob leaned out of the apartment. The city was thrumming. Bread-sellers were parading the busy streets, carrying on their head big trays of rolls and sweet pastries, and pretzels with sesame. Mopeds rode the pavements, avoiding dark-skinned schoolgirls with satchels.

Rob heard the bang again. He scanned the scene. A man was cutting baklava with a pizza-slicer in a shop across the way. And once more: *Bang!*

Then Rob saw a motorbike: an old, black, oily British Triumph. Backfiring. The owner was off the bike, and was now angrily hitting the machine with his left shoe. Rob was about to duck back inside when he saw something else.

The police. There were three policemen climbing out of two cars along the street. Two of them were in sweat-stained uniforms, the third in a dapper blue suit and a pale pink tie. The policemen walked to the front door of Christine's block, sixty feet below and paused. Then they pressed a button.

The bell in Christine's flat buzzed, very loudly.

Christine was already out of her bedroom, fully dressed.

'Christine the police are—'

'I know, I know!' she said. 'Good morning Robert!' Her face looked strained, but not frightened. She went to the intercom and buzzed the door open.

Rob pulled on his boots. Seconds later the police were in the flat – in the sitting room – and in Christine's face.

The dapperly-suited man was courteous, well-spoken, faintly sinister and barely thirty years old. He gazed curiously at Rob. 'You must be?'

'Rob Luttrell.'

'The British journalist?'

'Well, American, but I live in London . . .'

'*Perfect.* This is most convenient.' The officer smiled as if he had been given an unexpectedly large cheque. 'We are here to interview Miss Meyer about the terrible murder of her friend, Franz Breitner. But we would also like to talk with you, similarly. Perhaps afterwards?'

Rob nodded. He had anticipated a meeting with the police, but he felt oddly guilty being cornered here: in Christine's flat, at 9 a.m. The policeman was maybe playing on this guilt. His smile was suggestive and superior. He sidled to the desk, then flicked another supercilious glance at Rob. 'My name is Officer Kiribali. As we wish to speak with Miss Meyer first, in private, it would be beneficial if you could step outside for an hour or so?'

'Well, OK . . .'

'But don't go far. Just for one hour. Then we can proceed with you.' Another serpentine smile. 'Is that agreeable, Mr Luttrell?'

Rob looked at Christine. She nodded unhappily. Rob felt more guilt: at leaving Christine alone with this creepy guy. But he had no choice. Grabbing his jacket, he left the flat.

He spent the following hour on a sweaty plastic seat in a noisy internet café, trying to ignore the grunting older man, in baker's overalls, openly surfing lesbian porn on his right.

Rob worked the numbers from Breitner's book. He stuck them in every search engine possible: juggling them and rearranging them. What could the numbers be? They surely were a clue, maybe the key.

One likelihood was page numbers. But what book? And surely they went too high – 1013?

The Turkish baker had finished his surfing. He brushed past Rob with a petulant expression. Rob squinted into his screen, and juggled the numbers again. What was all this about? Were they geographical coordinates? Calendar years? Carbon dates? Rob had no idea.

He was sensing that the best method of cracking a puzzle like this was to let it lie: to let the subconscious get to work. Like a computer humming away in a backroom. The idea had a good pedigree. Rob had once read about a scientist called Kekule who had been striving to establish the molecular structure of Benzene. Kekule toiled for months with no success. But then one night he dreamed of a snake with its tail in its mouth: an ancient symbol called an ouroboros.

Kekule then woke, recalled the dream, and realized his unconscious mind was speaking to him: the molecule for Benzene was a ring, a circle, like a snake chewing its tail. Like the ouroboros. Kekule rushed to the laboratory to test the hypothesis. The solution he had dreamed was correct in all parts.

That was how powerful the unconscious was. So maybe Rob had to leave the problem in the mental cellar for a while, to let it ferment. Then the solution to Breitner's numbers might pop into his mind when he was thinking of something else: when he was showering, shaving, sleeping, or driving. Or being interviewed by the police . . .

The police! Rob checked his watch. An hour had passed. Thrusting his chair back, he paid the net café owner and walked swiftly to Christine's flat.

One of the uniformed policemen opened the door. Christine was sitting on the sofa, dabbing at her eyes. The other constable was handing out tissues. Rob bristled.

'Do not worry Mr Luttrell.' Officer Kiribali was sitting on the desk, his legs neatly crossed at the ankle. His tone-of-voice was casual and presumptuous. 'We are not Iraqis here. But Miss Meyer found talking of her friend's death rather . . . discomfiting.'

Christine glanced warily at the policeman and Rob detected plenty of resentment in her expression. Then she walked to her bedroom and slammed the door shut.

Kiribali shot his dazzling white cuffs, and wafted a manicured hand across the sofa, gesturing Rob to sit down. The two other policemen were standing across the room. Mute and sentinel. Kiribali smiled down at Rob. 'So you are a writer?'

'Yes.'

'How charming. I rarely get to meet genuine authors. This is such a primitive town. Because, you know, the Kurds . . .' He sighed. 'They are not exactly . . . scholars.' He tapped his chin with his pen. 'I studied English literature at Ankara. It is my private delight, Mr Luttrell.'

'Well, I'm just a journalist.'

'Hemingway was just a journalist!'

'Really. I'm just a hack.'

'But you are too modest. You are a gentlemen of letters. And of English letters, at that.' Kiribali's eyes were a very dark blue. Rob wondered if he was wearing tinted contacts. Vanity oozed from him. 'I always liked American poets. The women in particular. Emily Dickinson. And Sylvia Plath? You know them?' He looked at Rob, an inscrutable expression on his face. '*An engine, an engine, chuffing me off like a Jew. . . . I think I may well be a Jew!*' Kiribali smiled, urbanely. 'Aren't they some of the most frightening lines in literature?'

Rob didn't know what to say. He didn't want to discuss poetry with a policeman.

Kiribali sighed. 'Another time, maybe.' He waggled the pen between his fingers. 'I only have a few questions. I am aware you did not witness the alleged murder. Consequently . . .'

And so the interview proceeded. It was brief to the point of perfunctory. Almost pointless. Kiribali barely noted Rob's answers, one of the policemen turned a tape recorder on and off, in an apathetic way. Then Kiribali concluded with some more personal inquiries. He seemed more interested in Rob's relationship with Christine. 'She is a Jewess, is she not?'

Rob nodded. Kiribali smiled, contentedly, as if his biggest problem had been solved, then he laid the pen down. Resting it precisely in line with the edge of the desk. He clicked his fingers, the somnolent constables stirred; and the three policemen walked to the door. Pausing at the threshold, Kiribali asked Rob to tell Christine that she might be required for further questions, at 'some point in the future'. And then he was gone, with a final noxious waft of cologne.

Rob swivelled. Christine was standing in the bedroom doorway, looking cool and relaxed again in white shirt and khakis.

'What a total wanker.'

Christine shrugged acceptantly. '*Peut-être.* He was just doing his job.'

'He made you cry.'

'Talking about Franz. Yes . . . I haven't done that for a few days.'

Rob picked his jacket up. Then he put it down. He stared at Breitner's notebook on the desk. He didn't know what to do now. He didn't know where he was headed or where this story was going; he just knew he was involved and possibly even endangered. Or was that paranoia? Rob stared at the picture on the wall. The unusual tower. Christine followed his gaze.

'Haran.'

'Where is it?'

'Not so far away, an hour or so.' Her eyes sparkled. 'You know, I have an idea. Would you like to see it? Get out of Urfa again? I'd rather like to be somewhere else. Anywhere but here.'

Rob nodded keenly. He felt drawn to the desert more and more, the longer he was here in Kurdish Turkey. The starkness of the desert shadows, the silence in the empty valleys: he liked it all. And right now that desert emptiness was very preferable to the alternative: a day of skulking in hot and watchful Sanliurfa. 'Let's go.'

It was a long drive: the landscape south of Urfa was even more brutal than the desert surrounding Gobekli. Great yellow flatlands stretched to shimmering grey horizons; sandy wastes besieged the odd dilapidated Kurdish village. The sun was burning. Rob rolled the car window down as far as it would go but the breeze was still hot, as if a team of blowtorches had been turned on the Land Rover.

'In the summer it can reach 50° here,' Christine said, changing gear with a lusty crunch. 'In the shade.'

'I can believe it.'

'Didn't always used to be like that of course. The climate changed ten thousand years back. As Franz told you . . .'

For about fifty klicks they talked about Breitner's notebook: the map and the scrawl, and of course the numbers. But neither of them had any new ideas. Rob's subconscious was on vacation. His Kekule idea hadn't worked.

They passed an army roadblock. The blood-red flag of the Turkish state hung limp under the noontime sun. One of the soldiers stood up, wearily checked Rob's passport, leered briefly at Christine through the car window, then waved them on down the burning road.

Half an hour later Rob saw it, suddenly, the strange tower, looming. It was a broken pillar of a building constructed from burnt mud bricks seven storeys high, but shattered at the top. It was enormous.

'What is it?'

Christine swerved off the main road, towards the tower. 'It belongs to the oldest Islamic university in the world. Haran. A thousand years old at least. It's derelict now.'

'It looks like the tower on the Tarot cards. The tower hit by lightning?'

Christine nodded distantly, staring out of the window as she parked; she was staring at a row of little homes with mud domes for roofs. Three kids were kicking a football made of rags, in the yard that abutted the tiny houses. Goats bleated in the heat. 'See those?'

'The mud houses? Uh-huh?'

'They've been here since the third millennium BC maybe. Haran is vastly old. According to legend, Adam and Eve are meant to have come here, after being thrown out of Paradise.'

Rob thought of the name: Haran. It was triggering some deep memory of his father, reading out the Bible. 'And it's mentioned in Genesis.'

'What?'

'The Book of Genesis,' Rob repeated. 'Chapter 11 verse 31. Abraham lived here. In Haran.'

Christine smiled. 'I'm impressed.'

'I'm not. Wish I didn't remember any of that crap. Anyway,' he added. 'How can they be sure?'

'What?'

'How can they be sure it's the town where Adam and Eve lived after the Fall? Why not London? Or Hong Kong?'

'I don't know . . .' She smiled at his sarcasm. 'But it's pretty clear, as you say, that the early Abrahamic traditions date back to this area. Abraham is strongly linked with Sanliurfa. And, yes, Haran is where Abraham got the call from God.'

Rob yawned, and got out of the car, and gazed across the dust. Christine joined him. Together they watched a mangy black goat scratch itself against a rusty old bus; the bus, inexplicably, had blood down one side. Rob wondered if the local farmers used the bus as a makeshift abattoir. This was a strange place.

'So,' he said, 'we've established this is where Abraham came from. And he was the founder of . . . the three monotheistic religions, right?'

'Yes. Judaism, Christianity and Islam. He started them all. And when he left Haran he went down into the land of Canaan, spreading the new word of God, the single God of the Bible, the Talmud and the Koran.'

Rob listened to this with a vague but insistent sense of unease. He leaned against the car and pondered; he was getting more flashbacks to his childhood. His father reading from the Book of Mormon. His uncles quoting Ecclesiastes. *Glory O young man in thy youth.* That was the only line from the Bible Rob had ever really liked. He said the line aloud, then he added: 'What about the sacrifice? The slaying of the son?' He searched Christine's intelligent face for confirmation. 'I remember some story about Abraham and his son, right?'

Christine nodded. 'The slaying of Isaac. The Prophet Abraham was going to butcher his own son, as a sacrifice, a sacrifice ordered by Jehovah. But God stayed the knife.'

'There you go. Pretty decent of the old man.'

Christine laughed. 'Do you want to stay here, or shall I take you somewhere even weirder?'

'Hey, we're on a roll!'

They jumped back in the car. Christine shifted a gear and they sped away. Rob sat back, watching the landscape blur into dust. Every so often the mouldering hills were punctuated by the odd ruined building, or a crumbling Ottoman castle. Or a dust devil, whirring its solitary way across the wastes. And then, unbelievably, the desolation intensified. The road got rockier. Even the blue of the desert sky seemed to darken, to turn a brooding purple. The heat was almost insupportable. The car rattled around bleached yellow promontories, and along hot rutted tracks. Barely a tree disturbed the endless sterility.

'Sogmatar,' said Christine, at last.

They were approaching a tiny village, just a few concrete shacks, lost in a silent bare valley in the middle of the baked and mighty nothingness.

A big jeep was parked incongruously outside one shack and there were a few other cars; but the roads and yards were devoid of people; it reminded Rob instantly and queerly of Los Angeles. Big cars and endless sunshine – and no people.

Like a city hit by plague.

'A few rich Urfans have second homes here,' said Christine. 'Along with the Kurds.'

'Why the fuck would anyone live out here?'

'It's got a lot of atmosphere. You'll see.'

They stepped out of the car, into the kiln of dusty heat. Christine led the way, scrambling over decaying old walls, past scattered and carved blocks of marble. The latter looked like Roman capitals. 'Yes,' Christine said, sensing Rob's next question. 'The Romans were here, and the Assyrians. Everyone came here.'

They approached a big dark hole in an odd and very squat building: it was a building carved literally out of the rock face. They stepped inside the low-slung structure. It took a few seconds for Rob's eyes to adjust.

Inside, the smell of goat shit was oppressive. Pungent and dank, and oppressive.

'This is a pagan temple. To the moon gods,' said Christine. She pointed at some crudely carved figures cut into the walls of the shadowy interior. 'The moon god is here, you can see his horns – see – the curve of the new moon.'

The badly eroded effigy had a sort of helmet: two horns like a crescent moon balanced on his head. Rob ran a hand over the stone face. It was warm, and strangely clammy. He drew his hand back. The decaying effigies of the dead gods stared at him with their eroded eyes. It was so quiet in here: Rob could hear his own heartbeat. The noise of the outside world was barely perceptible: just the tinkling bells of goats, and the churning desert wind. Hot sunlight blazed at the door, making the dark room seem even darker.

'Are you OK?'

'Fine. I'm fine . . .'

She walked towards the opposite wall. 'The temple dates from the second century AD. Christianity was sweeping the region, but here they still worshipped the old gods. With the horns. I love it here.'

Rob gazed about him. 'Very nice. You should buy a condo.'

'Are you always sarcastic when you are uncomfortable?'

'Can we get latte?'

Christine chuckled. 'I've one more place to show you.' She led him out of the temple and Rob felt a serious relief as they exited the clammy, fetid darkness. They headed up a slope of scree and hot dust. Turning for a moment to take a breath, Rob saw a child staring at them from one of the humble houses. A small dark face in a broken window.

Christine scrambled up and over a final rise. 'The Temple of Venus.'

Rob climbed the last metres of scree to stand beside her. The wind was brisk up here, yet still burning hot. He could see for miles. It was an extraordinary landscape. Miles and miles of endless, rolling, blanched-out desolation. Dying hills of dead rocks. The mountains were marked with the black empty sockets of caves. These were, Rob presumed, more temples and pagan shrines, each more derelict than the last. He stared at the floor on which they stood, the floor of a temple, open to the sky. 'And all this was built when?'

'Possibly by the Assyrians, or the Canaanites. No one knows for certain. It's very old. The Greeks took it over, then the Romans. It was certainly a place of human sacrifice.' She pointed out some grooves in the carved rock beneath them, 'See. That was to let the blood flow out.'

'OK . . .'

'All these early Levantine religions were very keen on sacrifice.'

Rob looked out across the desert hills and down at the little village. The child with the face was gone; the broken window was empty. One of the cars was on the move: taking the valley road out of Sogmatar. The road ran alongside a dried up old river bed. The course of a dead river.

Rob imagined being sacrificed up here. Your legs tied with rough twine, your hands bound behind your back, the foul breath of the priest in your face; and then the thud of pain as the knife plunged into your ribcage . . .

He breathed deeply and wristed the sweat from his forehead. It was surely time to go. He gestured in the direction of their car. Christine nodded and they walked down the hill to the waiting Land Rover. But halfway down the slope, Rob stopped. He stared at the hill.

Suddenly: he *knew*. He had worked out what the numbers meant.

The numbers in Breitner's notebook.

19

The weather was still grim. The lead-grey sky was as sombre as the green and windswept fields beneath. Boijer, Forrester and Alisdair Harnaby were in a big dark car, speeding south across the Isle of Man. Ahead of them was another long black car: containing DCC Hayden and his colleagues.

Forrester was feeling the anxiety. Time was passing: slipping from his grasp. And every minute they lost brought them all closer to the next horror. The next inevitable murder.

He sighed, heavily. Almost angrily. But at least they were now onto something: following a proper lead. A farmer had spotted something odd in a remote corner of the Isle, way down in the south near Castletown. Forrester had urgently persuaded Alisdair Harnaby to come along for the interview, as he felt the man might be good for some more information. The historical angle. It seemed important.

But first Forrester wanted to know what the CNN woman had said; Boijer was keen to divulge. The Finnish DS explained that Angela Darvill had heard about the Craven Street case 'from some hack on the *Evening Standard*'.

'So she linked them,' said Forrester. 'Fair enough.'

'Yes that's right, sir. But she said something else. Apparently there was a similar case. New York State and Connecticut. In New England.'

'How similar?'

'Same kind of elaborate torture.'

'Star of David?'

Boijer said no, then added, 'But carvings in the skin, yes. And flayings. She said it was one of the most horrible cases she'd ever covered.'

Forrester sat back and looked out of the window. Low damp sober green hills stretched away on all sides. Small farms dotted the rural emptiness, and small hunched trees, with their branches shaved brusquely and bizarrely to an angle by the prevailing winds. The scenery reminded him of a holiday he'd once taken in Skye. There was a melancholy beauty to the landscape, a melancholy beauty which edged close to real, haunting sadness. Forrester drove the thought of his daughter from his mind, and asked: 'Who committed the murders?'

'They never found out. Weird though: the similarity, I mean . . .'

Ahead of them the road dwindled to little more than a rutted track, which led on through the wind-battered hedgerows to a farm. The two cars parked. The five policemen and the amateur historian walked down the track towards the low-slung white farmhouse. Boijer stared down at his shoes, now soggy with clay, and tutted with a young man's vanity. 'Damn. Look at that.'

'Should have brought your wellies, Boijer.'

'Didn't know we were going hiking, sir. Can I claim these on exes?'

Forrester was glad to laugh. 'See what I can do.'

One of the white helmeted constables accompanying Hayden knocked on the door of the farmhouse, and at last it was opened by a surprisingly young man. Forrester wondered why the word 'farmer' always conjured up an image of a middle aged gent brandishing a hoe, or a shotgun. This farmer was handsome and no more than twenty-five.

'Hello, hello. The Deputy . . . ?'

'Chief Constable,' supplied Hayden. 'Yes. And you must be Gary?'

'Yep. I'm Gary Spelding. We spoke on the blower. Come in, guys. Horrible day!'

They crowded into the warm, welcoming, and pinewoody farmhouse kitchen. Biscuits were arrayed on a plate: Boijer grabbed one with enthusiasm.

Forrester was suddenly conscious of their numbers. Five was too many. But they all wanted to know about the lead. What Spelding had seen. Over two potfuls of tea, provided by his smiling wife, Spelding told his story. The afternoon of the murder he had been fixing a gate on his farm. He was about to head back home, the job done, when he'd seen 'something strange'. Forrester let his tea go cold as he listened.

'It was a big four by four. Chelsea tractor.'

Hayden leaned over the kitchen table keenly. 'Where exactly?'

'Road at the end of the farm. Balladoole.'

Harnaby interrupted. 'I know it.'

'Course we get a few tourists there now and again. The beach is just beyond. But these guys were different . . .' Spelding swivelled his mug of tea, and smiled at Hayden. 'Five young men. In telecoms overalls.'

'Sorry?' said Boijer.

Spelding turned to Forrester's junior. 'They were all wearing big green overalls, with Manx telecom insignia. Mobile phone company.'

Forrester took over the questioning. 'And they were doing what?

'Just wandering around my fields. And I thought that was odd. Pretty odd. Yep.' Spelding sipped some tea. 'Not least because we have no masts down here, no reception. It's a deadzone for mobiles. So I wondered what they were doing. And they were all young. Young guys. But it was nearly dark and pretty cold so they weren't surfers.'

'Did you talk to them?'

Spelding blushed faintly. 'Well I was gonna. They were walking on my farm, for a start. But the way they looked at me when I went near . . .'

'Was?'

'Nasty. Just . . .' The farmer's blush deepened. 'Kind of nasty. Glaring.

So I thought discretion was the better option. Rather cowardly, sorry. And then I saw your press conference on the news and I started to wonder . . .'

DCC Hayden sank the rest of his tea. He looked at Forrester, then back at Spelding.

Over the next half hour they got the remaining information from Gary Spelding. Detailed descriptions of the men: all tall and young. Descriptions of the car: a black Toyota Landcruiser, though Spelding could remember no numberplate. But at least it was a lead. A break. Forrester knew these were likely to be the men they were looking for. Posing as telecoms workmen was a good cover. There were phone masts everywhere; everyone wanted mobile coverage, 24/7. You could work late at night without arousing suspicion. 'We've got a network failure.'

But the gang had come to an area without any mobile phone reception. Why had they done that? Was it possibly their first mistake? Forrester felt his hopes rising. You needed luck in this job. This might be his stroke of luck.

The interview was finished. The teapot was empty. Outside, the lid of grey clouds had partially lifted. Slants of sunshine shone down on the wet fields. The policemen lifted their trousers from the mud as they walked with the farmer down to the Balladoole Road.

'Just through here,' said Spelding. 'This is where I saw them.'

They all gazed across the rucked and muddy field, bordered by the small country road. A doleful cow was staring at Boijer. Beyond the cow was a long curve of grey sand, and then the frigid grey sea, lit by the occasional dazzle of sunshine.

Forrester indicated the lane. 'Where does that go?'

'To the sea. That's all.'

Forrester climbed the last gate; followed by Boijer and the rest, who showed rather less alacrity. He stood exactly where the car had parked. It was an odd place to stop if you were headed for the bay. It was half a mile back from the shoreline. So why did they park here? Why not drive the last half mile? Did they fancy a walk? Clearly not. So they must have been looking for something else.

Forrester climbed back on to the nearest gate. He was nine feet in the air now. He looked all around him. Just fields and stone walls and sandy meadows. And the unhappy sea. The only point of interest was the nearest field. Which, from Forrester's vantage, showed some shallow bumps, and stray rocks. He got down from the gate and turned to Harnaby, who was panting from the walk. 'What are they?' asked Forrester. 'Those little bumps?'

'Well . . .' Harnaby was smiling unsurely. 'I was going to mention it. Not many people know about it but that's the Balladoole burial site. Vikings. Eleventh century. It was dug up in the 1940s. They found brooches and the like. And . . . something else too . . .'

'What?'

'They also found a body.'

Harnaby elaborated. He told them about the great excavation during the war when scientists from the mainland had unearthed an entire Viking ship, interred with jewellery and swords. And the body of a Viking warrior. 'And there was also evidence of human sacrifice. At the warrior's feet, the archaeologists found the body of a teenage girl. She was probably a sacrificial victim.'

'How do they know?'

'Because she was buried without any grave goods. And she was garrotted. Vikings were quite partial to a bit of sacrifice. They would kill slave-girls to honour fallen men.'

Forrester felt a reflexive quickening. He looked at Boijer. He looked at the distant grey waves. He returned his gaze to Boijer. 'Ritual sacrifice,' he said at last. 'Yes. Ritual human sacrifice. Boijer! That's it!'

Boijer seemed puzzled. Forrester explained:

'Think about it. A man buried alive with his head in the soil. A man with his head shaved – and his tongue cut out. Ritual carvings on both bodies . . .'

'And now Balladoole,' said Harnaby.

Forrester gave a brisk assent. Jumping over a second gate, he crossed to the bumps and rocks in the field. His shoes were ruined by mud but he didn't care. He could hear the sounding waves from the beach; taste the tang of oceanic salt. Beneath him Vikings had interred a young woman, a woman who had been ritually slain. And these men, these murderers, had communed here: before committing their own ritualized execution: just a few hours later.

The clockwork was whirring. The machinery was engaged. Forrester inhaled the muggy moist air. Smirrs of grey cloud were racing in, from the roiled and choppy Irish Sea.

20

The Land Rover sped down the dirt track away from Sogmatar towards the main Sanliurfa road, twenty klicks alongside the ancient arroyo. Christine was staring ahead, concentrating on the road, her hand tight on the gearstick. They drove in silence.

Rob hadn't told her what he thought he had discovered about the numbers. He wanted to prove it to himself first. And for that he needed a book, and maybe a computer.

By the time they arrived back in the city the sun was an hour from sunset and Sanliurfa was notably busy. As soon as they reached the centre they went straight to Christine's flat, flung dusty jackets onto the wickerwork chair and flopped onto the sofa. And then Christine said, quite unexpectedly, and apropos of nothing, 'Do you think I should fly home?'

'What? Why?'

'The dig is over. My salary stops in a month. I could fly home now.'

'Without finding out what happened to Franz?'

'Yes.' She stared out of the window. 'He is . . . dead. Shouldn't I just accept it?'

The sun was dying outside. The muezzin were calling across the ancient city of Urfa. Rob got up, went to the window; creaked it open, and gazed out. The cucumber man was cycling down the pavement shouting his wares. Veiled women were in a group outside the Honda shop talking into mobile phones through their concealing black chadors. They looked like shades, like ghosts. The mourning brides of death.

He went back to the sofa and gazed at Christine. 'I don't think you should go. Not yet.'

'Why not?'

'I think I know what the numbers mean.'

Her face was motionless. 'Show me.'

'Do you have a Bible? An English one?'

'On that shelf.'

Rob paced to the shelf and checked the spines: art, poetry, politics, archaeology, history. More archaeology. There. He took down a big old black Bible. The proper authorized version.

At the same time Christine took Breitner's notebook from the desk.

'All right,' said Rob. 'I hope I'm right. I think I'm right. But here goes. Read out the numbers in the notebook. And tell me what they're next to on the page.'

'OK, here's . . . twenty-eight. Next to a compass sign, for east.'

'No, say it like the two numbers are separate. Two eight.'

Christine stared at Rob, perplexed. Maybe even amused. 'OK. Two eight. By an arrow pointing east.'

Rob opened the Bible to Genesis, thumbed through the thin, almost translucent pages and found the right page. He ran his finger down the dense columns of text.

'Chapter two, verse eight. 2:8 Genesis. "And the LORD God planted a garden eastward in Eden; and there he put the man whom he had formed".' Rob waited.

Christine was staring at the Bible. After a while she murmured, 'Eastward in Eden?'

'Read another one.'

Christine scanned the notebook. 'Two nine. Next to the tree.'

Rob went to the same page in the Bible and recited, 'Book of Genesis. Chapter two, verse nine. 2:9. "And out of the ground made the LORD God to grow every tree that is pleasant to the sight, and good for food; the tree of life also in the midst of the garden, and the tree of knowledge of good and evil".'

Christine said in a low voice, 'Two one zero. Two ten. By the river squiggly thing.'

'The line that turns into four rivers?'

'Yes.'

Rob looked down at the Bible. 'Chapter two, verse ten. "And a river went out of Eden to water the garden; and from thence it was parted, and became into four heads".'

'My God,' said Christine. 'You're right!'

'Let's try one more, to make sure. A different one, one of the big numbers.'

Christine went back to the notebook. 'OK. Here are some bigger numbers, at the end. Eleven thirty-one?'

Rob fanned through the pages and recited, feeling like a vicar in his pulpit, 'Genesis. Chapter eleven, verse thirty-one. "And Terah took Abraham his son, and Lot the son of Haran his son's son, and Sara his daughter-in-law, his son Abram's wife; and they went forth with them from Ur of the Chaldees, to go into the land of Canaan; and they came unto Haran, and dwelt there".'

'Haran?'

'Haran.' Rob paused, sitting down next to Christine. 'Let's try one more, one more of the others, one of the numbers next to a drawing.'

'Here's a number by a picture, seems to be a dog or a pig . . . or something.'

'What's the number?'

'Two hundred and nineteen. So, two nineteen?'

Rob found the relevant passage: ' "And out of the ground the LORD God formed every beast of the field, and every fowl of the air; and brought them unto Adam to see what he would call them . . ." '

Quietness filled the flat. Rob could still hear the cries of the cucumber seller floating up from the dusty streets below. Christine gazed at him intently. 'Breitner thought he was digging up—'

'Yes. *The Garden of Eden.*'

They stared across the sofa at each other.

21

Forrester was researching human sacrifice, in his London office. His coffee sat on his desk next to a photo of his son holding a beach ball and a picture of his snowy-blonde daughter, beaming and happy. It was a photo taken just before her death.

Sometimes when the black dog of depression was at his heels, Forrester would lay the photo of his daughter face down on the desk. Because it was just too painful, too piercing. Thinking about his daughter sometimes gave Forrester a kind of sharp chest pain, as if he had a fractured rib digging into his lungs. It was such a physical pain that he would almost vocalize it.

But most of the time it wasn't quite this bad. Usually, he was able to look past the pain – to other people's pain. This morning the photo stood on the desk ignored, his daughter's happy still-alive smile white and bright. Forrester was transfixed by his computer screen, Googling away at 'human sacrifice'.

He was reading about the Jews: the early Israelites who burned their children. Alive. They did this, Forrester learned, in a valley just south of Jerusalem – Ben-Hinnom. Wikipedia told the DCI that this valley was also known as Gehenna. The valley of Gehenna was Hell to the Canaanite, the 'valley of the shadow of death'.

Forrester read on. According to historians, in ancient times Israelite mothers and fathers would bring their firstborn children down to the valley, outside the gates of Jerusalem, and there they would place their screaming babies into the hollow brass stomach of a huge statue dedicated to the Canaanite demon god Moloch. The brass bowl in the centre of the enormous statue of Moloch also functioned as a brazier. Once the babies and children were in the brass bowl, fires were lit under the statue, which heated the brass, thereby roasting the children to death. As the children screamed to be saved, priests would pound enormous drums to drown out the shrieks and save the mothers from undue distress, from having to listen to their children burning alive.

Forrester sat back, his heart pounding like the drums of an Israelite ritual. How could anyone do such a thing? How could anyone sacrifice their own children? Unbidden, Forrester thought of his own children, his daughter, his dead daughter. The firstborn of the family.

Rubbing his eyes, he scrolled through some more pages.

The sacrifice of firstborn was a common motif in ancient history, it seemed. All kinds of peoples – Celts, Mayans, Goths, Vikings, Norsemen, Hindus, Sumerians, Scythians, American Indians, Incas, many others – sacrificed humans, and many of them sacrificed the first child. Often this was done as a so-called 'foundation sacrifice' when a strategically important or sacred structure was being built: before the main construction took place the community would sacrifice a child, usually a firstborn, and they would bury the corpse under the arch or pillar or door.

Forrester inhaled, and exhaled. He clicked another link. The sky outside was bright, the sunshine of late spring. The DCI was too absorbed in his macabre task to notice or care.

Aztec sacrifices were especially bloodthirsty. Homosexuals would be ritually killed by having their intestines ripped out through their rectums. Enemy warriors would have their living hearts torn from their chest cavities by priests whose heads were daubed with the human offal of their previous victims.

He read on. And on. Supposedly the Great Wall of China was built on thousands of cadavers: yet more foundation sacrifices. The Japanese once venerated a hitobashira – a human pillar – beneath which virgins were buried alive. Enormous cenotes, or water cisterns, were used by the Mayans of Mexico as drowning lakes for maidens and children. And there was more. The pre-Roman Celts would stab a victim in the heart and then divine the future from the death spasms of the thrashing body. The Phoenicians killed literally thousands of babies as atonement and buried them in 'tophets' – great baby cemeteries.

And on, and on. Forrester sat back feeling a little sick. Yet he also felt he was making progress. The ritual murder in the Isle of Man and the attempted murder in Craven Street had to be connected with sacrifice, not least because the murderers had gathered at the spot of a historically proven sacrifice. But what linked them?

He took a deep breath, like someone about to dive in a very cold pond, and Googled 'Star of David'.

After forty minutes of searching through Jewish history he found what he needed. It was on some lunatic American website, possibly a Satanist site. But lunacy was just what Forrester was investigating. The mad website told him the Star of David was also known as the Star of Solomon, as the ancient Jewish king had allegedly used it as his magical emblem. The symbol was abjured by some modern rabbinical authorities because of its occult associations. Solomon was reported to have used the Star on the temple he raised to Moloch, the Canaanite demon, where he committed animal and human sacrifice.

Forrester read the webpage again. And again. And for a third time. The Star of David was not what the murderers were etching into their victims. They were cutting the Star of Solomon. A symbol closely associated with human sacrifice.

And the head shaving?

That took only three minutes to Google.

Victims of sacrifice in many cultures were purified in various ways before the ritual. They were bathed, or required to fast, sometimes they would be shaved of all hair. Some would have their tongues cut out.

Forrester's thesis was confirmed. The murderers were obsessed or engaged with the concept of human sacrifice. But why?

He stood up and massaged his neck muscles. He'd been reading for three hours. His mind was buzzing with the pulse of the computer screen. All this was well and good. But they had no actual leads on the murder gang. All the Manx ports were being watched. The airport was under surveillance. But he had little hope they would catch the gang that way: they would surely have split up and fled the isle at once. Dozens of boats and ferries and airplanes left Man every day at all hours; most likely the gang had left Douglas before the corpse was even discovered. The only real hope was looking for CCTV images of the black Toyota. But it could take weeks for the available footage to be scanned.

Forrester sat down again and tugged his swivel chair nearer to the screen. He had three things left to research.

Jerusalem Whaley was a member of this club of roistering aristocrats: the Irish Hellfire Club. As the Manx historian had told him. But how was that fact linked to sacrifice? To the murders? Was it linked at all?

And the bones in Craven Street, in Benjamin Franklin's House, what was all that about?

These two queries led to his third question: everywhere they went, the gang dug something up. What were they looking for?

His initial search was simple and immediately successful. Forrester typed in Benjamin Franklin and Hellfire and the very first hit gave him his answer: Benjamin Franklin, the founding father of America, was a good friend of Sir Francis Dashwood, and Sir Francis Dashwood was the founder of the Hellfire Club. Indeed, according to some authorities, Benjamin Franklin was himself a member of the Hellfire Club.

The puzzle yielded. The Hellfire Club was obviously crucial. But precisely who or what were they?

As far as Forrester could tell from Google, the Hellfire Club, in both

Ireland and England, was a secret society of upper class ne'er-do-wells. But that was all. They were unsavoury and dangerous, maybe, indulged and hedonistic certainly; but truly Satanic and murderous? Most historians reckoned they were little more than a drinking club which sometimes got a little ribald. The rumours of devil worship were largely dismissed.

That said, there was one expert who disagreed. Forrester scribbled the name on a pad. A professor Hugo De Savary, at Cambridge University no less, reckoned that the Hellfires were serious occultists. Though he had been ridiculed for his views.

But even if De Savary was right it still didn't answer the rest of the awkward questions. What were the gang looking for? Why were they digging stuff up? How was it connected with the Hellfires? What was the point in turning over lawns and cellars? Were they seeking treasure? Demonic gewgaws? Old bones? Cursed diamonds? Sacrificed children? Forrester's mind was fizzing – a little too much. He had done enough for one morning. He had done well. He felt as if he had finally gathered all the main jigsaw pieces, or someone had tipped them all in his lap. The only problem was that he had lost the box and couldn't see the lid. So he didn't know what the jigsaw pieces were meant to represent, he didn't have a clue what picture he was trying to recreate. Still, at least he had the pieces . . .

Stifling a yawn, Forrester yanked his jacket from the back of the swivel chair and fed his arms into the sleeves. It was lunchtime. He'd earned a nice lunch – Italian maybe. Penne arrabiata at the trattoria down the road. With some good tiramisu to follow, and a nice long read of the sports pages.

On his way out of the office, he glanced down at his desk. His daughter smiled back at him, with her innocent face shining. Forrester paused, feeling a sharpness inside. He looked at the picture of his son, and then again at the picture of his daughter. He thought of her voice. Saying her first real words. Appull- App-ull. App-ull daddy! App-ull . . .

The pain was sharp. He laid the picture flat on the desk, and stepped through the door.

The first thing he saw was Boijer, breathless and excited.

'Sir, I think we have something!'

'What?'

'Toyota. The black Toyota.'

'Where?'

'Heysham, sir. In Lancashire.'

'When—'

'Two days ago.'

22

Rob and Christine were sitting in the tea-house by the Pool of Abraham. The honeyed stones of the Mevlid Halil mosque were glowing in the morning light: their mellow hues reflected placidly in the water of the fishpond.

They had spent the previous evening researching the Eden theory separately: Christine on the laptop in her flat, Rob in a net café: dividing their time to get more data more quickly. And now they had met to discuss it. They had come here for the anonymity: it felt safer to be sitting amongst the crowds. The strolling friends and off-duty soldiers, the kids eating fried mutton balls with one hand as their mothers gazed at the carp. The only jarring note was a police car parked discreetly at the edge of the tea-gardens.

Rob was remembering how he'd arrived at his solution. They had discussed Genesis when they were in Sogmatar and Haran. And Christine had also mentioned the Adam and Eve legend. This combination must, Rob realized, have triggered memories of his father reciting the Bible; so he had seen how the numbers could be read. Chapter x verse y. Digit followed by digit. But now they had to examine this solution, more deeply, and compare notes on the underlying logic.

'OK.' He took a gulp of tea. 'Let's go through it again. We know that agriculture began here. The first place in the world. In the area immediately surrounding Gobekli. Sometime around 8000 BC, yup?'

'Yes. And we know roughly when and where farming began . . .'

'Because of the archaeological evidence: "domestication is a shock to the system". I read that in the book in your flat. The skeletons of people change, they grow smaller and less healthy . . .'

'Yyyyes,' Christine agreed, hesitantly. 'As the human body adapts to a protein-poorer diet, and a more arduous lifestyle there is certainly a change in skeletal size, in the robustness of the physique. I have seen that in many sites.'

'So. Early domestication is a trial. Likewise, newly-domesticated animals get scrawnier.'

'Yes.'

'But . . .' Rob leaned forward. 'When this domestication happened, in 8000 BC, that was also the time when the local landscape began to alter. Around here. Right?'

'Yes, the trees were chopped down and the soil leached away and the area became very arid. As it is now. Whereas before, it was . . . paradisiacal.' She smiled meditatively. 'I remember Franz talking about Gobekli as it must have been. He said it was once a *prachtvolle Schafferegion* – a glorious pastoral region. It was a region of forests and meadows, rich with game, and wild grasses. And then the climate changed, as agriculture took over. And then it became a weary place – that had to be worked ever harder.'

Rob took out his notebook and recited, 'As God says to Adam: "cursed is the ground because of you; in toil you shall eat of it all the days of your life". Genesis Chapter 3, verse 17. Three seventeen.'

Christine rubbed her temples with her fingertips. She looked tired, which was unusual for her. But then she shook herself, and pressed on. 'I have heard this theory before: that the story of Eden is a folk-memory, and an allegory.'

'You mean, like, a metaphor?'

'According to some, yes. If you look at it one way the Eden story describes our hunter-gatherer past, when we had time to wander through the trees and pick fruit and gather wild grasses . . . like Adam and Eve, naked in paradise. And then we fell into farming and life got harder. And so we were expelled from Eden.'

Rob looked at two men holding hands, crossing the bridge over the little rivulet; the bridge that led to the teahouse. 'But why did we really start farming?'

Christine shrugged. 'No one knows. It is one of the great mysteries. But it certainly started here. In this corner of Anatolia. The very first pigs were domesticated at Cayonu, that's just seventy miles away. Cattle were domesticated at Catalhoyuk, to the west.'

'But how does Gobekli fit in precisely?'

'That's a difficult one. It's a miracle that hunters created such a site. Yet it shows that the life before farming was very leisured. These men, those hunters, they had time to learn the arts, to sculpt, to make exquisite carvings. It was a huge leap forward. Yet they didn't know how to make pots.' Christine's silver crucifix glinted in the sunshine as she spoke. 'It's bizarre. And of course sexuality developed, too. There are many erotic images in Gobekli. Animals and men with enlarged phalluses. Carvings of women, splayed and naked women . . .'

'Maybe they ate the fruit from the tree of knowledge?' said Rob.

Christine smiled politely. 'Maybe.'

They were quiet for a moment. Christine turned nervously to her left, as a swarthy policeman patrolled with his radio buzzing. Rob wondered why they were both so paranoid. Neither of them had done anything wrong. But Officer Kiribali had been so sinister. And what about the men staring up at the flat. What was that all about? He dismissed his fears. There was still ground to cover. 'Then there's the geography?'

'Yes.' Christine nodded. 'The topography. That's also important.'

'There aren't four rivers near Gobekli.'

'No. Just one. But it's the Euphrates.'

Rob remembered what he had read in the net café. 'And scholars have always reckoned that Eden, if it lay anywhere, must have been somewhere between the Tigris and the Euphrates. The fertile crescent. The earliest site of civilization. And the Euphrates is actually mentioned in Genesis, as rising in Eden.'

'It is. And also we have the mountains on the map.'

'The Taurus.'

'Source of the Euphrates, East of Eden,' Christine affirmed. 'There are strong legends that Eden is sheltered by mountains to the East. Gobekli has the Taurus to the east.'

Christine took out her own notebook: and read out some of her notes. 'OK, there's more. In ancient Assyrian texts, there is mention of a Beth Eden, a so-called House of Eden.'

'Which is?

'It is or rather it was a small Aramean statelet. Located on the bend of the Euphrates, just south of Charchemish. Which is fifty miles from Sanliurfa.'

Rob nodded, impressed. Christine's research had been better than his. 'Did you find anything else?'

'We know about Adam and Eve in Haran. But Eden isn't just described in Genesis, it is also mentioned in the Book of Kings.' She flicked a page in her notebook, and read the citation: ' "Have the gods of the nations delivered them which my fathers have destroyed; as Gozan, and Haran, and Rezeph, and the children of Eden which were in Thelasar?" '

'Haran again?'

'Yes. Haran.' She shrugged. 'And Thelasar is possibly a town called Rusafah in Northern Syria.'

'How far is that?'

'Two hundred miles south-west.'

Rob nodded, enthused. 'Making Gobekli just east. Eastward in Eden. And what about the name? The word Eden itself? It means delight in Hebrew . . .'

'But the Sumerian root is in fact "eddin". A steppe or plateau, or plain.'

'Like . . . the Plain of Haran?'

'Quite so. Like the Plain of Haran. In which we find . . .'

'Gobekli Tepe.' Rob felt the tingle of sweat on his back. It was a very hot morning, even in the cool of the teahouse gardens. 'OK then, the last thread is the actual Bible connection.'

'Abraham was meant to have lived here. He is certainly linked to Haran, in the Book of Genesis. Most Muslims believe Urfa is the Ur of the Chaldees. And that is also mentioned in Genesis. This small region has more links to Genesis than anywhere else in the Middle East.'

'So that's it.' Rob smiled, feeling satisfied. 'Taking into account the Biblical links, the history and legends, plus the topography of the region and the evidence of early domestication – and of course the data from the site itself – we have the solution. Right? At least we have Franz's solution . . .' Rob lifted his hands, like a magician about to do a trick: 'Gobekli Tepe is the Garden of Eden!'

Christine smiled. 'Metaphorically.'

'Metaphorically. But still, it is persuasive. This is where the Fall of Man took place. From the freedom of hunting, to the toil of agriculture. And that's the story recorded in Genesis.'

They were silent for a moment. Then Christine said, 'Though a better way of putting it is that Gobekli Tepe is . . . a temple in an Edenic landscape. Rather than the actual Garden of Eden.'

'Sure.' Rob grinned. 'Don't worry, Christine, I don't actually think Adam and Eve were wandering around Gobekli eating peaches. But I do think Franz reckoned he had found it. Allegorically.'

He gazed across the glittering pools, feeling a lot happier. Talking it through was helping; and he was also very excited about the journalistic possibilities. Even if it was a bizarre story it was astonishing, and surely very readable. A scientist who thought he was digging up Eden, even metaphorically and allegorically? It could be a double page headline. Easy.

Christine did not seem so happy about the success of their hypothesis. Her eyes misted for a second: a phase of emotion that swiftly passed.

'Yyessss . . . Let's say you are right. You probably are. It certainly explains the numbers. And his mysterious behaviour at the end, digging for things at night. Taking them away. He must have been very excited. He was very jumpy just before . . . just before it happened.'

Her mood touched Rob; he chided himself. Here he was thinking about his work and yet there was still a murder unsolved.

Christine was frowning. 'There's still many questions left.'

'Why did they kill him?'

'Exactly.'

Rob wondered aloud. 'Well, heck. Maybe . . . maybe some American evangelists found out what he was up to. Digging up Eden, I mean.'

Christine laughed. 'And they hired a hitman? Right. Those Methodists can be so touchy.'

There was nothing left in her tea glass. She picked it up and put it down, then said, 'Another problem is this: why did the hunters bury Gobekli? That's not explained by the Eden theory. It must have taken them decades to inter an entire temple. Why do that?'

Rob looked up at the blue Urfan sky for inspiration. 'Because it was the site of the Fall? Maybe it symbolized even at that early stage the error of mankind. Falling into farming. The beginning of wage slavery. So they hid it out of shame or anger or resentment or . . .'

Christine made a rather unimpressed pout.

'OK.' Rob smiled. 'It's a crap theory. But why *did* they do it?'

A shrug. '*C'est un mystère.*'

Another silence fell across their little table. A few yards away, through the rose bushes, little children were pointing excitedly at the fish in the pond. Rob looked at one girl: she was about eleven, with bright golden curls of hair. But her mother was shrouded in black veils and robes: a full chador. He felt a sadness: that soon this lovely girl would be concealed like her mother. Shrouded for ever in black.

And then a flash of real guilt crossed his mind. A flash of guilt about *his* daughter. On the one hand he was revelling in this mystery – and yet, inside, he still wanted to go home. He yearned to go home. To see Lizzie.

Christine was opening Breitner's notebook, and laying it on the table alongside her own notes. Shadows of sunlight, spangled by the teahouse lime trees, flickered across their little table. 'One final point. There is something I didn't tell you before. Remember the last line in his notebook?' She pointed to a line of handwriting, turning the notebook so that Rob could see.

It was the line about the skull. It said, *Cayonu skulls, cf Orra Keller.*

'I didn't mention it before because it was so confusing. It didn't seem relevant. But now . . . Well, take a look. I have an idea . . .'

He bent to read: but the line remained incomprehensible. 'But who is Orra Keller?'

'It's not a name!' said Christine. 'We just presumed it was a name because it's in capitals. But I think Franz was just mixing languages.'

'I still don't get it.'

'He's mixing English and German. And . . .'

Rob looked over Christine's shoulder suddenly. 'Jesus.'

Christine stiffened. 'What?'

'Don't look now. It's Officer Kiribali. He's seen us, and he's coming over.'

23

Kiribali appeared to be alone, though Rob could still see the parked police car, silent and waiting, at the edge of the Golbasi Gardens.

The Turkish detective was in another smart suit; this time of cream linen. He was wearing a very British tie, striped green and blue. As he crossed the little bridge and approached their table, his smile was wide and saurian. 'Good morning. My constables told me you were here.' He leaned and kissed Christine's hand, pulled up a chair. Then he turned to a hovering waiter and his demeanour changed: from obsequious to domineering. '*Lokoum!*' The waiter winced, fearfully, and nodded. Kiribali smiled across the table. 'I have ordered some Turkish delight! You must try it here in Golbasi. The best in Sanliurfa. Real Turkish delight is quite something. You know of course the story of its invention?'

Rob said no. This seemed to please Kiribali: who sat forward, pressing his manicured hands flat on the tablecloth. 'The story is that an Ottoman sheikh was tired of his arguing wives. His harem was in disorder. So the sheikh asked the court confectioner to come up with a sweetmeat so pleasing it would silence the women.' Kiribali sat back as the waiter set a plate of the sugar-floured sweets on the table. 'It worked. The wives were placated by the Turkish delight and serenity returned to the harem. However the concubines became so fat on these calorific delights that the sheikh was rendered impotent in their company. So . . . the sheikh had the confectioner castrated.' Kiribali laughed loudly at his own story, picked up the plate and offered it to Christine.

Rob felt, not for the first time, a strange ambivalence about Kiribali. The policeman was charming, but there was a very menacing element to him, too. His shirt was just too clean; the tie just too British, the eloquence too studied, and deft. Yet he was obviously very clever. Rob wondered if Kiribali was close to any solution: to Breitner's murder.

The Turkish delight was delicious. Kiribali was regaling them again: 'You have read the Narnia books.'

Christine nodded; Kiribali continued:

'Surely the most famous literary reference to Turkish delight. When the Snow Queen offers the sweetmeats . . .'

'*The Lion, the Witch and the Wardrobe*?'

'Indeed!' Kiribali chortled, then sipped piously at his glass thimble of tea. 'I often wonder why the British are so adept at children's literature. It is a peculiar gift of the island race.'

'Compared to Americans you mean?'

'Compared to anyone, Mr Luttrell. Consider. The most famous stories for children. Lewis Carroll, Beatrix Potter, Roald Dahl. Tolkien. Even the vile Harry Potter. All British.'

A welcome breeze was stealing over the Golbasi rosebushes. Kiribali averred: 'I think it is because the British are not afraid to scare children. And children love to be scared. Some of the greatest children's stories are truly macabre, wouldn't you say? A psychotic hatmaker poisoned by mercury. A reclusive chocolatier who employs miniature negroes.'

Rob raised a hand. 'Officer Kiribali—'

'Yes?'

'Is there any particular reason you have come here to talk to us?'

The policeman wiped his feminine lips with a fresh corner of napkin. 'I want you to leave. Both of you. Now.'

Christine was defiant. 'Why?'

'For your own sake. Because you are getting into things you do not understand. This is . . .' Kiribali wafted a hand at the cliffs behind them, a gesture that took in the citadel, the two Corinthian columns at the top, the dark caves underneath. 'This is such an ancient place. There are too many secrets here. Dark anxieties, which you cannot comprehend. The more you are involved, the more dangerous it will be.'

Christine shook her head. 'I'm not going to be chased away.'

Kiribali scowled. 'You are very foolish people. You are used to . . . to Starbucks and . . . laptops and . . . sofabeds. To comfortable lives. This is the ancient east. It is beyond your comprehension.'

'But you said you may want to question us—'

'You are not suspects!' The detective was scowling. 'I have no need for you.'

Christine was unabashed. 'I'm sorry, but I'm not going to be ordered about. Not by you, not by anyone.'

Kiribali turned to Rob. 'Then I must appeal to masculine logic. We know how women are . . .'

Christine sat up. 'I want to know what's in the vault. The museum!'

This outburst silenced the Turkish detective. An unusual and confused expression came over his face. Then his frown darkened. He glanced around as if he was expecting a friend to join them. But the café terrace was empty. Just a couple of fat besuited men were left, smoking shishas in a shady corner. They stared languidly at Rob, and smiled.

Kiribali stood up. Abruptly. He took some Turkish lire from a handsome leather wallet, and set the cash very carefully on the tablecloth. 'I'll say this quite clearly, so you understand. You were spotted breaking into the site, at Gobekli Tepe. Last week.'

Apprehension shivered through Rob. If Kiribali knew this, then they were in trouble.

The Turk went on. 'I have friends in the Kurdish villages.'

Christine tried to explain. 'We were just looking for—'

'You were just looking for the Devil. A Jewess should know better.'

Kiribali said the word *Jewess* with such sibilance that Rob got the impression of a snake: hissing.

'My forbearance . . . is not infinite. If you do not leave Sanliurfa by tomorrow you will find yourself in a Turkish prison cell. There you may discover that some of my colleagues in the judicial process of the Ataturk Republic do not share my humanitarian attitude to your well-being.' He smiled at them in the most insincere way possible, and then he was gone, brushing past the fat pink roses, which nodded, and shed a few scarlet petals.

For a minute Rob and Christine sat there. Rob felt the imminence of trouble: he could almost hear warning klaxons going off. What were they getting into? It was a good journalistic story, but was it worth real danger? The train of thought led Rob, reflexively, back to Iraq. Now he was remembering the suicide bomber in Baghdad. He could still see the woman's face. The bomber was a beautiful young woman, with dark long hair; and bright scarlet, lushly lipsticked lips. *A suicide bomber in lipstick.* And then she'd smiled at him, almost seductively: as she reached for her switch to kill them all.

Rob shuddered at the recollection. Yet this awful memory also gave him a kind of resolve: he'd had *enough* of being threatened. Of being chased away. Maybe this time he should stay, and get beyond the fears?

Christine was certainly undivided. 'I'm not leaving.'

'He will arrest us.'

'For what? Driving at night?'

'We broke into the dig.'

'He can't sling us in jail for that. It's a total bluff.'

Rob demurred, 'I'm really not so sure. I . . . dunno . . .'

'But he's so effete, surely? It's just a game—'

'*Effete?* Kiribali?' Rob shook his head, firmly. 'No, he's not that. I did a little research on him. Asked around. He's respected, even feared. They say he's an expert shot. He's not a good enemy to have.'

'But we can't go yet. Not until I know more!'

'You mean this vault thing? The museum? What was all that about?'

The waiter was hovering, expecting them to leave. But Christine ordered another two glasses of sweet, ruby-coloured cay. And then she said, 'The last line in the notebook. *Cayonu Skulls, cf Orra Keller.* You remember the Cayonu skulls?'

'No,' confessed Rob. 'Tell me.'

'Cayonu is another famous archaeological site. Almost as old as Gobekli. It's about a hundred miles north. It's where the pig was first domesticated.'

The waiter set two more glasses on the table and two silver spoons. Rob wondered if you could get tea-poisoning, from too much tea.

Christine continued, 'Cayonu is being dug up by an American team. A few years ago they found a layer of skulls and dismembered skeletons under one of the central rooms of the site.'

'Human skulls?'

Christine nodded. 'And animal bones too. Tests also showed a lot of human blood had been spilt. The site is now called the Skull Chamber. Franz was fascinated by Cayonu.'

'So?'

'The evidence at Cayonu points to some kind of human sacrifice. This is controversial. Kurds do not want to think their ancestors were . . . bloodthirsty. None of us wants to think that! But most experts now believe the bones in the skull room are the residue of many human sacrifices. The people of Cayonu built their houses on foundations made out of bones, the bones of their own victims.'

'Nice.'

Christine stirred some sugar into her tea. 'Hence the final line in the book. The Edessa Vault.'

'Sorry?'

'That's what the curators of Sanliurfa Museum use as a name for the most obscure archives in the museum, dedicated to pre-Islamic remains. That section is called the Edessa Vault.'

Rob grimaced. 'Sorry Christine, you're losing me.'

Christine elaborated. 'Sanliurfa has had many many names. The Crusaders called it Edessa, like the Greeks. The Kurds call it Riha. The Arabs, al-Ruha. The city of prophets. Orra is another name. It's a transliteration of the Greek name. So Edessa means Orra.'

'And Keller?'

'Is not a name!' Christine smiled, triumphantly. 'It's the German for cellar, basement, vault. Franz capitalized it because that's what Germans do, they capitalize nouns.'

'So . . . I think I see . . .'

'When he wrote "Orra Keller" he basically meant the Edessa Vault. In the basement of the Urfa museum!'

Christine sat back. Rob leaned forward. 'So he's telling us that something is in the Edessa Vault. But didn't we already know that?'

'But why put it in the notebook? Unless he is reminding himself? About something special? And then . . . what does "cf" mean?'

'Can find . . . er . . . can . . .'

'It is from the Latin. Confer. Meaning compare or contrast. It's an academic shorthand. Cf. He is saying compare the famous Cayonu Skulls with something in the museum vaults. But there is, or there was, nothing of significance down there. I went through the archives myself when I first came here. But remember,' she wagged a finger, in a teacherly way, 'Franz was digging up things at Gobekli, secretly, at night – just before he was murdered.' Her face was flushed with excitement, and maybe even anger.

'And you think he put his finds in there? In the pre-Islamic vaults?'

'It's an ideal place. The dustiest part of the museum basement, the furthest reach of the cellars. It's secure, concealed and virtually forgotten.'

'OK,' said Rob. 'But it's still a pretty wild theory. Tenuous.'

'Maybe. However . . .'

It dawned on Rob. 'You were testing Kiribali.'

'And you saw how he reacted! I was right. There's something in those cellars.'

The tea was nearly cold. Rob drained his glass and looked across the table. Christine had hidden depths. Hidden cunning. 'You want to go and look?'

She nodded. 'Yes, but it's locked. And the door is keycoded.'

'Another break-in? Way too dangerous.'

'I know that.'

The wind sussurated in the limes. Over the bridge, a woman in full chador was holding her baby and kissing the baby's fat pink fingers, one by one.

'Why do you want to do all this, Christine? Why go to these lengths? On a hunch?'

'I want to know how and why he died.'

'So do I. But I'm getting paid for it. This is my job. I'm on a story. You are taking big risks.'

'I do it . . .' She sighed. 'I do it because . . . he would have done it for me.'

A realization, half-formed, crept over Rob. 'Christine, forgive me. Were you and Franz . . . ever . . . ?'

'Lovers? Yes.' The Frenchwoman turned away, as if concealing her emotions. 'A few years ago. He gave me my first real chance in archaeology. This amazing site. Gobekli Tepe. There weren't any bones then. He didn't need an osteoarchaeologist. Yet he invited me because he admired my work. And a few months after I came we . . . fell in love. But then it ended. I felt guilty. The age difference was too much.'

'You ended it?'

'Yes.'

'Did he still love you?'

Christine nodded, and blushed. 'I think he did. He was so gracious and courteous about it. Never let it interfere. Could have asked me to go, but didn't. It must have been very difficult for him, having me there, still with those feelings. He was a fine archaeologist, but he was an ever finer man. One of the nicest men I have ever known. When he met his wife it was easier, thank God.'

'So you think you owe him this?'

'I do.'

They sat in silence for several minutes. The soldiers were feeding the carp in the pond. Rob watched a waterman on his donkey, loping down a path. But then, he had an idea. 'I think I know how you can get the code.'

'How?'

'The curators. At the museum. Your pals.'

'Casam? Beshet? The Kurdish guys?'

'Yes. Beshet particularly.'

'But . . .'

'He's got a huge crush on you.'

She blushed again, this time fiercely. 'Not possible'.

'Yes, yes possible. Totally.' Rob leaned across. 'Trust me, Christine, I know what pathetic male adoration looks like. I've seen how he stares at you, like a spaniel . . .' Christine looked mortified. Rob chuckled. 'I'm not sure you realize the effect you have on men.'

'But what does that matter?'

'Go to him! Ask him for the code! Odds on he'll give it you.'

The woman in the chador had stopped kissing her baby. The tea-house waiter was staring at them, wanting the table for new customers. Rob took out some money and laid it on the cloth. 'So you go and get the code. And then we'll go to the museum and see what's in there. And if there's nothing we go. Agreed?'

Christine nodded. 'Agreed.' Then she added, 'Tomorrow's a holiday.'

'Even better.'

They both stood. But Christine looked hesitant and troubled.

'What?' said Rob. 'What else?'

'I'm frightened, Robert. What could be so important that Franz hid it in the vault without telling us? What could be so horrifying that it had to be hidden? What was so terrible that it must be compared with the Cayonu skulls?'

24

Were they too late? Had they missed them, again?

DCI Forrester gazed across the stone circle at the brown-green moorlands of Cumbria beyond. He recalled another case that had seen a search for clues, in a place like this. A murderer who buried his wife on the Cornish moors. That homicide had been macabre: the head was never found. And yet, even that hideous crime lacked some of the sinister quality of this present mystery. There was a real danger in this sacrificial gang: psychopathic violence allied with subtle intelligence. A menacing combination.

Stepping over a low wooden stile, Forrester focused on his latest evidence. He knew the gang had fled the Isle of Man – just a few hours after the murder. He knew that they'd caught the first car ferry from Douglas to Heysham, on the Lancashire coastline, long before any alert had been sent to ports and airports. He knew all this because an observant docker at Heysham had remembered that he'd seen a black Toyota Landcruiser coming through the port on the early-morning ferry two days before, and he'd noticed five young men climbing out of the Toyota in the ferryport terminal car park. The men had gone for breakfast together. The docker had gone in for breakfast and sat next to the gang in the café.

Forrester approached one elegant grey standing stone, filigreed with lime-green moss. He reached in his pocket for his notebook, and flicked through his record of the interview with the docker. *The men were all tall and young. They had expensive clothes. Somehow they didn't look right.* The strangeness of this scenario had piqued the young docker's curiosity. Douglas to Heysham was not the most energetic of shipping lanes. The early morning car ferry from Douglas usually got farmers, the odd businessman and maybe some tourists. Five silent tall young men in a very expensive black Landcruiser? So he had tried to chat with them over their bacon and eggs. He hadn't had much luck.

Forrester scanned down the notes. *The men didn't want to talk. One of them said a very brief good morning. He maybe had a foreign accent. French or something. Could have been Italian, not sure. One of the others had a posh English accent. Then they just got up and left. As if I had ruined their breakfast.*

The docker hadn't taken down a number plate. But he had heard one of them say a word like 'Castleyig' as they walked out of the café, in the pale morning light, to their waiting car. Forrester and Boijer had rapidly researched Castleyig. To no one's surprise there was no such place. However, there was a Castlerigg not that far from Heysham. And it was quite well known.

Castlerigg turned out to be one of the better preserved stone circles in Britain. It comprised thirty-eight stones of variable sizes and shapes and was tenuously dated to 3200 BC. It was known also for a group of ten stones forming a rectangular enclosure, the purpose of which was 'unknown'. In his Scotland Yard office, Forrester had Googled 'Castlerigg' and 'human sacrifice' and found a long tradition associating the two. A stone axe had been discovered at the Castlerigg site in the 1880s. Some had surmised that it had been used in a Druidic sacrificial rite. Of course many scientists disputed this. Antiquarians and folklorists maintained that there was no disproof of sacrifice, either. And the tradition of sacred butchery was old. It was even cited by the famous local poet Wordsworth, in the 1800s.

With the Cumbrian breeze at his back, Forrester read through the stanza of the poem. He'd copied it down at Heysham library:

At noon I hied to gloomy glades
Religious woods and midnight shades
Where brooding superstition found
A cold and awful horror round
While with black arm and bending head
She wove a stole of sable thread
And hark, the ringing harp I hear
And lo! her Druid sons appear
Why roll on me your glaring eyes
Why fix on me for sacrifice?

It was a warm spring day up here on the Cumbrian hills, the late April sun was shining brightly on the surrounding, bare green hills, the dewy turf, the distant firwoods. And yet something in this poem made Forrester shiver.

'"At noon I hied to gloomy glades",' said Forrester.

Boijer, striding across the grass, looked nonplussed. 'Sir?'

'It's that poem by Wordsworth.'

Boijer smiled. 'Oh yeah. Must admit – didn't recognize it.'

'Likewise,' said Forrester, closing his notebook. The DCI recalled his inner city comprehensive, a struggling young English teacher trying to force-feed Shakespeare's *Macbeth* to a bunch of kids more interested in underage drinking, reggae music and shoplifting. An entirely pointless exercise. Might as well teach Latin to astronauts.

'Beautiful place,' said Boijer.

'Yes.'

'Are you sure they came here Sir? To this place?'

'Yes,' said Forrester. 'Where else were they going?'

'Liverpool maybe?'

'No.

'Blackpool?'

'No. And if they were going anywhere else they would have got the ferry to Birkenhead. That leads directly to the motorway. But they came to Heysham. Heysham leads practically nowhere. Except to the Lake District. And here. I can't believe they are doing a pleasant tour of the Lakes. They went to a Viking burial site on Man associated with sacrifice. Then they came here. To Castlerigg. Another place associated with sacrifice. And of course the docker overheard them. They were coming here.'

Boijer and Forrester walked to one of the tallest menhirs. The stone was mottled and patched with lichen. A sign of clear air. Forrester laid a flat palm against the ancient stone. The stone was just slightly warm to his touch. Warmed by the mountain sun, and old, so very old. 3200 BC.

Boijer sighed. 'But what really attracts them to these circles and ruins? What's the point?'

Forrester grunted. It was a good question. A question he had yet to answer. Down in the river valley, beneath the high plateau of Castlerigg, he could see the Cumbrian police squad cars; four of them parked in the sun by a picnic spot, and a couple of other police cars trundling down the narrow lakeland road, trawling the local farmsteads and villages to see if anyone had witnessed the gang. So far they had had no luck. Nothing at all. But Forrester was sure they had visited Castlerigg. It fitted too well. The circle was a notably atmospheric place. And intense. Whoever built this high and lonely circle in the shaved cradle of hills knew something about aesthetics. Feng shui even. The whole circle, standing on its table of dewy grass, was set in a kind of amphitheatre. A theatre in the round. The billowing hills were the terraces, the audience, the bleachers. And the stone circle itself was the stage, the altar, the *mise en scène*. But a stage-set for what?

Boijer's radio crackled. He pressed the button and talked to one of the Cumbrian officers. Forrester listened in. It was clear from Boijer's expression and his perfunctory words of acknowledgement that the

Cumbrian police were still drawing a blank. Maybe the gang hadn't come here after all.

Forrester walked on. A fox was stealing over a field and edging along a copse across the nearest valley: a furtive blur of brushy red. But then the fox turned and gazed behind it, staring directly at Forrester, showing a wild animal's fear and cruelty. Then it was gone, darting into the woodland.

The sky was clouding over: at least partly. Patches of black were scudding across the moorland hills.

Boijer caught up with Forrester. 'You know, sir, we had a weird case in Finland a few years back. Might be relevant.'

'Case of what?'

'It was called the Landfill Murder.'

'Because they buried the body in a dump?'

'Sort of. It started in October 1998. If I remember right, a man's left leg was found on a dumping ground near a little town called Hyvinkaa. North of Helsinki.'

Forrester was confused. 'Weren't you already living in England by then?'

'Yes, but I followed the news from home. As you do. Especially grisly murders.'

Forrester nodded. 'What happened?'

'Well, the police got nothing at first. Only clue they had was the leg. But then there were suddenly . . . well, all these headlines . . . The police claimed they had arrested three people suspected of the murder and they claimed there were indications of satanic worship.'

A wind was kicking up. Whistling across the ancient circle.

'In April 1999 the incident came back into the headlines, when the case went to court. Three kids, young people, were charged. The strange thing is, the judge ordered that the court records should be suppressed for forty years, and all the details kept quiet. Unusual for Finland. But some of the details leaked out, anyway. Horrible stuff. Torture, mutilation, necrophilia, cannibalism. You name it.'

'So who was the victim?'

'A guy of about twenty-three. He was tortured and killed by three of his friends. I think they were all in their early twenties or late teens.' Boijer frowned, trying to remember. 'The girl was seventeen – she was the youngest. Anyway the murder took place after a bout of drinking. Days of it. Home-made schnapps. *Brennivin* they call it in Iceland. The Black Death.'

Forrester was interested. 'Describe the murder.'

'He was slowly mutilated with knives and scissors. Killed over a period of many hours. Bits of him were progressively cut off. The judge called it a prolonged human sacrifice. After the victim died the three friends abused the body, ejaculated into his mouth and so on. Then they cut off his head, and I think his legs and arms. And they removed some of his internal organs, kidneys and the heart. They dismembered him, basically. And they ate some of the body.'

Forrester was watching a farmer, striding down a country lane, half a mile in the distance. He asked, 'And what does this tell you? I mean, what association do you make with this case?'

His junior shrugged. 'The kids were all Satan worshippers, death metal fans. And they had a history of sacrilege. Church burnings. Desecrating tombs, sort of thing.'

'And?'

'And they were into paganism, ancient sites. Places like this.'

'Though they buried the body in a landfill, not at Stonehenge.'

'Yes. We don't have a Stonehenge in Finland.'

Forrester nodded. The farmer had disappeared behind a rise in the landscape. The ancient standing stones were growing greyer and darker as the clouds covered the sun. Typical lakeland weather – from shining spring sun, to brooding, winter cold in half an hour. 'What were the murderers like? What's the sociology?'

'Definitely middle class. Rich kids even. Certainly not from the fringes.' Boijer zipped up his anorak against the gathering cold. 'Children of the élite.'

Forrester chewed a stalk of grass and regarded his junior. Boijer's bright red anorak brought a fierce and sudden image to Forrester's mind: a body gutted open, *unzipped,* oozing red blood. Forrester spat the stalk from his mouth.

'Do you miss Finland, Boijer?'

'No. Sometimes . . . Maybe a little.'

'What d'you miss?'

'Empty forests. Proper saunas. And I miss . . . cloudberries.'

'Cloudberries?'

'Finland's not very interesting, sir. We have ten thousands words for getting drunk. The winters are too cold, so all you do is drink.' The wind brushed the Finn's blonde hair over his eyes, he swept it back. 'There's even a joke. They tell it in Sweden. About how much the Finns drink.'

'Go on.'

'A Swede and a Finn agree to meet to drink together. They bring several bottles of very strong Finnish vodka. They sit across from each other in perfect silence, and pour glasses of vodka, not speaking. After three hours the Swede fills both glasses and says "Skol". The Finn looks at him in disgust, and asks: "Did we come to talk or did we come to drink?"'

Forrester laughed. He asked if Boijer was hungry and his junior eagerly nodded; with Forrester's assent, Boijer went off to eat his usual tuna sandwich in the car.

The DCI walked on alone, brooding, surveying his surroundings. The forests around here were government owned: Forestry Commission plantations. Strict squares of sterile firs marching across the landscape like Napoleonic regiments. Platoons of birches, marching silently and unobserved. He thought about Boijer's story. The Landfill Murders of Hyvinkaa. Was it possible that the Sacrifice Gang were burying corpses or bones or objects, not digging things up? But nothing appeared to have been buried in Craven Street. And nothing was buried in St Anne's Fort. But had they checked properly?

Forrester had reached the edge of the stone circle. The silent grey menhirs curved away from him on either side. Some seemed to be sleeping: prone and fallen like mighty warriors slain. Some were rigid and defiant. He remembered what he had read about Castlerigg; about the squarish enclosure of 'important but unknown purpose'. If you had come all this way to bury something, this was surely where you would do it – in the most symbolic part of the site. If Castlerigg mattered to you, this was your target.

The detective scanned the circle. It didn't take him long to find the enclosure: a rectangular site marked out by lower stones, besides the most eroded megaliths.

For twenty minutes Forrester examined these lower stones. He padded and prodded at the damp dark soil and the soggy, acidic turf. A soft lakeland rain started to fall. Forrester felt its cold drops on his neck. Maybe he was heading up another cul de sac.

Then he spotted something in the long wet grass: a small line of sliced earth. Dark soil disturbed, then replaced, barely visible to the naked eye – unless you knew what you were looking for. He knelt and dug at the sods with his bare hands. It was unscientific – Forensics would be appalled, but he had to know.

Within seconds his fingers touched something cold and hard – but not a stone. He dislodged the object from its little grave and brushed off the soil. It was a small glass vial. And inside the vial was a very intense-looking liquid the colour of dark red rum.

25

The streets were red with blood. Rob was walking through the old town to meet Christine, at the caravanserai. It was dusk. Everywhere he looked: he saw great splashes of blood – up the walls, along the pavements, outside the Vodafone outlet. The locals were slaughtering goats and sheep – and doing it publicly, in the streets. Rob presumed that it was part of the holiday Christine mentioned, but it was still unnerving.

He paused at the corner, by a clocktower, and watched as one man struggled to hold a white-skinned goat between his legs. The man wore baggy black pantaloons – shirwals, the traditional Kurdish dress. Setting the fuming cigarette on a stool beside him, the man picked up a long, glittering knife and plunged the blade into the lower stomach of the goat.

The animal screamed. The man was unfazed. He turned, picked up his cigarette, had another puff, put it down again. Blood was drooling from the stomach of the wounded goat. The man leaned further over, grimaced, then vigorously ripped the knife straight up the quivering, pink-white belly. Blood pissed out of the animal, showering the road in front. The goat no longer screamed and struggled but whimpered, sensuously. Its long-lashed eyelids fluttered as it died. The man yanked open the great gash, and viscera slithered out, the pastel-coloured organs tumbling neatly into a shallow plastic bowl on the pavement.

Rob walked on. He found Christine by the archway, that led to the caravanserai. His expression of surprise and perplexity obviously said it all.

'Kurban Bayram,' she said. 'The last day of hajj.'

'But why the goats?'

'And sheep.' Christine threaded her arm through his as they walked along the shuttered streets of the bazaar. Cooking smells wafted. Roasting goat and broiled sheep. 'It's called the Sacrifice Holiday. It commemorates Abraham and Isaac, the near sacrifice of Isaac.'

'Kurban Bayram, of course. They have that in Egypt and Lebanon; I know it well: it's called Eid. . . . But,' he shook his head, 'they don't kill animals in the street! They do it inside, and they slit the throats.'

'Yes,' she agreed. 'The Urfans treat it as a special, local festival. Because Abraham comes from here.' She smiled. 'And it is quite . . . bloodthirsty.'

They had reached a small square with cay houses and cafés in which men were smoking shishas. Many of them were wearing, for Kurban Bayram, the long black baggy Kurdish trousers. Others had special embroidered robes. Their women passed in front, decked in flashing jewellery, or sporting purple headscarves trimmed with silver. Some were tattooed with henna, their hands and feet liberally and gorgeously painted; their headscarves were hung with silver trinkets. The scene was pungently colourful.

But they weren't here to sight-see.

'There it is.' Christine nodded at a small house down a shady road. 'Beshet's address.'

The heat of the day was draining from the streets, like water after a flood. Rob squeezed Christine's hand. 'Good luck.'

Christine crossed the road and knocked on the door. Rob wondered how unorthodox and unsettling it would be for Beshet to have a white western woman come to his house. When Beshet opened the door, Rob scrutinized his expression and saw surprise and anxiety there, but also that puppydog languish again. Rob was confident Christine would get the keycode.

He walked back to the square and surveyed the scene. Some children, carrying firecrackers, greeted him.

'Hey you, American!'

'Hello . . .'

'Happy Bayram!'

The children laughed, as if they had stirred some exotic and slightly frightening beast in the zoo; then they scattered up the road. The pavements were still red with blood but the slaughter had stopped. Moustachioed Kurds, smoking their shishas at café tables, greeted him with a smile. Sanliurfa was, Rob decided, the strangest place. It was implacably exotic, and somehow hostile; yet the people were some of the friendliest Rob had ever encountered.

He barely noticed Christine as she stole up to him, and said: 'Hello.'

He turned, alerted. 'You got it?'

'I got it. He wasn't keen . . . but he gave it to me.'

'OK, so . . .'

'Let's wait until it's dark.'

A quick walk brought them to the main road out of the old town. A taxi took them to Christine's apartment, where they spent a nervous few hours surfing the net, trying not to worry, then worrying. At eleven they crept out of the apartment block and walked to the museum. The streets were much quieter now. The blood had been washed away; the holiday was nearly over. A scimitar of moon shone above them. Stars glittered like tiaras around the spires of the minarets.

At the gates to the museum Rob looked up and down the street. No one was about. He could hear Turkish TV voices from a shuttered house a block down. Otherwise, there was silence. Rob pushed and the gate swung open. At night the garden was an intensely atmospheric place. Moonlight silvered the wings of the desert demon Pazuzu. There were busts of Roman emperors, broken and crumbling; and Assyrian warlords, frozen in marble, their lion hunts never ending. The history of Sanliurfa was here, in this garden, dreaming in the moonlight. The demons of Sumeria screamed silently; stone beaks open for five thousand years.

'I need two codes,' said Christine. 'Beshet gave me both of them.'

She approached the front door of the museum. Rob hung back, checking that they were alone.

They were alone. There was a car parked under the fig trees. But it looked as if it hadn't been moved in a few days. Rotten figs were splattered across the windshield. A smear of jam and seeds.

The door clicked. Rob swivelled to find the front door was open. He paced up the steps and joined Christine inside. The air within the museum was hot: there was no one here to open windows or doors. And no air conditioning. Rob wiped the sweat from his forehead. He was wearing a jacket to carry everything they needed: flashlights, phones, notebooks. In the main room, the oldest statue in the world glowed dimly in the darkness, with his sad obsidian eyes staring mournfully into the gloom.

'Down here,' said Christine.

Rob saw, in the gloom, a small door in the far corner of the room. Beyond was a flight of stairs, leading down. He handed a flashlight to Christine and turned on his own. The two torch beams flickered in the dusty blackness as they descended the stairs.

The vaults were surprisingly big. Much bigger than the museum above. Doors and corridors led in all directions. Shelves of antiquities glimmered as Rob flicked his flashlight beam this way and that over broken pottery, chunks of gargoyle; spears, flints and vases.

'It's huge.'

'Yes. Sanliurfa is built on old caves and they converted the caves into cellars.'

Rob leaned and looked at a broken figurine lying on its back. Snarling at the shelf above. 'What's that?'

'The monster Asag. The demon that causes sickness. Sumerian.'

'OK . . .' Rob shivered, despite the stifling warmth. He wanted this over: the cold dread of what they were about to do was building up. 'Let's get a move on, Christine. Where's the Edessa Vault?'

'Down here.'

They doglegged down another corridor, past a Roman column, brutally truncated, and more shelves of vases and pots. The dust was thick and choking; Christine was leading them to the oldest part of the cave system.

But then a big steel door barred the way. Christine fumbled with the keycode. 'Shit.' Her hands were shaking.

Rob poised the flashlight so that she could see better as she keyed in the numbers; at last the lock snapped open. They were greeted with a rush of hot air as the Edessa Vault exhaled. There was badness in the breeze. Something indefinable, and remote, but organic and unpleasant. And old.

Rob tried to ignore it. They stepped inside the cellar. Blunt steel shelves led down the vast cavern. Most of the antiquities were in big plastic boxes with names and numbers scrawled on them. But some were left in their natural state. Christine named them as they walked. Syriac or Akkadian goddesses; a big head of Anzu; a chunk of a Hellenic nude. Ghostly hands and wings extended into the gloom.

Christine was walking up and down beside the shelves. 'There's nothing here.' She almost sounded relieved. 'It's all the same stuff I saw before.'

'Then we'd better go . . .'

'Wait.'

'What?'

Christine was gesturing into the darkness.

'Here. This is from Gobekli.'

Rob paused. He was getting the bad signals again. The suicide bomber in Iraq. He could never forget the bomber's face, staring over; just before the explosion.

Rob felt the urgent need to exit – to get out of here. Now.

Christine said: 'Shut the door.'

Reluctantly, Rob closed the door behind him. They were alone in the furthest vault, with whatever Franz had found. Whatever he felt should be compared with the horror of the Cayonu Skulls.

'Rob, come and look.'

Her torchlight was shining down on an extraordinary statue. A woman, with her legs open: the vagina heavily engraved, and obscenely large. Like the open wound in the fur of that goat.

Next to the woman stood a trio of animals: wild boars, perhaps. All of them had pronounced, erect penises; they were surrounding the splayed woman – like it was a gang-rape.

'This is from Gobekli,' Christine whispered.

'Is this what we were looking for?'

'No. I remember when we found this. Franz put it here. He must have been hoarding the . . . stranger discoveries in one place. So whatever it is he found should be here. Somewhere.'

Rob flicked his flashlight left and right and left. The dust whirled in the gloom. Faces of sombre gods and leering demons greeted him, then faded to black as he moved along. He couldn't see anything; he didn't even know what he was looking for. It was hopeless. Then his torchlight illuminated a large polystyrene box with the word *Gobekli* written on it in marker pen. Rob felt his heart thump. 'Christine,' he hissed.

The box was lodged at the back of the steel shelf, by the cave wall. It was obviously big and heavy; Christine struggled with it. Laying his torch on the shelf behind, Rob reached in and assisted her. Together they dragged the box out and set it on the floor.

Rob picked up his flashlight, his heart racing, and kept the beam high as Christine opened the box. Inside there were four old-fashioned olive jars about half a metre long, packed in bubblewrap. Rob felt a thudding pang of disappointment. Half of him had wanted to find something obscene and horrifying. The journalist half; the juvenile half of him, maybe.

Christine took one of the jars out.

'Is it from Gobekli?'

'For sure. And if it is, then it must be ten thousand years old. So they did have pottery . . .'

'Amazingly well preserved.'

'Yes.' Handling the jar with great care, Christine turned it over. There was a curious design on one side. A sort of stick with a bird at the top. 'I've seen that somewhere,' she said. Quietly.

Rob took his mobile out and took a brisk set of pictures. The flash from the phone-camera felt like an intrusion, in the sombre darkness of the vault. Djinns and emperors scowled in the brief and vulgar dazzle.

Pocketing the phone, Rob reached into the box and took out one of the long jars himself. It was surprisingly heavy. He wanted to know what was inside. Some kind of liquid? Grains? Honey? He tilted it and looked at the top. It was stoppered and sealed. 'Shall we open it?'

'Careful . . .'

Her warning came too late. Rob felt the jar suddenly sag in his hand: he had tilted it too brusquely. The neck of the jar seemed to sigh, and it fell onto the floor: then the crack in the neck opened further, ripping into the body of the ancient, rotting pottery. The jar was crumbling in Rob's hand. Just crumbling. The shards scattered on the floor, some of them shivering immediately into dust.

'Oh my God!' The smell was hideous. Rob put a sleeve to his nose.

Christine shone a torch on the contents of the jar. 'Fucking hell.'

A tiny body lay on the floor. A human body: a baby, forced into a foetal position. The corpse was half mummified, half viscous liquid. Still decomposing after all the centuries. The stench drilled into Rob's face till he gagged. Gurgles of liquid were pouring from the skull.

'Look at the face!' cried Christine. 'Look at the face!'

Rob shone his flashlight in the baby's face. It was locked in a silent scream. A scream of a dying child, echoing across twelve thousand years.

Suddenly lights filled the room. Lights, noises, voices. Rob spun and saw: a group of men standing in the back of the vault. Men with guns and knives, coming for them.

26

Hugo De Savary was very elegant for a professor. Forrester had expected someone dowdy: leather patches on the elbow, excess dandruff on his shoulders. But the Cambridge don was animated, cheerful, youngish, positively svelte, exuding an air of confident prosperity.

Presumably this was because his books – popular treatments of Satanism, cults, cannibalism, a whole roster of Gothic themes – had been so commercially successful. This had led him to be shunned by crustier members of the academic community, or so Forrester had guessed, judging by the reviews he had read.

It was De Savary who had suggested they lunch in this very fashionable Japanese restaurant near Soho. Forrester had requested they meet up, in an email, when the professor was next in town. De Savary had happily acceded, and even offered to pay, which was good, since the restaurant he had nominated was certainly not the sort of place Forrester normally used when soliciting information, being maybe five times too expensive.

De Savary was consuming his little dish of miso black cod with great enthusiasm. They were sitting on a bench of oak wood in front of a counter that surrounded a central kitchen space with a vast black grill, tended by frowning and ferocious Japanese chefs slicing obscure vegetables with frighteningly large knives. He turned to Forrester. 'How did your forensic people know the elixir was damu?'

The professor was talking about the liquid in the bottle from Castlerigg. Forrester tried to pick up some raw squid with his chopsticks and failed. 'We've had several muti murders in London. African child sacrifice. So the lab boys had come across damu before.'

'The headless torso of that poor child found in the Thames?'

'Yep.' Forrester sipped some of his warm sake. 'This damu stuff is apparently the concentrated blood of sacrificial victims. That's what Pathology tells me.'

'Well they're right.' Before them a large Japanese chef was gutting a lividly pink fish with great speed. 'Muti really is quite disgusting. Hundreds of children die every year in black Africa. You know exactly what they do to the children?'

'I know they chop off the limbs . . .'

'Yes. But they do it when the children are alive. And they cut off the genitals too.' De Savary sipped beer. 'The screams of the living victims are supposed to add to the potency of the muti. Shall we have some of that yellowfin tuna steak?'

'Sorry?'

The idea of this ultra-fashionable restaurant, it seemed, was that you kept ordering tiny bits of food. You didn't order everything at the start: you kept going until you were full. It was fun. Forrester had never been anywhere like it. He wondered who could afford the prices. Soft shell crab sushi, flown in from Alaska. Toro with asparagus and sevruga caviar. What was toro?

'The rock shrimp tempura is amazing,' said De Savary.

'Tell you what,' Forrester said, 'you order. Then tell me what you think about the gang . . .'

De Savary smiled gravely. 'Yes of course. My lecture is at three. Let's crack on.'

'So what do you think?'

'Your gang seems obsessed with human sacrifice.'

'That much we know.'

'But it's an eccentric congeries of praxes.'

'You what?'

'They are carrying out sacrifices from different cultures. The tongue excision is perhaps Nordic, the burying of the head Japanese, or Israelite. The shaving is clearly Aztec. The Star of David is Solomonic, as you say.'

A young Thai waitress approached them and De Savary ordered. The waitress gave a tiny curtsey and went away. De Savary faced Forrester again.

'And now we have the damu, buried at a spot dedicated to sacrifice. That's what African witch doctors do, before a major muti killing. They bury the damu in hallowed ground. Then they carry out the sacrifice.'

'So. . . . You think they'll kill again?'

'Naturally. Don't you?'

Forrester sighed, and assented. Of course the gang was going to strike again. 'So what's with the Hellfire stuff? How does that fit in?'

'I'm not quite sure. They are, self-evidently, seeking something to do with the Hellfires. What that might be is less obvious.'

Three plates were set on the oak counter before them. The aroma was delicious. Forrester yearned to be allowed a spoon.

De Savary went on, 'What I can tell you now is how these satanic cults work, the psychology of the groupuscule. They tend to come from the middle or even upper classes. Manson and his followers weren't scumbag lowlifes, they were rich kids. It is the bored, intelligent rich who commit the most terrible crimes. One can see a parallel with the Baader Meinhof terror gang in Germany. Sons and daughters of bankers, millionaires, businessmen. Children of the élite.'

'Then there's Bin Laden . . . ?'

'Exactly! Bin Laden is the smart, charismatic son of a famous billionaire, yet he was drawn to the most nihilistic, psychopathic brand of Islam.'

'So you see a parallel with the Hellfire Club?'

De Savary deftly chopsticked some of the yellowfin tuna. Forrester just about managed to do the same. It was unbelievably delicious.

'Again, quite right. The Hellfire Cub provided the template, if you like, for the *bon chic bon genre* death cults of today. A group of English aristocrats, many of them very talented – writers, statesmen, scientists – yet drawn to deliberately transgressive acts. To *épater les bourgeois*, perhaps?'

'But some people say the Hellfire Club was just a drinking club. A society of pranksters.'

De Savary shook his head. 'Sir Francis Dashwood was one of the better religious scholars of his time. He went to the Far East to pursue his more arcane interests – religious esoterica. That's not the action of a dilettante. And Benjamin Franklin was one of the finest minds of the century.'

'So they wouldn't have got together just to drink gin. And play naked Twister.'

'No I don't think so.' De Savary chuckled. The Japanese chef in front of them was using two knives at once. Filleting and dicing a slippery long eel. The eel's body danced on the chopping board as it was sliced, as if it was alive. Maybe it *was* alive. 'It's a matter of some dispute, what they got up to, the English Hellfire Club. We do know that the Irish Hellfires were hideously violent. They used to pour alcohol over cats, then set them on fire. The screams of the dying animals kept half of Georgian Dublin awake. And they murdered a servant in the same fashion. For a bet.' He paused. 'I think the Hellfire Club and some of the other Satanic cults we see in Europe can help us understand what your gang will be like. Hierarchically. Motivationally. Psychologically. There will be a definite leader. Charismatic and highly intelligent. Probably someone very well-born.'

'His followers?'

'Close friends; weaker personalities. But still intelligent. Seduced by the cult leader's Satanic charm. They are likely also to come from a privileged background.'

'That fits with the descriptions, posh voices etcetera.'

De Savary took a plate from the counter. He thought for a moment, staring at the food, then continued, 'However I think your gang leader is completely mad.'

'Sorry?'

'Don't forget what he is doing. The ahistorical mixture of sacrificial elements. Indeed the very idea of sacrifice – it's palpably insane. If he is looking for something connected with the Hellfires he could have done it in a much more discreet fashion. Rather than driving around the British Isles butchering people. Yes, the gang's murders are planned and executed with a certain finesse, they cover their tracks as you say, but why murder at all – if your intention is principally to retrieve? To uncover something hidden?' De Savary shrugged. '*Et voilà*. This is no louche but logical Francis Dashwood, this is more of a Charles Manson. A psychotic. A genius, but psychotic.'

'Which means?'

'You are the detective. I think it means he will go too far. They will make a mistake in their frenzy. The only question is . . .'

'How many people they will kill first?'

'Exactly. Now you've got to try this daikon. It's a kind of radish. Tastes like paradise.'

Back at Scotland Yard, Forrester relived the lunch with a happy burp. Then he sat in his swivel chair and spun around, like a kid. He was mildly drunk from the sake. But he could justify it. The lunch had been very useful. With his new friend Hugo. Forrester picked up the phone and called Boijer.

'Yes, sir?'

'Boijer, I need a search. A trawl.'

'What of?'

'Ring around the classier public schools.'

'OK . . .'

'Start with Eton. Winchester. Westminster. Don't go any lower than

Millfield. Do Harrow. Check the list with the Headmasters' Conference.'

'Right. And . . . what do we ask them?'

'For missing boys. Missing pupils. And try the better universities, too. Oxbridge, London, St Andrews. Durham. You know the roster.'

'Bristol.'

'Why not. And Exeter. And the agricultural college at Cirencester. We need to find students who dropped out, suddenly and recently. I want posh boys. With problems.'

27

The rotten, semi-mummified corpse of the baby lay on the floor. A reek of ancient decomposition swirled in the air. Bare bulbs flickered above the monuments and shelves of the museum vault. The approaching men were big, armed, and angry. Rob thought he recognized some from the dig. Kurds. They looked Kurdish.

There was only one door to the vault. And the route to the door was filled with these menacing figures. Eight or nine men. Some of them had guns: an old pistol; a shotgun; a brand new hunting rifle. The rest of them had large knives, one so big it was like a machete. Rob flashed an apologetic and hapless glance at Christine. She smiled, sadly, desperately. And then she walked over, reached out and squeezed Rob's hand.

They were captured, and separated. The men grabbed Rob by the collar and Christine by the arms. Rob watched as the largest of them, the apparent leader, gazed down the side aisle at the cracked-open urn and the pitiful little corpse with the strange pungent liquor drooling out around it. He hissed at his colleagues and immediately two of the Kurdish men peeled off from the main group and walked down the side aisle, perhaps to deal with the evidence, to do something with the obscene little heap of faintly rotting flesh.

Rob and Christine were marched out of the vault. One of the men holding Rob dug a pistol, hard, into his cheek. The cold muzzle smelled of grease. Another two men grasped Christine fiercely by her bare arms. The tall man with the hunting rifle brought up the rear with a couple of lieutenants.

Where were they taking them? Rob could sense that the Kurds were also scared: maybe as scared as he and Christine. But these men were also determined. They pushed and pulled Rob and Christine down the long lines of antiquities, past the desert monsters, the Roman generals and the Canaanite storm gods. Past Anzu, and Ishtar, and Nimrud.

They climbed the stairs to the main museum chamber. Christine was swearing bravely, in French. Rob felt a surge of protectiveness – for her – and a surge of shame – for himself. He was the man here. He should be able to do something. Be heroic. Kick the knives from the Kurdish hands, turn and wrestle the kidnappers to the ground: grab Christine's hand and save her, drag her to blazing freedom.

But life wasn't like that. They were being led, like captured animals, slowly but surely: to their certain fate. And that was . . . what exactly? Were they being kidnapped? Was this a stunt? Were these guys terrorists? What was going on? He hoped that the Kurds were somehow policemen. But he knew quite surely that they weren't. They couldn't be. This wasn't like an arrest. These guys looked furtive and guilty – and faintly murderous. Images of beheadings flooded his mind. All those poor guys in Iraq, Afghanistan and Chechnya. Held to the ground. The knife sawing across the cartilage and the windpipe. The gaseous exhalation as the headless body pumped air and blood, and then slumped to the ground. *Allahu Akhbar. Allahu Akhbar.* The grainy internet footage. The horror. A live human sacrifice, on the world wide web.

Christine was still swearing. Rob struggled and writhed but the men had him firmly. He couldn't be a hero. He could try shouting. 'Christine?' he called. 'Christine?'

Behind him he heard, 'Yes!'

'Are you OK? What the—'

A fist slammed into Rob's mouth. He felt his palate fill with hot salty blood. The pain was searing: his body sagged.

The leader came around, to face him. He lifted Rob's bleeding face and said, 'No talk! No speak!'

The leader's face wasn't cruel. His expression was more . . . resigned. As if this was something they had to do, but didn't necessarily want to. Something truly terrible . . .

Like an execution.

Rob watched as one of the Kurds slowly and carefully opened the main door of the museum. The sight of the door kicked off a procession of memories. The last few bizarre hours of his life: the sheep being slaughtered in the Urfan streets; the men in the black holiday pantaloons; their own stealthy ingress into the museum. And then the baby's silent scream. Buried alive twelve thousand years ago.

The Kurd at the door nodded at his compadres. The coast, it seemed, was clear.

'Go!' the leader was shouting at Rob. 'Go into car!'

Brusquely, the men escorted Rob through the sultry, moonlit car park. The car smeared with figs had been joined by three more vehicles. These were old cars: bashed-up local autos – clearly not police cars. Rob felt the last shred of hope disappear.

Their intent was obviously to take Rob and Christine somewhere a distance away. Out of the city maybe. To some lonely farmhouse. Where they would be chained to the seats. Rob imagined the sound of the knife as it ripped across his gullet. *Allahu Akhbar.* He shook the idea away. He had to stay lucid. Save Christine. Save himself for his daughter.

His daughter!!

Guilt pierced Rob's heart like a dagger of glass. His daughter Lizzie! He'd promised her just yesterday that he would be home in a week. Now he might never see her again. Stupid stupid stupid *stupid.*

A hand was pressing on Rob's head. They wanted him to stoop: to get into the musty backseat of the car. Rob resisted, feeling as if he was being taken to his death. He turned and saw Christine just behind him, a knife at her throat. She was being hauled across to the other car; there was nothing anyone could do.

Then: 'Stop!'

The moment froze. Bright lights dazzled across the car park.

'Stop!'

The lights were utterly blinding. Rob now sensed the presence of many more men. Sirens and sirens. Red and blue lights. Light and noise all about. The police. Was this the police? He wrenched an arm from his captor's grasp and shielded his face and stared into the dazzling blinding light . . .

It was Kiribali, with twenty or thirty policemen. They were running into the car park. Crouching. Taking position. Taking aim. But these weren't ordinary policemen. They wore black, almost paramilitary gear and carried submachine guns.

Kiribali was shouting in Turkish at the Kurds. And the Kurds were backing off. The one nearest Rob dropped his old pistol, then raised his hands. Rob saw Christine struggle from her captors and run across the car park to the safety of the police.

Rob wrenched his second arm free and walked across the car park to Kiribali, whose face was blank to the point of contempt. The officer snapped: 'Come with me.'

Rob and Christine were sharply led away to a big new BMW outside the museum grounds. Kiribali ordered Rob and Christine in the back: he got in the front, then turned and looked at them. 'I'm taking you to the airport.'

'But . . .' Rob started. His mouth throbbed with pain, where he had been punched.

Kiribali silenced him. 'I went to the apartment, your hotel room. Empty! Both empty. I knew you must have come here. You are so foolish. Such foolish people!' The BMW was speeding down the wide, lamp-lit road. Kiribali spoke in hurried Turkish to the driver; the driver answered obediently.

Then the officer flashed a very dark frown at Rob. 'You have a couple of bags in the back. Passports. Your laptops. We will send the rest of your possessions. You are leaving Turkey tonight.' He tossed two items into the back seat. 'Your tickets. For Istanbul, then London. One way only. Tonight.'

Christine protested, but her reply was faltering, and her voice tremulous. Kiribali gazed at her with infinite disdain, then he and the driver exchanged some more words. The car was now on the outskirts of town. The flat semi-desert was quiet in the night, the colour of tarnished silver in the moonlight.

When they reached the airport the driver handed them their bags from the boot. Inside the tiny airport, Kiribali watched them check in. Then he pointed at the departure gate. 'I do not expect to see either of you again. If you return the Kurds will probably kill you. Even if they don't, I will throw you both in jail. For a very long time.' He clicked his heels together, like a Prussian officer obeying an order, then he gave them another angry, contemptuous glare – and then he was gone.

Rob and Christine filed through security and boarded the plane. It taxied, and took off. Rob sank back into the seats, his whole body throbbing with pain and adrenaline. He could really feel it now: the surge of emotion, the fear; the eager fury. It was the same feeling he had experienced after the Iraqi suicide bomb. Rob clenched and unclenched his jaw muscles. His lip still hurt, his tooth was cracked. He tried to relax himself. His mind was racing, almost painfully. The story wasn't over. He was a journalist. A good journalist. That's all he was – but he could use it. He needed to channel this anger, this impotent anger, his humiliated masculinity. If they thought they could frighten him away with guns and knives they were wrong. He would get the story. He wouldn't be scared away. He had to relax, though he felt like shouting. He looked across at Christine.

And then, for the first time since the baby urn had broken open, she spoke directly to him. Quietly but clearly she said, 'Canaanites.'

'What?'

'That's what the ancient Canaanites did. They buried their children. Alive.' She turned and stared ahead. 'And in jars.'

28

Rob put down his phone and surveyed the tedious bustle of Istanbul airport. He'd spent an hour talking to his daughter: a happy, chatting, wistful, delightful hour. He'd then spent a slightly fractious and annoying ten minutes talking to her mother. His ex-wife, it turned out, was taking his daughter Lizzie to the country for a fortnight, starting today. Even if he flew home this minute he would miss her.

Rob rubbed the tiredness from his face. They'd arrived in the middle of the night and grabbed some frazzled sleep on the airport seats. It hadn't really de-stressed him. What an incredible twenty-four hours it had been. What a bizarre chain of events. And what was he going to do now?

'Hey soldier.' Christine was brandishing cans of Diet Coke. 'Thought you could use one of these.'

Rob took his can, gratefully, and cracked it open; the icy cola stung his broken lip.

'Is everything OK at home, Robert?'

'Yes . . .' He watched a Chinese businessman hawking exuberantly into a rubbish bin. 'No. Not really. Family stuff . . .'

'Ah.' She gazed levelly across the transit lounge. 'Look at it. All so ordinary. Starbucks. McDonald's . . . You'd never think we were nearly kidnapped. Just last night.'

Rob knew what she meant. He sighed, and gazed resentfully at the Departures screen. Their flight for London was many hours away. He really didn't want to be here, killing time. But he didn't want to go back to London if his daughter wasn't there. What was the point? What he wanted to do was to resolve the story, finish the deal. He'd already spoken to his editor and told him a slightly bowdlerized version of the latest developments. Steve had sworn, twice, and then asked Rob if he felt safe. Rob had said that, despite it all, he felt fine. So Steve had tentatively agreed that Rob could continue – 'as long as you avoid getting shot in the head'. He had even promised to put some more money in Rob's account to help things along. So the compass was pointing in one direction. Don't quit. Don't give up. Press on. Get the story.

But there was a big problem with pressing on: Rob didn't know how Christine was feeling. The ordeal at the museum had been extremely frightening. He felt he could deal with what had happened, because he was used to danger. He'd handled Iraq. Just about. Could he expect Christine to be equally stoical? Was it asking too much of her? She was a scientist, not a news journalist. He finished the Coke and wandered over to the rubbish bin to toss the can. When he came back Christine scrutinized him with a faint smile. 'You don't want to fly home, do you?'

'How did you guess?'

'The way you keep scowling at the departure board, like it's your worst enemy.'

'Sorry.'

'I feel exactly the same, Robert. Too many loose ends. We can't just run away can we?'

'So . . . what shall we do?'

'Let's go and see my friend, Isobel Previn. She lives here.'

Half an hour later they were hailing an airport cab; ten minutes after that, they were streaking along the motorway: heading into the hubbub of Istanbul. En route, Christine reprised the back-story of Isobel Previn.

'She lived in Konya for a long time. Working with James Mellaert. Catalhoyuk. And she was my tutor at Cambridge.'

'Right. I remember you saying.'

Rob gazed out of the cab window. Beyond the flyovers and housing estates he could see a huge dome surrounded by four lofty minarets: Hagia Sophia, the great cathedral of Constantinople. Fifteen hundred years old.

Istanbul, it seemed, was a curious and kinetic place. Ancient walls collided with shiny skyscrapers. The streets were filled with western-looking people: girls in short skirts, men in smart suits – but every so often they sped past some Levantine neighbourhood, with grimy blacksmiths, and veiled mothers, and lines of lurid washing. And surrounding it all, visible between the apartment blocks and the office towers, was the mighty Bosphorus, the great arc of water dividing Asia from Europe, and the West from the East. The barbarians from civilization. Depending on which side you lived.

Christine called her friend Isobel. Rob gleaned from the overheard conversation that Isobel was delighted to hear from her former student. He waited for the call to conclude, then asked, 'So where does she live?'

'She's got a house on one of the Princes Islands. We can get a ferry from the port.' Christine smiled. 'It's very pretty. And she's invited us to stay.'

Rob assented, happily.

Christine added, 'She might well be able to help with the . . . archaeological mysteries.'

The hideous little mummy in the amphora: the olive jar. As the cab driver shouted at the lorries, Rob asked Christine more about the Canaanites.

'I used to work at Tell Gezer,' Christine said. 'It's a site in the Judaean Hills, half an hour from Jerusalem. A Canaanite city.'

The car was heading downhill now. They'd turned off the road and were crawling through crowded, energetic streets.

'The Canaanites used to bury their firstborn children, alive, in jars. Some were found at the site. Babies in jars, just like the ones in the museum vault. So I think that's what we found in the cellar. A sacrifice.'

The horrible image of the baby's face filled Rob's thoughts. The terrible, silent scream on the baby's face. He shuddered. Who the hell would bury a child alive? In a jar? Why? What was the evolutionary purpose? What could drive you to do that? What kind of God demanded that? What *had* happened at Gobekli? Another thought occurred to him as the car turned onto a thrumming seafront. 'Wasn't Abraham linked with the Canaanites?'

'Yes,' said Christine. 'When he left Haran and Sanliurfa he descended into the land of the Canaanites. That's what the Bible says anyhow. Hey, I think we're here.'

They were just outside a ferry terminal. The concourse was heaving: with children, and girls on bicycles, and men carrying boxes of sesame biscuits. Again Rob sensed the fault line of civilization running right through the city: it was almost schizophrenic. Men in jeans stood by men with lavish Muslim beards; girls in mini-dresses laughed on their mobile phones next to silent girls in black chadors.

They bought tickets and headed for the top deck. Strolling by the taffrail, Rob felt his spirits lift. Water, sunlight, fresh air, cool breezes. How he had missed this. Sanliurfa was so ferociously landlocked, sweltering in the bowl of Kurdistan.

The boat chugged along. Christine pointed out some of the sights of the Istanbul skyline. The Golden Horn. The Blue Mosque. Topkapi Palace. A bar where she and Isobel once got very drunk on raki. Then she reminisced about Cambridge, and her university days. Rob laughed at her stories. Christine had been quite wild. Before he knew it, the ferry-horn blew: they'd reached the island.

The little pier was crowded with Turks, but Christine spotted Isobel immediately. It wasn't hard. The silvery-haired old woman was conspicuous amidst the darker faces. She was wearing swirling clothes. An orange silk scarf. And lorgnettes.

They walked down the gangplank. The two women hugged and then Christine introduced Rob. Isobel smiled, very graciously, and advised Rob that her house was a half-hour walk.

'I'm afraid we don't have cars on the islands, you see. They're not allowed. Thank God.'

As they threaded their way, Christine told Isobel the whole extraordinary story of the last few weeks. The horrible murder. The incredible finds. Isobel nodded. She sympathized over Franz. Rob detected an almost mother/daughter relationship between the two women. It was touching.

Considering this, he was reminded of Lizzie again. Lizzie would like this island, he decided. It was pretty, yet faintly mysterious too, with its wooden houses and tamarisk trees, its crumbling, Byzantine churches and cats sleeping in the sun. All around them was glittering water, and in the distance was the famous skyline of Istanbul. It was gorgeous. Rob firmly resolved to bring her here, one fine day.

Isobel's house was glamorously old: a cool summer retreat for Ottoman princelings. The white stone house stood by a well-shaded beach and looked across the water towards some of the other isles.

They sat down on cushioned sofas and Christine finished the narrative of Gobekli and the last few weeks. The whole house was quiet as she finished the tale with its outrageous coda: their near-kidnapping at the museum.

Silence sang in the air. Rob could hear the plash of water beyond the half-open shutters, and the creak of pine trees in the sun.

Isobel toyed languidly with her lorgnettes. They finished the tea. Christine shrugged at Rob as if to say, *maybe Isobel can't help. Maybe the puzzle is too difficult.*

Rob sighed, feeling tired. But then Isobel sat up: alert, with her eyes sparkling. She asked Rob to show her the mobile phone photo of the symbol on the jar.

Rob fished in his pocket, retrieved the phone and flicked to the image. Isobel contemplated the photo. 'Yes. As I thought. It's a sanjak. A symbol used by the Cult of Angels.'

'The cult of what?'

'The Cult of Angels, the Yezidi . . .' She smiled. 'I'd better explain. That remote part of Kurdistan around Sanliurfa is a remarkable breeding ground of beliefs. Christianity, Judaism and Islam all have strong roots there. But there are other, even older, faiths, that inhabit the Kurdish lands. Like Yarsenism, Alevism, and Yezidism. Together they are called the cult of angels. These religions are maybe five thousand years old, maybe older. They are unique to that part of the world.' She paused. 'And Yezidism is the oldest and strangest of all.'

'In what way?'

'The customs of the Yezidi are intensely peculiar. They honour sacred trees. Women must not cut their hair. They refuse to eat lettuce. They avoid wearing dark blue, because they say it is too holy. They are divided strictly into castes, who cannot marry each other. The upper castes are polygamous. Anyone of the faith who marries a non-Yezidi risks ostracism, or worse. So they never marry outside the faith. Ever.'

Christine interrupted. 'Hasn't the Cult of Angels basically died out, in Turkey?'

'Almost. The last of the Angelicans live mainly in Iraq, about half a million of them. But there are still a few thousand Yezidi in Turkey. They are fiercely persecuted everywhere, of course. By Muslims, Christians, dictators . . .'

Rob asked, 'But what do they believe?'

'Yezidism is syncretistic: it combines elements of many faiths. Like Hindus, they believe in reincarnation. Like ancient Mithraists, they sacrifice bulls. They believe in baptism, like Christians. When they pray they face the sun, like Zoroastrians.'

'Why do you think the symbol on the jar is a Yezidi symbol?'

'I'll show you.' Isobel walked to the bookshelf on the far wall and returned with a volume. Halfway through the book she found a picture showing a curious copper stick with a bird poised on the top. The book said the symbol was a 'Yezidi sanjak'. It was the exact same symbol inscribed on the jars.

Isobel shut the book and asked Christine, 'Now. Tell me the full names of the workmen, at the site. And the surname of Beshet at the museum.'

Christine closed her eyes, trying to remember: faltering a little, she recited a list of half a dozen names. Then a few more.

Isobel nodded. 'They are Yezidi. The workmen, at your site. They are Yezidi. And so is Beshet. And I presume the men who came to kidnap you were Yezidi too. They were protecting those jars in the museum.'

'That makes sense,' said Rob, quickly working it through in his mind. 'When you look at the sequence of events. What I mean is: when Christine went to Beshet for the keycode, he gave it to her. But then he must have called his fellow Yezidis and told them what we were doing. And so they came to the museum. They were tipped off!'

Christine interrupted. 'Sure. But why should the Yezidi be so worried about some old jars? However ghastly the contents? What's it got to do with them now? Why the hell were they so desperate to stop us?'

'That's the nub,' said Isobel.

The shutter had stopped creaking. The sun sparkled on the placid waters beyond the window.

'There's one more thing,' said Isobel. 'The Yezidi have a very strange god. He is represented as a peacock.'

'They worship a bird?'

'And they call him Melek Taus. The peacock angel. Another name for him is . . . Moloch. The demon god adored by the Canaanites. And another name for him is Satan. According to Christians and Muslims.'

Rob was nonplussed. 'You mean the Yezidi are *Satanists*?'

Isobel nodded cheerfully. 'Shaitan, the demon. The terrible god of the sacrifice.' She smiled. 'As we understand it, yes. The Yezidi worship the devil.'

29

Cloncurry. This was their very last name, and the very best hope. Forrester sorted through the papers and photos on his knee, as the rain spattered the windscreen. He and Boijer were in a hire car in northern France, heading south from Lille. Boijer was driving, Forrester was reading: fast. And hoping they were finally on the right track. It certainly looked good.

They'd spent the last few days talking to headmasters and rectors and student advisors, phoning reluctant doctors in university clinics. Quite a few likely candidates had emerged. A drop-out from Christ Church, Oxford. A couple of expellees from Eton and Marlborough. A schizophrenic student, missing from St Andrews. Forrester had been shocked at the number of students diagnosed as schizophrenic. Hundreds across the country.

But the candidates had all been ruled out, one way or another. The posh Oxford drop-out was in a mental hospital. The St Andrews student was known to be in Thailand. The Eton expellee had died. In the end they had drilled it down to one name: Jamie Cloncurry.

He had all the right credentials. His family was extremely wealthy, and of aristocratic descent. He'd been very expensively schooled at Westminster where his behaviour, according to his housemaster, was eccentric verging on violent. He had beaten another pupil and come perilously close to expulsion. But his academic brilliance had afforded him a second chance.

Cloncurry had then gone to Imperial College in London to study mathematics. One of the finest scientific universities in the world. But this grand opportunity hadn't solved his problems; indeed his wildness had only intensified. He'd dabbled in hard drugs and been caught with call-girls in his Hall of Residence. One of them had reported him to the police for brutality, but the Crown Prosecution Service had dropped the charge on the grounds of an unlikely conviction: she was a prostitute, he a gifted student at a top university.

Crucially, it seemed Cloncurry had gathered around him a number of extremely close friends – Italians, French and American. One of his fellow students said Cloncurry's social circle was 'a weird clique. Those guys worshipped him.' And, as Boijer and Forrester had established, in the last two or three weeks that clique had disappeared. They hadn't been seen at lectures. A concerned sibling had reported her brother as missing. The college had posters of him in the union bar. An Italian kid: Luca Marsinelli.

The young men had left no trace. Their student digs were empty of evidence. No one knew or even especially cared where they had gone. The clique members were disliked. Acquaintances and neighbours were bafflingly vague. 'Students come and go all the time.' 'I thought he'd gone back to Milan.' 'He just said he was taking a holiday.'

At Scotland Yard they had therefore been obliged to make some tough decisions. Forrester's team couldn't follow every lead with equal zeal. Time was running out. The Toyota Landcruiser had been found, abandoned, on the outskirts of Liverpool, the gang having evidently guessed that the car was a liability. The gang had gone to ground, but Forrester knew they would surely strike again, and soon. But where? There wasn't time for speculation. So Forrester had ordered his team to zero in on Cloncurry, the alleged leader.

The Cloncurry family lived, it turned out, in Picardy in northern

France. They had an ancestral home in Sussex, a large flat in London, and even a villa in Barbados. But for some reason they lived in the middle of Picardy. Near Albert. Which was why Forrester and Boijer had caught the first Eurostar this morning from London St Pancras to Lille.

Forrester surveyed the huge and rolling fields, the pinched little woods; the grey and steely sky of northern France. Every so often, one of the hills would be adorned by another British wartime cemetery: a lyrical but melancholy parade of chaste marble headstones. Thousands and thousands of graves. It was a depressing spectacle, not helped by the rain. The trees were in Maytime blossom, but even the blossom was wilted and helpless in the relentless drizzle.

'Not the most attractive part of France, is it, sir?'

'Hideous,' Forrester answered. 'All these cemeteries.'

'Lots of wars here, right?'

'Yes. And dying industries. That doesn't help.' He paused, then said, 'We used to come here on holiday.'

Boijer chuckled. 'Nice choice.'

'No not here. What I mean is we used to go camping in the south of France, when I was a kid. But we couldn't afford to fly, so we had to drive all the way down through France. From Le Havre. And we used to come through here, through Picardy. Past Albert and the Somme and the rest of it. And every time I would cry. Because it was so bloody ugly. The villages are so ugly because they were all rebuilt after the Great War. In concrete. Millions of men died in these wet fields, Boijer. Millions. In Flanders Fields.'

'I guess so.'

'I think the Finns were still living in igloos at the time.'

'Yes, sir. Eating moss.'

The two men laughed, quite laddishly. Forrester needed some light relief. The Eurostar journey had been equally sombre: they'd used the hours to go over the pathology reports one more time. To see if they'd missed anything. But nothing had jumped out at them. It was just the same chilling scientific analysis of the wounds. Extensive haemorrhage. Stab wound in the fifth intercostal. Death by traumatic asphyxia.

'Think this is it,' said Boijer.

Forrester checked the sign: Ribemont-sur-Ancre. 6km. 'You're right. This turn-off.'

The car swerved onto the slip road, scything through gathered pools of rainwater. Forrester wondered why it rained so much in north-east France. He remembered stories of Great War soldiers drowning in mud, literally drowning in their hundreds and thousands, in the churned wet rainy mud. What a way to die. 'And take a right here.'

He checked the address of the Cloncurrys. He'd rung the family and got their agreement to an interview just a day ago. The mother's voice was cold and slightly quavery on the phone. But she had given him instructions. Go past the rue Voltaire. A kilometre further on. Then take the left, towards Albert. 'Take this left . . .'

Boijer swung the wheel and the hire car crunched through a rutted puddle; the road was virtually a farm track.

Then they saw the house. It was large and impressive, shuttered and dormered, with a severely sloping roof in the French style. But it was also sombre, dark and oppressive. An odd place to come and live.

Jamie Cloncurry's mother was waiting for them at the end of the wide, looping driveway. Her accent was icily posh. Very English. Her husband was just inside the door, in an expensive tweed jacket and corduroys. His socks were bright red.

In the sitting room a maid served coffee. Mrs Cloncurry sat opposite them, with her knees pressed tightly together. 'So, Inspector Forrester. You wish to talk about my son Jamie . . .'

The interview was painful. Stilted and laborious. The parents claimed they had lost control of Jamie in his mid teens. By the time he reached university they had lost all contact, too. The mother's mouth twitched, very slightly, as she discussed Jamie's 'problems'.

She blamed drugs. And his friends. She confessed she blamed herself, as well, because they had sent him to boarding school – to be a boarder at Westminster. This had increased the young man's isolation within the family. 'And so he withdrew from us. And that was that.'

Forrester was frustrated. He could tell where the interview was going. The parents knew nothing: they had practically disclaimed their son.

As Boijer took over the questioning, the DCI scanned the large and silent sitting room. There were many family photos – of the daughter, Jamie's sister. Photos of her on holiday, on a pony, or at her graduation. Yet no photos of the son. Not one. And there were family portraits too. A military figure: a Cloncurry from the nineteenth century. A viscount in the Indian Army. And an admiral. Generations of distinguished forebears were staring from the walls. And now possibly – probably – there was a murderer in the family. A psychotic killer. Forrester could feel the shame of the Cloncurrys. He could feel the pain of the mother. The father was practically silent during the interview.

The two hours passed with elaborate slowness. At the end Mrs Cloncurry escorted them to the door. Her piercing blue eyes stared into Forrester, not at him, but into him. Her aquiline face matched the photo of Jamie Cloncurry that Forrester had already sourced from the Imperial College student records. The boy was handsome, in a high cheekboned way. The mother must have once been beautiful; she was still as thin as a model.

'Inspector,' she said, as they stood at the door. 'I wish I could tell you that Jamie didn't do these . . . these terrible things. But . . . but . . .' She fell quiet. The husband was still hovering behind his wife, his red socks glowing in the gloom of the hallway.

Forrester nodded and shook the woman's hand. At least they'd had their suspicions all but confirmed. But they weren't any nearer finding Jamie Cloncurry.

They scrunched to the car. The rain had finally relented, at least a little. 'So we know it's him,' said Forrester, climbing in.

Boijer keyed the engine. 'Reckon so.'

'But where the fuck is he?'

The car sludged through the damp gravel onto the winding road. They had to negotiate the narrow streets of the village to get to the autoroute. And Lille. On the way through Ribemont, Forrester spotted a little French café, a humble brasserie: its lights were inviting in the drizzly greyness.

'Shall we get some lunch?'

'Yes, please.'

They parked in the Place de la Revolution. An enormous and morbid memorial, to the Great War dead, dominated the silent square. This tiny village, Forrester reckoned, must have been right in the middle of the fighting during the war. He imagined the place during the height of the Somme offensive. Tommys loitering by the brothels. Wounded in ambulances racing to the tented hospitals. The ceaseless boom of the shelling, a few miles away.

'It's a funny place to live,' said Boijer. 'Isn't it? When you're so rich. Why live here?'

'I was wondering the same.' Forrester stared at the nobly agonized figure of a wounded French soldier, immortalized in marble. 'You'd think if they wanted to live in France, they'd live in Provence or somewhere. Corsica. Cannes. Somewhere sunny. Not this toilet.'

They walked to the café. As they pressed the door Boijer said, 'I don't believe it.'

'What do you mean?'

'I don't buy the weeping mother bit. I don't think they are ignorant as they say. There's something strange about it all.'

The cafe was virtually deserted. A waiter came over, wiping his hands on a grubby towel.

'Steak frites?' said Forrester. He had just enough French to order food. Boijer nodded. Forrester smiled at the waiter. '*Deux steak frites, s'il vous plaît. Et une bière pour moi, et un . . .* ?'

Boijer sighed. 'Pepsi.'

The waiter said a curt *merci*. And disappeared.

Boijer checked something on his BlackBerry. Forrester knew when his junior was having bright ideas because he stuck his tongue out like a schoolboy working on a sum. The DCI sipped his beer as Boijer Googled. Finally the Finn sat back. 'There. Now that's interesting.'

'What?'

'I Googled the name Cloncurry and Ribemont-sur-Ancre. And then I Googled it with just Ancre.'

'OK . . .'

Boijer smirked, a hint of victory on his face. 'Get this, sir. A Lord Cloncurry was a general in the First World War. And he was based near here. 1916.'

'We know that the family has a military background—'

'Yes, but . . .' Boijer smile's widened. 'Listen to this.' He read a note he had scrawled on the paper tablecloth. 'During the summer of 1916 Lord Cloncurry was notorious for his grotesquely wasteful attacks on impregnable German positions. More troops died under his command, proportionately, than under any other British general in the entire war. Cloncurry subsequently became known as the Butcher of Albert.'

This was more interesting. Forrester eyed his junior.

Boijer lifted a finger, and quoted: '"Such was the carnage under Cloncurry's leadership, sending wave after wave of infantry into the pitiless machine-gun fire of the well-trained, well-armed Hanover Division, his tactics were compared, by several historians, to the futility of . . . human sacrifice".'

The cafe was dead quiet. Then the door rattled as a customer stepped inside, shaking the rain from his umbrella.

'There's more,' said Boijer. 'There's a link from that entry. With a curious result. It's in Wikipedia.'

The waiter set two plates of steak frites on the table. Forrester ignored the food. He stared hard at Boijer. 'Go on.'

'Apparently during the war they were digging up trenches or something, or mass graves maybe . . . anyway, they found another site of human sacrifice. An iron age site. Celtic tribes. They found eighty skeletons.' Boijer quoted again. '"All headless, the skeletons had been piled up and tangled together along with weapons".' Boijer looked up at his boss. 'And the bodies were contorted into unnatural positions. It's apparently the biggest site of human sacrifice in France.'

'Where is this?'

'Here, sir. Right here. Ribemont-sur-Ancre.'

30

Rob stirred. Christine was besides him, still sleeping. In the night she had kicked half the sheets off. He looked at her glowing suntan. He caressed her neck, kissed her bare shoulder. She murmured his name, rolled over; and decorously snored.

It was nearly noon. The sunlight was streaming through the window. Rob got out of the bed and headed for the bathroom. As he sluiced the sleep from his face and hair, he thought about Christine: how it had happened. Them; the two of them; him and her.

He had never experienced a romance like this before: they seemed to have gone from being friends to holding hands, to kissing, to sleeping together as if it was the most obvious and natural thing in the world. A simple and expected evolution. He remembered when he had been nervous about her, reluctant to show his feelings. That felt ludicrous now.

But even if their relationship seemed obvious it was, paradoxically, still richly strange and marvellous. Maybe the best comparison, Rob decided, was with a brilliant new song you heard on the radio for the first time. Because the melody of a great song seems so right it makes you say: Ah, of course, yes, why didn't anyone think of that brilliant tune before? It just needed someone to write down the notes.

Rob rinsed his face and reached blindly for the towel. He dried himself, and stepped from the shower. He looked left. The bathroom window was wide open so that he was gazing across the Sea of Marmara to the other Princes Islands. Yassiadi. Sedef Adasi, with the villages and forests of Anatolia in the distance. White-sailed yachts drifted languidly across the blue. The scent of pine needles, warmed by the sun, filled the little bathroom.

Being here in this house had no doubt helped their love affair: had nurtured and developed it. The island was such a heavenly oasis, a vivid contrast to roiled and violent Sanliurfa. And Isobel's Ottoman home was so quiet: so winsome and untroubled. Sunlit and snoozing by the waves of Marmara; there weren't even cars to disturb the peace.

For ten days Rob and Christine had recuperated here. They'd also explored the other islands. They'd seen the grave of the first English Ambassador to the Ottoman Empire, sent by Elizabeth the First. They'd nodded as a local guide showed them the wooden house where Trotsky lived. They'd laughed over Turkish coffee in the waterfront cafés of Buyukada, and drunk heady glasses of raki with Isobel in her rose-scented garden, as the sun set over distant Troy.

And it was on one of those soft warm evenings, under the scattered jewellery of the Marmara stars, that Christine had leaned over and kissed him. And he had kissed her back. Three days later Isobel politely and subtly asked her maid to put the guest towels in just one room.

Rob padded through. The bedroom shutters were squeaking in the summer breeze. Christine was still asleep, her dark hair sprayed across the Egyptian cotton pillowslip. He crossed the parquet floor, barefoot, threw on his clothes and boots, and went quietly downstairs.

Isobel was on the phone. She smiled and waved at Rob and gestured him to the kitchen, where Andrea the maid was making coffee. Rob pulled a chair from under the kitchen table, and thanked the maid for his coffee. And then he sat there, absentmindedly, but happily, staring out of the wide-open kitchen door at the roses and the azaleas and the bougainvillea of the garden.

Ezekiel the cat – 'Ezzy', as Isobel called her – was chasing a butterfly around the kitchen floor. Rob teased the cat for a few idle minutes. Then he sat back and picked up a newspaper, a day old *Financial Times*, and read about some Kurdish suicide bombers in Ankara.

He set the paper down again. He didn't want to know about any of this. He didn't want to hear about violence or danger or politics. He wanted this idyll to persist; he wanted to stay here with Christine for ever, and bring Lizzie here, too.

But the idyll could not last: Steve his editor was making impatient noises. He either wanted the story done or Rob on another assignment. Rob had filed a couple of Turkish news items to keep things cool back at the office, but everyone knew that this state of grace was temporary.

Rob stepped into the garden and gazed out to sea. There was another alternative. He *could* just give up his job. Stay here with Christine. Charter a boat, hire it out to tourists. Become a squid fisherman like the Greeks on Burgazada. Join the Armenian café owners in Yassiada. Potter about Isobel's garden. Just give everything up, and live out his days in the sun. And somehow he could bring Lizzie here too. With his daughter here, laughing on the beach, he would be surrounded by the women he loved, and life would be perfect . . .

And now he sighed and smiled at his own fond delusions. Love was addling his brain. He had a job, he needed money, he had to be practical.

Rob watched a catamaran in the distance. The line of its white sail looked like a swan as it crossed the stretch of water.

A noise disturbed his reverie. Rob turned, and there was Isobel coming out of the kitchen.

'I've just had the most intriguing phone call from an old friend at Cambridge. Professor Hugo De Savary. Have you heard of him?'

'No . . .'

'Writes a lot. Does TV shows. But he's a very fine scholar nonetheless. Christine knows him. I think she did a term of his lectures at King's. In fact I think they were friends . . .' Isobel tilted a smile. 'Where is Christine anyway?'

'Still fast asleep.'

'Ah, young love!' She took Rob's arm. 'Let's go down to the beach. I'll tell you what Hugo said.'

The beach was rocky and small, but pretty; and almost completely isolated. They sat on a bench of rock and she told him about De Savary's phone call. The Cambridge historian had explained to Isobel everything he had learned from the police, and added everything he surmised himself about the gruesome murders across Britain. The gang of killers. The connection with the Hellfire Club and the link of human sacrifice in the murders.

'Why did De Savary ring you?'

'We're old friends. I was at Cambridge too, remember.'

'Yes, but what I mean is, how does this connect with everything we've discovered?'

'Hugo knows I am something of an expert on Turkish and Sumerian antiquity, on ancient religions of the Near East. Such as the Yezidi. He was asking my opinion on a theory. Connected with them. A strange little coincidence. Or maybe not.' She paused. 'Hugo believes this gang, the killers, are looking for something closely associated with the Hellfire Club.'

'Right. I understand that – they are digging up places associated with the club. But what are they looking for? And where do the Yez fit in?'

'It's very speculative. Hugo hasn't even told the police. But he thinks it might be connected with the Black Book. That's what the gang are pursuing, possibly . . .'

'The Black Book? Explain?'

Isobel ran through the story of Jerusalem Whaley: as a friend of Hugo De Savary she'd heard lots of juicy stories about the Hellfire Club. Endless stories of depravity. 'When he came back from the Holy Land, Thomas Whaley, or Jerusalem Whaley as he was thereafter known, brought with him a cache. A box. A hoard of some kind . . .'

'What was it?'

'Your guess is nearly as good as mine. But we do know he prized his find hugely, believed he'd proved a theory. He called it his "great evidence" in his many letters to friends. Supposedly he was given these materials by an old Yezidi priest. The Yezidi have a caste of priests, singing priests who hand down the oral tradition of the Yezidi. Because there isn't much of a literary tradition.'

'And he met with one of these priests, in Jerusalem? Who gave him something?'

'Presumably. We can't be sure because Whaley's memoirs are irritatingly vague. But some scholars think it might be the Black Book of the Yezidi. The sacred book of the Angelicans.'

'They have a Bible?'

'Not any more. But their oral traditions say there was, once, a great body of sacred and mystical writing that embodied Yezidi myths and beliefs. Contemporary legends also say that the only copy was taken by an Englishman hundreds of years ago. Might some exiled priest have given the Black Book to Whaley? For safe keeping? The Yezidi have always felt embattled. They might have wanted to preserve their most precious object somewhere safe. Like faraway England. Buck Whaley certainly brought something remarkable with him on his return from the Levant. Moreover, this item, whatever it was, eventually left him a broken man.'

'OK. So where is it now? The Black Book? If that's what it is?'

'Disappeared. Possibly destroyed. Possibly hidden.'

Rob's thoughts started to race. He looked into the older woman's serene grey eyes. Then he said: 'How can we find out what the gang are really looking for? How can we investigate this link to the Yezidi?'

'Lalesh,' said Isobel. 'That's the only place you could get real answers. The sacred capital of the Yezidi. *Lalesh*.'

Rob felt a shiver of disquiet. He knew he had to go to this place, Lalesh: to get answers, to finish the story. Steve was pressuring him to do the second and concluding article, and to write it properly Rob needed to tie up the straying ends: to find out about this 'Black Book'.

But Rob also knew where Lalesh was. He'd heard of it before, from other journalists. It had featured in the news, in recent years, more than once. For all the wrong reasons.

'I know Lalesh,' he said. 'That's in Kurdistan isn't it? South of the border?'

Isobel nodded gravely.

'Yes. It's in Iraq.'

31

That evening Rob told Christine that he had to go to Lalesh, and explained to her why.

She looked at him without saying anything. He told her, again, that Lalesh was the obvious place to finish the story. The answers to most of their puzzles lay with the Yezidi. The sacred capital was the only place he could find truly learned Yezidi. Scholars who could unwrap the enigma. And obviously it made sense for Rob to go alone. He knew Iraq. He knew the risks. He had contacts in that country. His paper would cover his enormous insurance bill, but they wouldn't pay for Christine. So he had to go to Lalesh – and he had to go alone.

Christine seemed to accede and accept. And then she turned and walked, wordless, into the garden.

Rob hesitated. Should he join her? Leave her alone?

His reverie of indecision was broken by Isobel, humming a song as she walked through the kitchen. The older woman glanced at Rob, and then at the silhouetted figure, sitting in the garden.

'You told her?'

'She seemed OK about it, but then . . .'

Isobel sighed. 'She was like this at Cambridge. When she's upset, she doesn't chuck things at walls, just bottles it up.'

Rob was torn. He hated to upset Christine, but the journey was a necessity: he was a foreign correspondent. He couldn't pick or choose where his stories led him.

'You know, I'm slightly surprised,' Isobel said.

'By what?'

'That she fell for you anyway. She doesn't normally go for men like you. With cheekbones and blue eyes. Dashing adventurers. It's usually older men. You do know she lost her dad when she was young, don't you? She's like any girl with that in her background. Always been attracted to the missing father figure. Advisors. Tutors.' Isobel looked Rob in the eye. 'Protectors.'

Across the waters came the hooting of a ferry. Rob listened to the echo rebounding. Then he stepped through the kitchen doorway, into the garden.

Christine was alone on the garden seat, staring through the moonlit pines. Without turning, she said, 'Isobel is very lucky. This house is so beautiful.'

He sat down beside her and took her hand. The moonlight made her fingers seem very pale. 'Christine, I need a favour.'

She turned to look at him.

He explained. 'While I am in Lalesh . . .' He paused. 'Lizzie. Watch over her a little. Can you?'

Christine's face was shadowed. A passing cloud had obscured the moon. 'But I don't understand. Lizzie's with her mother.'

Rob sighed. 'Sally works very hard at her job. Her studies. She's got legal exams. I just want someone I really trust to . . . keep another eye on her. You'll be staying with your sister, right? In Camden?'

Christine nodded.

'So that's barely three miles from Sally's house. Knowing you were there, or just nearby, would make it a lot easier for me. Then maybe you could email me. Or call. I'll ring Sally to make sure she knows who you are. She might even welcome the help. Maybe . . .'

The pine trees murmured; Christine nodded. 'I'll go and see her. OK. And I'll email you, every day . . . while you are in Iraq.'

When Christine said the word 'Iraq' Rob felt a shudder of fear. This was the *real* reason he wanted Christine to see and know his daughter: because he was worried for himself. Would he come back from this? Would he return and be a proper father? The Baghdad suicide bomber plagued his memories. He'd been lucky that time; maybe he wouldn't be so lucky again. And if he didn't come back – well then he wanted his daughter to meet and to know the woman he'd loved.

Iraq. Rob shuddered again. The word seemed to sum up all the danger he was about to face. The cities of death. The place of beheadings. The province of chanting men, and ancient stones, and terrible discoveries. And suicide bombers in bright red lipstick.

Christine squeezed his hand.

The next morning Rob got up without waking Christine. He left a note on the bedside table. Then he dressed, said goodbye to Andrea, hugged Isobel, stroked the cat, and took the sun-slanted path to the pier.

Twenty-four hours later, after one ferry ride, one cab ride, two plane trips and a gruelling service-taxi ride from Mardin airport, he arrived at the noisy tumult of the Iraqi-Turkey frontier post at Habur. It was a smoggy chaos of parked trucks and army tanks and impatient businessmen and bewildered pedestrians carrying shopping bags.

It took him five sweaty hours to cross the border. He was questioned for two of those hours by Turkish troops. Who was he? Why did he want to go to Iraq? Did he have links with the Kurdish rebels? Was he going to interview the PKK? Was he just stupid? A daredevil tourist? But they couldn't stop him for ever. He had the visa, the documents, the fax from his editor – and at last he made it through. A barrier went up and he stepped over the invisible line. The first thing he noticed was a striking red and green flag with a sunburst symbol, fluttering above: the flag of free Kurdistan. The flag was banned in Iran, and you could actually go to prison for flying it in Turkey. But here, in the autonomous province of Kurdish Iraq, it was fluttering proudly and freely, flying stark against the burning blue sky.

Rob gazed south. A man with no teeth was staring at him from a wooden bench. A dog was urinating on an old tyre. The road ahead slid through the yellow and sunburnt hills, snaking towards the Mesopotamian plains. Shouldering his bag, Rob walked over to a dinged and rusty blue taxi.

The unshaven driver looked up at him with a wall eye. The only available transport was a one-eyed cabdriver. Rob felt like laughing. Instead he leaned towards the driver's window and said, '*Salaam aleikum.* I want to go to Lalesh.'

32

Hugo De Savary got a taxi from the little station. In a few minutes he was speeding through gorgeous Dorset countryside in the full splendour of May. Hawthorn blossom and blowsy apple trees. Big clouds in a warm and smiling sky.

The taxi drove down a driveway ranked with large beech trees and came to a stop outside a grand manor house with rambling wings and gracious stone chimneys. All around the house overalled policemen were combing the lawns for evidence; others were coming out of the front door peeling off rubber gloves. He paid the cabbie, got out of the car, and glanced at the sign in front of the building: Canford School. From his research, done hastily on the train, he knew that the building had not long been a school: at least by the standards of its own history.

The estate itself dated back to Saxon times, when it encompassed large parts of Canford Magna, the nearby village. But only the Norman church and the fourteenth century 'John of Gaunt's' kitchen survived from those earliest years. The rest of the building was late eighteenth or early nineteenth century. But nonetheless beautiful for that. The manor, converted to a school in the 1920s, stood in fine parkland beside the River Stour. De Savary could smell the freshness of the air, despite the warmth of this gorgeous day: the river was evidently close at hand.

'Professor De Savary!' It was DCI Forrester. 'Great you could come at such short notice.'

De Savary shrugged. 'I'm not sure I can be of that much use.'

Forrester smiled, though,.as De Savary noted, the policeman looked very haggard.

How bad was this murder, De Savary wondered? On the phone this morning all Forrester had said was that it had 'some sacrificial elements', which was why the professor had agreed to come. De Savary's professional interest was piqued: he was vaguely wondering if the theme – of contemporary human sacrifice – might make another book. Or maybe even a TV series. 'When was the body discovered?' he asked.

'Yesterday. Sheer luck. It's half term so the school's closed. The only person here was the caretaker. The victim. But there was a delivery . . . some sports equipment. An inquisitive kid thought something was up and poked his nose around.'

'He found the body?'

'Poor bastard. He's still being counselled.' Forrester eyed the professor. 'Mr De Savary—'

'Call me Hugo.'

'It's a bloody unpleasant sight. I'm a detecting police officer, I've seen a fair few gruesome murders but this one . . .'

'Whereas I am just an innocent from the groves of academe?' De Savary smiled. 'Please, Mark, I have been studying Satanic cults and psychotic impulses for more than a decade. I am used to handling some quite disturbing materials. And have a fairly strong constitution, I rather hope. I even ate a Southwest Trains prawn sandwich on the way down.'

The policeman didn't laugh. Or even smile. He just nodded, blankly. Again De Savary noted the harrowed quality of his expression. The detective had seen something awful. For the first time De Savary got an inkling of apprehension.

The policeman cleared his throat:

'I haven't told you what you are about to see because I don't want to nudge you. I want your honest opinion what you think is going on. Without any preconceptions . . .'

The front door was opened by an obedient constable. Inside it was very much the normal entrance to an English public school: roll calls of honour from the war: lists of boys who gave their lives. There were trophies and noticeboards and some desultory antiques, badly scuffed and damaged by generations of eager schoolboys running past, rugby boots slung over young shoulders. It was nostalgic for De Savary. He remembered his own schooldays at Stowe.

The entrance hall was dominated by a big door at the end. The door was shut, and guarded by another policeman. Forrester looked down at De Savary's feet. And gave him some plastic overshoes.

'There's a lot of blood,' the DCI said quietly, then he motioned to the constable standing by the large inner doors. The constable gave a sort-of salute, and swung open the door, allowing them to step inside.

Beyond was a very baronial space. Wood panelling and heraldic coats of arms: a Victorian pastiche of a medieval nobleman's grand hall. But it was quite well done, thought De Savary. He could imagine minstrels at one end, on the first floor balcony, serenading the feasting duke, sitting above the high table at the other end. But what *was* at the other end? The police had erected a big screen.

Forrester led the way across the creaking floorboards. The nearer they got the more sound their footsteps made: but they weren't creaking now, but squelching. This, De Savary realized, was because he was walking into patches of splashed blood. The polished wooden floor seemed to be sticky with splashes of blood.

Forrester rolled the movable screen out of the way and De Savary gasped. In front of him was a portable soccer goal. A portable wooden frame, which had been wheeled in from the sports pitches outside. Stretched between the goal post and the bar, tied to the bar and the posts by leather straps, was a man.

Or rather, what was left of a man. The naked victim had been suspended upside down from the frame by the ankles. His arms were stretched and tied to each of the posts by the wrists. The hideous grimace of pain on the face of the man, down there by the bloodied floorboards, showed the torment he had been through.

He had been flayed. Flayed alive, it seemed, very slowly and diligently, the skin peeled, or scraped, strip by strip, flap by anguished flap, from the man's body. The raw pulsing flesh had been left uncovered at each stage, leaving blobs of yellow fat; though sometimes this fat had been flensed away, exposing the raw red muscles underneath. You could actually see the organs and the bones in certain places.

De Savary put a forefinger to his nose. He could smell the body, smell the muscles and the lustrous fat. He could see the neck muscles taut with agony, the grey-and-white lungs, the curving definition of the ribcage. It was like an illustration of the muscles and tendons of the human body in a biology textbook. The genitals were missing, of course. A dark and scarlet socket was left where the penis and testicles should have been. De Savary guessed they had been forced into the victim's mouth: he had probably been obliged to eat them.

He stepped around. It looked like the work of more than one person. To do it this carefully, without killing the victim at once, needed care and skill. If you flayed a person correctly they could live for hours, as the muscles and organs slowly dried and crinkled. Sometimes the victim might faint with pain, De Savary imagined, but you could bring them round, before starting again. He didn't want to reconfigure the scene. But he had to. The terrified caretaker brought in here. Tied upside-down. Hanging by his feet from the bar. Then lashed with his arms to either post. Like an inverted crucifixion.

And then – then De Savary imagined it – the terrible horror that must have overcome the victim as he realized what they were doing: the initial tentative scrape of flesh at the ankle or on his feet. Then the searing pain as the skin was peeled away, leaving the pulp exposed to cold and heat. If anything had touched the raw flesh the pain would have been virtually unendurable. He must have screamed as the gang worked their way down his quivering, agonized body, working like expert butchers, making a pelt of his skin. Perhaps he had screamed too loudly at one point, so they had chopped off his genitals, folded the bloody handful of flesh into the screaming mouth, to shut him up.

Then the major flaying: the chest, the arms. Technically quite difficult. They must have practised beforehand, on sheep, goats or maybe cats. Getting it right.

He turned away, shuddering.

Forrester put an arm around the academic's shoulder. 'Yes, I'm sorry.'

'How old was he? It's hard to tell when there's no . . . skin on the face.'

'In his forties,' Forrester said. 'Shall we go outside?'

'Please.'

The policeman led the way. As soon as they were outside they made for the garden bench. De Savary was pleased to sit down. 'Just ghastly,' he said.

The sun was still warm. Forrester took his overshoes off with a grunt. They sat there in a heavy silence. The sweetness of the early summer air seemed sickly now.

After a while De Savary said, 'I think I can help.'

'You can?'

De Savary rephrased. 'That is to say, I think I understand what their psychology might have been . . .'

'So?'

'Clearly there are Aztec themes. The Aztecs had . . . many methods of human sacrifice. The most famous, of course, is live heart excision. The priest would plunge the obsidian knife into the chest, rip open the chest cavity, and yank out the beating heart.'

They both watched as a police car pulled up the driveway. Two officers stepped out, carrying metal suitcases. They nodded briskly at Forrester, and he nodded back.

'Pathology,' said Forrester. 'Go on Hugo, the Aztecs . . . ?'

'They would feed people to jaguars. They would bleed them to death. They would fire little arrows into warriors until they died. But one of the most elaborate methods was *flaying*. They even had a special day for it, the Feast of the Flaying of Men.'

'A special day for flaying?'

'They would strip the skins of enemy prisoners. And then they would dance through the streets of the city, wearing the flayed skins. Aztec nobles often wore the flayed skins of their victims: they considered it an honour for the victim. Indeed there is a story that they once captured an enemy princess, then a few weeks later they invited her father, an enemy king, to a feast, to make peace. The king presumed they were going to hand back his daughter, alive, as part of that peacemaking. But the Aztec emperor clapped his hands after dinner and a priest walked in, wearing the slain princess's skin. The Aztecs thought this was a great honour for the enemy king. I think the peace overture was not a great success.'

Forrester had gone very pale. 'You don't think they are wearing this skin? That Cloncurry is driving around in this guy's fucking skin?'

'It's very possible. That's what the Aztecs would do. Wear the human skin of their victims, like a suit, until it literally rotted away from them. The stench must have been appalling.'

'We certainly haven't found the skin yet. We've called in the dog unit.'

'That's a good idea. I consider it entirely possible they are wearing the skin. As they are following the Aztec method so closely.'

They both fell silent once more. De Savary gazed across the rolling parkland, the lofty trees bending over the river; the beautiful scene of tranquil, bucolic Englishness. It was hard to reconcile with that . . . that thing suspended on a wooden frame, just yards away. The pink and inverted cadaver; with its hideous grin of pain.

The detective stood up. 'So what were they looking for? The gang. I've been searching. There's no connection with the Hellfire Club at all.'

'No,' said De Savary. 'But there is a curious connection between this school and the Middle East.'

'And that is what?'

De Savary smiled, very hesitantly.

'If I recall from what I read on the train, the tuck shop should be down here.' He strode around the front of the building, Forrester following. At the far end of the south wing there was a curious gabled building adjoining the main elevation. It looked like a chapel. De Savary stopped.

Forrester gazed at the red-and-black design of the impressive doors: a motif of winged metal lions. 'What's that?'

'This is the Nineveh Porch. It has a profound association with Iraq and Sumeria. Shall we see if our guys were down this end?'

Forrester nodded.

De Savary prodded the metal door and it swung open easily. Inside, apart from some peculiar stained glass windows, it looked like a normal tuck shop for a rich school. There was a Pepsi machine. A till. And boxes of snacks and crisps chaotically scattered on the floor. But the boxes were scattered too randomly. The unlit room had been ransacked. On closer examination, the wooden panelling along one wall had been ripped away; a window was broken. Someone had been in here, vigorously searching for something. Whether they had taken anything was a different matter. De Savary guessed they hadn't. The scattering of items in the tuck shop looked angry: frustrated and thwarted.

They stepped out into the peaceful sunshine and walked along the pathway. Pollen drifted languidly on the mild sunny air as De Savary told the tale of the Nineveh Porch. 'The porch was ordered by Lady Charlotte Guest and her husband Sir John around 1850. It was built after a design by the architect Charles Barry, better known as the creator of—'

'The Houses of Parliament,' said Forrester. And he smiled shyly. 'Architecture is a private hobby.'

'Quite so! The Houses of Parliament. Anyway the Nineveh Porch was a private loggia, built expressly for the purpose of housing some famous Assyrian reliefs gathered from Victorian explorations of Mesopotamia. Hence the rather unusual doors, with the Assyrian lions.'

'Right.'

'These reliefs, housed in the porch, had been excavated by Austen Henry Layard, a cousin of Lady Charlotte Guest. The reliefs were significant and substantial. Each weighed several tons. They had originally adorned important thresholds in Nimrud.'

'And Layard and Barry put them here?'

'Yes. And together with a number of other reliefs they remained here, in the Nineveh Porch, until shortly after the First World War. Then the whole collection was offered for sale.'

'So there's nothing left?'

'Hold on! The antiquities in the porch were replaced by humble casts. In 1923 Canford Hall itself was sold by the Guest family and it became a boys' school. At that point, the Nineveh Porch, now robbed of its ancient treasures, was turned into a tuck shop. Selling sandwiches and Snickers bars.'

'So our guys must have known this? That nothing was left. Why come here again?'

'There is a slightly odd denouement to the story. In 1992 two academics came here. Both experts in Assyriology. They were on their way to a conference in Bournemouth but they had some time, so they decided to make a quick pilgrimage to this place so important in their discipline. They didn't expect to find anything. But they looked at the stained glass windows, with their pictures of Sumeria, and they admired the vaguely Assyrian detailing of the architecture. And then they looked behind the Pepsi machine – and they found an original relief.'

'You're joking.'

'No. Only the casts were supposed to be left. But lo and behold! One more piece remained. It was recognized as the real thing, although covered by layers of white vinyl emulsion. The relief was taken down and sent to London, where it was offered for sale at auction by Christie's. It was bought by a Japanese dealer, apparently acting on behalf of a religious sect. The price was, I think, around eight million pounds. The highest amount ever paid for an antiquity anywhere in the world. *Et voilà.*'

They had reached the riverbank. The rushing River Stour was before them; sunlight dappled across the waters, spangled by the arch of leaves above.

'I still don't get it,' said Forrester. He picked up a stick and threw it into the river. 'What links this with the Hellfire stuff?'

'You remember what I told you on the phone the other day?'

'About the Yezidi and the Black Book? How that might be what they are seeking?'

'Precisely. Austen Henry Layard, you see, was one of the first ever westerners to meet the Yezidi, in 1847. He was excavating in northern Iraq, in Ur and Nineveh. The early years of modern archaeology. Then he heard about this strange sect that lived near Mosul, around Dahuk. Layard made contact with the Yezidi. Then he was invited to their sacred capital Lalesh. In the mountains. It's a dangerous place, hostile to this day.'

'What did he do there?'

'Now that's a question. We know he was invited to witness some of their most secret ceremonies. A privilege, as far as I know, afforded to no one else before or since.'

'Did they give him the Black Book?'

De Savary smiled. 'Detective! First rate work. Yes, that's one theory. Scholars have speculated that Layard must have had a very close relationship with the Yezidi, to be treated the way he was. Some think he may have taken the Black Book with him. Thus giving rise to their legends that it came to England.'

'So, if he had brought it back he might have brought it here, to the building designed for the best antiquities, the ones he kept to himself? Right?'

'*Vraiment!*'

Forrester frowned. 'But I thought we established that Jerusalem Whaley already had the Black Book. How does Layard get involved?'

De Savary shrugged. 'Who knows? Maybe Jerusalem Whaley thought he had the Book, but didn't. Maybe he gave the Book back to the Yezidi and Layard went to get it again, a century later. Shuttling back and forth! My personal hunch, for what it is worth, is that Jerusalem Whaley had the Book all along, and Layard is just a diversion.'

'But the main thing is we can assume that this is what the gang are after. Otherwise they wouldn't have come here. So it's not necessarily anything to do with the Hellfire Club in itself. The gang are actually after the Black Book of the Yezidi. That's their real prize.'

'Yes.'

Forrester whistled, almost cheerfully. He slapped De Savary on the back. 'Thanks for coming, Hugo.'

De Savary smiled, though he felt guilty for doing so. The smell of the man's exposed flesh had not quite left his nostrils.

A loud shout ripped through the silent wood.

'Angus! *Angus!*'

Something was up. Another shout echoed across the parkland. The shout was coming nearer.

De Savary and Forrester scrambled up the rise. A constable was running across the lawns, chasing something. Shouting out the name *Angus*.

'That's the dog handler,' said Forrester. 'Lost his dog. Hey, Johnson! Where's the dog?'

'Sir! Sir!' The constable kept running. 'Just gone past you, sir. Over there!'

De Savary swivelled and saw a large dog galloping towards the school buildings. It was having trouble running. Because it was dragging something. Something long, and slippery, and sullen grey. What was that? It looked very strange. For a moment the professor got the surreal and sickening idea that the dog was dragging a kind of ghost. He ran across to it. The dog turned, guarding its prize. It growled as De Savary approached.

The professor shuddered as he looked down. The dog was drooling over a long and stinking sheath, frayed into ribbons and strips.

It was a complete human skin.

33

Rob had been in Dahuk for ten days. The taxi driver from Habur had refused to go any further.

At first Rob had been reasonably content with this. Dahuk was a likeable and animated Kurdish city: poorer than Sanliurfa, but without the sense of brooding Turkish oversight. Dahuk was also enticing because the Yezidi were a visible presence. There was even a Yezidi cultural centre – a big old Ottoman house on the outskirts of town, ramshackle and noisy. Rob spent the first few days hanging around the centre. It was full of beautiful dark-haired girls with shy smiles and long embroidered dresses and laughing lads with Barcelona football shirts.

On the wall inside the centre's hall was a striking picture of the peacock angel, Melek Taus. When he first saw it, Rob had stared at it for a good ten minutes. It was a strangely serene image, the demon-god, the fallen angel, with his splendid tail of emerald and aquamarine. The tail of a thousand eyes.

The Yezidi at the centre were wary but not that unfriendly. The moustachioed Yezidi men gave him tea and pistachios. A couple of them spoke faltering English, more than a few spoke German. They told him this was because there was a strong Yezidi presence in Germany. 'We have been destroyed everywhere else, we have no future here, now only you Christians can help us . . .'

What the Yezidi would not do was discuss the finer points of their faith. As soon as Rob started asking about the Black Book, or Sanliurfa, or the sanjak, or the worship of Melek Taus, the expressions turned to scowls, or disdain, or a defensive incomprehension. And then the moustached men got shirty, and stopped handing over saucers of pistachios.

The other sticking point was Lalesh itself. It turned out – and Rob was annoyed at himself for his lack of prior information, for rushing into this so impetuously – that no one actually lived in Lalesh. It was a sacred city in the truest sense of the phrase: a ghost town for angels, a city for exclusively sacred things: holy spirits, ancient texts, venerable shrines. The villages around Lalesh were busy and thronging, but the Yezidi only went into Lalesh itself to pray or worship, or for festivals, which would make any outsider conspicuous.

Moreover, just getting to Lalesh for a non-Yezidi was a difficult and even dangerous task, it seemed. Certainly no one wanted to take Rob. Not even after a hundred-dollar bribe. Rob tried more than once. The taxi drivers just looked at his money mistrustfully, and said a curt '*La!*'

By the tenth night Rob felt like giving up. He was lying on his bed in his hotel room. The city was noisy and fervid outside. He went to his open window and gazed across the concrete rooftops and the dark winding alleys. The hot Iraqi sun was going down over the grey-gold Zagros Mountains. Old women in pink headscarves were hanging out washing next to enormous satellite dishes. Rob could see plenty of church spires amongst the minarets. Churches of the Gnostics maybe. Or the Mandeans. Or the Assyrian Christians. The Chaldeans. There were so many ancient sects here.

Closing the window to block out the evening call to prayer, Rob returned to his bed and picked up his mobile. He found a good Kurdish network and called England. After a few long beeps Sally came on the line. Rob expected his ex-wife to be her usual curt but polite self. But Sally was oddly warm and enthusiastic: then she explained why. She told Rob she had met his 'new girlfriend' and actually liked her, a lot. Sally told Rob she approved of Christine, and that he must have finally returned to his senses if he'd started dating real women, not those bimbos he normally went for.

Rob laughed and said he'd never regarded Sally as a bimbo; there was a pause, and then Sally laughed, too. It was the first laughter they had exchanged since the divorce. They chatted some more, as they had not chatted in quite a while. And then Rob's ex-wife handed the phone to their daughter. Rob felt piercingly sad when he heard his daughter's voice. Lizzie told her dad that she had been to the zoo to see 'nanimals'. She said she could raise her arms right above her head. Rob listened with a mixture of joy and grief and he said he loved her and Lizzie demanded daddy come home. Then he asked her if she had met the French lady Christine. Lizzie said yes and she really liked her and mummy liked her too. Rob said that was great, and then he blew a kiss to his giggling daughter. He rang off. It felt slightly weird, his new girlfriend and his ex-wife making friends. But it was better than mutual animosity. And it meant there were more people looking after his daughter when he wasn't there.

But then it occurred to him that maybe it was time he was 'there': maybe it was time he went back home. Maybe he should just quit. The story hadn't panned out as he'd hoped. He hadn't even made it to Lalesh, but it didn't look like there was any point anyway. The Yezidi were too opaque. He couldn't speak enough Arabic or Kurdish to get beyond their ancient obscurantism. How could he hope to unlock the secrets of a six thousand year old faith by just pottering around this ancient city saying 'Salaam'? He was stymied; his hopes were dwindling by the hour. Sometimes that happened. Sometimes you didn't get the story.

Grabbing his door key, Rob left his hotel room. He was hot and bothered and he needed a beer. And there was a nice bar on the corner of his street. He slumped into his usual plastic seat outside the Suleiman Café. Rob's temporary friend, Rawaz the café owner, brought him some chilled Turkish beer, and a saucer of green olives. The life of the

Dahuk streets passed on by. Rob rested his forehead in his hands and thought again about the article. Looking back on his determined and impulsive excitement at Isobel's house, he wondered what he had really wanted. Some mysterious priest to explain everything, perhaps in a secret temple, with savage carvings on the wall. And flickering flames from the oil lamps. And of course a couple of handy devil worshippers, happy to be photographed. But instead of realizing his naive journalistic dream Rob was drinking Efes beer and listening to gaudy Kurdish pop from the music store next door. He might as well have been in Sanliurfa. Or London.

'Hello?'

Rob looked up. A young man was standing, slightly hesitantly, by his table. He wore clean jeans and a well-pressed shirt. He had a round face. He looked scholarly. Geeky even. Yet prosperous and kind. Rob asked the man to sit down. His name was Karwan.

Karwan smiled. 'I am a Yezidi.'

'OK . . .'

'Today I go to the Yezidi cultural centre and some women told me about you. An American journalist. Wanting to know about Melek Taus?'

Rob nodded: mildly embarrassed.

Karwan went on. 'They said you were staying here. But they say you might go soon, because you were not happy.'

'I'm not unhappy. I'm just . . . frustrated.'

'Why?'

'Because I am writing an article. About the Yezidi faith. You know, what you guys really believe. It's for a British newspaper. But no one will tell me, so it's a little frustrating.'

'You must understand why this is.' Karwan leaned forward with an earnest expression on his face. 'For many thousands of years, mister, we have been killed and attacked for what we believe. What people say we believe. The Muslims kill us, the Hindus, the Tartars. Everyone says we worship Shaitan, the devil. They kill us and drive us away. Even

Saddam killed us, even our fellow Kurds they kill us, Sunni and Shiite, they all kill us. Everyone.'

'But that's why I want to write my article. Tell the real story. What the Yezidi really believe.'

Karwan frowned, as if he was deciding something. He was silent for more than a minute. And then he said, 'Yes, OK. This is how I see it. You Americans, the great eagle, you helped the Kurds, and you have protected the Yezidi people. I see American soldiers, they are good. They really try to help us. So . . . now I will help you. Because you are American.'

'You will?'

'Yes.'

'Yes and I will help you because I studied one year in America at Texas University. This is why my English is not so bad. Americans they were good to me.'

'You were at UT?'

'Yes, you know? The Longhorns. In Austin.'

'Great music in Austin.'

'Yes. A nice place. Except,' Karwan nibbled an olive, 'except women in Texas have the most enormous asses. This is problem for me.'

Rob laughed. 'What did you study, at UT?'

'Religious anthropology. So, you understand, I can tell you everything you need to know. And then you can go away and tell everyone we are not . . . Satanists. Shall we start?'

Rob reached for his notebook; he ordered two more beers. And for an hour he plied Karwan with questions. Most of the information he already knew, from Isobel, and from his own research. The origins of Yezidism and the Cult of Angels. Rob was slightly disappointed. But then Karwan said something which made him sit up, very straight.

'The tale of the Yezidis' origin comes from the Black Book. Of course the Black Book has gone now but the story is handed on. It tells us we have a distinct . . . bloodline, it shows how we are different from all other races.'

'How?'

'Maybe it is best expressed in a myth, in Yezidi myth. In one of our creation legends there were seventy-two Adams, each Adam more perfect than the one before. Then the seventy-second Adam married Eve. And Adam and Eve deposited their seed in two jars.'

Rob interrupted, his pen poised over his notebook. 'Two jars?'

Karwan nodded. 'These jars were sealed for nine months. When the jars were opened, the jar containing Eve's seed was full of insects and terrible things, snakes and scorpions. But when Adam's jar was opened, they found a lovely boy child.' Karwan smiled. 'The boy was called Shahid ibn Jayar – "the Son of the Jar". And this name is also used for the Yezidi. You see: we are the Sons of the Jar. These children of Adam became the ancestors of the Yezidis. Adam is our grandfather. Whereas all other nations are descended through Eve.'

Rob finished scribbling his notes. A white UN Chevrolet was trundling across the junction opposite the café.

Karwan said, quite abruptly, 'OK. That is that! Now I must go. But, mister, the Yezidi at the centre, they also tell me you want to go to Lalesh, as well? Yes?'

'Yes. I do! But everyone says it's dangerous. They just won't take me. Can it possibly be arranged?'

Karwan curved a smile. He was nibbling discreetly on another olive; he cupped his hand, and deposited the olive stone on the edge of the ashtray. 'I can take you there. We are having a festival. It is not so dangerous.'

'When?'

'Tomorrow. Five a.m. I will meet you here. And then I will bring you back. And then you can go and write about us, in that famous newspaper *The Times*, in England.'

'That's great. That's fantastic – *shukran!*'

'Good.' The young man leaned and shook Rob's hand. 'Tomorrow we meet. Five a.m. So we must sleep now. Goodbye.' And with that he stood up and disappeared along the sultry road.

Rob guzzled the last of his beer. He was happy. He was almost very happy. He was going to get the story. The first man to visit the sacred capital of the Yezidi! Our man with the Cultists of Iraq. He almost ran back to the hotel. Then he phoned Christine and excitedly told her the news; her voice sounded worried and pleased at the same time. Rob lay back on the bed with a smile, as they talked: he was going home soon, and he would see his daughter, and his girlfriend – with the job safely done.

The next morning Rob found Karwan waiting, as promised, by the café tables. Parked by the shuttered café was an old Ford pickup truck: loaded with flat bread, and fruit in plastic sacks.

'Fruit for the festival,' said Karwan. 'Come. Is not very much room.'

There were three of them squeezed in the cabin of the truck. Karwan, Rob, and a whiskery old guy. The driver was Karwan's uncle, it seemed. Rob shook hands with Karwan's uncle, and Karwan said, 'He has only crashed three times this year. So we should be OK.'

The truck rattled out of Dahuk up into the mountains. It was a long and spine-jarring journey, but Rob didn't care. He was surely close to his story.

The road led up into pine forests and oak woods. As they ascended, the grey morning air began to clear. The sun was coming up bright and warm. Then the road dipped into a vivid green valley. Poor but pretty stone houses stood over rushing streams. Dirty children with dazzling smiles rushed down to the truck and waved. Rob waved back and thought about his daughter.

The road went on, and on. It snaked around a great mountain. Karwan told Rob the mountain was one of the Seven Pillars of Satan. Rob nodded. The road negotiated rushing rivers, on rickety wooden bridges. And then at last they stopped.

Karwan nudged him. 'Lalesh!'

He'd made it. The first thing he saw was a strange conical building, its roof oddly fluted. There were more of these conical buildings, placed around a central square. This central plaza of Lalesh was alive with people: parading and chanting and singing. Old men were walking in single file, playing long wooden flutes. Rob got out of the truck, along with Karwan, and watched.

A black-cloaked figure emerged from a grimy building. He walked over to an array of stone pots from which small fires were billowing. More men, in white robes, processed behind.

'These are the sacred fires,' said Karwan, gesturing at the yellow flames dancing in the stone pots. 'The men must circle the sacred fires seven times.'

Now the crowd pressed forward, calling out a name. 'Melek Taus, Melek Taus!'

Karwan nodded. 'They are praising the peacock angel, of course.'

The ceremony continued. It was picturesque, and strange, and oddly touching. Rob watched the bystanders and the onlookers: after the initial flurry of ceremonial, many ordinary Yezidi had moved on to nearby patches of grass and the hillsides overlooking the conical towers of Lalesh: they were laying out picnics of tomatoes, cheese, flatbread and plums. The sun was high in the sky. It was a warm mountain day.

'Every Yezidi,' Karwan told Rob, 'must, at some point in life, come here to Lalesh. To make a pilgrimage to the tomb of Sheikh Mussafir. He established the ceremonies of the Yezidis.'

Rob edged closer to peer through the dingy doorway of a temple. Inside it was dark: but Rob could just discern pilgrims wrapping coloured cloths around wooden pillars. Others were laying bread on low shelves. On one wall Rob saw writing that was distinctly cuneiform: it had to be cuneiform: the very oldest, most primitive alphabet in the world. Dating back to Sumerian times.

Cuneiform! As he ducked out of the temple again, Rob felt a thrill of privilege just to be here. It was a miraculous survival: the city, the faith, the people, the liturgy and ritual. And it was an admirable survival, too. The whole atmosphere of Lalesh, the festival, was lyrical, poetic, and preciously pastoral. The only menacing aspects were the lurid and sneering images of Melek Taus, the ubiquitous devil-god, who was pictured on walls and doors, even on posters. Yet the people themselves seemed friendly, happy to be out in the sun, happy to be practising their peculiar religion.

Rob wanted to talk to some Yezidi. He persuaded Karwan to interpret: on one patch of grass, they found a jocular, middle-aged woman pouring tea for her children.

Rob leaned in and said, 'Tell me about the Black Book?

The woman smiled, jabbing a finger at Rob quite vigorously.

Karwan interpreted her words. 'She says that the Black Book is the Bible of the Yezidi, and it is written in gold. She says you Christians have it! You English. She says you took our holy book. And that is why the westerners have science and education. Because you have the book, that came from the sky.'

The woman smiled warmly at Rob. And then she bit into a fat tomato, spilling vivid red seeds down her shirt, making her husband laugh very loudly.

The ceremony in the square was nearly over. Young girls and boys in white were in the central space, finishing their spiralling dances around the sacred flames. Rob regarded them. He took some discreet photos with his camera-phone. He scribbled some notes. And then, when he looked up, he noticed something else. Quite unremarked by the bystanders all the elite old men were ducking, one by one, into a low building at the far end of the square. Their action seemed somehow furtive, clandestine. Or at least significant. There was a guard at the door of this low building, though there were no guards on any of the other doors. Why was that? And the door they were using was itself marked out from the others. It had an odd black snake set beside it in stone. A long snake symbol right by the door.

Rob felt the tingle. This was it. Rob had to find out what was going on. He had to get in that mysterious door. But could he get away with it? He glanced around. Karwan was now lying back on the grass, dozing. The truck driver was nowhere. Probably asleep in his cabin. It had been a long day.

This was Rob's chance. Right now. Sloping down the hill, he crossed the square briskly. One of the chanting boys had dropped his white headdress by the well beneath the spring. Rob checked left and right, and snatched the garment up and put it over his head. Again he checked. No one was looking. He slunk towards the low building. The guard was on the door: he was about to close the door. Rob had just one chance. He muffled and concealed his lower face with the white cloth, then darted over the threshold into the temple.

The yawning guard stared vaguely at Rob. For a moment he seemed puzzled. Then he shrugged and shut the door behind them. Rob was inside the temple.

It was very dark. The acrid smoke of the oil lamps fugged the air. The Yezidi elders were lined up in rows, chanting, murmuring and singing very quietly. Reciting prayers. Others were on their knees, kowtowing and bending: touching the floor with their foreheads. A blaze of light filled the far end of the temple. Rob squinted to see through the smoke. A door had briefly opened. A white-robed girl was bringing an object covered in a rough blanket. The chanting grew a little louder. The girl set the object down on an altar. Above the altar the gleaming image of the peacock angel stared down at them all, serene and superior, disdainful and cruel.

Rob moved forward to get as close as he could without drawing attention to himself, desperate to see what was hidden underneath the blanket. He edged closer and closer. The praying and chanting grew louder, yet darker. Lower in tone. A hypnotic mantra. The lampsmoke was so thick it was making Rob's eyes itch and weep. He rubbed at his face and strained to see.

And then the girl whipped away the blanket, and the chanting stopped.

Sitting on the altar was a skull. But it was like no skull Rob had seen. It was human, yet not human. It had curved slanted eye sockets. High cheekbones. It looked like the skull of a monstrous bird, or a bizarre snake. Yet still it was human.

Then Rob felt a hard knife blade: pressed cold against his throat.

34

Everyone was shouting and jostling. The knife bit at Rob's throat, pressing hard against his windpipe. Someone thrust a hood over his head: Rob blinked in the darkness.

Doors slammed and opened and he felt himself being jostled into another room: he sensed it because the noises were different, the echoes smaller. He was definitely in a more confined space. But the voices were still angry and shouting, babbling fiercely in Kurdish. Threatening and yelling.

A boot kicked him in the back of the knees. Rob crumpled to the floor. Images drove through his mind: victims on internet videos. Orange bodysuits. *Allahu Akhbar.* The sound of a knife slicing at a windpipe and the creamy froth of blood. *Allahu Akhbar.*

No. Rob struggled. He writhed this way and that but there were hands all over him, holding him down. The hood was made of old sacking; it smelled of stale breath. Rob could just perceive light through the weft of the cloth wrapped over his face. He could make out the shapes of shouting men.

A second door opened somewhere. The voices got louder and Rob could hear a woman calling a question and some men yelling back at her. It was all confusion. Rob tried to breathe slowly: to calm himself.

He was pushed on his side now: lying down: and he could see Yezidi robes, dimly, through the cloth. Robes and sandals and men.

They were binding his wrists behind him. Rough twine was biting into his flesh. He winced at the pain. Then he heard a man growling at him – was that Arabic? Did he recognize these words? He twisted his body and strained his eyes to see through the rough cloth of the hood, and he gulped: what was that flash: was that the knife again? The big knife they had put to his throat?

The fear was searing. He thought of his daughter. Her lovely laugh. Her blonde hair on a sunny day: blonde as sunshine itself. Her blue eyes uplifted. *Daddy. Nanimals. Daddy.* And now he was probably going to die. He would never see her again. He would ruin her life by not seeing her again. He would be the father she never had.

The grief welled in him. He nearly wept. The cloth was hot and his heart was pounding, and he had to stop panicking. Because he wasn't dead. They hadn't done anything more than manhandle him. And scare him.

But then as soon as Rob's hopes arose he thought of Franz Breitner. They'd killed *him*; that hadn't been a problem for the Yezidi workers at Gobekli. They had pushed him onto the spike, skewering him like a frog in a laboratory. Just like that. He remembered the gush of blood from Franz's chest wound. Blood squirting onto the yellow Gobekli dust. And then he remembered the trembling goat being slaughtered in the Sanliurfa streets.

Rob screamed. His only hope was Karwan. His friend. His Yezidi friend. Maybe he would hear. His shouts echoed around the room. Then the Kurdish voices came back, cursing him. He was jostled and kicked. A hand gripped his neck, almost throttling him; he felt another hand tight on his arm. But Rob angrily thrashed out with his boots: he was angry now. He bit the hood. If they were going to kill him, he was going to fight, he was going to try, he was going to make it hard for them—

And then the hood was whipped off.

Rob gasped, blinking in the light. A face was staring down at him. It was Karwan.

But this wasn't the Karwan of before: the friendly, round-faced guy. This was Karwan unsmiling, grim-faced, angry; and yet commanding.

Karwan was ordering the older men around him: snapping at them, in Kurdish. Telling them what to do. And the older men in robes were evidently obeying him: they were practically kowtowing to him. One of the older men rubbed a wet cloth over Rob's face. The smell of the dampness was vile. But the coolness was also refreshing. Another man was helping Rob to sit up straight; they had propped Rob against the rear wall.

Karwan barked another order. He seemed to be telling the robed men to go: they were obediently filing out of the room. One by one they left, and the door slammed shut, leaving Karwan and Rob alone in the little room. Rob looked around. It was a dingy space with bare painted walls and two high, slitted windows letting in a poor amount of light. It was some kind of store room maybe; an antechamber for the temple.

The cords around his wrist were still painful. They'd taken off the hood but he was still bound. Rob urgently rubbed his wrists together as best he could to restore some circulation. Then he gazed at Karwan. The young Yezidi man was squatting on a faded but richly embroidered rug. Staring back at Rob. He sighed. 'I tried to help you, Mr Luttrell. We thought if we let you come here you would be satisfied. But you had to go looking for more. Always. Always you western people want more.'

Rob was nonplussed: what was he talking about? Karwan was rubbing his eyes with finger and thumb. The Yezidi man seemed tired. Through the slitted windows Rob could hear the faint noises of Lalesh: children laughing and giggling, and the gurgle of the fountain.

Karwan sat forward. 'What is it with you people? Why do you want to know everything? Breitner was the same. The German. Just the same.' Rob's eyes widened. Karwan nodded. 'Yes. Breitner. At Gobekli Tepe . . .'

The young Yezidi man moodily traced the pattern of the rug in front of him. His forefinger followed the scarlet maze of the embroidery. He seemed to be meditating: deciding something important. Rob waited. His throat was very dry; his wrists were throbbing from the ropes. Then he asked, 'Can I have a drink, Karwan?'

The Yezidi man reached over, to grab a small plastic bottle of mineral water. Then he put the bottle to Rob's mouth and Rob drank, shuddering and gasping and gulping. The bottle was set on the concrete floor between them, and Karwan sighed for a second time.

'I am going to tell you the truth. There is no point in hiding it any more. Maybe the truth can help the Yezidi. Because the lies and deceptions, they are hurting us. I am the son of a Yezidi sheikh. A chief. But I am also someone who has studied our faith from the outside. So I am in a special position, Mr Luttrell. Maybe that allows me a certain . . . discretion.' His eyes avoided Rob's. A guilt reflex? He went on: 'What I am about to tell you has never been revealed to a non-Yezidi, not for thousands of years. Maybe not ever.'

Rob listened intently. Karwan's voice was level, almost monotonous. As if this was a prepared monologue, or something he had been thinking about for many years: a rehearsed speech.

'The Yezidi believe that Gobekli Tepe is the site of the Garden of Eden. I think maybe you know this. And I think our beliefs have . . . informed other religions.' He shrugged and exhaled profoundly. 'As I told you, we believe we are direct descendants of Adam. We are the Sons of the Jar. Gobekli Tepe is, therefore, the home of our ancestors. Every Yezidi in the priestly caste, the upper class, like myself, is told that we must protect Gobekli Tepe. Protect and defend the temple of our ancestors. For the same reason, we are taught by our fathers, and our fathers' fathers, that we must keep the secrets of Gobekli safe. Anything taken from there we must conceal or destroy. Like those . . . remains . . . in the Sanliurfa Museum. This is our task, as Yezidi. Because our forefathers buried Gobekli Tepe under all that earth . . . for a reason.' Karwan took up the bottle and sipped some water; he gazed directly at

Rob, his dark brown Kurdish eyes burning in the gloom of the little storeroom. 'Of course I see your question, Mr Luttrell. Why? Why did my Yezidi ancestors bury Gobekli Tepe? Why must we protect it? What happened there?' Karwan smiled, but the smile was pained, even agonized. 'That is something we are not taught. No one tells us. We do not have a written religion. Everything is handed down orally, from mouth to mouth, from ear to ear, from father to son. When I was very young I would ask my father, why do we have these traditions? He would say, because they are traditions, that is all.'

Rob made to speak but Karwan raised an impatient hand to silence him. 'None of this mattered, of course. Not for many centuries. No one threatened Gobekli Tepe. No one even knew it was there, apart from the Yezidi. It remained buried in its ancient earth. But then the German came along, the archaeologists with their shovels and their diggers and their machines, testing and digging, digging and exposing. For the Yezidi, uncovering Gobekli is a terrible thing. Like exposing a terrible wound. It pains us. What our ancestors buried has to be kept buried, what was exposed to the air has to be concealed and protected. So we, the Yezidi, we had ourselves hired by him, we became his workmen so we could delay the digging, stop the endless digging. But still, he carried on. Carried on exposing the wound—'

'So you killed Franz and then you—'

Karwan growled, 'No! We are not devils. We are not killers. We tried to frighten him. To scare him off, to scare you all away. But he must have fallen. That is all.'

'And . . . the Pulsa Dinura?'

'Yes. Yes of course. And the troubles at the temple. We tried to . . . what is the word . . . we tried to hamper the dig, to stop it. But the German was so determined. He kept on digging. Digging up the Garden of Eden, the garden of jars. He even dug it up at night. So there was an argument. And he fell. It was an accident I think.'

Rob made to protest. Karwan shrugged. 'You can believe this, or you can choose not to believe it. As you wish. I am tired of lies.'

'So what is the skull?'

Karwan exhaled, slowly. 'I do not know. When I went to Texas, I studied my own religion. I saw the . . . structure of its myths. From a different perspective. And I do not know. I do not know who Melek Taus is and I don't know what the skull is. All I know is that we must worship the skull and the peacock. And that we must never reveal these secrets. And that we must never ever breed with non-Yezidi, we must never marry outside the faith. Because you – the non-Yezidi – are polluted.'

'Is it an animal? The skull?'

'I do not know! Believe me. I think . . .' Karwan was struggling with the words. 'I think something happened at Gobekli Tepe. To our temple in Eden. Something terrible, ten thousand years ago. Otherwise why did we bury it? Why bury that beautiful place unless it was a place of shame or of suffering? There had to be a reason. To bury it.'

'Why are you telling me this now? Why now? Why me?'

'Because you kept on coming. You would not give up. So now I am telling you everything. You found the jars. With those terrible remains. What is that for? Why were those babies put there? It scares me. There is too much I do not know. All we have is myth and traditions. We do not have a book to tell us. Not any more.'

Outside, voices were calling again. It sounded like farewells. The voices were joined by car engines starting up. It seemed as if people were leaving Lalesh. Rob wanted to write down Karwan's words: he felt a physical hunger to get this down; but the cords were still tight around his wrist. All he could do was ask, 'So where does the Black Book fit in?'

Karwan shook his head. 'Ah yes. The Black Book. What is that? I am not so sure it is a book. I think it was some proof, some key, something that explained the great mystery. But it has gone. It was taken from us. And now we are left with . . . with our fairy tales. And our peacock angel. Enough. I have told you things that I should never tell anyone. But I had no choice. The world despises the Yezidi. We are abused and persecuted. Called devil-worshippers. How can it get any worse? Maybe if the world knows more of the truth, they will treat us better.' He took another deliberate sip of mineral water. 'We are keepers of a secret, Mr Luttrell, a terrible secret we do not understand. Yet we must cleave to our silence. And protect the buried past. It is our burden. Through the ages. We are the Sons of the Jar.'

'And now—'

'And now I am going to take you back to Turkey. We are going to drive you back to the border and you can fly home and then you can tell everyone about us. Tell them we are not Satanists. Tell them of our sadness. Tell them what you like. But do not lie.'

The Yezidi man stood and shouted through the window. The door swung open and more men came in. Rob was jostled again, but this time it was with a purpose and a calm determination. He was shunted outside through the temple. He glanced at the altar as he was pushed along: the skull was gone. Then he was out in the sun. Kids were pointing at him. Rob saw women staring, hands over their mouths. He was being led to the Ford pickup truck.

The driver was ready. Rob's bag was on the passenger seat, waiting. Rob was still tied by the wrists. Two men helped him up into the cabin. He stared out of the window as another man got into the cab: a dark, bearded man, younger than Karwan. Strong and muscular, and silent. He was going to sit between Rob and the truck door; Rob was in the middle seat.

The Ford pulled out, wheels spinning in the dust. Rob's last glimpse of Lalesh was of Karwan, standing amongst the staring children, beside one of the conical towers. His expression was enormously sad.

Then Lalesh disappeared behind a slope as the truck tore down the hillside, heading for the Turkish border.

35

As soon as Rob was shoved across the Turkish border at Habur he phoned Christine, then jumped in a taxi for the nearest city. Mardin. Seven arduous hours later he booked into a hotel room, phoned Christine again, phoned his daughter; then he fell asleep with the phone in his hand, he was so tired.

The next morning he sat down at his laptop and wrote – immediately, passionately, and in one session – his story.

Kidnapped by the Cults of Kurdistan.

He felt that writing the piece quickly and unthinkingly was the only way. There were so many disparate elements that, if he sat down and cogitated, if he tried to form a coherent narrative, there was a risk he would get lost in the many details and the endless byways. Also, the article might seem contrived if he toiled over it: the story was so bizarre it had to sound simple and heartfelt for it to work. Very immediate. Very honest. As if he was telling someone a long and astonishing anecdote over a coffee. So Rob just banged it down in one go. Gobekli Tepe and the jars in the museum, the Yezidi and the Cult of Angels and the worship of Melek Taus. The ceremonies in Lalesh and the skull on the altar and the mystery of the Black Book. All of it, the whole story, spiced with violence and murder. And it now had a good ending: it concluded with him lying on his side, a hood over his head, in a filthy little room in the mountains of Kurdistan: thinking he was going to die.

The article took five hours to write. Five hours in which he barely looked up from his laptop, he was so focused. In the zone.

After six minutes of spellchecking, Rob copied the piece on to a data stick, walked out of the hotel and went straight to an internet café. Then he plugged in the data stick and emailed the piece to Steve, in London, who was impatiently awaiting his copy.

He sat nervously in the quiet internet café by the computer, hoping that Steve would phone back soon with his response. The hot Mardin sun was bright in the streets outside, but in here it was almost sepulchral. Only one other guy was in the internet café, drinking an obscure Turkish soda, playing some computer game. The boy had big fat headphones on. He was eviscerating an onscreen monster with a virtual AK47. The monster had purple claws and sad eyes. Its intestines spilled out, vivid and green.

Rob returned to his own screen. He checked the weather in Spain for no reason. He Googled his own name. He Googled Christine's name. He discovered that she was the author of 'Neanderthal Cannibalism in Ice Age Euskera' in a recent issue of *American Archaeology.* He also found a nice picture of her receiving an obscure award in Berlin.

Rob stared at the picture. He missed Christine. Not as much as he missed his daughter, but he missed her. The decorous conversation; her perfume; her graciousness. The way she smiled when they had sex, with her eyes shut, as if she was dreaming of something very sweet that had happened very long ago.

His mobile rang.

'Robbie!'

'Steve . . .' His heart was thumping. He hated this bit. 'Well?'

'Well,' said Steve. 'I don't know what to say . . .'

Rob's spirits sagged. 'You don't like it?'

Pause. 'Nah, you arse. I fucking love it!'

Rob's spirits rocketed.

Steve was laughing. 'Jesus, Rob I only sent you to do a fucking history piece. Thought it might be nice for you. Bit of a break. But you witness a murder. You get assaulted by Satanists. You discover a Stone Age toddler in a pickle jar. You find some more devil-worshippers. You hear evil Kurdish death prayers. You . . . you . . . you . . .' Steve was running out of breath. 'Then you go to Iraq and you meet some mystery bloke who takes you to a sacred capital where his people worship a fucking pigeon and you find them all bowing down to some alien skull at which point the Yezzers run in and try to stab you before telling you they are all directly descended from Adam and Eve.'

Rob was silent. Then he burst out laughing. His laughter was very loud – so loud that the monster-slaughtering kid on the computer across the room looked up and tapped his headphones to see if they were working properly. 'So you think the story is OK? I've tried to be fair to the Yezidi . . . Maybe too fair, but I just—'

Steve interrupted:

'It's more than OK! I love it. And so does the boss. We're gonna run it tomorrow in the centre, dps, and we'll have a teaser on the front.'

'Tomorrow?'

'Yup. Straight into print. We've got your pics too. You've done a grand job.'

'That's great. That's . . .'

'Bloody great, yeah I know. Now when are you heading back?'

'I'm not sure . . . I mean, I'm trying to get the first flight I can, but they're booked solid. And I don't fancy a twenty-hour bus ride to Ankara. Certainly I'll be in London by the weekend.'

'Good man. Come in to the office and I'll buy you lunch. Might even go to a proper restaurant. With pizzas.'

Rob chuckled. He said his goodbyes to his boss. Then he paid the internet café owner and walked out into Mardin.

It was a nice city, Mardin. From what little Rob had seen of it, the city seemed poor but very historic and atmospheric. It was said to date from the Flood: it had Roman streets, and Byzantine remains, and

Syriac goldsmiths. It had weird lanes that ran under the houses. But Rob didn't care any more. He'd had enough historic and Oriental fantasies. He wanted to get home now: to cool, modern, rainy, beautiful, hi-tech European London. To hug his daughter and kiss Christine.

Standing by the doorway to a bakery, he called Christine. He'd already rung her twice today – but he just liked talking to her. She picked up at once. He told her the story had gone down well at the newspaper and she said that was great and told Rob she wanted him back in England. He said he would be there as soon as he possibly could, five days max. Then she told him she was still seeing a lot of his daughter, becoming firm friends. Indeed, Sally had asked Christine if she'd like to help out with Lizzie. Sally had a day-long law course to do in Cambridge so Christine had agreed to look after Rob's daughter. They were going to spend the afternoon seeing De Savary, Christine's old friend and lecturer; that is, if Rob didn't mind. She wanted to talk to De Savary about the link with the murders in England, since he seemed to know so much of what the police were doing. And Lizzie was keen to go see some cows and sheep.

The Frenchwoman told him she missed him, a lot, and Rob said he was longing to see her, and then they both rang off. He walked down the road back to his hotel, thinking of lunch. Ambling happily. But as soon as he put the phone back in his pocket a sharp and sudden realization brought him up short. De Savary. Cambridge. The murders.

There was still one half of the story entirely unsolved. The British half. The story hadn't finished. It had just shifted.

From feeling happy and contented, Rob was now tensed and hungry again. Pumped for action. Ready for the next instalment. More than ready: he was worried that something might happen when he wasn't around. He needed to fly back to England as fast as he could. Maybe he could get a new flight via Istanbul. Maybe he could hire a plane . . .

Rob felt the prickle of a new anxiety.

36

Forrester and Boijer were staring at the River Styx.

'I remember this from school,' said Boijer. 'The River Styx is the river surrounding the underworld. We have to cross it, to get to the land of ghosts.'

Forrester peered into the dank and subterranean gloom. The River Styx was not very wide, but it was vigorous: it tumbled along its ancient channel, then turned a rocky corner and disappeared further into the caves and caverns. It was a suitable spot to forsake this earthly life. The only jarring note was the old packet of Kettle Chips on the opposite shore.

'Course,' the guide broke in, 'the River Styx is just a name they gave it. Actually it's an artificial river, constructed by the second Baronet, Francis Dashwood, when they were converting the caves. Though there are lots of real rivers and aquifers in these chalk and flint cave systems. It's an endless labyrinth.'

The guide, Kevin Bigglestone, smoothed back his floppy brown hair, and smiled at the policemen. 'Shall I show you the rest?'

'Lead on.'

Bigglestone began his guided tour of the Hellfire Caves, six miles from the Dashwood Estate at West Wycombe. 'OK,' he said, 'here we are.'

He lifted his umbrella as if he was leading a tour group. Boijer sniggered; Forrester shot his junior a warning glance: they needed this guy. They needed the cooperation of everyone in West Wycombe, if their plan was to work.

'So,' said Bigglestone, his podgy face barely visible in the darkness of the caves. 'What do we know of the eighteenth century Hellfire Club? Why did they meet here? In these cold and clammy caverns? During the sixteenth century various secret societies arose in Europe, such as the Rosicrucians. All of them were committed to freethinking, to occult lore, to investigating the mysteries of belief. By the eighteenth century élite members of these societies were seized by the idea that evidence could be found in the Holy Land, texts and materials which undermined the historical and theological basis of Christianity. Maybe of all the major creeds.' The guide lifted his umbrella again. 'Of course, it was wishful thinking, in an age of anti-clericalism and revolutionary secularism. But these legends and traditions were enough to tantalize some very rich men . . .' He walked to the bridge that crossed the Styx and turned. 'Certain maverick members of the English aristocracy were particularly intrigued by these rumours. One of them, the second Baron Le Despencer, Sir Francis Dashwood, actually travelled across Turkey in the eighteenth century in search of the truth. When he came back he was so inspired by what he found that he established first the Divan Club, and then the Hellfire Club. And one of the *raisons d'être* of the Hellfire Club was contempt and refutation of established faith.'

Forrester interrupted. 'How do we know this?'

'There are plentiful clues, in this area, that reveal Dashwood's disdain for orthodox faith. For instance, he adopted the motto "*Fay ce que voudras*", or "Do as you wish". This was taken from Rabelais, a great satirist of the church. The motto was later co-opted by the diabolist Aleister Crowley in the twentieth century and is now commonly used by Satanists across the world. Dashwood had this motto inscribed over the archway at the entrance of Medmenham Abbey, a ruined abbey, near here, that he rented for parties.'

'That's right sir,' said Boijer, looking at Forrester. 'I saw it. This morning.'

Bigglestone invited them to follow, still giving them his guided tour speech. 'In 1752 Dashwood made another eastern journey, this time to Italy. The trip was made in secret: no one is sure where he went. One theory is that he went to Venice, to buy books about magic. Other experts believe he may have visited Naples, to see the excavations of a Roman brothel.'

'Why would he do that?'

'Dashwood was a highly libidinous man, Detective Forrester! In the gardens at West Wycombe is a statue of Priapus, the Greek god who suffers a constant erection.'

Boijer laughed. 'Gotta cut down on the Viagra.'

Bigglestone ignored the interruption. 'Underneath the statue to Priapus Dashwood had his sculptor engrave *Peni Tento Non Penitenti*. That is to say: "A tense penis, not penitence", confirming, you see, Detective Forrester, his outright rejection of Christianity. Of religious morality.' They were walking quickly down the main cavern now. Bigglestone jabbed at the clammy air with his umbrella, as if he was fending off a footpad. 'See here. According to Horace Walpole, these smaller caves were fitted with beds so the brothers could have their sport with young women. Sex parties were common in the caves in Dashwood's time. As were drinking parties. We also hear rumours of devil-worship, group masturbation and so forth.'

They had emerged into a larger cave, this time carved into Gothic and religious shapes: a faintly mocking version of a church.

The guide pointed the umbrella high. 'Right above us is the church of St Lawrence, built by the same Francis Dashwood. The church ceiling is a precise facsimile of the ceiling in the ruined Temple of the Sun at Palmyra, in Syria. Francis Dashwood was not only influenced by the ancient mysteries but also by the ancient sun cults. But what did he really believe? A matter of dispute. Some assert that his political and spiritual vision can be summed up thusly: that Britain should be ruled by an élite; and that this noble élite should practice a pagan religion.' He smiled. 'And yet, allied to these views was a definite tendency to libertinism: drunken orgies, abusive blasphemy, and so forth. All of which begs the question. What was the true rationale for the Club?'

'What do you think?' Forrester asked.

'You ask that question as if you expect a succinct answer! I'm afraid that's impossible, Detective. All we know is that, in its heyday, the Hellfire Club numbered the most prominent figures of British society amongst its members. Indeed by 1762, the Friars of Medmenham, as they called themselves, dominated the highest circles of the British government, and thus the nascent British Empire.' Bigglestone began the walk back through the higher caves to the car park; explaining as he went. 'In 1762 the existence of the club was finally made public. It was revealed that the Prime Minister, the Chancellor of the Exchequer, plus various lords, nobles, and Cabinet ministers, were all members. This revelation meant that the Hellfire Club became a byword for aristocratic wickedness and lubricious exclusivity.' Bigglestone chuckled. 'Following this scandal, many of the most famous members, like Walpole, Wilkes, Hogarth and Benjamin Franklin, decided to quit. The very last meeting of the club was convened in 1774.'

They were in the narrow rock corridor that led from the cave system to the entrance and the ticket office; the walls were close and dripping wet.

'From this point the Hellfire caves entered centuries of neglect, but they remained a poignant and sometimes troubling memory. But they are unlikely to ever reveal their final secret – because the club members took pains to bury their mysteries with their own corpses. It is said that the last steward of the Order, Paul Whitehead, spent the three days before his death burning all relevant papers. So, what really went on inside the caves is a question whose answer may only be found . . . in the fires of hell!'

He stopped. Boijer was clapping politely. The guide did a little bow, then looked at his watch. 'Gosh, it's nearly six. I have to go! I do hope tomorrow's plan comes off, officers. The twelfth baronet is very keen to help the police catch those awful murderers.'

He hurried across the tarmac and disappeared down a hillside path. Boijer and Forrester walked slowly to their police car, parked in the shade of an oak tree.

As they walked, they went over their plan. Hugo De Savary had, by phone and email, convinced Forrester that the gang was bound to visit the Hellfire caves, because if the gang were looking for the Black Book, the treasure Whaley had brought back from the Holy Land – this was one place they just had to search: in the epicentre of the Hellfire Club phenomenon.

But when would the gang visit the caves? Forrester had worked out that they only hit a target when it was most likely to be deserted. Craven Street in the middle of a weekend night; Canford School one early morning at half term.

So the police had set a trap. Forrester had paid a visit to the present owner of West Wycombe Estate, the 12th Baronet Edward Francis Dashwood, direct descendant of the Hellfire lord, and had got permission to close the caves for one day. The unexpected closure would be spuriously publicized, as being 'in celebration of the baronet's wedding anniversary, and to give the loyal staff of West Wycombe a holiday'. Adverts to this effect had been put in all the local papers. The news had been posted on relevant websites. Scotland Yard had even persuaded the BBC to run a small TV item, focusing on the scandalous history of the site, but mentioning the temporary closure. Consequently, as far as the general public were concerned, the Hellfire caves were going to be completely empty. The trap had been baited.

Would the gang turn up? It was a long shot, Forrester knew, but this idea was all they had. Forrester felt a definite pessimism as Boijer raced their car along the country roads to their hotel.

The only other lead they had of any sort was a CCTV shot of Cloncurry from Canford School. The gang had disabled the rest of the school's cameras by snipping the cables. But one camera had been overlooked, and it had yielded a blurry image of Cloncurry walking through the school. Cloncurry had stared chillingly at the camera as he walked past. As if he knew he was being filmed. And didn't care.

Forrester had stared at the grainy image of Cloncurry for hours, trying to get inside the young man's mind. It was difficult: this was a man who could flay a pinioned victim, alive. A man who could cheerily cut out a tongue, and bury a screaming face in soil. A man who could do anything.

He was strikingly handsome, with high cheekbones and almost oriental eyes. An angular and dashing profile. And somehow this made his intense wickedness all the more sinister.

Boijer was parking the car. They were staying at the High Wycombe Holiday Inn, just off the M40. It was a fitful night. Forrester had a tiny bit of spliff after dinner, but it didn't help him sleep. He dreamed, sweatily, all night, of caves and naked women and lurid parties; he dreamed of a small girl lost amongst the laughing adults, a small girl crying for her father, lost in the caves.

He woke up early, dry-mouthed. Leaning across the bed, he picked up the phone and called Boijer, stirring his junior from sleep. They drove straight to their Portakabin.

The little cabin was concealed around the hill at the far side of the main cave entrance. The cave system was empty. The ticket office was locked. The Dashwood Estate was largely deserted: all the staff had been asked to stay away.

Boijer and Forrester had three constables with them in the cabin. They took it in turns to look at the CCTV images. The day was hot: cloudless and perfect. As the hours dragged by, Forrester stared out of the little window and thought about the newspaper article he had read, a *Times* piece about the Yezidi and the Black Book. Some journalist in Turkey was, it seemed, onto another thread of the same bizarre story.

Forrester had read the article again last night, and then called De

Savary to ask his opinion. De Savary had confirmed that he'd read the article and agreed that it was a peculiar and rather intriguing echo: and then he told Forrester there was a further link. The journalist's French girlfriend, mentioned in the article, was actually an ex-student and a friend. And she was coming to visit him the following day.

DCI Forrester had asked De Savary to question the girl. To find out what the possible connection was, between Turkey and England. Between there and here. Between the Yezidis' sudden fear and Cloncurry's sudden violence. De Savary had agreed to ask the questions. And, at that moment, Forester had felt a certain hope. Maybe they *could* crack this. But now, fifteen hours later, that optimism had gone again. Nothing was happening.

Forrester sighed. Boijer was telling a salacious story about a colleague in a swimming pool. Everyone chuckled. Someone handed out some more coffee. The day trudged by and the Portakabin grew stuffier. Where were these guys? What were they doing? Was Cloncurry just teasing them?

Dusk came, soft and balmy. A serene and tranquil May evening. But Forrester's mood was bleak. He went for a walk. It was now 10 p.m. The gang wasn't coming: it hadn't worked. The detective scuffed along in the darkness, glaring at the moon. He kicked an old Appletise bottle with his shoe. He thought of his daughter. *App-ull. App-ull. App-ull dadd-ee.* His heart filled with the mercury of grief. He fought back the sense of purposelessness: the sense of cold anger going nowhere; the bleakness of everything.

Maybe the old Sir Francis Dashwood was right. Where was God anyway? Why did He allow such terrible things? Why did He allow death? Why did He allow the death of children? Why did He allow people like Cloncurry? There was no God. There was nothing. Just a small child lost in the caves, then silence.

'Sir!'

It was Boijer, running out of the Portakabin followed by three armed constables.

'Sir. Big Beamer, in the car park – right now!'

Forrester's energy returned instantly. He chased after Boijer and the armed cops. They sprinted around the corner, towards the car park. Someone had switched the lights on: the anti-burglary lights they had installed on the fencing all around the car park. The entrance to the caves was flooded with dazzling light.

In the middle of the bare car park was a big, new, glossy black BMW. The windows of the car were tinted, but Forrester could see large figures inside.

The constables trained their rifles on the car. Forrester took the megaphone from Boijer, his amplified voice booming across the floodlit emptiness: 'Stop. You are surrounded by armed police.' He counted the dark shapes in the car. Five, or six?

The car remained motionless.

'Get out of the car. Very slowly. Do it now.'

The car doors stayed shut.

'You are surrounded by armed police. You must get out of the car. Now.'

The constables crouched lower, training their rifles. The driver's side car door was opening, very slowly. Forrester leaned forward, to catch his first glimpse of the gang.

A can of cider rolled onto the concrete with a clatter. The driver emerged from the car. He was about seventeen, visibly drunk, and visibly terrified. Two more figures got out and raised their shaking hands. They were also seventeen, eighteen. They had strings from party poppers draped pinkly over their shoulders. One of them had a red lipstick kiss on his cheek. The tallest of them was wetting himself, a big stain of urine spreading across the front of his jeans.

Kids. They were just *kids.* Students on a prank. Probably trying to spook themselves in the evil caves.

'For fuck's sake!' Forrester snapped at Boijer. 'For fuck's *sake.*' He spat onto the ground and cursed his luck. Then he told Boijer to go and arrest the kids. For something. Anything. Drunk driving.

'Jesus!' The DCI slouched back to the Portakabin, feeling like an idiot. He was being made a fool of by this bastard Cloncurry. The posh young psychopath had escaped them again: he was too smart to fall for a dumb trick like this. So what would happen next? Who would he kill? And how would he do it?

A piercing and terrible idea gripped the DCI. Of course.

Forrester ran to the police car, grabbed his jacket and found his mobile. With shaking hands he keyed in the number. He lifted the phone to his ear, urging the signal to kick in. *Come on come on come on.* Forrester was ardently praying he wasn't too late.

But the phone just kept ringing.

37

By the time Hugo De Savary woke up his boyfriend was already half-way out of the door. Mumbling about an anthropology lecture at St John's.

When De Savary got downstairs, he saw that his handsome young lover had left behind the usual mess in the kitchen: breadcrumbs everywhere, an eviscerated *Guardian*, marmalade smeared on an uncleared plate and coffee grounds dark and soggy in the sink. Yet De Savary didn't mind. He was happy. His boyfriend had kissed him passionately this morning: kissed him awake. They were really getting on well. And, even better, De Savary had one of his favourite days ahead of him: a day of pure research. No stressful writing; no boring meetings in Cambridge, let alone London; no important phone calls to make. All he had to do was sit in the garden of his country cottage, go through some papers and read an unpublished thesis or two. A very nice day of leisured reading and thinking. Later he might drive over to Grantchester and do some chores and some book shopping: at about 3 p.m. he had his only social engagement, with his old pupil, Christine Meyer. She was coming for the afternoon, and she was bringing the daughter of her boyfriend, the journalist who had written the richly intriguing piece in *The Times* about the Yezidi and the Black Book and this strange place called

Gobekli Tepe. When she had contacted him Christine had said she wanted to talk about the links between her boyfriend's story and the murders across England.

De Savary was keen to talk about this. But he was also simply keen to see Christine again. She had been one of his brightest students – his favourite student – and she was doing good work at Gobekli Tepe, it seemed. Good but rather hair-raising work, judging by the more excitable elements of *The Times* article.

He spent a quick ten minutes clearing up the breakfast things. Then he texted his lover: *Is it utterly impossible to slice bread without destroying the kitchen? Hugo xx*

As he sluiced the dark coffee grounds down the sink, he got a text back. *Dont napalm my village ok Ive got finals xxx*

De Savary laughed out loud. He wondered if he was falling in love with Andrew Halloran. He knew it was foolish if so: the lad was only twenty-one. De Savary was forty-five. But Andrew was so very handsome, in a seductively uncaring way. He just threw clothes on and seemed to look perfect every morning. Especially with a little stubble to offset the deep blue eyes. And De Savary quite liked the fact that Andrew was probably seeing other men, too. A little mustard on the sandwich: it helped. The sweet torment of jealousy . . .

Collecting his papers and books, he walked out into his garden. It was a beautiful day. Almost distractingly so: the birdsong was too sweet. The scent of late May blossom too heady. De Savary could hear children laughing in a garden across the Cambridgeshire meadows, though his cottage was very isolated.

He tried to concentrate on his work. He was researching a long and rather learned *TLS* article on violence as a part of English culture. But as he sat in the morning sunshine his mind kept wandering back to the themes that had dominated his thoughts lately. The gang murdering their way across Britain. And the links to the curious story coming out of Turkey.

Picking up his sun-warmed phone from the lawn, De Savary contemplated calling Detective Chief Inspector Forrester to see if the police were having any luck at West Wycombe caves. But then he thought better of it, and put the phone back down. He was confident that the gang would, at some point, search out the caves. If they were so frenziedly seeking the Black Book, then the Hellfire Caves were an obvious place to look. Whether the police trap would work was an entirely different matter. It was a gamble. But gambles sometime paid off.

The sun was very warm now. De Savary dropped his papers onto the grass, stretched out on his deckchair and closed his eyes. The children were still laughing, somewhere across the water meadows. He thought about the Yezidi. Clearly this journalist, Rob Luttrell, had discovered something. The Black Book of the Yezidi must once have revealed some crucial information about this extraordinary temple, Gobekli Tepe, which appeared to be so central to their faith and their ancestry. A tiny hint of disquiet trilled through him as he thought about *The Times* piece. The gang had surely seen it – seen it and absorbed it. They weren't stupid. The article implied that Rob Luttrell had garnered vital information about the Black Book. The article also mentioned Christine by name. The gang might therefore come looking for the couple at some point down the line. De Savary reminded himself to tell Christine when she came over that she could conceivably be in danger. The two of them, Rob and Christine, needed to take care: until the gang was caught.

De Savary leaned from his deckchair and picked up his photocopied thesis: *Fear of the Mob: Riots and Revelry in Regency London.* The birds chirruped in the apple tree behind him. He read and took notes; then read some more, and took some more notes.

Three hours later he had finished. He slipped some shoes on, climbed in his little sports car and thrummed over to Grantchester. He went to the bookshop and idled between the shelves for a pleasant hour; after that he strolled to the computer shop and bought some ink cartridges for his printer. Then he remembered that Christine was coming over, so he stopped off at a supermarket and bought some fresh lemonade and three punnets of strawberries. They could sit in the garden, and have strawberries in the sun.

On the drive back to his cottage De Savary hummed a tune. The Bach Double Violin Concerto. Such a beautiful piece of music. He resolved to download a new version when he had time.

For another hour he Googled in his study; then the doorknocker went and there was Christine. Smiling and suntanned, with an angelic little blonde girl in tow. De Savary beamed with pleasure: he had always thought that if he hadn't been gay Christine was the sort of girl he could have loved: dreamy and sexy, but demure and somehow innocent too. And of course deeply gifted and clever. And this suntan suited her. As did the little girl by her side.

Christine placed a hand on the girl's shoulder. 'This is Lizzie, Robert's daughter. Her mum's in town doing a course . . . and I am her adopted mother for the day!'

The girl did a sweet sort-of curtsey as if she was meeting the Queen and then giggled and solemnly shook De Savary's hand.

As Christine followed him through to the garden she was already telling him gossip and stories and theories: it was as if they were back in his rooms at King's. Laughing and talking, passionately: about archaeology and love, about Sutton Hoo and James Joyce, about the prince of Palenque and the meaning of sex.

In the garden De Savary poured the lemonade and offered the strawberries. Christine was animatedly describing Rob. De Savary could see the romance in her eyes. They talked about him for a short while and Lizzie said she was looking forward to seeing her daddy coz he was bringing her a lion. And a llama. Then she asked if she could play on the computer and De Savary happily agreed, as long as she stayed where they could see her; the little girl skipped inside the cottage, and sat by the open French windows, absorbed in her computer game.

De Savary was pleased he and Christine could now talk more freely. Because he wanted to talk about something else. 'So, Christine,' he said. 'Tell me about Gobekli. It sounds *incroyable*.'

For the next hour Christine outlined the whole remarkable story. By the time she had finished the sun was just edging the treetops over by the water meadows. The professor shook his head. They discussed the strange interring of the site. Then they moved on to the Hellfire Club and the Black Book, conversing as they used to do: two engaged and lively minds with similar cultural interests: literature, history, archaeology, painting. De Savary was really enjoying the dialogue. Christine told him, as an aside, that she was trying to teach Rob the daunting delights of James Joyce, the great Irish modernist, and De Savary's eyes sparkled. This cued him up for one of his latest theories. He decided to tell her. 'You know, Christine, I was looking at James Joyce again the other day, and something struck me . . .'

'Yes?'

'There's a passage in *A Portrait of the Artist as a Young Man*. I've just wondered if—'

'What?'

'Sorry?'

'What was that?!'

Then he heard it. A loud thump behind them. Coming from the cottage. A strange, loud and ominous crash.

De Savary's immediate thought was for Lizzie. He stood and turned, but Christine was already rushing past him. He dropped his glass of lemonade onto the lawn and ran after her, and as he did so he heard something worse: a muffled shriek.

He found Christine inside the house and in the hands of several young men wearing dark jeans and ski masks. Only one man was unmasked. He was black-haired and handsome. De Savary knew him immediately. He'd seen the CCTV image in an email from Forrester.

It was Jamie Cloncurry.

De Savary felt like crying out: at the idiocy of it all. The gang had knives and guns. One of the guns was pointed at him. This was clearly ludicrous. This was Cambridgeshire. On a sweet Maytime afternoon. He had just been to the supermarket to buy some strawberries. On the way home he had whistled some Bach. And now there were armed psychopaths in his cottage!

Christine was trying to cry out and she was wriggling: but then one of the men punched her very hard in the stomach and she stopped writhing. She moaned. Her eyes were wild and wide. She stared at De Savary and he saw her total fear.

The tallest man, Jamie Cloncurry, waved his pistol languidly at De Savary. 'Tie him to the chair.'

The voice was very educated: chillingly so. De Savary could hear stifled cries from the kitchen. Lizzie was in there, and she was crying. Then the girlish crying ceased.

Two of the gang members strapped De Savary to the chair. They put a sweaty gag around his mouth and tied it ferociously tight, making his lips bleed as the gag pressed his lips against his incisors. But it wasn't this pain that was most troubling De Savary. It was the way they were tying him to the dining chair. They were tying him so he was sitting on the chair the wrong way round: straddling the seat, his chest pressed against the wooden chair back. Big straps were lashed around him. His ankles were bound, very tightly, under the chair. His wrists were twined viciously together also under the chair; his chin was painfully propped on the chair back. Everything hurt. He couldn't move. He couldn't see Christine or Lizzie: his ears detected a faint whimpering, in another room. But then his thoughts were drowned by mental terror when he heard the next words of Jamie Cloncurry, standing somewhere behind him.

'Have you ever heard of blood eagling, Professor De Savary?'

He gulped – and then he couldn't help it: he started to cry. The tears ran down his face. He had guessed they were going to kill him. But this? Blood eagling?

Jamie Cloncurry came around and looked close at him, his pale and handsome face very slightly flushed. 'Of course you have heard of blood eagling, haven't you? After all, you wrote that book. That rather alarming piece of pop history. *The Fury of the Northmen*.' Cloncurry was sneering. 'All about Viking rites and beliefs. Rather lurid, if you don't mind my saying so. But I suppose that's how you accrue sales . . .' The young man was holding a book in his hands, quoting from a page: '"And now we come to one of the most repellent concepts in the annals of Viking cruelty: the so-called blood eagle. Some scholars dispute that this gruesome rite of sacrifice ever existed, but various references in the sagas and in skaldic poetry can leave an open mind in little doubt: the rite of the blood eagle existed. It was an authentic sacrificial ceremony of the North".' Cloncurry smiled in De Savary's direction, and then went on, '"The notorious blood eagle rite was performed, according to Norse accounts, on various eminent personages, including King Ella of Northumbria, Halfdan son of King Harfagri of Norway, and King Edmund of England".'

De Savary felt his bowels begin to liquefy. He wondered if he was going to soil himself.

Cloncurry turned a page, and read on. '"Accounts of blood eagling differ in detail, but essential elements remain the same. The victim first has his back sliced open close to the backbone. Sometimes the skin is peeled away beforehand. Then the exposed ribs are broken at the spine, perhaps with a hammer or mallet; maybe they are cut. The shattered ribs are then splayed out like a spatchcocked chicken, revealing the grey lungs beneath. The victim remains fully conscious as his pulsing lungs are yanked from the chest cavity and flung out across the shoulders, so that the victim resembles an eagle with its wings outspread. Salt is sometimes sprinkled in the enormous wounds. Death must have come sooner or later, perhaps from asphyxiation or blood loss; or a simple heart attack from the sheer terror induced by the cruelty of the act. The Irish poet Seamus Heaney cites the blood eagle in his poem "Viking Dublin": "With a butcher's aplomb they spread out your lungs, and made you warm wings for your shoulders".'

Cloncurry snapped shut the book and laid it on the dining table. De Savary was quivering with fear. The tall young man smiled widely. '"Death must have come sooner rather than later". Shall we see if that is true, Professor De Savary?'

The professor closed his eyes. He could hear the men behind him. His bowels were empty: he had soiled himself in terror. A vile faecal smell offended his own nostrils. There was some murmuring behind him. Then De Savary felt the first crippling pain: as the knife plunged into his back and ripped downwards. The shock made him almost vomit. He rocked back and forth in his chair. A man laughed in the background.

Jamie Cloncurry spoke. 'I am going to have to cut your ribs with some humble pliers. I'm afraid we don't have a mallet . . .'

Another laugh. De Savary heard a cracking noise and felt a hammering pain near his heart as if he had been shot; he realized they were cutting his ribs one by one. He felt them bend, then break. *Crack*. Like something very taut being snapped. He heard another crack; and then another. He vomited around the gag. He hoped he would choke on his own vomit, and he hoped he would die very soon.

But he wasn't dead yet: he could actually *feel* Cloncurry's hands as they rummaged in his chest cavity. He could feel the surreal sense of someone pulling out his lungs, and then the agonizing rapture of pain as the lungs were exposed to the air. His own lungs came flopping over his own shoulders, greasy and hot. His own lungs . . . A strange smell filled the air. Half fishy, half metallic: the smell of his own lungs. De Savary nearly blacked out.

But he didn't black out. The gang had done the job well: keeping him alive and quite conscious. So as to suffer.

De Savary watched in a mirror as the girl and Christine were bundled out of the room. They were being taken away. The gang was packing up: they were going to leave De Savary here, to die alone. With his ribs cracked and bent apart, and his own lungs draped over his shoulders.

The door slammed shut; the gang was gone.

Strapped to his chair, De Savary stilled his gasps of pain, and the anguish of frustration. He had been going to tell Christine – but he hadn't had time. And now he was dying. There was no one to save him.

Then he noticed. There was a pen lying on the table very close, next to his book about Vikings. He could maybe reach the pen with his mouth. And write something; make some use of his final moments.

The tears of pain blurred his eyes as he stretched and struggled; the title of his own book stared back at him.

The Fury of the Northmen, by Hugo De Savary.

38

Rob was sitting in DCI Forrester's office in Scotland Yard. The window was open and a chilly breeze was whistling through. It was an unseasonably cool, wet and overcast day. Rob thought about his daughter and fought back the anger and despair.

But the anger and despair were so powerful. He felt as if he was standing thigh deep in rushing floodwater: any moment he would lose it, lose his grip, and get swept away by his emotions. Like those people caught in the Asian tsunami. Rob had to concentrate on keeping upright.

He had told the police officers everything he knew about the Yezidi and the Black Book. Forrester's junior, Boijer, had taken notes while Forrester stared directly and seriously at Rob. When Rob finished the senior officer sighed, and swivelled in his chair.

'Well it's pretty obvious how and why they kidnapped them.'

Boijer nodded. Rob said, bleakly, 'Is it?'

Rob had only been aware of his daughter's abduction for a few hours: since landing at Heathrow from Istanbul. He had rushed straight to his ex-wife's house, then come straight to meet these policemen. So he hadn't had time to work out how it had happened.

The policeman said, 'Obviously Cloncurry read your article in *The Times* a few days ago.'

'I guess . . .' The words felt dry and pointless in Rob's mouth. Everything felt dry and pointless. He recalled something Christine had told him – the Assyrian name for Hell: the Desert of Anguish.

That was where he was. The Desert of Anguish.

The policeman was still talking. 'They obviously think, Mr Luttrell, you have some knowledge of the Black Book. So they must have traced your name. Googled you. And found out the address of your ex-wife. That was your old home, right? Where you were registered to vote?'

'Yes. I never changed it.'

'So. That was easy for them. They must have been watching that address for a good few days. Waiting and watching.'

Rob murmured, 'And then Christine turned up . . .'

Boijer intervened. 'She made it easier for them. All of them went off to Cambridge, followed by the gang, no doubt. And then your girlfriend took your daughter to a remote cottage for the afternoon. The worst possible place.'

'They may have known of De Savary already,' Forrester added. 'He was a bestselling writer, with books on sacrifice and the Hellfire Club to his name. Cloncurry must surely have read him. Or seen him on TV.'

'Then . . .' Rob was still swaying in the grey floodwater. He forced his mind to focus. 'Then they waited outside the cottage. Knowing they could get Christine and my daughter all at once.'

'Yeah,' said Boijer. 'They must have been waiting for hours. And then they rushed the house.'

Rob glared at Forrester. 'She's going to die isn't she? My daughter? Isn't she? They've killed everyone else.'

Forrester winced. And shook his head. 'No . . . Not at all. We don't know anything of the sort . . .'

'Oh come on.'

'Please.'

'No!' Rob was almost shouting. He stood up and stared down at the policeman. 'How can you say that? "We don't know anything of the fucking sort"? You don't know what it is like, Detective. You can't know what it is fucking like. My daughter has been abducted by some fucking killers. I will lose my only child.'

Boijer motioned at Rob: calm down. Sit down. Calm down.

Rob inhaled and exhaled, deliberately and slowly. He knew he was making a scene but he didn't care. He had to vent his emotions. He couldn't bottle them up. For a few moments Rob just stood there, his eyes blurred with anger. At last, he sat down again.

DCI Forrester continued, very calmly, 'I know this is very difficult for you to appreciate right now, but the fact is the gang did not harm, as far as we know, either your daughter Lizzie or Christine Meyer.'

Rob nodded, grimly, and said nothing. He didn't trust himself to speak.

The policeman pursued his logic. 'We've found no blood, other than De Savary's, at the scene of the crime. Every other time the gang has struck they have, as you say, killed without compunction. But this time they didn't. They abducted. Why? Because they want to get to you.'

The waters swirling around Rob seemed to weaken. He gazed attentively and even hopefully at Forrester. There was some logic here, some lucidity. Rob wanted to believe: he really wanted to trust this guy.

'You gave an email address at the end of your article?' Forrester asked.

'Yes,' Rob replied. 'It's standard practise. A *Times* email address.'

Boijer was writing on his pad. Forrester concluded, 'I predict Jamie Cloncurry will be in touch with you. Very soon. He wants the Black Book. Desperately.'

'And if he does get in touch? What the fuck do I do then?'

'Then you call me immediately. Here's my mobile number.' He handed a card to Rob. 'We need to string him along. Convince the gang you have the book. The Yezidi materials.'

Rob was confused. 'Even though I haven't got anything?'

'They don't know that. If we imply that you do have what they want, that buys us time. Precious time – for us to catch Cloncurry.'

Rob gazed across Forrester's shirt-sleeved shoulder at the glass partition beyond. He thought of all the hundreds of policemen working away right now, in this building. Dozens of them on this case. Surely they must be able to find a gang of murderers? The trail of blood and cruelty was all over the papers now. Rob wanted to go out into that wider office and shout at people: *Catch them! Do your job. Catch these fucking people! How hard can it be?*

'Where do you think they are?' he said instead.

'We have a few leads,' said Boijer. 'The Italian, Luca Marsinelli, has a private pilot's licence. Maybe they are using planes to get in and out of the country, private jets.'

'But these are just kids . . .'

Forrester shook his head. 'Not just kids. Not just average kids anyway. These are rich kids. Marsinelli is an orphan. But he inherited a Milanese textile fortune. Immensely wealthy. Another gang member, we think, is the son of a hedge fund manager in Connecticut. These boys have trust funds, private fortunes, Jersey bank accounts. They can buy new cars just like that.' Forrester clicked his fingers. 'There are a lot of private airfields in East Anglia, old American airstrips from the war. Maybe they flew your daughter out of the country: we think Italy is the obvious place, given Marsinelli's connections. He has an estate near the Italian lakes. Then there's Cloncurry's family in Picardy. Also being watched. The French and Italian police are up to speed on all of this.'

Rob actually yawned. It was a weird yawn of frustration and bitterness, not fatigue. It was a yawn from too much adrenalin. He felt thirsty and tired and wired-up and furious. The two women he most loved: Lizzie and Christine. Kidnapped; weeping; suffering: lost in the Desert of Anguish. He couldn't bear to think about it.

Rob stood up. 'OK, Detective, I'll keep checking my emails.'

'Good. And you can call me any time, Mr Luttrell. Five a.m. I don't mind.' The policeman's eyes seemed to mist for a moment. 'Rob, I do understand a little of what you are going through. Believe me.' He coughed, then continued, 'Cloncurry is an arrogant young man, as well as psychotic. He thinks he is smarter than everyone. People like that can't resist taunting the police with their cleverness. And that's how they get caught.'

He shook Rob's hand. There was a firmness in the policeman's handshake which, Rob felt, went beyond professional reassurance: there was an empathy there. And there was something in the policeman's glance, as well: a distinct pity, even pain, in the detective's eyes.

Rob said thanks, then he turned and left the building, walking like a zombie to the bus-stop and then he caught the bus home to his tiny flat in Islington. The journey was gruelling. Everywhere he looked he saw young kids, little girls: playing with friends, skipping along pavements, shopping with their mothers. He wanted to keep looking at them in case, just in case one was Lizzie: even though he knew this was ludicrous. But he also wanted to avert his face: to not look at these girls. Because they reminded him of Lizzie. The smell of her hair after he had bathed her as a baby. The eyes of trusting blue. Rob felt the tidal wave of agony all over again: enormous and crushing.

When he got to the flat he ignored his unpacked suitcases and the decomposing milk on the kitchen counter and he walked straight to his laptop, plugged it in, booted it up, and checked his emails.

Nothing. He checked again, by refreshing the screen; still nothing.

He took a shower, then started to dress and stopped. He unpacked one suitcase, then stopped. He tried not to think about Lizzie and failed; he was so angry and tense. But all he could do was this one ludicrous thing: keep checking his emails.

Shirtless and barefoot he went back to the laptop and clicked. He flinched. There it was, sent ten minutes ago. An email from Jamie Cloncurry.

Rob stared in fear and hope at the title. *Your Daughter.*

Was it going to be some hideous image of her corpse? Burned or headless? Buried and dead? Or was it going to say she was safe?

The tension and anxiety was unfeasible. Perspiring heavily, Rob opened the email. There was no photo; just writing. It began tersely enough:

We have your daughter, Rob. If you want her back you must give us the Black Book. Or tell us exactly where it is. Otherwise she will die, in a manner I shall not confide. I am sure your imagination can do the rest. Your girlfriend is similarly unharmed, but we will likewise kill her if you do not assist us.

Rob wanted to throw the laptop at the wall. But he read on: there was more. A lot more.

By the by, I read your piece about the Palestinians. Very moving. Heart-wrenching. You do write some quite effective prose, when you aren't being so predictably liberal. But I wonder if you have ever really thought about the Israeli situation, and what underlies it. Have you, Rob?

Look at it this way: who are you most scared of? In terms of race? Which race most unnerves you, deep down? I'd hazard a guess that it's blacks – Africans – yes? I'm right, aren't I? Do you cross the road when you see a gang of black youths in their hoodies, on the streets of London? If you do, you are hardly alone, Rob. We all do it. And fear of black men is statistically sensible – in terms of petty street crime. You are far more likely to be assaulted and robbed by a black man than by a white man, let alone a Japanese or a Korean – given the proportion of black people in the general populace.

But think a little deeper.

I've read your articles and I know you are not stupid. You may be an idiot in terms of politics, but you are not stupid. So think. Which race really kills the most? Which one of the human races is the most lethal?

It's the smart ones, isn't it?

Let's go through it. You are scared of black people. But, really, how many people have been killed by Africans, globally? By African armies? By African power? A few thousand? Maybe a few hundred thousand? And that's for the whole of Africa. So you see, Africans, per capita, are actually not that dangerous. They are wholly chaotic, and clearly incapable of self-government, but they are not dangerous on a global scale. Now take the Arabs. The Arabs have barely mastered the computer. They haven't successfully invaded anyone since the 15th century. 9/11 was their best attempt at killing lots of people in two hundred years. And they killed three thousand. The Americans could napalm that many in a minute. By remote control.

So who are the organized people who do the real killing, Rob? For this we need to go north. Where the smart people live.

Amongst the European nations the British and the Germans have killed more than anyone else. Behold the British Empire. The British wiped out the Tasmanian aborigines, in toto. Completely killed them all. The British in Tasmania actually had a sport whereby they went out and hunted them down. A bloodsport: like foxhunting.

The only European people who can match the British in terms of sheer lethality, Rob, are the Germans. They were slow to catch up, not having an empire and all, but they did rather well in the 20th century. They butchered six million Jews. They killed five million Poles, maybe ten to twenty million Russians. Too many to count.

And what are the IQ levels of the British and the Germans? Around 102–105: significantly above average, and well above most other races. This small margin is significant enough to make the British and the Germans some of the most lethal people in the world, as well as some of the cleverest.

But let's look further afield. Who is even smarter than the British and the Germans, Rob? The Chinese. They have an average IQ of 107. And the Chinese killed maybe 100 million in the 20th century alone. Of course they killed their own people, but there's no accounting for taste.

Now let's go straight to the top.

Per head of population, who is most likely to kill you? Is it the Krauts or the British? Is it a black man or a Chinaman? A Korean or a Kazakh? A nigger or a wop?

No, it's the Jews. The Jews have killed more people on this planet than anyone else. Of course, given the tiny size of the Jewish population, they have had to do their massacring by proxy, as it were: by harnessing the power of other nations, or getting other countries to fight each other. They live and they kill by weaponizing their cleverness: and there's no denying how many they have put to the sword. Think about it. Jews invented Christianity: how many died for and by the cross? Fifty million? Jews dreamed up communism. Another 100 million. Then there is the atom bomb. Invented by Jews. How many will that kill?

Jews, in the guise of neo-conservatives, even came up with the second Iraq war. Yes that was a small-time operation by their standards: only killed a million. Positively picayune. But at least they are keeping their hand in. Perhaps because they are rehearsing for the big war between Islam and Christianity. Which we all know is coming, and which we all know the Jews will start. Because they start all wars; because they are so very clever.

What is the average Ashkenazim Jewish IQ? 115. They are by far the smartest race on earth. And Jews are more likely to take your life, historically, than anyone else. They just don't do it on the street, with a knife, looking for ten bucks to buy crack.

Rob stared at the email. The racist filth was almost concussive in its psychosis. It was dizzyingly insane. Yet there might be clues in it.

He reread it twice. Then he picked up the phone and called Detective Forrester.

39

DCI Forrester was on the phone, arranging a meeting with Janice Edwards; he wanted to ask her opinion on the Cloncurry case, because she was an expert in evolutionary psychology: she had written dense but well-received books on the subject.

The therapist's secretary was evasive. She told him that Janice was very busy and that the only time she could spare in the coming week was tomorrow, when she was at the Royal College of Surgeons, for the monthly meetings of the College Trust.

'So. That's fine. I'll meet her there then?'

The secretary sighed. 'I'll make a note.'

The next morning Forrester caught the Tube to Holborn, and waited in the pillared hallway of the Royal College until Janice arrived to guide him into the large, shiny, steel-and-glass museum of the college as being a 'good place to talk'.

The museum was impressive. A maze of enormous glass shelves, arrayed with jars and specimens.

'This is called the Crystal Gallery,' said Janice, gesturing at the glittering racks of dissections. 'It was refurbished a couple of years ago: we're very proud of it. Cost millions.'

Forrester nodded politely.

'Here's one of my favourite exhibits,' said his doctor. 'See. The preserved throat of a suicide. This man slashed his own throat – you can actually see the explosion in the flesh. Hunter was a brilliant dissector.' She smiled at Forrester. 'Now. What were you saying, Mark?'

'Do you think there can be a gene for murder?'

She shook her head. 'Nope.'

'Not at all?'

'Not one gene, no. But perhaps a gene cluster. Yes. I don't see why that is impossible. But we can't know for sure. This is still a fledgling science.'

'Right.'

'We've only just begun to crack genetics. For instance: have you ever noticed how gayness and high intelligence are interlinked?'

'They are?'

'Yes.' She smiled. 'Gay people have an IQ about ten points higher than average. There is clearly some genetic element at play here. A gene cluster. But we are not remotely sure of the mechanics.'

Forrester nodded. He glanced at some animal specimens. A jar containing a hagfish. The pale grey stomach of a swan.

Janice Edwards went on, 'As for the heritability of homicidality, well . . . it depends how these genes interact. With each other and the environment. Someone who had the trait might still live a perfectly normal life, if their urges weren't catalysed or provoked in some way.'

'But . . .' Forester was confused. 'You do think murderousness could be inherited?'

'Let's take musical ability. That seems to be partially heritable. Consider the Bach family – brilliant composers over several generations. Of course environment played a part but genes must surely be involved. So, if something as complex as musical composition is heritable then, yes, why not a fairly primal urge like murder?'

'And what about human sacrifice? Could you inherit a desire to commit human sacrifice?'

She frowned. 'Not sure about that. Rather a bizarre concept. What's the background?'

Forrester recounted the story of the Cloncurrys. An aristocratic family with a history of martial values, some of whom took their aggression to lurid lengths approaching human sacrifice. And now they had begat Jamie Cloncurry: a murderer who sacrificed without apology or rationale. Even more bizarrely, the family appeared to be attracted to sites of human sacrifice: they lived near the biggest sacrificial death-pit in France and the Great War battlefields blooded by their appalling forefather, General Cloncurry.

Janice nodded, thoughtfully. 'Interesting. I suppose murderers often return to the scene of the crime, don't they?' She shrugged: 'But that is rather odd. Why live there? Near the battlefields? Could be coincidence. Maybe they are in some way honouring their ancestors. You'd need to ask an anthropologist about that.'

She walked on down the Crystal Gallery. Two girls were sitting cross-legged on the floor with sketch pads on their laps and little tins of paint at the side. Student artists, Forrester surmised. One of the girls was Chinese – she was squinting with great concentration, at five eerily preserved foetuses: deformed human quintuplets.

Janice Edwards turned to Forrester: 'What it sounds like to me, actually, is an inherited and homicidal psychosis that possibly presents as sacrifice in certain situations.'

'Which means?'

'I think a psychosis that predisposed you to extreme violence could be inherited. How might such a trait survive, in Darwinian terms? Generally in history, a tendency towards outrageous violence might not always be a bad thing: for instance, if the bloodlust and brutality was channelled, it might be adaptive.'

'How?'

'If, for instance, there was a military tradition in the family. The most violent offspring could be sent straight into the army, where their aggressions and bloodlust would prove an asset.'

They walked on, past the students. Further along the gallery was another array of tiny foetuses showing the development of the embryo from four weeks to nine months. They were remarkably well preserved, floating in their space of clear liquid like tiny aliens in zero gravity. Their expressions were human from an early stage: grimacing and shouting. Silently.

Forrester coughed, and looked at his notebook. 'So, Janice, if these guys carried these genes for murder and sadism, they might have been disguised until now? Because of, say, Britain's imperialist history? All the wars we've fought?'

'Very possibly. But these days such a trait would be problematic. Intense aggression has no outlet in an era of smoking bans and smart bombs. We often kill by proxy if we kill at all. And now we have young Jamie Cloncurry, who is maybe what we call a "genetic celebrity". He carries the sadistic genes of his forefathers but in the most outrageous way. What can he do with his talents? Apart from murder? I see his dilemma, if that doesn't sound callous.'

Forrester stared at half a pickled human brain. It looked like a withered old cauliflower. He read the accompanying sign. The brain belonged to Charles Babbage, 'inventor of the computer'.

'What about a propensity for sacrifice then? Are you sure you couldn't, you know, inherit that, as a trait?'

'Maybe in historic times this gene cluster might have led you to commit human sacrifice, in a religious society already structured for such acts.'

Forrester pondered this for a moment. Then he retrieved a slip of paper from his pocket: a print-out of the email that had been sent to Rob Luttrell. He showed it to Janice, who scanned it very quickly.

'Anti-Semitism. Yes, yes. This sort of thing is a fairly common symptom of psychosis. Especially if the victim is very bright. The dimmer kind of psychotics just think aliens are living in the toaster, but a clever man, going mad, will perceive more intriguing patterns and conspiracies. And anti-Semitism is a pretty regular feature. Remember the mathematician, John Nash?'

'The guy in that film? *A Beautiful Mind*?

'One of the greatest mathematical thinkers of his time. Won the Nobel I believe. He was totally schizophrenic in his twenties and thirties, and he was obsessively anti-Semitic. Thought the Jews were everywhere, taking over the world. High intelligence is no defence against dangerous lunacy. The average IQ of Nazi leaders was about 138. Very high.'

Forrester took the sheaf of paper and folded it back into his pocket. He had one last question. A very long shot. He gave it a try. 'Maybe you could help with one last thing. When we found that poor guy De Savary he had written a word, a single word on the front page of a book. The paper was soaked with flecks of aspirated blood.'

'Sorry?'

'He was writing with his mouth. The pen was in his mouth, and he was coughing blood as he wrote.'

The doctor grimaced. 'That's horrible.'

Forrester nodded, 'Not surprisingly, the writing is barely legible.'

'OK . . .'

'But the word seems to be "Undish".'

'Undish?'

'Undish.'

'I have absolutely no idea what that means.'

The DCI sighed. 'I did a search on it, and there is a Polish death metal band called Undish.'

'Right. Well . . . there's your answer no? Aren't these satanic cults often influenced by this awful music? Goth metal or whatever?'

'Yes,' Forrester agreed. Janice was heading for the exit, past ancient dark planks, smeared with dissected veins. He followed, adding, 'But why would someone like De Savary know about a death metal band? And why tell us about them anyway? If he had one last word to write, when he was in massive pain, why write *that*?'

Dr Edwards checked her watch. 'Sorry, I have to go. We have another meeting.' She smiled. 'If you like we can have a proper session next week: call my secretary.'

Forrester made his farewells and walked down the stairs, past its plinths and pedestals, and the sombre unsmiling busts of famous medical men. Then he strode, with a certain relief, into the sunny streets of Bloomsbury. His conversation with Janice had given him some intriguing ideas. He wanted to sort through them. Right now. The phrase his doctor had used: *honouring their ancestors*, had set him thinking. Hard. It chimed with something in Rob Luttrell's report in *The Times*. Something about ancestors. And where you chose to live.

He strode to Holborn station, hummed impatiently on the Tube train, barrelled his way through the crowded shopping streets of Victoria. When he reached Scotland Yard he sprinted up the stairs and slammed into his office. He would have knocked over the photo of his dead daughter if it hadn't already been laid face down on the desk.

Straight away he booted up his computer and Googled 'ancestors buried house'.

He found it. Bang to rights. His prize. What he wanted; what he remembered being mentioned in *The Times* article.

Cayonu and Catalhoyuk. Two ancient Turkish sites, near the temple of Gobekli Tepe.

The crucial aspect of these sites, for Forrester, was what had happened beneath the houses and buildings. Because the inhabitants had buried the human bones of their sacrificial victims in the floors beneath their homes. Consequently, these people lived and worked and slept and fucked and ate and talked right above their own victims. And this, it seemed, would go on for centuries: new layers of human bones and corpses, then another floor, then more bones. Living above the sacrificial victims of your ancestors. In the Skull Chamber.

He took a victorious glug of water from an Evian bottle. Why would you want to live near or even above your own victims? Why did so many killers want to do this? He stared out of the window at the sunny London sky and considered the curious echo in so many modern murder cases. Like Fred West in England, burying his murdered daughters in the backyard. Or John Wayne Gacy in Indiana, who buried dozens of the boys he killed, right under his own house. Whenever you got a mass murder the first place you looked for bodies was in the murderer's house or under his floorboards. It was standard police procedure. Because murderers so often hid their victims nearby.

Forrester had never properly considered this phenomenon in the round before: but now that he did he was struck by the strangeness of it. There was obviously a deep, maybe subconscious urge – to live near or above your dead victims, an urge that had been arguably present in humanity ten thousand years back. And maybe that was what the Cloncurrys were doing. Living above the bodies of their own victims: all those soldiers killed by the Butcher of Albert.

Yes.

He swallowed another mouthful of lukewarm Evian. What about the death-pit? Maybe the Cloncurry family fancied some affinity with those victims, too: after all, the victims in the Ribemont death-pit were Celtic. Gaulish warriors . . .

Forrester sat straight. Something was tugging at his thoughts like a loose nail pulling a thread. Unravelling a pullover. Celtic. Celts. Celts? Where did the Cloncurrys come from originally? He decided to search under 'Cloncurry ancestors'.

Within barely two minutes he found it. The Cloncurry family were descended, by marriage, from an old Irish family. But not just any old Irish family. Their forefathers were . . . the Whaleys.

The Cloncurrys were descended from Buck and Burnchapel Whaley, from the founders of the Irish Hellfire Club!

He beamed at the screen. He was on a roll, on a high. He felt he could crack the whole thing. He was hitting the sweet spot. Knocking every ball for six. He could solve the damn thing now. Here and now. Right here – at his desk.

So where could the gang be? Where could they be hiding? For a long time he and Boijer and the rest of the squad had presumed the gang was slipping in and out of Britain, going to Italy, or France. On a private plane, or maybe by boat. But maybe he and Boijer were looking in the wrong place. Just because certain gang members were Italian or French didn't mean they were going to France or Italy. They might be in another country: but they could be in the one country you didn't need a passport to get to when you left Britain. Forrester looked up. Boijer was coming through the door.

'My Finnish friend!'

'Sir?'

'I think I know.'

'What?'

'Where they are hiding, Boijer. I think I know where they are hiding.'

40

Rob sat in his flat and watched the video obsessively. Cloncurry had sent it three days before, in an email.

The video showed his daughter and Christine in a nondescript little room. Lizzie's mouth was gagged, as was Christine's. They were tied, firmly and lavishly, to wooden chairs.

And that's all it showed of them. They were in clean clothes. They didn't look injured. But the tight leather gags around their mouths and the terror welling in their eyes made the video almost unwatchable, for Rob.

So he watched it every ten or fifteen minutes. He watched it and watched it, and then he wandered around his flat, in his underwear, unshaven, unshowered, in a daze of despair. He felt like a deranged old saint in the Desert of Anguish. He tried to eat some toast and then gave up. He hadn't eaten a proper meal in a long time. Apart from the breakfast his ex-wife had cooked him a few days back.

He'd been over to Sally's to discuss their daughter's fate and Sally had, in her generous way, made him bacon and eggs, and for the first time in ages Rob had felt hungry and he had got halfway through the meal but then Sally had started crying. So Rob had stood up and comforted her with a hug: but that just made it worse: she had shoved him away and said it was all his fault and she yelled and cried and slapped him. And Rob had just stood there as she slapped him and then thumped him in the stomach, flailing. He took the blows, placidly, because he felt she was right. She was *right* to be angry. He had brought this terrible situation upon them. His ceaseless pursuit of the story, his selfish desire for journalistic fame, his mindless denial of the increasing danger. The mere fact he wasn't in the country to protect Lizzie. All of it.

The drenching guilt and the self-hatred Rob felt at that moment felt almost good. A least it was real: a genuine, searing emotion. Something to pierce the oddly numb despair he felt so much of the time.

His only other lifeline to sanity was the phone. Rob spent hours gazing morosely at it, willing it to ring. And the phone did ring, many times. Sometimes he got calls from friends, sometimes from colleagues at work, sometimes from Isobel in Turkey. The callers were all trying to help, but Rob was impatient – for the one communication he wanted: the call from the police.

He already knew they had a promising lead: Forrester had rung four days back saying they now reckoned the gang was possibly somewhere around Montpelier House, south of Dublin. The home of the Irish Hellfire Club. The detective had explained Scotland Yard's route to this conclusion: how the killers were surely moving in and out of the country, because of their ability to totally disappear, yet they weren't being traced by Customs and passport checks. That meant they must be escaping to the one foreign country for which you didn't need passport checks – when leaving the UK.

They must have driven or flown to Ireland.

All that was very plausible. But Forrester had felt it necessary, when talking to Rob, to add some strange supporting theory – about buried victims and the Ribemont death-pit and Catalhoyuk and a murderer called Gacy, and the fact that Cloncurry would choose somewhere near his ancestors' victims . . . And Rob had switched off at that point.

He was far from convinced that Forrester was right with these psychological speculations. It just seemed to be a hunch and Rob didn't trust hunches. He didn't trust anyone. He didn't trust himself. The only thing he could trust was the sincerity of his own self-loathing, and the fierceness of his anguish.

That night he went to bed and slept for three hours. He dreamed of a crucified animal, screaming on a cross, a pig or a dog maybe. When he woke it was dawn. The image of the nailed animal persisted in his mind. He took some Valium. When he woke again it was noon. His mobile phone was ringing. *Ringing!* He ran to the table and picked up.

'Hello? Hello.'

'Rob.'

It was . . . Isobel. Rob felt his mood dive precipitously; he liked and admired Isobel, he craved her wisdom and succour, but right now he just wanted to hear from the police, the police, the police.

'Isobel . . .'

'No news then?'

He exhaled. 'Not since last time, no. Nothing. Just . . . just these fucking emails. From Cloncurry. The videos . . .'

'Robert, I'm sorry. I'm *so* sorry. But . . .' She paused. Rob could picture her in her gracious wooden house, staring at the blue Turkish sea. The mental image was piercing, reminding Rob of how he and Christine had fallen in love. There, under the Marmara stars.

'Robert, I have an idea.'

'Uhn.'

'About the Black Book.'

'OK . . .' He could barely muster any interest.

Isobel was not dissuaded. 'Listen, Rob. The Book. That's what these bastards are looking for, right? The Black Book? They are absolutely desperate. And you've told them you can find it, or you've found it, or whatever, to keep them going . . . Correct?'

'Yes, but . . . Isobel we *haven't* got it. We have no idea where it is.'

'But that's it! Imagine if we do find it. If we do locate the Black Book then we've got some real leverage over them, haven't we? We can . . . swap . . . negotiate . . . you see my meaning?'

Rob assented gruffly. He wanted to be energized and excited by this phone call. But he felt so tired.

Isobel talked on. As she did, Rob wandered barefoot through the flat, cradling the phone under his chin. Then he sat at his desk and gazed at the shining laptop. There was no email from Cloncurry. No new email, at least.

Isobel was still talking; Rob tried to focus. 'Isobel, I'm not with you. Sorry. Say again?'

'*Of course* . . .' She sighed. 'Let me explain. I think they – the gang – might be barking up the wrong tree. *Vis à vis* the book.'

'Why?'

'I've been doing some research. We know, at one point, the gang were interested in Layard. The Assyriologist, who met the Yezidi. Correct?'

A dim memory wafted across Rob's distractions. 'The break-in, at the school, you mean?'

'Yes.' Isobel's voice was crisp now. 'Austen Henry Layard, who instigated the Nineveh Porch. At Canford School. He is famous for meeting the Yezidi. In 1847.'

'OK . . . we know that . . .'

'But the truth is he met them twice! He met them again in 1850.'

'Rrright . . . so . . .'

'It's all in this book I've got – I've only just remembered. Here. *The Conquest of Assyria*. Here's what it says: Layard went to Lalesh in 1847. As we know. Then he returned to Constantinople and there he met the British ambassador to the Sublime Porte.'

'Sublime . . .'

'Porte. The Ottoman Empire. The ambassador was called Sir Stratford Canning. And that's when it all changes. Two years later, Layard goes back to the Yezidi again – and this time is met with inexplicable triumph, and he finds all the antiquities that made him famous. And all this is true. It's in the history books. So you see . . . ?'

Rob forced the image of his daughter from his mind. The leather gags . . . 'Actually, no, I haven't the foggiest what you're on about.'

'OK, Rob, I'm sorry. I'll get right to the point. On his first expedition Layard went to Lalesh. My guess is that when he was there he was told by the Yezidi about the Black Book, how it had been taken from them by an Englishman, Jerusalem Whaley. Layard was the first Brit the Yezidi had met, probably the first westerner – since Whaley's visit – so it makes perfect sense. They must have told him they wanted the Book returned.'

'Mmmmaybe . . .'

'So, Layard then goes to Constantinople and tells the ambassador, Canning, about his findings. We certainly know they met. And we also know Sir Stratford Canning was Anglo-Irish, of the Protestant ascendancy.'

Rob dimly discerned, at last, where this might be going. 'Canning was Irish?'

'Yes! The Anglo-Irish aristocracy. A tiny coterie. People like Whaley and Lord Saint Leger. The Hellfires. They are all related.'

'Well yes, that's curious. I s'pose. But how does it all fit in?'

'Around the same time, rumours were flying around Ireland, about a certain Edward Hincks.'

'Sorry? Right over my head.'

'Hincks was an obscure Irish parson from Cork. Who single-handedly managed to decipher cuneiform! All this is true, Rob. Google it. This is one of the great mysteries of Assyriology. The whole of educated Europe was trying to decipher cuneiform, then this rural Irish vicar beats them to it.' Isobel was rushing her words in her enthusiasm. 'So let's put two and two together. How did Hincks suddenly decipher cuneiform? He was an obscure Protestant cleric from the middle of nowhere. The bogs of Eire.'

'You think he found the Book?'

'I think Hincks found the Black Book. The book was almost certainly written in cuneiform – so Hincks must have somehow found it, in Ireland, and translated it, and deciphered cuneiform, and realized he'd found the Whaley treasure. The famous text of the Yezidi, once owned by the Hellfires. Maybe he tried to keep it secret – only a few Protestant Irish toffs would have known what Hincks had found, people already aware of the Whaley story, and the Irish Hellfires, in the first place.'

'You mean Irish aristos. People like . . . *Canning*?'

Isobel almost yelped. 'That's it, Rob. Sir Stratford Canning was hugely important in Anglo-Irish circles. Like many of his type he was no doubt ashamed of the Hellfire past. So when he heard that Whaley's book had been found Canning had the perfect idea to solve all their problems. They wanted rid of the Book. And he knew that Layard needed the Book to give to the Yezidi. And Hincks had just found the Book.'

'So the Black Book was sent back to Constantinople . . .'

'And then finally it was returned to the Yezidi . . . via Austen Layard!'

The phone went silent. Rob pondered the concept. He tried not to think about his daughter. 'Well. It's a theory . . .'

'It's more than a theory, Rob. Listen to this!' Rob could hear the pages of a book being flipped. 'Here. *Listen.* Here's the actual account of Layard's second visit to the Yezidi. "When it was rumoured among the Yezidi that Layard was back in Constantinople, it was decided to send four Yezidi priests and a chief" – and they went all the way to Constantinople.'

'So—'

'There's more. After some "secret negotiations" with Layard and Canning in the Ottoman capital, Layard and the Yezidi then headed east into Kurdistan, back to the lands of the Yezidi.' Isobel drew breath, then quoted directly: '"The journey from Lake Van to Mosul became a triumphal procession . . . Warm feelings of gratitude poured over Layard. It was to him the Yezidi had turned and he had proven worthy of their confidence." After that the group made their way through the Yezidi villages, to Urfa, accompanied by "hundreds of singing and shouting people".'

Rob could sense Isobel's excitement, but he couldn't share it. Staring glumly at the cloudy London sky he said, 'OK. I get it. You could be right. The Black Book is therefore in Kurdistan. Somewhere. Not Britain, not Ireland. It was returned by Layard after all. The gang are wrong. Sure.'

'Of course, darling,' Isobel said. 'But it's not just in Kurdistan, it's in *Urfa*. You see? The book says Urfa. Lalesh is of course the sacred capital of the Yezidi. But the ancient administrative capital, the political capital, is Urfa. The Book is in Sanliurfa! Hidden away somewhere. So Layard took it there, to the Yezidi. And in return the Yezidi told him where to find the great antiquities, the obelisk of Nineveh, and so on. And Canning and Layard got the fame they wanted. It all fits!'

Rob's mouth was dry. He felt a surge of sarcastic despair. 'OK. That's great, Izzy. It's possible. But how the hell do we get hold of it? How? The Yezidi just tried to kill us. Sanliurfa is a place where we are not wanted. You suggest we just march back in and demand they hand over their sacred text? Anything else we should do while we're at it? Walk across Lake Van perhaps?'

'I'm not talking about you,' Isobel sighed, firmly. 'I mean me. This gives *me* a chance! I have friends in Urfa. And if I can get to the Black Book first – even just borrow it for a few hours, just make a copy – then we have something on Cloncurry. We can exchange our knowledge for Lizzie and Christine. And I really do know Yezidi people. I believe I can find it. Find the Book.'

'Isobel—'

'You can't dissuade me! I'm going to Sanliurfa, Rob. I'm going to find the Book for you. Christine is my friend. And your daughter feels like my daughter. I want to help. I can do it. Trust me.'

'But, Isobel, it's dangerous. It's a wild theory. And the Yezidi I met certainly thought the Book was still in Britain. What's that about? And then there's Kiribali—'

The older woman chuckled. 'Kiribali doesn't know *me*. And anyway I'm sixty-eight. If I get beheaded by some psychotic Nestorians so be it,

I won't have to worry about a new prescription for my spectacles. But I think I'll be all right, Rob. I already have an idea where the Book might be. And I'm flying to Urfa tonight.'

Rob demurred. The hope Isobel offered was faint, very faint, yet it also appealed to him – perhaps because he had no other real hopes. And he also knew Isobel was risking her life, whatever the outcome. 'Thank you, Isobel. Thank you. Whatever happens. Thank you for this.'

'*De nada*. We're going to save those girls, Rob. I will see you soon. All three of you!'

Rob sat back and rubbed his eyes. Then he went out for the afternoon, and drank alone in a pub. Then he came back, for a few minutes, and couldn't bear the silence so he returned to the streets and carried on drinking. He went from pub to pub, drinking slowly and alone, staring at his mobile every five minutes. He did the same the next day. And the next. Sally rang five times. His friends from *The Times* rang. Steve rang. Sally rang. The police didn't ring.

And through it all Isobel called, almost every other hour, giving him her progress in Urfa. She said she felt she was 'close to the truth, close to the Book'. She said some of the Yezidi denied they had the Book, yet some thought she was right, that the Book had been returned, but they didn't know where it was kept. 'I'm close, Rob,' she said. 'I'm very close.'

Rob could hear the sound of the muezzin in the background of this last call, behind Isobel's earnestly encouraging voice. It was a strangely horrible feeling, hearing the hubbub of Sanliurfa. If he'd never gone there in the first place none of this would have happened. He never wanted to think about Kurdistan ever again.

For two more days Rob did nothing but agonize. Isobel stopped calling. Steve stopped calling so much. The silence was unendurable. He tried to drink tea and he tried to reassure Sally and he went to the supermarket to buy some vodka; then he got back home and went straight to his laptop, yet again. He was doing it by rote, now: expecting nothing.

But this time there was the little symbol of an envelope on his screen. A new email had arrived, and the new email was from . . . *Cloncurry.*

Rob opened up the message, his teeth gritted with tension.

The email was empty: apart from a link to a video. Rob clicked the videolink: the screen fizzed and cleared, and then Rob saw Christine and his daughter in a bare room, again tied to chairs. The room was a little different, smaller than the last one. The prisoners' clothes had changed. Obviously Christine and Lizzie had been moved.

But it wasn't any of this that caused Rob to shiver, with a harsh new fear, and a deeper anguish: it was the fact the two hostages were *hooded.* Someone had put thick black hoods over the heads of the girls.

Rob grimaced. He remembered his own terror in that foul black hood in Lalesh. *Staring at the darkness.*

These new, chilling scenes on the video – of Lizzie and Christine, silent, hooded, and lashed to the chairs – lasted a long three minutes. After then Cloncurry appeared, talking directly to the webcam.

Rob stared at the lean and handsome face.

'Hello, Rob! As you can see we've moved to more exciting accommodation. The girls have got hoods on because we want to frighten the living fuck out of them. So. *Do* tell me about the Black Book. Are you really on to it? I need to know. I need to be kept fully informed. Please don't keep secrets. I don't like secrets. Family secrets are such terrible things, don't you think? So tell me. If you still want a family, if you don't want your family dead, tell me. Tell me soon. Don't make me do what I don't want to do.'

Cloncurry turned away. He seemed to be talking to someone behind the webcam. Murmuring. Rob could hear laughter from somewhere off-cam. Then Cloncurry faced the camera again. 'I mean, let's get down to basics, Rob. You know what I like to do, you know my metier. It's sacrifice, isn't it? Human sacrifice. But the trouble is I am spoiled for choice. I mean: how *shall* I kill your daughter? And Christine? Because there are so many methods of sacrifice, aren't there? What are your favourites, Rob? I rather like the Viking ones. Don't you? The blood eagling, for example. The professor was quite alarmed I believe, when we took out his lungs. Alarmed and somewhat impressed, if I say so myself. But we could have been so much . . . *crueller.*' Cloncurry smiled.

Rob sat in his flat, sweating.

Cloncurry edged nearer the camera. 'For instance, there is a delightful rite the Celts had. They would impale their victims. Especially young women. First they would strip them naked, then they would carry them to a field, lift them up on top of a sharp wooden stake, and pull their legs apart, and then – well then just kind of yank them down, onto the stick. Impaling them. Through the vagina. Or the anus maybe.' Cloncurry yawned, then continued, 'I really don't want to do that to your lovely girlfriend, Rob. I mean, if I did shove a pike up her snatch she would just bleed all over the rug. And then we'll have to buy a big carpet cleaner. A needless expense!' He smiled again. 'So just give me the fucking Black Book. The Tom Whaley shit. Stuff you found in Lalesh. Give it over. Now.'

The webcam wobbled slightly. Cloncurry reached out and steadied it. Then he said, direct to camera, 'And as for *child* sacrifice, with little Lizzie over here. Well now . . .'

He got up and walked over to Lizzie's chair. With a magician's flourish, Cloncurry whipped off the hood – and there was Lizzie. Staring, terrified, at the camera, the leather gag tight around her mouth.

Cloncurry stroked the girl's hair. 'So many methods, just the one little girl. Which one shall we choose? The Incans would take children up mountains and just kill them by exposure. But that's rather slow, I feel. Rather . . . *boring.* But how about one of the more refined Aztec methods? You may, for instance, have heard of the god Tlaloc?'

He moved around Lizzie's chair. 'The god Tlaloc was a bit of a cunt, to be perfectly frank, Rob. He wanted his thirst slaked with human tears. So the Aztec priests had to make the children cry. So they did this by tearing off the children's fingernails. Very slowly. One by one.'

Cloncurry was unstrapping one of Lizzie's hands now; Rob saw that his daughter's hand was shaking with fear. 'Yes, Rob, they would rip out the nails, then cut off little fingers like these.' He caressed her fingers. 'And that made the children cry, of course. Having their fingernails ripped away. And then as they tore off the nails the Aztecs would capture the tears of the sobbing children, and give the liquid to Tlaloc. Then the kids were decapitated.'

Cloncurry smiled. Then, brusquely, he tied Lizzie's hand to the arm of the chair again. 'So that's what I may do, Rob, I may follow the old Aztec method. But I really think you should try and dissuade me. Don't make me rip off her nails, slice off her fingers, and then chop her head off. But if I am forced by your obstinacy to do any of that, I shall be sure to send her tears to you in a little plastic pot. So get cracking, get moving, get working.' He smiled. 'Chop chop!'

The killer leaned forward, looking for a switch. The video paused; the clip was frozen.

Rob stared at the silent computer for ten minutes afterwards. At the final frozen image of Cloncurry's half smile. His high cheekbones; his glittering green eyes; his dark hair. Sitting in the room behind him were Rob's daughter and Rob's girlfriend, tied to chairs, waiting to be impaled, to be mutilated and killed. Rob had no doubt that Cloncurry would do these things. He'd read the report of De Savary's murder.

The following day Rob spent with Sally. And then he got another email. With another video. And this one was so grotesque that Rob vomited as he watched.

41

As soon as he'd got the new email with the new video Rob went to Scotland Yard, to Forrester's office. He didn't even ring first, he didn't text or email, he wiped the puke from his mouth and washed his face with cold water, and hailed a cab.

On the way to Victoria he looked at all the happy people. Shopping; walking; climbing on and off buses; staring in shop windows. It was hard to reconcile the ordinariness of the street scene with the obscenity of what Rob had just witnessed in the video.

He tried not to think about it. He had to control his anger. They could still save his daughter; even if it was too late for Christine. Rob sat in the back of the taxi and felt like punching out the cab window, but he wasn't going to lose control. Not yet, anyway. What he would do, if he ever got the chance, was slaughter Cloncurry. And not just slaughter him with a knife or a hatchet: Rob was going to take a poker to Cloncurry's head, smash the back of his skull until brain came ejaculating out of his eyes. No, worse than that, he would burn Cloncurry slowly with acid, rotting away that handsome face. Anything. Anything anything anything ANYTHING ANYTHING.

Rob wanted payback for what he'd just seen Cloncurry do to Christine in the video. He wanted homicidal revenge. *Now.*

The taxi pulled up at the glass and steel atrium of New Scotland Yard and Rob paid the taxi driver with a fierce grunt and went in through the glass doors. The girls on reception tried to stop him but he glared at them so angrily they didn't know what to do; then Boijer spotted him in the lobby.

'There's something you need to see,' said Rob.

The friendly-faced Finn offered a smile but Rob didn't smile back. The Finn's expression darkened; Rob scowled in return.

The lift journey was quiet. They paced to Forrester's corridor. Boijer knocked on his superior's door but Rob shoved right in. Forrester was sipping from a mug of tea and staring at folders and he jumped, startled, as Rob burst into the office and sat down in the chair besides Forrester's. Rob said, bluntly, 'Check this webmail. Email from Cloncurry.'

'But why didn't you call us we could have—'

'*Look at it.*'

With a worried glance at Boijer, Forrester leaned forward to his screen and opened up a search engine. He went to Rob's email; Rob gave him the password.

'There,' said Rob. 'It's just a video link. Open it.'

Forrester clicked and the video fizzed into life, showing the same scene as before. Christine and Lizzie tied to a chair. Same clothes, same hoods, a room as nondescript as the last. Hard to tell.

'I've seen this,' said Forrester, gently. 'We're working on it, Rob. We think he's hooding them so they can't blink at you and send messages, some people can do that – send signals by blinking. Anyway there's something I wanted to mention—'

'Detective.'

'I've been researching the Cloncurrys and the Whaleys, their ancestry, it's a new angle and—

'*Detective*!' Rob was full of righteous anger. And grief. 'I want you to shut up. *Just watch the clip.*'

The two policemen swapped another anxious glance. Boijer stepped round so he could look at the screen. The three men stared at the computer as the little video clip rolled into action.

A figure emerged from the left of the screen. It was Cloncurry. He was carrying a big saucepan – a huge, grey metal saucepan, full of steaming water. He set the saucepan down, then disappeared off-screen again. Christine and Lizzie sat there in their vile black hoods, presumably oblivious. Not sensing what Cloncurry was doing.

Now Cloncurry was back. With a kind of metal tripod, and a camping gas stove – already emitting an eager blue flame. He set up the tripod in front of Christine and put the burning gas stove between the legs of the metal stand; then he picked up the steaming tureen of water, and placed it on top. With the blazing flame directly beneath it, the water started to bubble, and to boil.

Apparently satisfied, Cloncurry turned to the camera. 'Those Swedes are an odd bunch, aren't they, Rob? I mean, look at their cooking. Open sandwiches. Gravadlax. All that stuff with herrings. And now this! Anyway, we're all set. I hope you appreciate the expense we've gone to, Robert. This saucepan cost fifty quid. I may take it back afterwards, swap it for a toast rack.' He looked away from the camera. 'OK. So. Guys. Has someone got the knife?' He was looking offscreen. 'Hell-o? Big knife for cutting up people? Yes. That's it. Thank you so much.'

Taking the blade from an unseen assistant, Cloncurry tilted the knife in his hand, and ran a thumb down the edge. 'Perfect.'

Now he was staring at the camera again. 'Of course I'm not talking about modern Sweden, Rob. No. I don't mean Ikea dining chairs. Or Volvos and Saabs and indoor tennis centres.' Cloncurry laughed. 'I mean Sweden before they went all gay on us. Real Sweden. Medieval Sweden. The long-haired barbarians who really knew how to deal with victims, who know how to sacrifice . . . to Odin. And Thor. *You know.* 'Cause that's what we're going to do, in a very special way. We're going all Swedish this morning. Old time Swedish sacrifice. The Boiling of the Innards.' The knife flashed in the air. 'We're going to cut open one of your girls and boil her lights and vitals, alive, in this big old pot here. But which one shall we sacrifice? Which one do you fancy?' His eyes twinkled. 'Which one? The little girl or the big girl? Mmm? I think maybe we should save the best to last, don't you? And much as you love pretty Christine here with that adorable birthmark near her nipple – yes, that one – I imagine you are more attached to your daughter. So I think we should spare your daughter for a different ritual, later on, maybe tomorrow, and instead we should slice open the Frenchwoman. She has such a nice tummy, after all. Shall we cut your friend open? Yes I think so.'

The killer leaned towards Christine's hooded figure. She was straining and arching against her bonds, pointlessly. Rob could see the hood inflating and deflating as Christine panted with fear under her shroud.

Cloncurry lifted up her jumper a couple of inches and Christine jerked away from his touch.

'Goodness. She doesn't seem very keen, does she? All I'm going to do is carve out her intestines and her stomach and maybe her bladder and boil them slowly in this pot so she dies over thirty minutes or more. Anyone would think she was at the dentist. What's wrong with that, Christine?'

In the fetid tension of the office, Forrester leaned to turn the video off.

Rob snapped. 'No! *Watch it.* I want you to watch it. I had to fucking watch it. Watch it!'

Forrester sat back. Rob saw the glint of tears in the policeman's eyes. Rob didn't care. He'd had to watch it. Now *they* had to watch it.

They watched.

Cloncurry's initial slicing movement was quick. With a professional ease, as if he was practised at butchery, Cloncurry stabbed the knife into Christine's exposed stomach, and ripped the blade laterally. Blood seeped out, down the blade and onto Christine's lap. A moan was distinctly audible, despite the gag and the hood, muffling Christine's voice. The blood was seeping slowly, and the pink and red inner organs were beginning to ooze and poke out of the horizontal slash, like the smeared pink heads of weird babies.

'Well lookie here,' said Cloncurry, forcing open the huge wound to peer inside. 'Who's that pushing in front. Mrs Uterus? Come on gal, give someone else a chance.'

Dropping the knife, the murderer reached his hands, deep into the lateral gash in Christine's stomach. Rob couldn't help noticing how pale Christine's stomach was. Her tan had faded from her imprisonment; her skin looked almost white. But the whiteness was coloured by the slowly dripping blood. And the moans were escalating into whines of pain, as Cloncurry gently drew out Christine's intestines: coils of pastel grey and greasy blue, like links of obscenely raw sausages.

Carefully Cloncurry extracted more of Christine's organs, still attached to her body by veins, arteries and muscles, and grey-white ganglions; then he carried the great handful of innards to the pot, and he dropped the organs with a plop, into the steaming vat of water.

Christine writhed.

'Now you see how clever those Swedes were. You can extract all the lower organs, but the victim lives on. Because she's still attached to her major organs, so she's still metabolizing. It's just that she's *also* being boiled to death.' Cloncurry was smirking. 'Hey. Shall we pop some pepper in? Make it spicy. A lovely hotpot of girlfriend.'

Christine's muffled voice was a strange, sobbing, urgent moan of pain. Smothered by the gag and the hood, it was a noise Rob had never heard anyone make before.

Cloncurry had picked up a large wooden spoon from somewhere and was stirring Christine's innards in the pot. The stirring went on for a few searing minutes, punctuated by the victim's desperate groaning. Cloncurry sighed in frustration. 'Jesus. She's a bit of a moaner, isn't she? She never moaned like this when I fucked her. Do you think she's enjoying it? Hmm.' He smiled. 'I know, let's cheer her up with a proper Swedish singsong!' Cloncurry started humming, then burst into song. 'Mamma Mia don't you let me go, my my, how could I forget you! Yes,

I was broken-hearted, blue since the day we parted, but now you've – put me in a pressure cooker!'

He stopped singing. The moaning became a low murmur, then virtually a whimper. Cloncurry gave the pot another stir. 'Chin up, Christine, not long to go now. Think the gravy is thickening.' He smiled. 'Ah look, what's this here? Look at this! *Mr Kidney.*'

Cloncurry turned to the camera and held up the wooden spoon. Balanced in the bowl of the spoon was one of Christine's dark brown kidneys, draped with veins and arteries, like blood-red spaghetti.

Forrester stared down at the floor.

'That's it,' said Rob. 'The video ends around now. Christine slumps. She just . . . she just *dies.*'

Boijer leaned forward and shut down the email. Then he turned to Rob. He said nothing, but there was a definite wetness in his eyes.

For a while the men sat around the room. Barely able to speak. Rob shrugged, desolately, at the policemen; and he got up to go.

And then the phone rang.

Forrester took the call. His gaze met Rob's across the room, as he spoke, low, on the phone. At last, the detective put the phone down. 'It may be too late for . . . for Christine. But we can still save your daughter.'

Rob stared at him, from the open door.

Forrester nodded, grimly. 'That was the Gardai. In Ireland. *They've found the gang.*'

42

Forrester and Rob met at Dublin Airport. The policeman was accompanied by several Irish officers with gold star cap badges.

There was little small talk. Forrester and the Irish police led Rob straight through the arrivals lounge into a breezy car park; they climbed wordlessly into a minivan.

It was Rob who broke the sombre and frightening silence. 'My ex-wife is here?'

Forrester nodded. 'Arrived on the flight an hour before you. She's at the scene.'

'It was the last seat on that flight,' said Rob. He felt a need to explain himself. He felt guilty all the time now. Guilty about Christine's death; guilty about Lizzie's impending fate. Guilt about his own lethal stupidity. 'So . . .' he said, trying to control his emotions. 'I got the next flight. I let her go first.'

The cops all nodded. Rob didn't know what else to say. He sighed and bit his knuckles and tried not to think about Christine. Then he lifted his gaze and told Forrester and Boijer about Isobel and her attempts to find the Black Book. He hadn't heard from her in a day or more, he told them, and he couldn't get her on the phone; but that silence might mean that she was close to her prize. Out there in the desert, beyond the reach of a signal.

The policemen shrugged as if trying to be impressed, but failing. Rob couldn't blame them: it seemed a long shot, and pretty obscure, and so very far away, compared to the reality of cold, rainy Ireland. And a cornered gang of murderers. And an eviscerated corpse. And a daughter about to be dismembered.

At last he said, 'So, what's the latest . . . ?'

The senior Irish officer introduced himself. He had greying hair and a serious, firm-jawed face. 'Detective Liam Dooley.'

They shook hands.

'We've been staking them out. Obviously, we can't go straight in. Heavily-armed buncha guys. They've killed . . . the woman . . . your friend. I'm sorry. But the girl is still alive and we want to save her. We will save her. But we have to be careful.'

'Yes,' said Rob. They were struck in traffic on the busy Dublin ringroads. He gazed through the rain-smeared van windows.

Dooley leaned forward and tapped the police driver's shoulder: he turned on the siren and the Gardai minivan swung through the traffic, which peeled away to let the police vehicle pass.

'OK,' said Dooley, talking loudly above the siren. 'I'm sure DCI Forrester has filled you in but this is the scene now. We snatched one of them, the Italian—'

'Marsinelli,' said Forrester.

'Yes, him. Marsinelli. We snatched him yesterday. Of course that's alerted the rest of the gang: they know we are surrounding them and they're heavily armed.'

Rob nodded, and sighed, then he gave into his feelings and slumped forward, his head hard against the seat in front. Thinking of Christine. The way she must have heard her own organs boiling . . .

Forrester put a calming hand on Rob's shoulder. 'We'll get them, don't worry, Rob. The Gardai know what they are doing. They dealt with Irish terrorism for thirty years. We'll get Lizzie out.'

Rob grunted: he wasn't just feeling sad and scared, he was also feeling a rising resentment, at the police. The police had snatched just one gang member, and his daughter was still inside the cottage, still in the hands of Cloncurry. And Christine was already dead. *The Irish cops were screwing up*. 'What you're telling me then,' he said, 'is that it's a total stalemate? You've got the place surrounded so they can't get out but you can't get in either, in case they do anything to my daughter. But he's already butchered my girlfriend! And we know he has killed before. So how do we know he isn't killing Lizzie right now? Right this fucking minute?'

Dooley shook his head. 'We know your daughter is OK. Because we are speaking to Cloncurry all the time.'

'How?'

'By webcam. He's got another webcam set up – a two-way webcam this time. We've seen your daughter and she's OK. Uninjured. Tied up. As before.'

Rob turned to Forrester for reassurance. The DCI nodded. 'Cloncurry is rambling on a lot. He may be on drugs.'

'But what if he suddenly snaps?'

There was a weighty silence in the minivan. The siren had been switched off. No one spoke. Then Dooley said, 'For some reason he seems determined to get something out of you. He wants this Black Book or whatever it is. He goes on and on about it. We think he is convinced you have it. He won't kill your daughter while he thinks that.'

Rob couldn't follow the logic. He couldn't follow anything.

They turned off the motorway, leaving the last of the Dublin suburbs behind, and sped along open country roads, heading into green, well-wooded hills. White-painted farmsteads dotted the fields. A sign said *Wicklow Mountains 5km*. It was still drizzling.

Dooley added quietly, 'And of course, if there is any sign that he is going to harm your daughter we will go in, whatever the risk. We've got armed Gardai all over. I promise.'

Rob closed his eyes. He could imagine the scene: the police rushing in, the melee and the chaos. And Cloncurry silently smiling and slitting his daughter's throat with a kitchen knife, or shooting her in the temple, just before the police smashed through the door. What was to stop him? Why would a lunatic like Jamie Cloncurry keep Rob's daughter alive? But perhaps the police were right. Cloncurry must be desperate to find the Black Book: that was what Isobel had surmised. And Cloncurry must have believed Rob when he said he could find it. Otherwise he'd have just killed Lizzie as well as Christine.

The problem was that Rob had no idea where the Book was. And unless Isobel came up with something, very quickly, this fact would soon become apparent. And what then? When Cloncurry guessed that Rob had nothing, *what happened then*? Rob didn't have to guess. When that happened, Cloncurry would do what he had done so many times: kill his victim. Get that grim and macabre satisfaction, and silence the blood-lusting voice inside him. He would placate his Whaley demons – and kill with great cruelty.

Rob gazed at the sodden green countryside. He saw another sign, half-hidden by dripping oak branches. *Hellfire Wood, owned by the Irish Forestry Commission, Coillte.* They were nearly there.

He had studied the history of the place on the train to Stansted Airport, simply to give himself something to do. To distract himself from his horrible imaginings. On the top of a hill near here was an old stone hunting lodge: Montpelier House. Built on a hilltop also graced by a Neolithic stone circle. Montpelier had a reputation for being haunted. It was celebrated by occultists, cider-drinking kids and local historians alike. The lodge was one of the main places where the Irish Hellfire members had got together. To drink their scultheen and burn those black cats and play whist with the devil.

Much of what happened in the house was, as far as Rob could tell, legend and myth. But the rumours of murder were not entirely unsubstantiated. A house in the valley beneath Montpelier had also, according to legend, been used by the Hellfirers. By Buck Egan, and Jerusalem

Whaley, and Jack St Leger and all the rest of the eighteenth century sadists.

Killakee House, it was called. And when Killakee House was being refurbished decades ago they had dug up a skeleton of a child or a dwarf, next to a small brass statue of a demon.

Rob turned and looked out of the other window. He could actually see Montpelier House now: a sombre grey presence on top of the hills, even darker and greyer than the grey clouds beyond. It was a vile day for June. Suitably rainy and satanic. Rob thought of his daughter shivering in the cottage somewhere near here. He had to get a grip. Think positive, even in the smallest way. He hadn't congratulated Forrester on his coup.

'By the way, well done.'

The DCI frowned. 'Sorry?'

'On the hunch, you know, finding these guys.'

Forrester shook his head. 'It was nothing. Just a reasonable guess. I tried to think with his brain. Cloncurry's deluded brain. He likes the historical resonance. Check his family. Where they live. He would hide out somewhere that meant something to him. And of course they are looking for the Black Book, for Whaley's treasure. This is where Burnchapel Whaley came from, where Jerusalem Whaley came from. They would have started looking here, so why not base yourself here?'

The van scrunched to a halt outside a farmhouse with a large tent erected in the forecourt and they all climbed out. Rob walked into the crowded tent and saw his ex-wife in the corner, sitting with a Gardai policewoman drinking a mug of tea. There were lots of policemen here, lots of sonorous Irish accents, flashing gold cap badges and screens of TV monitors.

Dooley took Rob by the arm and talked him through the situation. The gang's cottage was just a few hundred yards away down the hill. If you walked three minutes to the left, out of the farmhouse back door, you could see it, tucked into a narrow green valley. Montpelier House was right on top of the lofty hill behind them.

'Cloncurry rented the croft months ago,' said Dooley. 'From the farmer's wife. She was the one who informed us, when we were doing door to door. Said she'd seen strange comings and goings. So we put the cottage under surveillance. We've been watching them for twenty hours now. Think we've counted five men inside. We seized Marsinelli as he drove to the shops.'

Rob nodded, dumbly. He felt very dumb. He was in some dumb stupid stand-off: policemen with rifles were apparently stationed around the fields and hills, gunsights aimed at the cottage. Inside were four men led by a fucking lunatic. Rob wanted to run down the hill and just . . . do something. *Anything.* Instead he glanced at the TV screens. It seemed the Gardai had several cameras, one of them infra-red, directed at the gang's hide-out. Every movement was scrutinized and noted, day and night. Though nothing serious had been seen for hours: the curtains were shut; the doors self-evidently shut.

On a desk in front of the TV monitors was a laptop. Rob guessed this was the computer set up to receive communications from Cloncurry via the webcam. The laptop had a webcam of its own.

Feeling as if someone had filled his lungs with frozen leadshot Rob crossed to Sally. They exchanged words, and a hug.

And then Dooley called to Rob across the tent. 'It's Cloncurry! He's on the webcam again. We told him you were here. He wants to speak to you.'

Rob ran across the tent and stood in front of the laptop screen. There it was. That angular face: almost likeable, yet so utterly chilling. The intelligent yet serpentine eyes. Behind Cloncurry was Lizzie, in fresh clothes; still tied to a chair; this time unhooded.

'Ah, the gentleman from *The Times.*'

Rob stared mutely at the screen. He felt a nudge from somewhere. Dooley was gesturing and mouthing: *talk to him, keep him talking.* 'Hello,' said Rob.

'Hello!' Cloncurry laughed. 'I'm sorry we had to parboil your fiancée, but your little girl is perfectly unharmed. Indeed I like to think she's in tiptop condition! We're giving her lots of fruit. So she thrives.

Of course I'm not sure quite how long we can maintain the status quo, but that's up to you.'

'You've . . .' Rob said. 'You've . . .' He tried again. It was no good; he didn't know what to say. In despair he turned and looked at Dooley, but as he did, he realized something. He *did* have something to say. He had one card in his hand and now he had to play it. He stared directly at the screen. 'OK, Cloncurry, this is the deal. If you give me Lizzie. I can get you the Book. I can do that.'

Jamie Cloncurry winced. It was the first flash of insecurity, however subtle, that Rob had ever seen on his face. It gave him hope.

'Of course,' said Cloncurry. 'Of course you can.' The smile was sarcastic; unconvinced. 'I suppose you got it in Lalesh?'

'No.'

'So where did you get it? What the fuck are you on about, Luttrell?'

'Ireland. It's here in Ireland. The Yezidi told me where. They told me in Lalesh, where to find it.'

It was a blatant gamble – and yet it seemed to work. There was a hint of worry and doubt on Cloncurry's face, worry disguised by a sneer. 'Right. But of course you can't tell me *where* it is. Even though I might slice off your daughter's nose with a cigar cutter.'

'It doesn't matter *where* it is. But I'll bring it here. In a day or two. Then you can have your Book and you can give me back my daughter.' He gazed into Cloncurry's eyes. 'Whether you shoot your way out after that, I don't care.'

'No. Nor do I.' Cloncurry laughed. 'Nor do I, Robbee. I just want the Book.'

The two men stared at each other. Rob felt a surge of curiosity, the old journalistic intrigue. 'But *why*? Why are you so obsessed by it? Why all of . . . *this*?'

Cloncurry looked off-camera, as if thinking. His green eyes flashed as he glanced back. 'I may as well tell you a little, I suppose. What do you journalists call it? A teaser?'

Rob sensed the policemen moving on his left: something was happening. Was this the signal? Were the police moving in? Was his daughter's fate going to be decided *right now*?

Forrester made a hand gesture: *keep him talking.*

But it was Cloncurry who kept talking. 'Three hundred years ago, Rob, Jerusalem Whaley came back from the Holy Land with a cache of materials brought back from the Yezidi. He should have been a happy man. Because he had found precisely what the Hellfire Club had been looking for, what Francis Dashwood had sought all those years. He had found the final proof that all the religions, all the faiths, the Koran and the Talmud and the Bible, all that rancid, imaginary piffle, all of it was bullshit. Religion is just the stale reek of urine from the orphanage of the human soul. For an atheist, for a priest-hater like my forefather, that final proof was the Holy Grail. The big one. El Gordo. The lottery win. God isn't just dead, *the fucker never lived.*' Cloncurry smiled. 'And yet, Rob, what Whaley found went further than that. What he found was so mortifying it actually broke his heart. What's the saying? Be careful what you wish for. Isn't that how it goes?'

'So what was it? What did he find?'

'Ah.' Cloncurry chuckled. 'Wouldn't you like to know, Robbie, my little tabloid hack? But I'm not going to tell you. If you really know where the Book is you can have a read yourself. Except if you tell anyone I shall slice up your daughter with a set of steak-knives from eBay. All I can say for now is that Thomas Buck Whaley concealed the Book. And he told a few of his friends what was in it. And that in certain circumstances the Book must be destroyed.'

'Why didn't he destroy it himself?'

'Who knows? The Black Book is such an extraordinary . . . treasure trove. Such a terrifying revelation, Rob, maybe he couldn't quite bring himself to do it. He must have had some pride in its discovery. He had found what the great Dashwood didn't. Him. Humble Tom Whaley from the boondocks of colonial Ireland had outdone the British Chancellor. He must have been proud, despite himself. So instead of destroying it, he hid it. Where exactly has been forgotten over time. Hence our heroic search for my brave ancestor's discovery. But here's the clever bit, Rob. Are you listening?'

The police were definitely doing something. Rob could see armed men walking out of the tent. He heard whispered commands. There was a sense of action: the videoscreens were flickering with movement. At the same time the gang seemed to be erecting something in the garden. It was a big wooden stake. Like something you'd use for an impaling.

Rob knew he had to keep Cloncurry talking; stay calm and keep the killer talking. 'Go on. Go on, I'm listening.'

'Whaley said that if ever a temple was dug up in Turkey—'

'Gobekli Tepe?!'

'Clever boy. Gobekli Tepe. Whaley told his confidants precisely what the Yezidi had told him: that if ever Gobekli Tepe was dug up then the Black Book must be destroyed.'

'Why?'

'That's the damn point, you halfwit. Because the Book is, in the right hands, seen the right way, combined with evidence from Gobekli, something that would overturn the world, Rob: it would change everything. It would demean and degrade society. Not just religions. The whole structure of our lives, the way the world exists, would be endangered if the truth was revealed.' Cloncurry was leaning very close to the webcam. His face filled the entire screen. 'That is the rich, rich irony here, Rob. All along I've just been trying to protect you from yourself, you jerks, protect all of humanity. That is the job of the Cloncurrys. To protect you all. To find the Book if necessary, and destroy it. To save you all! You know, we are practically saints. I am expecting an e-vite from the Pope any day now.' The snakelike smile had returned.

Rob glanced up at the screens behind the laptop. He could see movement. One of the cameras showed three figures, obviously armed, crawling towards the cottage garden: it had to be the police. Going in.

As he tried to concentrate on the dialogue with Cloncurry he realized that Cloncurry was probably trying to do exactly the same in reverse: to distract Rob and the police.

But Dooley and his men had seen the wooden stake: they knew this was the moment. Rob stared at the profile of his daughter. Tied to her chair, visible over Cloncurry's shoulder. With a physical effort, Rob got hold of his emotions. 'So why all the violence? Why all the killing? If you just wanted the Yezidi Book, why all the sacrifices?'

The face on the laptop scowled. 'Because I am a Cloncurry. We descend from the Whaleys. They descend from Oliver Cromwell. *Capisce?* Notice the theme of burning people there? Burning people in churches? With a nice big audience? Cromwell was heard to laugh when he killed people in battle.'

'So?'

'So just blame my fucking haplotype. Ask my double helix. Take a look at Dysbindin gene sequence DTNBP-1.'

Rob tried not to think of his daughter: impaled. 'So, you're saying you inherited this trait?'

Cloncurry applauded, sarcastically. 'Brilliant, Holmes. Yes. Quite clearly I am a psychopath. How much proof do you want? Stay tuned to this channel and you might see me eat your daughter's brain. With some oven chips. That proof enough?'

Rob swallowed his anger. He just had to keep Cloncurry here, and keep Lizzie in view, via the webcam. And that meant listening to the madman, ranting. He nodded.

'Of course I have the fucking genes for violence, Rob. And funnily enough I have the genes for very high intelligence, too. You know what my IQ is? 147. Yes, 147. That makes me a genius, even by the standards of geniuses. The average IQ of a Nobel Prize winner is 145. I'm smart, Rob. Very smart. I'm probably too smart for you to realize how smart I am. That's the problem with very high intelligence. For me, relating to ordinary folk is like trying to have a serious chat with a mollusc.'

'Yet we caught you.'

'Oh, well done. You and your piffling post-grad IQ of, what, 125? 130? Jesus Christ. I am a Cloncurry. I carry the noble genes of the Cromwells and the Whaleys. Unfortunately for you and your daughter I also carry their propensity for flamboyant violence. Which we are about to see. Nonetheless—'

Cloncurry turned to his left. Rob looked up and checked the video monitors. The police were moving in: at last the guns had opened up. The shots and the echoes resounded along the valley.

There were shouts and noises and gunshots everywhere. From the laptop, from the monitors, from the valley. The laptop screen fuzzed and then came back, as if the camera had been knocked. Cloncurry was standing. Another shot was audible across the valley, then four more – and then it happened. Rob watched as a second team of police made a move, firing as they went. Shooting with speed and verve.

The Gardai snipers were taking out the gang. He saw the dark figures of the gang members on the TV monitors crumple to the ground. Two bodies fell. Then he heard another scream. He didn't know if it was coming from the TVs or the laptop or real life outside, but the noises were unnerving: these were high-velocity rifles. There was a shout: perhaps one of the policemen was down. And then another? But the assault went on – live on the TV monitors all over the tent.

The police were pouring over the back wall of the cottage garden and vaulting over the fences. As Rob watched the screens the backyard of the cottage was filled with policemen in black ski-masks and black helmets, yelling out orders. Screaming at the gang.

It was all happening with stunning and incredible speed. At least one of the gang looked seriously injured, sprawled and barely moving; another might have been dead. Then someone jumped forward and threw a stun grenade into the cottage and Rob heard an enormous bang; clouds of black smoke came streaming out of the broken cottage window.

Through the smoke and the deafening noise and confusion it was nonetheless clear: the police were *winning* – but could they take Cloncurry *as well*? Rob stared at the laptop. Cloncurry had Lizzie, wriggling, in his arms. He was frowning, backing off, retreating out of the room. As he ran from the room Cloncurry's hand came out and snatched the laptop shut and the picture went black.

43

Apart from its leader the gang was finished, its members dead, seriously injured or in custody; two policemen were wounded. Ambulances were parked along the roads behind them; doctors and nurses and paramedics were everywhere.

Now the cottage was filling with police for the final stake-out. Cloncurry was apparently barricaded in the rear upstairs bedroom: he'd turned his laptop on again; Lizzie was once more lashed to a chair. Rob could see all this through the webcam. The room in which she was being held had been prepared for a final shoot-out.

Rob was gazing at Cloncurry's leering face. Staring at that smile so thin and well-bred and sneering it was as if someone had sliced his mouth slightly wider with a knife. His mineral-green eyes glinted in the half-light of the cottage bedroom.

The police had been urgently discussing what to do. Forrester reckoned they should just charge in, blasting the door: every second they delayed endangered Lizzie's life. The Gardai were much more reticent: Dooley felt they should talk some more. Maybe find a way of breaking in through the roof, clandestinely. Rob wanted them to go in now. He felt sure he'd worked out Cloncurry's psychology. The gang leader surely knew he was dead: he knew he wasn't going to get the Book, but he wanted to take Lizzie down with him, in the most disgusting way – by making her father watch his daughter die. Rob shuddered, to the depths of his spine, when he considered the ways Cloncurry might butcher his daughter. Right now. Live. On camera.

Forrester grasped Rob's shoulder, trying to reassure him. The Gardai officers were urgently examining, once more, the plans of the cottage: the chimney; the windows, everything. Could they throw stun grenades through the upper floor windows? Could a marksman take a shot through the window? Their deliberations infuriated Rob. Yet he knew that as soon as they tried anything Cloncurry would kill Lizzie. The doors to the last room were surely bolted, locked, and sturdy. It was a stand-off with only one possible outcome. It would take at least two or three minutes to break in. As soon as they began to break in, Cloncurry would take one of his gleaming knives and cut her tongue out. Slice her eyes out. Slice an artery in her pale young throat . . .

Rob thought of his daughter's head detached from her body. He tried not to think about this. Sally was silently crying. So was their daughter, it seemed. In the background of the vidpicture Rob could see Lizzie's shoulders shaking.

Sally wiped her running nose with the back of her hand, and said what Rob was thinking. 'It's just a stalemate. He's going to kill her. Oh Jesus . . .'

Rob clenched his teeth at his ex-wife's tearful and jagged remark. She was right.

On the laptop screen Cloncurry was rambling. Talking to the webcam. He'd been doing this on and off for twenty minutes. Since the shootings in the cottage, and the backyard. The ramblings were bizarre.

This time he was talking about the Holocaust.

'Haven't you ever thought, Rob, about Hitler, why he did what he did? That was a big sacrifice, wasn't it? The Holocaust? A big human sacrifice. That's that the Jews call it, did you know that? The Shoah. The burnt offering. Shoah means a burnt offering, like the sacrifice.

Hitler sacrificed them. They were burnt offerings, like the little children the Yids gave to Moloch. In the tophet. Ben hinnom. The valley of the shadow of death. In the place of burning. Yes. That's where we are Rob, in the Valley of the Shadow of Death. Where the little children get burned.'

Cloncurry licked his lips. He had a gun in one hand and a knife in the other. The killer's speech rambled on. 'Great men always sacrifice. Don't they? Napoleon used to march across rivers on the bodies of his drowned men. He would order them into the rivers, to drown, so he could use their stiffened corpses as a bridge. A truly great man. Then there's Pol Pot, he butchered two million of his people in Cambodia *as an experiment,* Rob. Two million. That's what the Khmer Rouge did. And they were the *haute bourgeoisie*: the upper middle classes. The educated and enlightened.'

Rob shook his head and looked away from the laptop.

Cloncurry sneered. 'Oh, you don't want to talk about it. How convenient. But you're going to have to talk about it, Rob. Face facts. Every political leader in the world has some urge towards violence, is a sadist of sorts. The Iraq war, we fought that for freedom, didn't we? But how many did we kill with our cluster bombs? Two hundred thousand? Half a million? We just can't help ourselves, can we? The more advanced societies just keep on killing. But killing more efficiently. That's all we humans are good for, because we are always led by killers. Always. What is it with our leaders, Rob? Why do they always kill? What is that urge? They seem insane, but are they really any different from you and me? What urges have you had towards me, Rob? Have you imagined how you might kill me? Boil me in oil? Stab me with razors? I bet you have. All the smart people, all the clever guys, they're all killers. We're all killers. So what is wrong with us, Rob? Is there something . . . buried in us, do you think? Hmm?' Another lick of the lips. Cloncurry stopped smiling. 'But I'm tired of this, Rob. I don't for a minute believe you've got the Book, or know where it is. I think the time has come to end this silly melodrama.'

He stood up, turned from the webcam and walked to the chair. In full view of the webcam, he undid the cords that bound Lizzie to the chair.

Rob watched his daughter wriggling in Cloncurry's arms. She was still gagged. Cloncurry brought the girl over to the laptop and sat her on his knee; then he spoke to the webcam again.

'Have you ever heard of the Scythians, Rob? They had some strange habits. They would sacrifice their horses. Herd them onto burning ships. Then burn them alive. Most amusing. They were equally cruel to shipwrecked sailors: if you managed to survive a disaster at sea the Scythians would run down to the shore, grab you by the arms, then lead you to a cliff and throw you off again. Such an admirable people.'

Lizzie writhed in Cloncurry's grasp. Her eyes sought her father's on the screen in front of her. Sally was sobbing as she watched their daughter struggle for life.

'So now I'm going to roast her head alive. It's a Scythian thing. It's the way they sacrificed the firstborn. She is your firstborn, isn't she? In fact she's your only child right? So I'm going to light a little fire and then—'

Rob snapped. 'Fuck you, Cloncurry! *Fuck you.*'

Cloncurry laughed. 'Oh yeah?'

'Fuck you. If you so much as touch her I'll—'

'You'll *what,* Robbie? What will you do? You'll what? Bang on the door like a pussy while I slit her throat? Shout naughty words through the letterbox as I fuck her then shoot her? What? What? What are you gonna do you snivelling little he-she? You pathetic ladyboy. Come on? What? *What?* Why don't you come and get me? Hey? Run down here right now and get me, you stupid tranny. Come on *down,* Robbie. I'm *waiting*—'

Rob felt the anger overwhelm him. He leapt from his chair and ran out of the tent. An Irish policeman went to stop him but Rob just punched him out of the way. He was sprinting now. Running down the green, wet, skiddy Irish hill, to save his daughter. Running as fast as he could. His heartbeat was like a mad bass drum thumping in his ears. He ran and ran, he half fell on the soggy turf then got up again and he threw himself down the hill and pushed past some more policemen with guns and black helmets who tried to stop him, but he screamed at them and they fell back and then Rob was at the cottage door and he was inside the cottage.

Police were running up the narrow cottage stairs but Rob overtook them. He dragged one policeman out of the way, feeling as if he could throw someone off a cliff if he had to. He felt stronger than he had ever felt in his life, and angrier than was possible: he was going to slay Cloncurry and he was going to do it now.

Moments later he was at the locked and sealed door and the cops were shouting at him to get out of the way but Rob ignored them: he kicked and kicked at the door, and somehow it gave way: the locks buckled. He kicked again. He could feel the bones in his ankle almost crack but he kicked a final time and the door groaned and the hinges snapped and Rob was in.

He was in the bedroom. And there was . . .

Nothing. The room was . . . *empty.*

There was no chair, no laptop, no Cloncurry; no Lizzie. The floor was scattered with the signs of a squalid occupation. Half-opened tins of food. Some clothes and dirty coffee cups. A newspaper or two; and there, in the corner, a pile of Christine's clothes.

Rob felt his mind orbiting close to insanity. Being pulled into some vortex of illogic. Where was Cloncurry? Where was the chair? The discarded hood? *Where was his daughter?*

The questions whirled in his mind as police filed into the room. They tried to usher Rob out, to take him away, but he didn't want to go. He needed to solve this dark and concussing puzzle. He felt fooled, humiliated and griefstruck. He felt a serious proximity to madness.

Rob looked frantically around the room. He saw little cameras, trained on the space. Was Cloncurry somewhere else? Watching them? Laughing at them? Rob could somehow *feel* the hideous buzz of

Cloncurry's laughter, somewhere, out there on the internet, laughing at him.

And then he heard it. A real noise. A muffled noise coming from the wardrobe in the corner of the room. It was a human voice, but gagged and muffled: Rob knew that sound very well by now.

He pushed another Gardai officer aside, went straight to the wardrobe and opened the door.

Two wide frightened eyes stared at him from the darkness. A muffled voice of pleading, and relief, and even love, moaning from behind a gag.

It was Christine.

44

Rob was sitting in a swivel chair at Dooley's desk. Dooley's office was on the tenth floor of a gleaming new building overlooking the River Liffey. The views from the picture windows were stupefying, from the junction of the river and the Irish Sea in the east, to the soft Wicklow Hills beyond the city, to the south. The hills looked green and innocent under clearing skies. If Rob squinted he could actually discern the low, sullen shape of Montpelier House on top of its wooded hill, a dozen miles away.

The view of Montpelier returned him to stark reality. He swivelled to face the room: the office was full of people. Just ninety minutes had elapsed since the terrifying drama at the cottage under Hellfire Wood. They'd had one brief message from Cloncurry showing that Lizzie was still alive. But where? Where was she? Rob bit a fingernail, trying to work it out, desperately trying to piece the puzzle together.

Christine was talking animatedly and lucidly. Dooley leant towards her. 'Are you sure you don't need the paramedics to—'

'No!' she snapped. 'I'm fine. I told you. They didn't harm me.'

Boijer interrupted. 'So how did they get you to Ireland?'

'Boot of a car. In a car ferry. Judging by the rancid smell of diesel and seawater.'

'You were stuck in the boot?'

'I survived. It was only a few hours in the car, and then the boat. And then here.'

Forrester nodded. 'Well, that's what we guessed. They were driving between Britain and Ireland, taking the ferry, avoiding customs controls. Miss Meyer, I know it's traumatic but we need to know as much as we can, as soon as we can.'

'As I said, I'm not traumatized, Detective. Ask me anything.'

'OK. What do you recall? Do you know when the gang split? We know they kept you and Lizzie together, for a day or two in England: any idea where?'

'Sorry.' Christine was talking in an odd way, Rob noticed: staccato, sharp. 'I have no idea where they kept me, sorry. Somewhere near Cambridge perhaps? The first drive wasn't long, maybe an hour. Lizzie and I were both in a car boot. But then they took us out. Hooded and gagged. They were talking a lot, and I guess then they split up. After about a day and a half maybe? It's hard to tell when you are in a gag and hooded and fairly terrified.'

Forrester smiled, quietly and apologetically. Rob could sense him trying to work through the logic. Boijer said, 'But I still don't get it. What was the whole drama for? The poor woman in the video, the stick in the garden, when he threatened to kill the girl. What was that about?'

'He saw it as an opportunity to torture Rob. Psychologically,' said Christine. 'That's Cloncurry's style. He's a psychotic. Flamboyant and theatrical. Remember, I was with him a while. Not the best hours of my life.'

Rob glanced her way; she stared right back. 'He never touched me. I wonder if he's asexual. Either way, I do know he's an exhibitionist. A show-off. He likes to make people watch what he does. Make the victims suffer, and make those who love them suffer too . . .'

Forrester had stood, and walked to the window. The soft Irish sun was on his face. He turned and said quietly, 'And human sacrifice was traditionally performed in front of an audience. De Savary told me that. What was the word he used . . . the *propitiatory* power of sacrifice comes from its being watched. The Aztecs would haul people to the top of pyramids so the whole town could see their hearts being pulled out. Right?'

'Yes,' Christine added. 'Like the Viking ship burials – very public ceremonies of sacrifice. And the impaling of the Carpathians – again, a big public ritual. Sacrifice is meant to be observed. By the people, by the kings, by the gods. A theatre of cruelty. That's the appeal for Cloncurry. Prolonged, public and very *elaborate* cruelty.'

'And that's what he was planning for you, Christine,' Forrester said gently. 'A public impaling. In the cottage garden. I guess the gang in Ireland fucked up.'

'How?'

'They started arguing and shooting,' Dooley said. 'I think the gang lost control, without him – without the leader.'

'But there's another thing,' Boijer added. 'Why did Cloncurry leave the gang in Ireland when he must have known they would get caught, get shot even?'

Rob laughed bitterly. '*Another sacrifice.* He sacrificed his own men. In public. He was probably watching as the Gardai killed them. He had those cameras everywhere in the cottage. I imagine he enjoyed the whole thing, watching it on his computer screen.'

The central question had been raised. Boijer voiced it.

'So. Where is Cloncurry? Where the hell is he now?'

Rob glanced at the policemen in turn. At last Dooley said, 'Surely he must be in England?'

'Or Ireland,' Boijer replied.

Christine suggested, 'I think maybe he's in France.'

Forrester frowned. 'Sorry?'

'When I was tied up and hooded I'd hear him going on and on about France and his family there. He loathed his family, family secrets, all that. His horrible inheritance. That's what he kept saying. How much he hated his family – his mother, in particular . . . In her stupid house in France.'

'I wonder . . .' Boijer stared at Forrester with a significant expression. The DCI nodded sombrely. 'Maybe the woman in the video, the one he killed, might be his mother.'

'Christ.'

The room fell silent. Then Rob said, 'But the French police are staking the place out. No? Watching the parents?'

'Supposedly,' Boijer answered. 'But we aren't in touch with them hourly. And they wouldn't have been tracing the mother if she went away.'

Sally suddenly interrupted angrily. 'But how would he have got there? Private planes? You said you were following that up!'

Forrester raised a hand. 'We've scoured air traffic control reports. Contacted *every* private airfield in eastern England.' He shrugged. 'We know they had the money for a plane, we know Marsinelli had a licence, and possibly Cloncurry too. The problem with that line of enquiry is . . .' He sighed. 'There are thousands of private planes in the UK, tens of thousands in western Europe. If Cloncurry has been flying successfully under a false name for months, a year, who knows, no one would necessarily challenge him. He'd have clearance, by rote. And another problem is that everyone is looking for a gang of men, in a car, on a private jet. Not a single guy, *flying alone* . . .' He rubbed his chin, pensively. 'But I *still* don't think the French would have let him slip through their hands. Every major airfield and port was alerted. But I suppose it's possible.'

'All this speculation doesn't get us very far, does it?' Rob snapped. 'Cloncurry may be in Britain, France or Ireland. Great. Just three countries to search. And he still has my daughter. And maybe he's butchered his mom. So what are we gonna do?'

'What about your friend in Turkey, Isobel Previn? Has she had any luck with finding the Black Book?' Forrester asked.

Rob felt a pang of hope mixed with despair. 'I got a text from her last night. She says she's close. That's all I know.'

Sally sat forward, the sun flashing on her yellow hair. 'But what about *Lizzie*? Enough of this Black Book. Who *cares* about that? What's he going to do to Lizzie now? *To my daughter?*'

Christine moved along the sofa and hugged Sally. 'Lizzie is safe for now. He didn't need me because I'm just Rob's girlfriend. I was a toy. A bonus. Disposable.' She hugged Sally again. '*But the guy is not an idiot*. He is going to use Lizzie, use her against Rob. Until he gets what he wants. And what he wants is the Black Book. He thinks Rob has it.'

'But the fact is, I *don't* know anything,' Rob said despondently. 'I lied to him, told him I knew something, but why would he believe me? He's not stupid. As you say.'

'You went to Lalesh,' Christine answered. 'I heard him talking about that, too. Lalesh. How many non-Yezidis have been there? Maybe a few dozen, in a hundred years? That's what's bugging him.' She sat back. 'He's obsessed with the Book and he is sure you know something. Because of Lalesh. So I think Lizzie is relatively safe, for now.'

Silence ensued. Then the general conversation wandered, helplessly, between planes and airfields and car ferries for a couple more minutes. And then the laptop chimed.

Cloncurry had come online.

Rob waved a hand, wordlessly, at the people in the room and they gathered around and stared at the laptop screen.

There, in the webcam image, was Cloncurry. The image was clear and distinct. The audio was good. The killer was smiling. Chuckling.

'Hello again! Thought we should catch up. Have a little chat. So, you managed to catch my cognitively deficient operatives. My brothers in Eire. How tiresome. I had a nice impaling planned as well. As you probably know. Did you see the big stick in the garden?'

Dooley nodded. 'We saw.'

'Ah, Detective Doohickey. How are you? Shame we didn't get to kebab the French bitch. All that whittling for nothing. I should have at least tortured the slut, as I intended. But I had other things on my mind. It doesn't really matter. Because I still have my friends. In fact I've got one right here. Say hello to my little friend.'

Cloncurry reached off camera and picked up something.

It was a severed human head.

To be precise, it was Isobel Previn's head, white and faintly rotting. Grey nerves and greenish arteries dangled flaccidly from the neck.

'Isobel! Say something. Say hello to everyone.' With a jaggle of the hand he made the head nod.

Christine began to cry. Rob stared, aghast, at the screen.

Cloncurry was beaming with a kind of sardonic pride. 'There. She says hi. But now I think she wants to go to her special place. I've made a special place for her head, out of respect for her archaeological achievements.' Cloncurry stood, took a step forward and then kicked the head across the room, toe-punting it expertly. The head flew towards a rubbish bin in the corner, landing neatly in it with a chunky clatter. 'Slam fucking *dunk*!' He turned back to the camera. 'I've been practising that for hours. Now, where was I? Ah yes. Robert the journalist. So-called. Hello. So pleased you could be with us. Don't worry, as I said before, your daughter is still safe. Look—' he leaned forward and twisted the webcam until it showed Lizzie. Still lashed to a chair; but alive and healthy, it seemed. The webcam was shifted back.

'So you see, Robbeeeee. She's just fine. Fit as a fucking fiddle. Unlike Isobel Previn. I'm *so* sorry about my little joke with her vital organs. But I just couldn't resist the gag. Think I must have a bit of film director in me. And it was such a rare opportunity. There I was, mooching around these pissy little Turkish streets, and there's Isobel Previn! The great archaeologist! On her own! Wearing lorgnettes! What the fuck are lorgnettes? So I had a little think, for about a second. I know my archaeologists, I *know* she was a colleague of De Savary, I *know* she taught the prize-winning Christine Meyer, I *know* she is an expert in Assyria and the Yezidi in particular. Yet she's meant to be retired to her dildos in Istanbul?'

Cloncurry chortled. 'Yeah right. Too much of a coincidence. So we grabbed her, sorry, and smacked her around a bit, and she told us quite a lot, Robbie, quite a lot of *interesting detail.* And then I had a flash, if I say so myself, of aesthetic insight. I came up with our little drama. With the hoods. And the saucepan. And her small intestine. Did you appreciate *that*? I so hoped to make you think that Christine was dying in front of you, under that hood, having her uterus boiled in gravy, and then – this is the beauty of it – then you would actually get to Ireland and see Christine die *again*, in the most grotesque fashion, impaled on a stake, in Ireland. How good is that? How many people get to see their loved ones tortured to death *twice*? First turned into *soup*? *Then impaled?* West End producers get paid millions for that kind of thing. A *coup de theâtre*!' He gestured excitedly. 'And that's just half of it. What about the sheer directorial beauty of the whole gory drama in Ireland? Can I not have a little applause? For my Oscar-winning scenario?!'

He gazed out at them as if he seriously expected a round of cheers and bravos. 'Oh, come on. Did you not have a sneaking admiration for the production values? In one go, I throw you off the scent and put you through the worst mental torture, you believe you are about to see your daughter impaled but then it would turn out to be Christine being impaled, and meanwhile I'm here, safe and sound and watching it all on high definition telly.' The smile faded, slightly. 'But then my cretinous assistants go and start shooting and fuck it all up before managing to skewer Christine. Tsk tsk. I tell you, you can't get the staff these days. It would have been *so* good. *So* good. But still. Where were we? Where . . . you . . . you . . . were . . .'

Cloncurry's voice drifted, his eyes seemed unfocused. His expression was odd, detached. Rob glanced meaningfully at Forrester, who nodded back.

'No, I'm not going fucking mad,' Cloncurry chuckled. 'I'm already mad. You surely have noticed that, Detective Forrest Gump. But I'm also several times smarter than you, no matter how mad I am. So I know what you know. For instance, you've already worked out in your slow-witted way I am in Kurdistan. Given that I got hold of poor Isobel and her pancreas, that much must be obvious. And I have to say, what a shitty place this is. The Turks are so *mean* to the Kurds. Really. It's disgraceful.' Cloncurry shook his head, and exhaled, 'I'm serious, they're racist. And I hate racists. Really. You maybe think I'm some heartless psychotic but I'm not. I utterly despise *racists*. The only people I hate more than racists are *niggers*.' Cloncurry spun around in his swivel chair, spun round twice, then stopped to face the camera again. 'Why are the darkies so dim? Guys, come on, admit it. Haven't you ever wondered? The sooties? They just fuck everywhere up, don't they? Is that a plan they've got? Do the niggers get together and think – hey, let's see if we can emigrate somewhere nice and turn it into a toilet? We can go and live in crappy houses and start robbing and shooting. Again. Then we'll complain about white people. And as for Pakis! Pakis! And Arabs! God help us. Why don't they just piss off and put their women in binliners *at home*? And stop all the yelling from mosques? No one cares. And what about the Yiddos, whining about the Holocaust?' Cloncurry was chortling now. 'Whining and mewling like a bunch of girls. *Holocaust this, Holocaust that, please don't hit me, it's a Holocaust*. Holocaust schmolocaust. Listen up, Johnny Kike, isn't it time you got over it? Move on. And anyway was the Holocaust really that bad? Really? At least it was *punctual*. Those Germans can stick to a timetable. Even with cattle trucks. Can you imagine the chaos if the Brits had been in charge? They can't even run a commuter line from Clapham let alone a pan-European Railway of Death.' Cloncurry went into a fake Cockney accent. '"We'd like to apologize for the late running of the Auschwitz service. An alternative bus service has been provided. The buffet car will reopen at Treblinka."' Another chortle. 'Jesus, the *Brits*. Screw the Brits. Arrogant drunken idiots always brawling in the fog. And what about the *Yanks*? God save us from the Yanks and their buttocks! Fucking Yanks with their *ginormous asses*. What is that about? Why are their arses so big? Haven't they worked out the link between their failure in Iraq and their *massive great butts*? Hey, here's a clue, America. Wanna know what happened to those weapons of mass destruction? Some fat bitch in LA is *sitting on them* in Dunkin Donuts. Only she doesn't even realize it, because her ass is the size of Neptune and she can't feel a thing.' Cloncurry swivelled again. 'As for the Japs, they are just devious trolls with a gift for wiring. And the Chinks: seven ways to cook broccoli, and they look like gonks. Fish-eating fuckers.' He paused, considering. 'I quite like the Poles.'

Cloncurry grinned. 'Anyway, you get the picture. You know what I want. You've realized I have Lizzie and that I'm keeping her alive for just one reason, and one reason only – I want the Black Book – and I know you know where it is Rob, because Isobel told me that you know. She told me what happened in Lalesh. We had to cut one of her ears off to elicit the info, but she told us. I ate the ear. No I didn't. I fed it to the chickens. No I didn't. Who gives a flying fig? Point is: she told us everything. She told us you sent her here to get the Book, because you can't come yourself, because the local police chappie, that stylish Mr Kiribali, will put you in jail. So you sent Isobel Previn to do the job. Unfortunately I was here already and I scooped her liver out and cooked it up *á la Provençale*. So now, Rob, you have one more day. My patience is running out. Where is the Book? Haran? Mardin? Sogmatar? Where is it? Where was Isobel going? We tortured her as much as we could but she was a brave old lesbian and wouldn't give us that final clue. So I need to know. And if you don't tell me within twenty-four hours, then it'll be little Lizzie's turn for the jam-jars, I'm afraid. Because my patience will have snapped.' He nodded, soberly. 'I'm a reasonable man, as you know, Robbie, but don't let my obvious kindness deceive you. Truth be told, I do have a bit of a temper, and I can sometimes get . . . *snitty*. Now I'm talking to you, Sally, yes you, the ex-Mrs Luttrell, dear weeping Sally – I can see you, peeping over the camera with your little piggy eyes, Sally, are you listening? Stop crying, you liquidizing whore. One day is what you've got, twenty-four little hours, to think it all over, and then, well then your daughter gets shoved in a jar and buried alive. So I expect to hear from you very soon.' He leaned towards the camera switch. 'Or it's *pickling time*.'

45

The videolink fizzed and shut down. Sally had retreated to the sofa, once more, and was quietly crying. Rob went over and put an arm around her.

It was Christine who got it together first. She dried her eyes and said, 'So. We know he's in Urfa. That means Cloncurry must have been thinking along the same lines as . . .' she sighed, profoundly, 'as poor Isobel.'

'You mean the Austen Layard theory?' asked Rob.

'Surely. What else? Cloncurry must have reached the same conclusion concerning the Book. So I guess he flew to Kurdistan, with Lizzie, in that private plane.'

Forrester nodded. 'Yup. Might have been doing it for months. False name, etc. We'll get onto Turkish air traffic control.'

Rob shook his head. 'You don't know Kurdistan! If Cloncurry is clever – and he is – then he could have landed almost unnoticed. In some areas the Turks barely have control. And of course he could have flown to *Iraqi* Kurdistan and crossed the border. It's a huge and lawless region. Not exactly Suffolk.'

Sally made an imploring gesture. 'So what do we *do*?'

'We look here. We look in *Ireland*,' said Christine.

'Sorry?'

'The Black Book. It's *not* in Urfa. I think poor Isobel was wrong. I think the Book is still *here*.'

The policemen exchanged glances. Rob frowned.

'How come?'

'I had several days in a wardrobe to think about the Black Book. And I know the Layard story. But I reckon Layard was just buying off the Yezidi with money and that was why he returned. So I reckon that's a dead end.'

'So where is it, then?'

'Let's go outside,' she said. 'I need fresh air to think it through. Just give me a few minutes.'

Obediently, they trooped out of the office and took the steel lift to the ground floor and exited into the mild summer air. The Dublin sky was now bluish and pale; the breeze was gentle off the river. Tourists were staring at an old boat moored by the quays. A strange parade of gaunt bronze statues blocked half the pavement. The group walked slowly down the quayside.

Dooley pointed to the statues. 'Memorial for the Famine. Starvelings from the Famine would queue on these docks, waiting for boats to New York.' He turned and gestured at the shiny new office buildings and the glittery glass atria: ranked along the quays. 'And all that used to be brothels and wharves and terrible slums, the old red light district. Monto. Where James Joyce went whoring.' He paused, then added, 'Now it's all fusion bistros.'

'All is changed, changed utterly . . .' murmured Christine. And then she went very quiet.

Rob looked at her and could tell at once that she *knew* something. Her fine mind was engaged.

They stopped at a glamorous new footbridge and watched the grey river water surging torpidly to the Irish Sea.

Then Christine asked Forrester to tell her again the strange word De Savary had written just before he died.

'"Undish".'

'Undish?' said Rob, bemused.

'Yeah. Spelled as it sounds. U N D I S H.'

The group was silent. A few seagulls cawed. Sally asked the question that hovered between them. 'What the hell does *undish* mean?'

'We don't have any idea,' Forrester replied. 'It's got some musical connection but that doesn't seem relevant.'

Rob observed Christine and saw that she was half smiling. Then she said, 'James Joyce! That's it. *James Joyce.* That's the answer.'

Rob frowned. 'I don't see the relevance.'

'That's what Hugo was talking to me about, that was the last thing he said to me, before the gang arrived. In Cambridgeshire.' She was talking fast, and walking just as fast – towards the footbridge. 'When I last saw him – De Savary – he said he had a new theory. About the Whaley evidence, the Black Book. And he mentioned Joyce.' She looked at Rob. 'And he knew that I was trying to get you to read *Ulysses* or *Portrait*—'

'Without much luck!'

'Sure. But, still. I've been thinking about this while I was imprisoned. And now . . . Undish.' She snatched a pen from her handbag and scrawled the word on an opened notebook.

UNDISH.

She looked down at the handiwork. 'Undish undish undish. There's no such word. But that's because De Savary was trying to deceive the killers.'

'What?'

'If he'd written the whole word they might have seen it and Cloncurry would have worked it out. He couldn't have known if they were coming back. So instead he wrote a nonsense word. But a nonsense word that he reckoned someone might work out. Maybe you, Rob. If you ever heard it.'

Rob shrugged. 'Still don't get it.'

'Of course not. You never did read Joyce, despite my enthusiasm! And you'd need to know the books well. Hugo and I loved talking about Joyce. Endless discussions.'

Dooley interrupted impatiently, 'All right then, so what does *undish* mean?'

'It doesn't mean anything. But it just needs one letter to complete it. The letter T. Then it becomes . . .' She scrawled an extra letter next to the word on her notebook and showed it to them. 'Tundish!'

Rob sighed. 'That's great, Christine. But who or what's a *tundish*? How the hell does that help Lizzie?'

'It's not a common word. It occurs only once, as far as I know, in major English literature. And that's the point. Because the passage in which it occurs is in Joyce's first masterpiece. *A Portrait of the Artist as a Young Man*. And I think there may be a serious clue in there. To help us.' She looked at the faces all around her. 'Remember that Joyce knew more about Dublin than any man. He knew everything: every legend, every scrap of information, every tiny anecdote, and he poured them into his books.'

'OK,' said Rob, dubiously.

'Joyce would have known every secret and myth about the Irish Hellfires. And what they did.' Christine snapped her notebook shut. 'So I'm guessing that passage might just tell us where to find what we need, to save Lizzie.' She stared across the river. 'And there, I believe, is a bookshop.'

Rob swivelled. Just across the spindly new footbridge, on the other side of the torpid Liffey, was a branch of Eason's bookstore.

The five of them crossed the river and entered the store *en masse*, rather to the surprise of the young sales assistant. Immediately Christine went to the Irish Classics section. 'Here.' She pounced on a copy of *Portrait of the Artist as a Young Man* and flicked feverishly through it. 'And here . . . are . . . the tundish pages.'

'Read it out.'

'The tundish passage occurs about halfway through the book. Stephen Dedalus, the hero, the artist of the title, has gone to see his tutor, a Jesuit dean of English studies at University College Dublin. They have a debate about philology. And that's where we come in. Here's what it says: "To return to the lamp, he said, the feeding of it is also a nice problem. You must choose the pure oil . . . using the funnel".' She looked up at the assembled, expectant faces. 'I'm doing dialogue here. Don't expect an accent.' Returning to the book, she recited: '"What funnel? asked Stephen. – The funnel through which you pour the oil into your lamp. – That? said Stephen. Is that called a funnel? Is it not a tundish?"' Christine stopped reading.

Rob nodded slowly. 'So they talk about funnels. Where's the Hellfire stuff?'

'The precise passage we want is a page or two back.' Christine flicked and scanned. 'Here it is. "But the trees in Stephen's Green were fragrant of rain and the rain-sodden earth gave forth its mortal odour, a faint incense rising upward through the mould from many hearts . . . he knew that in a moment when he entered the sombre college he would be conscious of a corruption other than Buck Egan and Burnchapel Whaley".'

Rob nodded eagerly now.

'Wait, there's more.' She turned another page and calmly recited. '"It was too late to go upstairs to the French class. He crossed the hall and took the corridor to the left which led to the physics theatre. The corridor was dark and silent but not unwatchful. Why did he feel that it was not unwatchful? Was it because he had heard that in Buck Whaley's time there was a secret staircase there?"' She closed the book.

The bookshop was quiet.

'*Ah*.' Said Dooley.

'Yes!' said Boijer.

'But surely it can't be that obvious,' Sally said, frowning. 'A secret staircase. Just like that? Why wouldn't that horrible gang have had a look?'

'Maybe they don't read Joyce,' said Forrester.

'It makes sense,' Dooley surmised. 'Historically. The Whaley connection is true. There are two great big houses on St Stephen's Green. And I am sure one of them was built for Richard Burnchapel Whaley.'

'The building still exists?' asked Rob.

'Of course. I think they are still used by University College even now.'

Rob was heading for the door. 'Come on, guys. What are we waiting for? Please. We've got *one day*.'

Just a couple of minutes of urgent walking brought them to a large Georgian square where lofty terraces overlooked a noble green space. The gardens and lawns had an inviting aspect, sunlight glittering through the greenery. For a moment Rob imagined his daughter playing happily in the gardens. He stifled his piercing sadness. His fear was unquenchable.

The old university college turned out to be one of the largest houses on the square: elegant and chaste, in grey Portland stone. Rob found it difficult to link this impressive building with the homicidal depravities of Burnchapel Whaley and his even crazier son. The sign outside read *Newman House: part of University College Dublin.*

Dooley buzzed the bell while Christine and Rob loitered on the pavement below. Sally elected to wait on a bench in the square itself: Forrester assigned Boijer to stay with her. There was some debate over the intercom: then Dooley gave his full police title, and the door opened smartly. The hallway beyond was nearly as spectacular as the exterior: with scrolling Georgian plasterwork, grey and white, and exquisite.

'Wow,' said Dooley.

'Yes we're very proud of it.'

It was a New England American accent. A neatly-suited, middle-aged man trotted along the hallway and extended a hand to Dooley. 'Ryan Matthewson, Principal of Newman House. Hello, officer . . . and hello . . .'

They exchanged names; Forrester showed his badge. The principal took them into the receptionist's cluttered office.

'But officers, the break-in was last week, I'm not sure why they've sent you now?' he said.

Rob felt a lowering feeling.

'Break-in?' said Dooley. 'When? Sorry?'

'It was nothing important. Some days back a group of kids broke into a cellar. Probably drug addicts. We never caught them. They positively brutalized the cellar stairs. God knows why.' Matthewson shrugged his uninterest. 'But the Gardai sent a constable at the time. We've already been over this. He took all the details . . .'

Rob and Christine exchanged a melancholy glance. But Dooley and Forrester were not, it seemed, so easily disheartened. Forrester gave the principal the essence of the Burnchapel story, and the Cloncurry search. Rob sensed, by the way he phrased his monologue, that he was trying not to say too much lest he totally confuse and frighten the man. Even so, by the end of the explanation, the principal looked both confused and frightened. At last he said, 'Extraordinary. So you think these people were looking for the secret stairs? Mentioned in *Portrait*?'

'Yes,' said Christine. 'Which means we're probably too late. If the gang didn't find anything that means there's nothing here. *Merde*.'

The principal shook his head, vigorously. 'Actually, there was no need for them to break in. They could have just come to one of our open days.'

'Your what?'

'It's not a mystery. Not at all. Yes there was a secret staircase here, but it was uncovered in 1999. During the major refurbishment. It's now the main service stairs at the back of the building. There's nothing secret about it these days.'

'So the gang looked in the wrong place?' Dooley said.

Matthewson nodded. 'Well, yes. I imagine they did. What a cruel irony! They could have just come and asked me where the secret staircase was, and I would have told them. But I guess that's not the modus operandi of these gangs, is it? Polite inquiry? Well, well.'

'So where are the stairs?' Rob asked.

'Follow me.'

Three minutes later they were at the rear of the building, staring at a narrow wooden staircase that led from the ground floor to a kind of mezzanine level. The staircase was dark and badly lit, hemmed in by sombre oak panelling on either side.

Rob crouched over the wooden planks. He rapped the lowest tread of the stairs with his knuckles. The sound was disappointingly solid. Christine rapped the second tread.

The principal leaned over with an anxious expression. 'What are you doing?'

Rob shrugged. 'I just thought, if there is something hidden it must be under one of the treads. So if I hear a hollow sound, maybe . . .'

'You intend to rip up the stairs?'

'Yes,' Rob said. 'Of course. What else?'

The principal blushed. 'But this is one of the most protected buildings in Dublin. You can't just come in here and take a crowbar to the fittings. I'm so sorry I do understand your predicament but . . .'

Rob scowled, and sat down on the stairs, trying to repress his anger. Forrester had a short private discussion with Dooley, who turned to Matthewson. 'You know, it looks like it could do with a lick of paint.'

'Sorry?'

'The stairs,' said Dooley. 'Bit spartan. Need a touch-up.'

The principal sighed. 'Well of course we didn't have enough money to do everything. The plasterwork in the hallway took most of the funds.'

'We have,' said Dooley.

'What?'

'We have the money, the Gardai. If we have to crack a few stair-rods in pursuit of a legitimate inquiry we will of course reimburse your college for any damage.' Dooley patted Matthewson on the back. 'And I think you will find that police refunds can be very generous.'

Matthewson managed a smile. 'Enough to repair and paint a few stairs? And maybe a classroom or two?'

'Oh I should think so.'

The principal's smile broadened: he seemed intensely relieved. 'OK. I think I can explain that to the Trustees. So yes, let's do it.' He paused. 'Though I wonder if you are actually looking in quite the right place.'

'You have another idea?'

'Tentatively . . . Just a notion.'

'Tell us!!'

'Well. I've always thought . . .' He lifted his gaze up the stairs. 'I have sometimes wondered why this little stairway dog-legs at the top. See there, look, it just turns about. At the top. For no apparent architectural reason. Annoying if you are carrying lots of books: you can trip. It's so dark. We had a student break an ankle just this Christmas.'

Rob was already running up the stairs with Christine after him. The stairs did indeed turn. They led up to a panelled wall and then shifted abruptly left. Rob stared at the panelled wall, then slapped it. It sounded hollow.

They all looked at each other. Matthewson was now noticeably flushed. 'Extraordinary! I guess we need to open it up and have a look? We've got a chisel and a flashlight in the cellar, I'll just go and fetch—'

'Bugger that.'

Reaching in his pocket, Rob produced a Swiss Army Knife and unclasped the sturdiest blade.

Christine, Dooley, Forrester and Matthewson were silent as Rob slammed the blade straight into the panel. The wood was easily pierced. It was thin, like a false panel. Rob rotated the blade to get some purchase, then sliced down and the panel began to give way. Forrester reached in and grabbed the corner of the wooden square, and the two men peeled the complete, yardwide section from its frame.

A dark, receding alcove lay beyond, and a musty smell exhaled from the blackness. Rob leaned in, and rummaged. 'Jesus. It's dark, it's too dark . . . I can't see . . .'

Christine took out her mobile phone, switched on the phonelight and flashed it into the hidden space, over Rob's shoulder.

Rob and Forrester stared; Dooley swore; Christine put a shocked hand to her mouth.

Right at the back of the alcove, swathed in cobwebs and grey dust, was a large and very battered leather box.

46

Reaching in to the echoey darkness, and slightly grunting from the exertion, Rob pulled the box along the planks and dragged it onto the stairway.

The round, flat-topped box was made of ancient leather, cracked, worn and battered black leather. It had the distinct air of something from the eighteenth century, something aristocratic. Like the luggage of a lord on the Grand Tour. The case seemed to match the architectural style of the house wherein it had lain, secretly concealed, for so long.

The box was also covered with thick cobwebby dust. Christine brushed away the top layers of grease and dirt, and a series of letters and words appeared on the lid, inscribed in a thin, delicate gold:

TW, Anno Domini. 1791

The lovers exchanged glances. Christine said, 'Thomas Whaley.'

'Before he went to Israel. And became *Jerusalem* Whaley . . .'

The principal of the college was looking agitated. Hopping from one elegantly-shod foot to another. 'Guys, look, sorry, but do you mind if we take this somewhere else? We have students coming up and down these stairs all the time, and . . . Not sure I want all the . . . brouhaha?'

Forrester and Dooley saw the point; they all agreed to shift elsewhere. Rob picked up the box again, holding it like a drum in front of him. The box wasn't that heavy: just unwieldy. Something quite large was rattling inside it. He tried to hold it as steady as possible as they walked. Every second that passed, every second they wasted, he thought of Lizzie. Every second took her closer to death.

Rob was finding it hard not to shout at people; setting his jaw into determined silence, he followed Principal Matthewson up the rest of the stairs and along a short corridor. And then at last they were in a bright, elegant office: the principal's study, overlooking the trees and sunlit lawns of St Stephen's Green.

Forrester glanced through the windows at Sally and Boijer sitting there, on a bench, in the Green. Waiting. 'Just a moment,' he said. He took out his mobile.

The box was clunked on Mathewson's desk, sending a cloud of dust flying out of the venerable leather casing.

'OK,' said Dooley. 'Let's open it.'

Christine was already examining the box. 'These old straps and buckles,' she muttered, trying one. 'They won't undo.'

Dooley struggled with another buckle. 'Totally rusted.'

Rob stepped forward, his knife out. 'My daughter is waiting!' He knelt and slashed the straps open. The very last strap was the toughest of all: he had to saw at it for a while: viciously; then at last it gave up, and flopped away.

He stood back. Forrester was lifting off the black leather lid, with the printed gold lettering. They all peered into the depths of the historic box and found themselves looking down at the Black Book, the first time it had been seen in two hundred and fifty years.

Except that it was not a book that stared back at them; but a face.

'Jesus!' said Dooley.

Sitting at the bottom of the box was a skull.

It was a very strange skull. Obviously human, yet not quite human. It had slanting cheekbones, and almost birdlike, snakelike eyes, handsome and Asiatic, yet oddly broad, and cruelly smiling.

Rob recognized it immediately. 'That's exactly what I saw in Lalesh.

The same kind of skull. Sort of half man . . . half bird. What the hell is that? Christine, you're an osteo . . . expert. What is it?'

With a confident dexterity, Christine reached inside the black leather case, and took out the skull. 'It's very well preserved,' she said, examining the cranium and the lower jawbone. 'Someone has had it treated to prevent it from decaying.'

'But how old is it? What is it? Is it human? What's with the eyes?'

Christine walked to the light of the long sash windows. She held the skull up, in the slanting sunshine. 'It's definitely hominid. But it's hybrid.'

The door to the office pushed open. It was Sally and Boijer. They stared in shock, at the skull in Christine's hands.

'That's it?' said Boijer. 'That's the Black Book? *A human skull?*'

Rob nodded. 'Yep.'

'Not *quite* human.' Christine twisted the skull in her hands. 'It's hominid, but there are stark differences between this and a normal *Homo sapiens* skull. Here, look. The large braincase size, the sagittal size, and the orbitals, very intriguing . . .'

'So it's a crossbreed between humans and . . . and what?' asked Rob.

'No idea. Not Neanderthals. Not *Homo habilis.* This seems to be some unknown human type; and one with a very large braincase.'

Rob was still in the dark. 'But I thought humans couldn't breed with other species? I thought different species couldn't breed?'

Christine shook her head. 'Not necessarily. Some species can interbreed. Tigers and lions, for instance. It's rare but it happens. And this kind of hybridization is not unknown in human evolution. Various experts think we interbred with the Neanderthals.' She set the skull on the table. Its white teeth glittered in the lamplight. The skull was yellowy cream, and very large.

Dooley was still looking in the musty leather case. 'There's something else.' He reached in, and pulled out a folded document. Rob watched, transfixed, as the Irish detective carried the document to the principal's desk and laid it next to the skull.

The document was weathered and creased, and made from some form of robust parchment. Yellowed and old: maybe hundreds of years old.

Very carefully, Rob unfolded it; as he did so, the parchment creaked and gave off a distinct and not unpleasant fragrance. Of sadness, and age, and funeral flowers.

They leaned over the parchment as Rob flattened it out. Christine looked down, frowning. The parchment was inscribed with very dark ink, showing a cursory map, and a few lines in a scrawled and archaic script.

'Aramaic,' said Christine, almost immediately. 'It's Aramaic. Seems to be a fairly unusual form . . . Let me have a proper look.'

Rob sighed with frustration: the passing of every second was painful. He glanced at the skull, sitting there on the desk next to the parchment. It seemed to be sneering at him. Sneering like Jamie Cloncurry.

Cloncurry! Rob shook himself. They had the Black Book! And Cloncurry needed to know this at once. Rob asked Matthewson if he could use the office computer and the principal nodded his assent.

Rob went to the principal's desk, logged on the computer, and got straight through to Cloncurry. The videolink buzzed into life. The webcam was working. Within a few seconds Cloncurry came briskly and suddenly into view. He was grinning, maliciously. 'Ah, so I suppose you have found it. In a bus stop perhaps? Maybe in a bingo hall?'

Rob silenced him by lifting up the skull.

Cloncurry stared. He swallowed, and stared. Rob had never seen the gang-leader nonplussed like this: but the killer seemed discomfited, anxious, almost stunned.

'You have it, you actually *have it*.' Cloncurry's voice was phlegmy with anxiety. He started again. 'And what about . . . the documents, was there anything else? *In the box?*'

Sally handed across the parchment. Rob lifted it up and showed it to him. Cloncurry breathed out, long and hard, as if he had been relieved of a terrible burden. 'All this time. All this time. *And in Ireland!* So

Previn was wrong. *I* was wrong. Layard was a dead end. And it's not even in cuneiform!' Cloncurry shook his head. 'So. Where was it exactly?'

'Newman House.'

Cloncurry went quiet. Then he shook his head and laughed, bitterly. 'Christ. Under the secret stairs!? Jesus Christ. I told them to search properly. Those rancid imbeciles.' Now he stopped laughing and gazed insolently and contemptuously at the webcam. 'Still, nothing to be done about it now. My colleagues are lying in coffins. But you can save your daughter's life – as long as you bring me the Book – the skull and the document. OK? And I want it here within . . . oh God. Here we go again. Another deadline. How long will it take you morons to get here?'

Rob started to speak but Cloncurry lifted a hand. 'Shut up. Here's the deal. I'll give you three more days. That's surely enough time. Possibly too generous. But that's me for you, super generous. But please believe me, my patience is running out. Recall that I am psychotic.' He chortled, and did an exaggerated facial tic, mimicking his own madness. 'And, guys, when you come, don't bother bringing your police chums. They'll be of no use to you. Will they? Because they won't get much help from Kiribali, or the Kurds. As I think you realize very well. So get on with it, Rob. Fly here, bring the Book, and you can have your Lizzie back, unpickled. You've seventy-two hours, and that's that. The final deadline. *Ciaociao*.'

The screen went black.

Forrester broke the silence. 'Of course, we will have to go through the local police, in Turkey. I'll speak to the Home Office. We can't have you guys just flying out there. This is a murder case. It's very complex. As I'm sure you realize.'

Rob narrowed his eyes. 'Of course.'

'I'm sorry if this seems bureaucratic, but we'll be quick, very quick. I promise. It's just that we need to be careful. And this guy is a nutcase, if you go in alone there's no guarantee he won't just, *you know*. We need local back up. And that means official involvement, approval from Ankara, liaisons with Dublin. All that.'

Rob thought about Kiribali. His lizardly smile. His threats at the airport. 'Of course.'

Matthewson was hopping from foot to foot again. He evidently wanted this troublesome entourage out of his office but was too polite to say as much. Obediently they all filed outside, led by Rob, carrying the 'Black Book' – the skull and the map in the old leather box. Sally and Christine came behind, talking quietly. The police, bringing up the rear, were animatedly conversing, almost arguing.

Rob watched the London detective jabbing a finger at Boijer. 'What the hell are they arguing about?'

Christine shrugged. 'Who knows?' Her expression was sardonic. They walked on ahead.

Rob glanced to his left, at Sally, and to his right, at Christine. Then he said, 'Are you thinking what I'm thinking?'

'Yes,' said Christine. 'The police will screw it all up.'

'Exactly. All that "talk to the Home Office" stuff. Jesus.' Rob felt the anger and frustration surge inside him. 'And talk to bloody Kiribali? What are they on? Kiribali is probably in league with Cloncurry anyway. Who else is helping that bastard?'

'And if they go through Ankara it will take ages,' Christine went on, 'and they will antagonize the Kurds, the whole thing will be a terrible fiasco. They don't understand. They've never been there, never seen Sanliurfa . . .'

'So maybe you have to go. Now.' Sally leaned and squeezed Rob's hand. '*Just do it.* Take the Black Book, the skull – whatever it is – just take it to Cloncurry, and give it to him. Just fly there, now, tomorrow: the police can't stop you. Do what Cloncurry wants. She's our daughter.'

Rob nodded slowly. 'Absolutely. And I know someone who can help . . . in Sanliurfa.'

Christine raised a hand. 'But we still can't trust Cloncurry. Can we? Forrester is right about *that*, at least.' With the last rays of the setting sun soft on her face, Christine looked earnestly at Rob and then at Sally. 'Sure he's hunting for the Book. But once he's got it, once we give him the Black Book he may just . . . do what he wants anyway. You see? He's psychotic. As he says. He *enjoys* killing.'

'So what do we do?' Rob said despairingly.

"There may be a way. I saw the map.'

'What?'

'When we were in the office,' Christine explained. 'The parchment is written in Late Ancient Aramaic. The language used by the Canaanites. And I think I can read that. Just about.'

'And?'

Christine looked down at the leather box, sitting at Rob's feet. 'Show me again.'

Rob bent and opened the box, retrieved the parchment and flattened it on his knee. Christine nodded. 'That's what I thought.' She pointed at a line of ancient handwriting. 'It says the "great skull of the ancestors" comes from . . . "the Valley of the Slaughter".'

'So, what's that then?'

'It doesn't say.'

'Great. OK. So what about the writing? Here. What does that mean?'

'It mentions the Book of Enoch. It doesn't quote it.' She frowned. 'But it refers to it. And then it says, here: "The Valley of the Slaughter is where our forefathers died". Yes. Yes, *yes*.' Christine pointed at one line on the parchment. 'And here it says the valley is a day's walk towards the setting sun, from the "place of worship".'

'And this . . . ?'

'That shows a river and the valleys. And here's another clue. It says the place of worship is also called "the hill of the navel"! That's it!'

Rob's mind was blank. He felt so tired, and so stressed about Lizzie. He glanced at Christine. Her expression was the opposite of his: alert and eager.

She eyed him. 'The hill of the navel. You don't remember?'

Rob shook his head, feeling an idiot.

'Hill of the Navel is the English meaning of the Turkish phrase . . . *Gobekli Tepe.*'

A light dawned in Rob's head.

Across the lawns, the police were evidently concluding their debate, and shaking hands. Christine went on, 'So. According to this parchment, a day's walk from Gobekli Tepe, walking west, away from the sun, is the Valley of the Slaughter. And that's where this skull comes from. And that's where, I suspect, we will find many others like it. We have to be proactive. Think a few moves ahead. We can bring Cloncurry to *us*. We need to have something so powerful that he *has* to hand Lizzie over unharmed. If we actually unearth the secret, implied by the Black Book, contained in the skull and the map, if we dig up the Valley of the Slaughter and find out the truth behind all of this, then he will come to us in supplication. *Because that valley is where the secret is hidden.* The secret he keeps banging on about. The secret revealed to Jerusalem Whaley that ruined his life. The secret that Cloncurry wants hidden for ever. If we want to have power over Cloncurry we need to go right past him, dig up this valley, find out the secret, and threaten to reveal the mystery, unless he hands over Lizzie. That's how we *win*.'

The police were walking towards them now, their debate apparently concluded.

Rob squeezed Sally's hand, and Christine's too. He whispered to them both. 'OK. Let's do it. Christine and I will fly to Sanliurfa immediately. We do it alone. And we dig up this secret.'

'And we don't tell the police,' said Christine.

Rob turned to Sally. 'Are you sure about this, Sally? I need your agreement.'

She stared at Rob. 'I'm . . . going to trust you, Rob Luttrell.' Her eyes filled with tears: she fought them back. 'I'm going to trust you to bring back our daughter. So, yes. Please do it. Please, please, please. Just *bring Lizzie back*.'

Forrester was rubbing his hands as he approached them. 'Getting a bit nippy, shall we head for the airport? Have to get the Home Office onto it. We'll pile the pressure on, I promise.'

Rob nodded. Behind the DCI loomed the sombre grey elevations of Newman House. For a second Rob had an image of the house as it had been when Buck Egan and Buck Whaley had held their roistering parties in the guttering light of Georgian lamps; the tall young men laughing and roaring as they set fire to black cats soaked in whisky.

47

Christine and Rob flew to Turkey straight from London the same evening, after telling blatant lies to Forrester and Boijer.

They decided to take the Black Book with them: Christine was obliged to show her archaeological credentials at Heathrow and flash her most charming smile to get a strange and arguably human skull past London customs. In Turkey they had to be even more careful. They flew to Dyarbakir, via Istanbul, then made a long, dusty, six-hour cab-ride to Sanliurfa, through the night and the dawn. They didn't want to announce their arrival to Kiribali by turning up at Sanliurfa Airport, conspicuous, Western and unwanted; indeed they didn't want Kiribali to know they were anywhere near Turkey.

Just being here, in Kurdistan, was risky enough.

In the thrumming heart of broiling Urfa they headed for the Hotel Haran. Right outside the lobby Rob found his man – Radevan – sheltering from the hot morning sun, arguing noisily about football with the other cab drivers, and acting a little grouchy. But the grumpiness was due to Ramadan: everyone was grouchy, hungry and thirsty through the hours of daylight.

Rob went straight for it and asked Radevan if he could find some friends to help them dig the Valley of the Slaughter. He also quietly asked him to procure some guns, as well. Rob wanted to be ready for anything.

Initially, Radevan was moody and unsure: he went off to 'consult' with his numberless cousins. But an hour later he returned with seven friends and relatives, all smiling Kurdish lads. In the meantime Rob had bought some second-hand shovels and hired a couple of very old Land Rovers.

This was probably going to be the most makeshift archaeological dig of the last two hundred years, but they had no choice. They had only two days to unearth the final answer to all their questions, two days to unearth the Valley of the Slaughter, and lure Cloncurry into a position in which he would have to give up Lizzie. And Radevan had done his job with the guns: they were concealed in a shabby old sack: two shotguns and a German pistol. Radevan winked at Rob as they made the transaction. 'You see I help you, Mr Robbie. I like Englishman, they help the Kurds.' He grinned, luxuriously, as Rob handed over the wad of dollars.

As soon as everything was stowed in the cars, Rob jumped in the driver's seat and keyed the engine. His impatience was almost unbearable. Just being in the same city as Lizzie, yet not knowing where she was or how she was suffering made him feel as if he was having a serious heart attack. He had pains shooting up his arm; palpitations of anguish. His jaw hurt. He thought of Lizzie, tied to a chair, as the last of Urfa's suburbs became a haze of dust and greyness in the rearview mirror.

Christine was in the seat beside him. Three Kurdish men were in the back. Radevan was driving the second Land Rover, right behind. The guns were hidden in their sack, under Rob's seat. The Black Book, in its worn leather box, was firmly wedged in the boot.

As they rattled along, the familiar talkativeness of the Kurds lapsed into whispers, and then into silence. Their silence was matched by the deadness of the landscape as they headed out into the vastness of the desert. The yellow and desolate wastes.

The heat was quite incredible: high summer on the edge of the

Syriac wilderness. Rob sensed the nearness of Gobekli as they motored south. But this time they drove straight past the Gobekli turn off, and were waved through several army checkpoints further down the hot Damascus road. Christine had bought a detailed map: she reckoned she knew precisely where to find the valley.

'Here,' she said, at one turning, very authoritatively. They took a right and barrelled for half an hour along unmetalled dirt tracks. And then at last they crested a rise. The two cars halted, and everyone climbed out: the Kurds looking dirty, sweaty and mildly mutinous. The shovels were unloaded, the trowels, ropes and backpacks were dumped on the sandy hilltop.

To their left was a bare and narrow valley.

'That's it,' said Christine. 'The Valley of the Slaughter. They still call it the Valley of Killing. It's actually marked on the map.'

Rob gazed and listened. He could hear – nothing. Nothing but the mournful desert wind. The site – the entire region – was strangely hushed, even for the deserts near Gobekli.

'Where is everyone?' he said.

'Gone. *Evacuated.* Moved by the government,' replied Christine.

'Huh?'

'That's why.' She was pointing left where an expanse of silver flatness glistened in the distance. 'That's the water from the Great Anatolian Project. The Euphrates. They are flooding the whole region, for irrigation. Several major archaeological sites have already flooded – it's very controversial.'

'Christ – it's only a few klicks away!'

'And it's coming in our direction. But that levee will stop it. The earthbank over there.' Christine pointed, and frowned. Her white shirt was freckled with yellow dust. 'But we need to be careful: these inundations can be very quick. And unpredictable.'

'We need to be quick *anyway*,' said Rob.

They turned and descended the hill into the valley. Within a few minutes Christine had got the Kurds digging. As they worked, the size of the task assailed Rob. The valley was a mile long, at least. In two days, their team would only be able to turn over a fraction of it. Maybe twenty per cent. Maybe thirty. And they wouldn't be able to dig very deep.

So they were going to have to be lucky to find anything. The sombreness and fear that Rob had been feeling since they had returned to the Kurdish desert were joined by a rising surge of ennui. A great tide of pointlessness. Lizzie was going to die. *She was going to die.* And Rob felt useless: he felt he would drown in the futility of it all, be entombed like the thirsty lands around him, awaiting that vast silver coffinlid of water. The Great Anatolian Project.

But he knew he had to stay strong, to see this through and so he tried to improve his mood. He reminded himself what Breitner had said of Christine: that she was 'one of the best archaeologists of her generation'. He reminded himself that the great Isobel Previn had taught Christine at Cambridge.

And the Frenchwoman certainly seemed confident: she was calmly but firmly telling the men where to dig, ordering them this way and that, up and down the valley. For an hour or two the dust rose and settled; the spades rang and shovelled. The hot, joyless wind whirred over the Valley of Killings.

And then one man dropped his shovel. It was Radevan's second cousin, Mumtaz.

'Miss Meyer!' he cried. 'Miss Meyer!'

She ran over; Rob followed.

A portion of white bone was lying in the dusty earth. It was the curve of a skull: small but human. Even Rob could tell that. Christine seemed intrigued, but not triumphant. She nodded.

'OK, good. Now dig laterally.'

The Kurds did not understand. Christine told Radevan, again, in Kurdish: *dig straight across. Don't bother digging any deeper.* It was a matter of covering the ground now: they had less than two days left.

The men worked to order, apparently charmed by Christine's wilfulness. Rob joined the shovelling once more. Every few minutes they uncovered a new skull. Rob helped them scrape the earth away with feverish energy. Another skull; another skeleton. Whenever they found the ruins of another body, they didn't bother uncovering the whole thing – as soon as they got the sense of one skeleton, Christine told them to move on.

Another skull; another skeleton. These, Rob noted, were quite small people. Typical hunter-gatherers, as Christine explained, five foot tall at most. Sturdy men of the caves and the deserts, with healthy physiques: but no more than averagely tall for the time.

They dug, quicker and quicker. It was messy and slipshod. The sun was past its zenith and Rob also sensed the great wall of water was getting nearer. The incoming flood was just a few days away.

Still they dug.

And then Rob heard another shout, this time from Radevan.

'Mr Rob,' Radevan said. 'Look at this! A very big man. Like American.' He was scraping earth from a femur bone. 'Like American who eat many McNuggets.' The femur was almost twice as large as any of the others.

Christine jumped down into the trench; Rob joined her. They helped to unearth the rest of the skeleton. It took time because the skeleton was huge: seven foot six at least. They all scraped earth from the pelvis. From the ribs. From the spine, unearthing large white bones in the grimy yellow dust. And then they came to the skull. Radevan pulled it out in one go, and held it up.

Rob gawped. It was enormous.

Christine took the great skull from Radevan's hands and examined it. It was not an obvious human skull: it was much larger, with slanting, birdlike eyes, stark cheekbones, a smaller jaw and a very large braincase.

Rob looked closer at the grinning jaw, with its teeth still intact.

'This is . . .' He wiped the sweat, salt and dust from his face. 'This is a hominid, right?'

'Yes,' said Christine. 'But . . .' She turned it in the shadeless sun.

The skull was filled with dark yellow earth, giving the large slanted eye sockets a blank and hostile stare. Rob could hear a bird somewhere, calling – a lonely bird circling languidly in the sky. Probably a buzzard, attracted by the bones.

Christine brushed some adhering yellow dust from the skull. 'Clearly hominid. Clearly non-*Homo sapiens*. Like nothing we have ever found. Very large braincase, presumably highly intelligent.'

'It looks kind of . . . Asiatic. No?'

Christine nodded. 'Mongoloid in certain aspects, yes. But . . . but look at the eyes, and the cranium. *Amazing.* Yet it fits. Because I think . . .' She looked at Rob. 'I think we have the answer here, to the hybridization. This is the *other* species of hominid. The one that inter-bred with the smaller people here, to produce the skull from the Black Book.'

The Kurds were still digging. Skeleton after skeleton. The number of bones they had uncovered was almost sickening. The sun was nearing the horizon: the day's fast would soon be over and the men were keen to get home for the feast, the end of the day's Ramadan famine.

When he was too exhausted to continue, too nauseated by the white of the bones, and the grins of the enormous skulls, Rob lay back on the dusty slope and just watched. Then he took out his notebook and began to scribble. To piece the story together. This was the only way he knew to unlock a puzzle: to write it down; set it out. And thereby piece together a narrative. He sensed the light fading as he wrote.

After he'd finished his notes he looked up: Christine was measuring bones, and taking photos of the skeletons. But the day was over. The desert breeze was mild, and freshening. The inundating water was now so near that Rob could smell it in the air. Probably no more than two or three miles away. He gazed down the trenches with his tired eyes. They had uncovered an enormous and mournful graveyard: a charnel house of proto-humans, lying next to near-human giants. But the real puzzle remained hidden; Rob hadn't worked it out; his notes didn't make sense. They hadn't yet managed to solve the secret. And the darkness of the desert meant they had just one day left.

Rob's heart cried out for his daughter.

48

On the drive back to Sanliurfa they talked about the document, the reference to the Book of Enoch. Rob shifted gears, vigorously, as Christine shouted her theories across the rattling car.

'The Book of Enoch is a piece of . . . pseudo-scripture.'

'Which means?'

'That means it's not part of the official Bible but it is regarded by some ancient branches of Christianity, like the Ethiopic Church, as being truly sacred.'

'OK . . .'

'The Book of Enoch is about 2200 years old and was probably written by Israelis, though we are not entirely sure.' She stared ahead at the unrolling desert. 'It was found amongst those documents preserved in what we know as "The Dead Sea Scrolls".

'The Book of Enoch describes a time when five fallen angels – the Five Satans, or the Watchers – and their minions came amongst early men. These angels were supposedly close to God but they could not resist the beauty of women. The daughters of Eve. So the bad angels took these women, and in return promised the human males the secrets of writing and building, of artistry and carving. These . . . demons also taught the women to "kiss the phallus".'

Rob gazed across the car and managed a smile. Christine smiled back. 'That's the exact phrase the Book of Enoch uses,' Christine said, drinking some water from a bottle. 'Yuk. This water's warm.'

'Go on,' said Rob. 'The Book of Enoch.'

'OK. Well . . . this intermarrying between demons and men created a race of evil raging giants, the Nephilim, again according to the Book of Enoch.'

Rob stared at the twilit road ahead. He wanted to comprehend what she was saying. He really wanted to. He tried hard. He got her to repeat it . . . but then he gave up. He couldn't stop thinking about Lizzie. He wondered if they should call Cloncurry. But he knew that was stupid; they had to surprise him. They had to announce suddenly that they had unearthed the secret – if they ever unearthed it: that was the way their plan worked.

But he was tired, sunburnt and frightened, and still feeling that spookiness of the desert. He could sense the nearness of the stones of Gobekli. Still out there in the wilderness. He remembered that carving of the woman, staked and pinioned, ready to be raped by the wild boars with the penises. He thought about the babies, screaming in their ancient jars.

And then he thought of Lizzie again, and Cloncurry – and tried to shunt the thought from his mind.

The conclusion of the drive was silent. And anxious. The Kurds said a muttered goodbye and went off to eat and drink; Rob and Christine parked the cars, wearily, and sloped quietly into the Hotel Haran. Rob carried the Black Book close to his chest, the exhaustion rippling through his arms.

But they didn't have time to relax. Rob was tired, but he was febrile with determination, and he wanted to talk through his notes. As soon as they reached their hotel room, before Christine had even showered, he quizzed her again.

'One thing I don't understand is the jars. The jars with the babies, in Gobekli.'

Christine looked at him. Her deep brown eyes were loving, but bloodshot with tiredness but Rob persisted.

'You mean . . . the mere fact they were jars. That confuses you?'

'Yes. I always thought the culture around Gobekli Tepe was . . . what was the word Breitner used . . . *aceramic*? Without pottery. But then, suddenly, someone came along and taught these guys how to make jars, long before any other culture in the region. Long before anywhere else on earth.'

'Yes, it's true . . .' Christine paused. 'Except one place . . . There was one place that had pottery before Gobekli.'

'Yeah?'

'Japan.' Christine was frowning. 'The Jomon of Japan.'

'The what?'

'A very early culture. Aboriginal Japanese. The Ainu, who still live in northernmost Japan, may be related . . .' She stood and rubbed her aching back, then went to the minibar, took out a cold bottle of water and drank, thirstily. Lying back down on the bed, she explained, 'The Jomon came literally from nowhere. They were maybe the first to cultivate rice. And then they started producing sophisticated pottery – cordware it is called.'

'How long ago?'

'Sixteen thousand years ago.'

'*Sixteen thousand years ago?*' Rob stared across the room. 'That's more than three thousand years before Gobekli.'

'Yes. And some people think the Jomons of East Asia may have learned their techniques from an even *earlier* culture. Like the Kondons of the Amur. Maybe. The Amur is a river north of Mongolia, where there are arguably signs of pottery going back even further. It is most mysterious. They come and they go, these peculiarly advanced peoples of the north. They are basic hunter-gatherers, yet suddenly they make a wild and irrational technological leap.'

'What do you mean? *Irrational?*'

'This is not the most promising territory for early civilization. Siberia, inner Mongolia, the far north of Japan. These places are not the warm, sunny fertile crescent. These are the freezing and intractable lands of north Asia. The Amur basin is one of the coldest places on earth in the winter.' She gazed at the bare hotel ceiling. 'In fact I've sometimes wondered, could there have been one protoculture north of there? In Siberia? Now lost to us? Some culture that was influencing all these tribes? Because otherwise it is too bizarre . . .'

Rob shook his head. He had his notebook flat on his lap; pen poised. 'But maybe they didn't go, Christine. These cultures. Mmm? Maybe they didn't disappear.'

'Sorry?'

'The skulls, they look Asiatic. Mongoloid. Maybe these eastern cultures didn't vanish. They just moved . . . west. Could there be some link between these advanced Asiatic tribes and Gobekli?'

Christine nodded, and yawned. 'Yes, I suppose so. Yes, I guess. Jesus, Rob, I'm tired.'

Rob mentally admonished himself. They hadn't slept in twenty-four hours; they'd done as much as they could. He was pushing Christine too hard. He said sorry and came over, and lay down besides her on the bed.

'Robbie, we *will* save her,' said Christine. 'I promise.' She hugged him. 'I promise.'

Rob shut his eyes. 'Let's sleep.'

The next morning Rob was woken by a dream of great violence. He dreamed for a few moments he was being hit, being pummelled by Cloncurry, but when he woke he realized it was drumming: real drumming. Men were walking down the dark streets of Sanliurfa, outside the hotel, banging big bass drums, rousing people for the pre-dawn meal. The traditional Ramadan ritual.

Rob sighed and tilted his wristwatch, which was lying on the bedside table. It was just 4 a.m. He stared at the ceiling and listened to the thumping and booming of the drums, while Christine snored gently next to him.

Two hours later Christine was nudging him awake in return. He stirred, feeling sluggish. He got up and showered in bracingly cold water.

Radevan and his friends were waiting outside. They helped stow the Black Book in the boot. Rob ate a hardboiled egg and some pitta bread in the car as they rattled across the desert to the Valley of the Slaughter. They didn't have time to linger for breakfast at the hotel.

Rob watched the Kurds as they dug. It was as if they knew their job was nearly over, whatever happened: they were demob happy. This was the last day. Tomorrow morning the time was up. *Whatever happened.* Rob's stomach twisted with the tension.

At eleven Rob climbed the hill next to the valley and gazed across the flat, silvery lakewater of the Great Anatolian Project. It was no longer in the distance but only about a mile away, and the water seemed to be accelerating, pouring over hills and filling the dales. The levee would defend them, but the encroaching flood was still a menacing sight. There was a small shepherd's hut on top of the levee. Like a sentinel, protecting them from the waters.

He sat down on a boulder and made some more notes, threading the precious pearls of evidence onto the necklace of the narrative. One quote kept striking home. He remembered his father, in the Mormon church, reciting it. From Genesis Chapter 6: '*And it came to pass, when men began to multiply on the face of the earth, and daughters were born unto them . . . that the sons of God saw the daughters of men that they were fair; and they took them wives of all which they chose . . .*'

For half an hour he scribbled, and crossed out, and scribbled again. He was nearly there; the story was nearly finished. Shutting the notebook, he turned and paced down the hill into the valley. He found Christine lying flat on the ground, as if she was asleep. But she wasn't asleep: she was staring hard and flat across the dust.

'I'm looking for anomalies,' she said, looking up at him. 'And I've found some. There!' She stood up and clapped her hands and the young Kurds stared at her. 'Please, gentlemen,' she said. 'Soon you can go home to your families and forget about the madwoman from France. But just one more effort, please. Over there.'

Radevan and his friends picked up their shovels and followed Christine to another corner of the valley.

'Dig down straight down. Here. And not too deep. Dig wide and shallow. Thank you.'

Rob went to find his spade so he could join in. He liked digging with the Kurds. It gave him something to do other than worry about the possible pointlessness of what they were doing. And Lizzie. And Lizzie and Lizzie and Lizzie.

As they dug, Rob asked Christine about the Neanderthals. She had been explaining how she had worked on several sites where Neanderthals had lived. Like Moula-Guercy, on the banks of the Rhone, in France.

'Do you think they interbred with *Homo sapiens*?'

'Possibly.'

'But I thought there was a theory that they just died out? The Neanderthals?'

'There was. But we also have evidence that they may have bred with humans.' Christine sleeved the sweat from her face. 'The Neanderthals may even have raped their way into the human gene pool. If they were dying out, unable to compete for food or whatever, they would have been desperate to preserve their own species. And they were bigger than *Homo sapiens*. Albeit possibly more stupid . . .'

Rob watched a bird circling in the air: another vulture. He asked a second question. 'If they did interbreed, might that have altered the way humans behaved? Human culture?'

'Yes. One possibility is cannibalism. There is no record of organized cannibalism in the human repertoire before about 300,000 BC. Yet the Neanderthals were definitely cannibalistic. So . . .' She tilted her head, thinking. 'So it is possible the Neanderthals might have introduced some traits of their own. Like cannibalism.'

A Turkish Air Force plane streaked across the sky. Christine added one more thought. 'I was wondering, this morning, about the size of the hominids, the large ones. The bones we found.'

'Go on . . .'

'Well . . . Your theory that there might be a link with Central Asia, that fits. In a way.'

'How?'

'The largest hominid ever found was in Central Asia. Gigantopithecus. Absolutely enormous: an apeman maybe nine foot tall. Like a kind of . . . yeti . . .'

'Seriously?'

His girlfriend nodded. 'They lived around three hundred thousand years ago. They might have survived longer – and some think that Gigantopithecus might have survived long enough – for memories to persist in *Homo sapiens*. Memories of enormous apemen.' She shook her head. 'But of course this is very fanciful. What's more likely is that Gigantopithecus died out due to competition from *Homo sapiens*. No one is quite sure what happened to Gigantopithecus. However . . .' She paused, leaning on her spade like a farmer contemplating his fields.

The obvious conclusion dawned on Rob. He took out his notebook, and scribbled excitedly. 'What you mean is, maybe there is a *third* explanation, right? Maybe Gigantopithecus *did* evolve – but into a much more serious rival to *Homo sapiens*. Isn't that possible, too?'

Christine nodded, frowning. 'Yes. It is possible. We have no evidence either way.'

Rob went on. 'So. Let's just say that *did* happen. Then that new hominid – that would be a very large, aggressive and highly intelligent hominid, wouldn't it? Something evolved to cope with harsh and brutal conditions. A fierce competitor for resources.'

'Yes. I agree. It would.'

'And this large, aggressive hominid would also have an instinctive fear of nature, of endless lethal winters, of a cruel and severe God. And it would have a desperate need to *propitiate*.'

Christine shrugged, as if she didn't quite follow this latest concept; but she didn't have time to reply, because Radevan was calling them over. Even as Rob reached the scene, Christine was already on her hands and knees, scraping at more remains.

Three large dirty jars were lying by Radevan's feet.

They were marked with sanjaks.

Rob knew at once what the jars would contain. And he didn't have to tell Christine, but she was cracking one of the jars open, anyway, with the handle of a trowel. The ancient jar crumbled and a slimy, fetid-smelling thing oozed into the dust: a half-mummified, half-liquefied baby. The face was not quite as intact as the babies they had found in the Edessa Vault. But the scream of terror and pain on the tiny child's face was just the same. It was another child sacrifice. Another infant buried alive in a jar.

Rob tried not to think of Lizzie.

Some of the Kurds had spotted the jar, and the remains. The dead and rotting baby. They were pointing, and arguing. Christine asked them to continue digging. But they were shouting now.

Mumtaz approached Rob. 'They say it is dangerous here. This place is cursed. They see the baby and they say they must go. The water will be here soon.'

Christine pleaded with the men, in English and Kurdish.

The men gabbled at Mumtaz and he interpreted. 'They say the water comes. To bury these bodies and that is good. They say they go now!'

Christine protested again. The argument continued. Some of the Kurds dug, some just stood and debated. The sun rose all the time, hot and menacing. The spades and trowels lay unused, glinting in the merciless light. The sun was baking the small slimy corpse of the baby. That obscene little package of flesh. Rob had an enormous urge to bury it again, to cover up the obscenity. He knew he was close to unlocking the puzzle, but he also felt close to some kind of nervous surrender. The tension was hideous.

And then the tension worsened. Some of the Kurds, led by Mumtaz, came to a decision: they refused to go on. Despite Christine's pleadings, three of them climbed the slopes of the valley, and got into the second Land Rover.

Mumtaz looked in Rob's direction as they left, a strange, wistful glance. Then the car accelerated away into the dust and the haze.

But four men still remained, including Radevan. And with the last of her charm, and the last of Rob's dollars, Christine persuaded them to complete the task. So they all picked up the discarded shovels, and together they dug. They dug for five hours, sideways across the valley, shifting enough dry, yellow soil to expose what was necessary, and then moving on.

They uncovered parts of maybe thirty skeletons lying next to the jars. But these were no ordinary skeletons. They were a mixture of the large hominids and the hybrid men *and* the little hunter-gatherers. All jumbled together, promiscuously and wildly. And all of the skeletons showed damage: signs of violent death. Vicious cracks in the skull, spear-holes in pelvic bones. Broken arms, broken femurs, broken heads.

They had uncovered a battlefield. A terrible site of slaughter and conflict. They had uncovered the Valley of Killing.

Christine looked at Rob. He looked back and said, 'I think we're done here. Don't you?'

Christine nodded solemnly.

Rob reached into his pocket and pulled out his phone. The sensation was almost elation. He felt it in his lungs and in his heart. He had *worked it out:* he had deciphered the great secret Cloncurry had been born to conceal. The Genesis Secret. And that meant Rob had power over Cloncurry, at last. Rob was going to win his daughter back.

Anxious – but hopeful for the first time in these bitter weeks – he keyed in the number. He was about to phone Cloncurry and demand his daughter's immediate return when he heard a voice.

'Well, hello.'

Rob swivelled. A figure was standing on the crest of the hill above them, between the valley and the westering sun. The sun behind the figure was so bright Rob couldn't make out who it was. He squinted and raised his arm.

'Have I put on weight? How depressing. Surely you recognize me?'

Rob felt his blood congeal with fear.

Jamie Cloncurry was standing on the hill above them, with a gun in his hand. The gun was aimed at Rob. The killer had two large men beside him. Big Kurds with black moustaches, also conspicuously armed. These two thugs were holding a small figure between them bound and strapped.

Lizzie! Alive, but evidently frightened, and gagged very tightly.

Rob stared to his left and right at Radevan and his friends – seeking their help.

Cloncurry chortled. 'Oh, I shouldn't expect any assistance there, Mr Robbie.' With a languid gesture, he signalled at Radevan.

Radevan nodded, obediently. He turned and stared at Rob and Christine, and then rubbed his thumb and forefinger together. 'Englishman much money. Dollars and euros. Dollars and euros . . .' Then he gestured to his friends and the rest of the Kurds dropped their tools and walked away from Rob and Christine, nonchalantly deserting the couple. Leaving Rob and Christine to their fate.

Rob watched – slack-jawed, defeated, and desolate – as the Kurds calmly loped up the hill towards the last Land Rover. Radevan reached in the boot of the car and took out the Black Book. He carried it over to Cloncurry and laid it in the dust beside Lizzie. Cloncurry smiled and nodded, and Radevan walked back to the car, jumped in the front seat, and the car was driven away with a spin of wheel dust, taking with it the shotguns and the pistol.

The orange dust hung in the air, reproachfully, as the vehicle disappeared over the sunburnt horizon, leaving Rob and Christine alone and defenceless in the bottom of the valley.

Above them stood Cloncurry, armed, with the other two Kurds. The killer had his four-wheel-drive parked a few hundred yards away, silver and glittering in the desert light. He had obviously approached on foot, to surprise them. And it had worked.

They were trapped. Lizzie knelt, gagged and bound, in the dust, staring at her father with wild and puzzled eyes. Imploring him to save her.

But Rob knew he couldn't save her. He knew what was going to happen next. And it wasn't going to be a heroic rescue.

Cloncurry was going to kill Lizzie in front of him. He was going to sacrifice Rob's firstborn, here in this wilderness, as the crows and the buzzards circled in the sky. His daughter was going to die, cruelly and brutally, in the next few minutes, and Rob would be forced to watch.

49

Cloncurry waved the gun at Rob and Christine. 'More over there, *lovebirds*.'

Rob gazed at his daughter kneeling there in the dust, feeling perplexed, and utterly anguished. Then he stared with fierce anger at Cloncurry. He'd never felt such a lust to hurt someone – he wanted to dismember Cloncurry with his bare hands, with his teeth. Dig out his eyes with his thumbs.

But Rob and Christine were trapped and unarmed: they had to obey; following Cloncurry's languid directions, they moved up a slight rise in the middle of the valley, onto a kind of sandy knoll, though Rob had no idea why Cloncurry wanted them on this isolated hillock.

The wind was whispering and melancholy. Christine looked as if she was about to cry. Rob glanced left and right, desperate for some escape. There was no escape.

What was Cloncurry doing? Rob squinted, visoring his gaze against the sun with a hand. It seemed that Cloncurry had some kind of phone or other gadget in his hand. He was pointing it left, towards the encroaching floods. Where the levee protected them from the inundations.

At last Cloncurry spoke. 'It's not every day one gets to mutilate and kill a child in front of her daddy, so I think some celebrations are in order. Indeed, some fireworks. So. Here we go. *Surf's up!*'

He pressed a button on the device he was holding. A fraction of a second later the boom of an explosion ripped across the desert – followed by a tangible blast wave: Cloncurry had blown up the little shepherd's hut on the levee. As the smoke and the flames cleared, Rob saw why.

It wasn't just the hut that Cloncurry had sent hurtling into the sky: half the levee had gone too. And now floodwater was pouring through the gap: it had found this lower channel, and the floodwater was tumbling, down the sides of the valley, tons of water spouting and screaming. Coming their way, *very fast*.

Rob grabbed Christine hard, and pulled her to the top of the knoll. The water was already gushing beside them; tons of water, some of it lapping at their ankles. Rob looked up at the crest: Cloncurry was laughing.

'Do hope you can swim.'

The water was cascading now, filling the valley, splashing at Rob's feet. A wall of water, roaring and engulfing, carrying with it a repulsive scum. Bobbing on the surface were bones, and slops of mummified baby, and some of the warrior skulls: floating and tumbling. Soon the scummy and turbulent waters had completely surrounded Rob and Christine on their little hill. If it continued to rise they were going to drown.

'Perfect!' exclaimed Cloncurry. 'Can't tell you how difficult that was. We had to come out here in the middle of the night to set it all up. In that nasty little hut. Lots of explosives. Tricky. But it worked to perfection! How *enormously* gratifying.'

Rob stared across the waters at Cloncurry, safe on his elevation. He didn't know what to think about this man, the utter madness mixed with this . . . devious subtlety. And then Cloncurry made his usual near-telepathic remark:

'I guess you're a tad confused, little Robbie.'

Rob stayed silent; Cloncurry smiled.

'Can't work out how such a total psycho like me should end up on this side of the water? Eh? While the good guys, all you guys, you're on *that side.* The drowning side.'

Again, Rob said nothing. His enemy grinned wider.

'I'm rather afraid I've been using *everyone* all along. I got you to find me the Black Book. I harnessed the fine and famous minds of Christine Meyer and Isobel Previn to the cause. OK, I sliced Isobel's head off but she'd done her job by then. Showed me the Book surely wasn't in Kurdistan.' Cloncurry was gleaming with pride. 'And then, by simply sitting back and doing nothing, I got you lovely people to do the *rest* of the work, as well: to decipher the Book, to locate the Valley of the Slaughter, to find the only evidence of the Genesis Secret. Because, you see, I needed to know for sure where all the evidence *is*, so it can be destroyed forever.' He gestured across the frothing floodwater. 'And now I am going to erase all of this . . . along with the only people who know.' He looked down, very happily. 'Oh yes, nearly forgot, and I have the Black Book, too! At least I think I do. Let me just make sure . . .'

Stooping to the dust, Cloncurry grabbed the box and wrenched the leather lid away. He peered down, reached inside, and took out the hybrid skull. For a moment he cradled the skull, caressing the smoothness of the cranium. Then he turned the skull so it met his gaze.

'Alas, poor Yorick. You had fucking weird eyes. But quite superb cheekbones! Hah.'

He set the skull to the side, and took out the document and spread it across his knee so that he could read.

'Fascinating. Truly fascinating. I fully expected cuneiform. We *all* expected cuneiform. But late ancient Aramaic? A wonderful discovery.' Cloncurry glanced at Christine and Rob. 'Thank you, chaps. So kind of you to bring it all the way here. And to dig everything up.'

He folded the document, put it back in the box and replaced the skull on top of the document; the leather lid followed.

Rob watched all this with a kind of sullen, hate-filled resentment.

The most disgusting flavour in this banquet of defeat was the sense that Cloncurry was *right*. The killer's whole gameplan had a kind of glistening, alien *perfection*. Cloncurry had outwitted and out-thought them all the way through. From the Kurds to the cottage and back again, Cloncurry hadn't just won, he had *triumphed*.

And now his triumph would be honoured in blood.

Rob stared at his daughter's shining, crying eyes; and he shouted across the water that he loved her.

Lizzie's eyes implored her helpless father: *help me*.

Cloncurry was giggling. 'Very touching. If you like that kind of thing. Makes me want to spew, personally. Either way, I think we should now proceed to the final drama, don't you? Before you actually drown. Enough of the preamble.' The killer regarded the wavelets lapping at Christine's ankles. As he gazed, one particularly enormous skull bobbed along the burbling floodwaters, like an obscene kind of bath toy. 'Oooh, look, there's one of the wrinklies. Say hello to granddad, Lizzie.'

Another chuckle. Lizzie wept louder.

'Yes, yes.' Cloncurry sighed loudly. 'I never liked my family either.' He turned and called across to Rob. 'You have a nice view from your hillock? Excellent. Because we're going to do the Aztec thing, and I want to make sure you can see. I'm sure you know the rigmarole, Robert. We splay your daughter over a rock, then we rip into her chest and yank out the beating heart. Can be a bit messy but I think my friend Navda has some Kleenex.'

Cloncurry nudged one of his followers. The moustached Kurd on his left grunted, but said nothing. The gang-leader sighed. 'Not the most expressive of chaps, but the best available. I do wonder about the moustaches though. Just a tiny bit . . . *sincere,* aren't they?' He smiled. 'Anyway, could you two chatty Kurdish gaylords take this little girl and *drape* her over that rock?' He mimed it for them.

The Kurds nodded, and obeyed. They picked up Lizzie and carried her over to a small boulder and laid her out with the boulder under her back, her feet held by one Kurd, her hands held by the other henchman; and all the while Lizzie sobbed, and struggled. And all the while Cloncurry smirked.

'Very good, very good. Now to the best bit. By rights, Mr Robbie, we should have a chac mool, one of those weird stone bowls, into which I can drop your daughter's bloody, still-beating heart, but we haven't got a chac mool. I suppose I shall feed her heart to the crows.'

He handed his pistol to one of the Kurds, then reached into his jacket pocket and took a huge steel blade from inside his jacket. This, he brandished exultantly, admiring it, his eyes bright and keen and loving. Then he looked over, and winked at Rob.

'We should really be using obsidian: that's what the Aztecs used. Dark obsidian daggers. But a big thick knife like this will do nicely, a big thick rather memorable knife. You do recognize it?' Cloncurry lifted the knife in the dusty sunlight. It flashed as he turned it. 'Christine? Any ideas?'

'Fuck you,' said the Frenchwoman.

'Well, quite. It's the knife I used to fillet your old friend, Isobel. I think I can still see some of her elderly blood on the handle. And a tiny bit of spleen!' He grinned. '*Also*, as the Germans say. To our task. I see the water is now at your knees and you will drown within about ten minutes. But I so want the last thing you witness to be your daughter having her heart literally *torn* from her tiny chest as she screams *helplessly* for her pathetic, useless and *cowardly* father. So we'd better get cracking. Guys, hold the girl tighter, yes, like that. Yes, yes. Very good.'

Cloncurry lifted the knife in his two hands and the vicious blade sparkled in the sun. He paused. 'The Aztecs were so weird, weren't they? Apparently they came from Asia, over the Bering Straits. Like you me and Rob. All the way from North Asia.' The knife glittered; Cloncurry's eyes were likewise shining. 'They just loved to kill children. They *lusted* for it. Originally they killed the kids of all their enemies, their conquered foes. Yet I understand that by the end of their empire they were so nuts they started killing all their *own* children. No joke. The priests would pay poor Aztec families to hand over babies and infants to be ritually slaughtered. An entire civilization literally murdering itself, devouring its own offspring. Fantastic! And what a way to do it, to rip out the heart by smashing into the ribcage, then hold the still-beating organ in front of the living victim. So.' Cloncurry sighed happily. 'Are you ready, Lillibet? Little Betsy? My little Betty Boo? Mmm? Chesty open time?'

Cloncurry beamed down at Rob's daughter. Rob watched, with desolate disgust: Cloncurry was actually drooling, a line of spittle dribbling from his mouth onto Lizzie's gagged and screaming face.

And then the moment came: Cloncurry's two hands took a grip at the furthest end of the handle and raised the knife higher . . . and Rob closed his eyes in the sadness of uttermost defeat . . .

. . . as a shot cracked the air. A shot from nowhere. A shot from heaven.

Rob opened his eyes. A bullet had whipped across the waters and slammed into Cloncurry – a bullet so violent it had clean ripped off the killer's hand.

He blinked and stared. Cloncurry had lost a hand! Arterial blood was pumping from the severed wrist. The knife had been sent spinning into the water.

Cloncurry gazed at the hideous wound, nonplussed. His expression was one of deep curiosity. And then a second shot snapped out, again from nowhere – who was doing the shooting? – and this one nearly took off Cloncurry's arm at the shoulder. His left arm, already handless, was now dangling by a few red muscles, and blood was pissing into the dust from the gaping shoulder-wound.

The two Kurds immediately dropped Lizzie, turned with panic on their faces and, as a third shot cracked through the desert air, ran.

Cloncurry fell to his knees. The third shot had obviously hit him in the leg. He knelt, bleeding, on the sand, scrabbling anxiously around. What was he looking for? His own severed hand? The knife? Lizzie was next to him lying gagged and hogtied. Rob stood knee-deep in the water. Who was shooting who? And where was Cloncurry's gun? Rob glanced left: he could see dust in the distance. Maybe a car was coming their way, but the dust obscured his view. Were they going to shoot Lizzie too?

Rob realized he had one chance. *Now.* He dived into the water, plunged and swam, swimming for Lizzie's life, swimming between the bones and skulls. He had never swum so hard, had never battled such surging, dangerous waters . . . He kicked and crawled, swallowing whole mouthfuls of cold water, and then he slapped a hand on dry hot earth, and hauled himself up. When he rose from the water, gasping and spitting, he saw Cloncurry a few yards away.

Cloncurry was lying down, using Lizzie's body as a shield from any further gunshots; but his mouth was wide open and drooling – and he was closing his jaw over Lizzie's soft throat. Like a tiger killing a gazelle. Jamie Cloncurry was going to bite into Lizzie's neck, and chew out her jugular.

A surge of fury ran through Rob. He flung himself across the sand and ran at Cloncurry just as the killer's sharp white teeth closed over his daughter's windpipe, and he kicked Cloncurry in the head, kicking him straight off his daughter. Then Rob did it again: he kicked the killer away for a second time, and then a third time, and Cloncurry sprawled with a yell of pain into the dust, his half-severed arm hanging useless and obscene.

Rob leapt on the gang-leader, lodging a knee on Cloncurry's uninjured shoulder so that he couldn't move. Now he had Cloncurry at his mercy. He could hold him here as long as he liked.

But Rob had no intention of showing mercy.

'*Your turn,*' said Rob.

He reached into his pocket for his Swiss Army knife. Slowly and carefully he unclasped the biggest blade and twisted it in the air for a moment, then he looked down.

Rob found himself *smiling.* He was wondering what to do first, how to torture and maim Cloncurry so that it would cause the maximum pain, before the killer's inevitable death. Stab him in the eye? Carve off an ear? Slit the scalp open? What? But as Rob lifted the knife, he saw something in Cloncurry's leering expression. A kind of shared and exultant shame, a hopeful yet defiant evil. The bile of revulsion rose in Rob's throat.

Shaking his head, Rob closed the knife and put it back in his pocket. Cloncurry wasn't going anywhere: he was bleeding to death right here. His leg was shattered, his hand was gone, the arm was hanging off. He was unarmed, and mutilated, dying from the shock of the pain and blood-loss. Rob didn't need to do anything.

Rolling off the killer, Rob turned to his daughter.

He ungagged her immediately. She cried out *Daddy daddy daddy* and then she said *Christine!* and Rob turned, ashamed. He'd quite forgotten Christine in his urge to save Lizzie; but Christine was saving herself, and a moment later Rob reached down to the waters to grab her hand and help her out of the surging water. He hauled her up onto the dust, and she lay there, panting.

Then Rob heard a noise. Turning, he saw Cloncurry dragging himself along in the dust, creaking and slow, his half-severed arm hanging at his side, the wound in his thigh gaping wide and raw. As he crawled, he left a trail of blood behind him. He was heading straight for the water.

He was going to make the last sacrifice: suicide. Jamie Cloncurry was going to drown himself. Rob watched, transfixed and appalled. Cloncurry was at the water's edge now. With a grunt of great pain he hauled himself the final yard, and then he flopped down into the scummy cold waves with a great splash. For a moment his head bobbed amongst the grinning skulls, and his bright eyes stared straight at Rob.

And then he sank beneath the waves. Gently spiralling down, to join the bones of his ancestors.

Christine sat upright, shaking her phone, making sure it was still working. At last, miraculously, she got a signal and rang Sally and began telling her the good news. Rob listened, half-dazed, half-happy, half-dreaming. He found himself scanning the horizon and did not know why. Then, a minute later, he realized *why* he was scanning the horizon.

There were police cars speeding across the dust, negotiating their way between the fingers of floodwater. A few moments later the hilltop was alive with policemen and officers and soldiers – and there was Kiribali. In his dustless suit, wearing a wide bright smile. He was snapping orders into his radio, and pointing directions to his men.

Rob sat on the sand and hugged his daughter close.

50

Two hours later they drove slowly back to Sanliurfa. Rob and Christine and Lizzie were wrapped in blankets in the back of the biggest police car, one of a long convoy of police vehicles.

Evening was falling. Rob's clothes were drying in the desert warmth, the fine mellow breeze whistling through the car windows. The last rays of sun were streaks of crimson against the purple and black of the darkening west.

Kiribali was in the passenger seat in the front of the car; he turned and looked at Rob, and at Christine, and then he smiled at Lizzie. He said to Rob, 'Cloncurry was of course paying the Kurds all along. Paying more than us, paying more than you. We had known something was up for a while. The Breitner murder, for instance. The Yezidi didn't mean to kill him, just frighten him. But he *was* killed. Why? Someone had persuaded the men at the dig to . . . go that extra mile. Your friend *Cloncurry.*'

'OK. And then . . . ?'

Kiribali sighed, and flicked some dust from his shoulder. 'I have to confess, we didn't know anything for a time. We were perplexed and confounded. But then I got a call, very recently, from your excellent policemen at Scotland Yard. But we were still in the pickle, Robert.

Because we didn't know where *you* were.' Kiribali smiled. 'And then Mumtaz! The little one, he came to me. He told us everything, just in time. It is always so good to have . . . *contacts*.'

Rob looked at Kiribali, barely registering what he was saying. Then he looked down at his hands. They were still slightly rusty with dried blood: Cloncurry's blood. But Rob didn't care, he didn't give a damn: he had saved his daughter's life! That was all that mattered. Rob's thoughts were a jangle of anxiety and relief and a weird bruising joy.

They drove on, quietly. And then Kiribali spoke again. 'You do know I am going to take the parchment, with the map, don't you? And the skull. I shall take that too. The whole Black Book.'

'Where are you going to put them?'

'With all the other evidence.'

'You mean the museum vaults.'

'Of course. And we have changed the keycode!'

A large police van overtook them, its brake lights ruby in the dusk.

'Please understand,' said Kiribali. 'You are safe. That is good. We shall hold the Kurds for a while, then let them go. Radevan and his foolish friends.' He smiled urbanely. 'I shall let them go because I have to keep the peace here. Between the Turks and the Kurds. But everything else will be locked away, forever.'

The car drove on. The warm evening air was delicious as it breezed through the windows: sweet and soft. Rob inhaled and exhaled; he stroked his daughter's hair. She was half asleep now. And then Rob noticed that they were passing the Gobekli turn off. It was just visible in the rising moonlight.

Rob hesitated. Then he asked Kiribali if they could go and look at Gobekli Tepe, *one last time*.

Kiribali asked the driver to stop the car, and he gazed across at Rob and Christine and Lizzie. The two girls were asleep: the policeman's smile was indulgent. He nodded, and radioed the other vehicles – informing them that they would all meet later, in Urfa. Then the driver turned the car and drove off-road.

It was the same familiar route. Over the shallow hills, past the Kurdish villages with their open sewers and straying goats and minarets floodlit a lurid green. A dog yapped, and chased the car. It chased them for a half a mile, then ran off into the gloom.

They drove further into the darkness. Then they crested the rise and were on the low hill, overlooking the temple. Rob got out of the police car, leaving Lizzie with her head laid in Christine's lap; both of them asleep.

Kiribali got out too. Together, the two men strolled the rolling path that led to the temple.

'So,' said Kiribali. 'Tell me.'

'Tell you *what*?'

'What you were doing in the valley? The Valley of Killing?'

Rob thought for a moment, and then he explained, tentatively. He gave a brief outline of the Genesis Secret, the most cursory sketch. But it was enough to intrigue: in the moonlight Rob could see Kiribali's eyes widening.

The detective smiled. 'And you believe you understood? That you really worked it all *out*?'

'Maybe . . . But we don't have any photos. It was all lost in the flood. No one would believe us. So it doesn't matter.'

Kiribali sighed, rather cheerfully. They had reached the top of the little hill, by the single mulberry tree. The megaliths were visible, casting a shadow by moonshine. Kiribali slapped Rob on the back. 'My writer friend. It matters to *me*. You know I love English literature. Tell me what you think . . . Tell me the *Genesis Secret*!'

Rob demurred; Kiribali insisted.

Rob sat down on a rocky bench. He took out his notebook and strained to read his notes in the moonlight. Then he closed the book, and stared across the undulating plains. Kiribali sat beside him, and listened to Rob's account.

'The Biblical accounts of the Fallen Angels, the passages in the Book of Enoch, the secret imparted in Genesis 6: I believe these are a folk memory of interbreeding between hominid species, the first men . . .'

'I see.' Kiribali smiled.

'And this, I believe, is how the folk memory arose. Sometime around 10,000 BC a species of man migrated from the north to Kurdish Turkey. These invading hominids were physically large. They may ultimately have evolved from Gigantopithecus, the largest hominid ever known. Certainly, judging by cultural influences nearby, these larger hominids came from central east Asia.'

Kiribali nodded. Rob went on, 'Whatever their origin, let's call these invading hominids the Northern men. Compared to *Homo sapiens*, the Northern men were more advanced, and certainly more aggressive. They had mastered pottery, and building, carving and sculpting, maybe even writing; whereas *Homo sapiens* were still living in caves.'

The detective remained silent, thinking. Rob elaborated. 'Why were the Northern men smarter and more ruthless? The solution is in their origin: they came from the north. Scientists have long speculated that fiercer climates produce a sharper, more strategic intelligence. In an Ice Age you need to plan ahead, merely to survive. You also need to compete more brutally for what resources there are. By contrast, warmer and kinder climates maybe produce a higher social intelligence, and more friendly co-operation . . .

'But the Northmen had a problem; hence their migration. We can speculate that they were dying out, like the Neanderthals before them. It seems, indeed, that the Northmen suffered a genetic flaw which predisposed them to intense and evil violence. Perhaps the harshness of their environment instilled in them a fear, of a vengeful God. A deity who hungered for blood, for the propitiation of *human sacrifice*.

'Whatever the reason: the Northern men were killing themselves, sacrificing their own kind. A dying civilization, like the Aztecs. In desperation they sought a kinder locale and climate: the Edenic climate of the fertile crescent. They migrated south and west. Once there they began to breed with the humbler peoples of the Kurdish plains; and as they intermingled with the hunter-gatherers, the humble cavemen, they taught them the arts of building, carving, religion, society: hence the startling advance in culture represented by Gobekli Tepe. In fact, I suspect Gobekli was a temple built by the supermen to inspire awe in the hunter-gatherers.'

A goat bleated, somewhere in the gloom.

'For a while, Gobekli Tepe must have seemed to the little hunter-gatherers like paradise. A Garden of Eden, a place where the gods walked amongst men. But things began to change. Food resources may have run low. As a result the Northern giants put the little hunters to work: to reap the wild grasses of the Kurdish plain, to toil as farmers. The mysterious move to agriculture had begun. The Neolithic revolution. And we humans were the helots. The slaves. The toilers in the field.'

'You mean *this* was the Fall of Man,' Kiribali said. 'The expulsion from Eden?'

'Perhaps. To deepen the mystery, we also have strange hints of changes in sexual behaviour around this time. Maybe the Northern men liked to rape the small cavewomen, rape them with pigs like the statue in your museum, maybe they taught the women to "kiss the phallus" as the Book of Enoch has it. The women certainly became aware of their sexuality – like Eve, found naked in Eden – as they copulated with the newcomers. And as the two hominids interbred, the unhappy genes of violence and sacrifice were passed on, albeit in a diluted form. The genes were inherited by the children born of these unions.'

A lorry hooted in the far distance as it took the main road south to Damascus.

'So yes, it was the Fall of Man. The community of Gobekli and the surrounding plains was now thoroughly brutalized, traumatized and hypersexualized. This was no Eden any more. Moreover, the farming itself was coarsening the landscape. Making life harder. And the reaction of the Northern men to these ominous signs? It was to take up the old traits again: they began to sacrifice, to appease the cruel gods of nature, or the demons in their minds. And they needed to appease these gods with human blood. *To fill jars with living babies.*' Rob glanced at the empty deserts to the east.

Kiribali leaned forward. 'And then?'

'Now we reach recorded history. Around 8000 BC the suffering, sacrifice and violence must have become too much. The local hunter-gatherers turned on the Northern invaders. They fought back. There was a huge battle. In desperation, the ordinary cavemen slaughtered the last of the invading Northmen, whom they greatly outnumbered. And then they buried all those bodies in a valley, close to the graves of the sacrificed children. Creating one great death-pit – not far from here, from Gobekli. The Valley of Killing.'

'And then they buried the temple!'

Rob nodded. 'And then Gobekli Tepe was interred, laboriously, to hide the shame of this cross-breeding, and to entomb the evil seed. The hunter-gatherers deliberately buried the great temple to eradicate the memory: the memory of the horrors, of the Fall from Eden, of their encounter with evil.

'But the burial didn't work. It was too late. The violent and sacrificial genes of the Northern men had entered the DNA of *Homo sapiens.* The Gobekli gene was now part of the human inheritance. And it was spreading. Using the Bible and other sources we can actually trace the gene, trace the exiles from Gobekli wandering south, to Sumer, Canaan and Israel; because as they went they spread the genes of sacrifice and violence. Hence the early evidence for sacrifice in these lands. The lands of Canaan, Israel and Sumer.'

'The lands of Abraham,' said Kiribali.

'Yes. The prophet Abraham, born near Sanliurfa, must have been partly descended from the Gobekli Northmen: he was intelligent, a leader, charismatic. And he was also obsessed with sacrifice. In the Bible he was prepared to slay his own son, in obedience to some wrathful god. Abraham was also, of course, the founder of the three great religions: Judaism, Christianity and Islam. The Abrahamic faiths. And Abraham founded these faiths on the folk memory he shared with those around him.

'All these great monotheistic religions spring from the trauma of what happened at Gobekli Tepe. All religions are based on a fear of great angels and a wrathful god: a subconscious and mass recollection of what happened in the Kurdish desert: when powerful and violent beings came amongst us. Significantly, all these religions are still based on the principal of human sacrifice: in Judaism there is the mock fleshly sacrifice of circumcision, in Islam we have the sacrifice of jihad—'

'Or maybe the butchered captives of al-Qaeda?'

'Maybe. And in Christianity we have the repetitive sacrifice of Christ, the firstborn of God, forever dying on the cross. So all these religions are a stress syndrome, a kind of nightmare, in which we constantly relive the trauma of the northern incursions, the time when we humans were cast out of Eden, and forced to give up our life of leisure. Forced to farm. Forced to kiss the phallus. Forced to kill our own children to please the wrathful gods.'

'But, Robert . . . How do the *Yezidi* fit in?'

'They are vitally important. Because there are only two sources of knowledge as to what really happened at Gobekli. The first are the Kurdish cultists, the Yarsens, Alevis *and the Yezidi.* These tribes like to believe they are directly descended from the purebred Gobekli cavemen. They are the Sons of the Jar. The sons of Adam. The rest of humanity, they say, comes from Eve, from the second jar of quarterbreeds and halfbreeds: the jar full of scorpions and snakes.'

'I see . . .'

'These cultists share many myths about the Garden of Eden. But even to the cultists, what happened at Gobekli is just a vague, frightening memory, of some sneering, birdlike angels that demanded worship. But the hazy folk-memory is potent. This is why the Yezidi, in particular, don't outmarry. They have a mythic fear that they might taint their own bloodline with the traits of the violence and sacrifice they see in wider humanity. In the rest of us. The peoples who carry the Gobekli gene.'

Kiribali was silent, taking this in.

Rob continued. 'The cursed Yezidi also bear a terrible burden. A mortification. They may claim to be pure, but deep down they sense the truth: that some of their forefathers interbred with the evil Northmen, allowing the Northmen to spread the Gobekli gene, and so the ills of the world are essentially their fault. Hence their inhibition, their secrecy, the Yezidis' peculiar sense of shame. Hence also the fact they have not spread far from the temple whence they come. They need to protect it. They still fear that if the truth is ever properly uncovered, and their deeds revealed to the world, they will be exterminated by the rest of humanity, in anger. Their forefathers failed to protect humanity from the Northmen. Their women lay with the Northern demons. Like the horizontal collaborators of occupied France.'

'And this,' Kiribali said, 'would explain their god. The peacock angel.'

'Yes. The Yezidis' knowledge of the truth makes it impossible for them to worship the normal gods. Which is why they worship the Devil, Melek Taus – the Moloch of the child-burnings. A symbolic reworking of the evil supermen, with their birdlike eyes. And for many thousands of years this strange faith and credo was a hidden mystery. The Gobekli gene spread around the world, it had already spread across the Bering Straits into America. But the actual Yezidi secret, the Genesis Secret, was perfectly safe. As long as Gobekli Tepe remained undisturbed.'

'And who was the other source? You said that there were two . . . wellsprings of knowledge?'

'The secret societies of Europe that arose in the sixteenth century. The Freemasons, and so forth. People intrigued by rumours and traditions, traditions which told of evidence, even documents, which existed in the Near East, and which threatened the historical and theological basis of Christianity, and of religion in general.'

The stars were high now; high and glittering.

'The loucher members of the anti-clerical English aristocracy,' Rob explained, 'were especially intrigued by these rumours. One of them, Francis Dashwood, travelled across Anatolia. What he learned there convinced him that Christianity was a charade. He then established the Hellfire Club, along with other likeminded intellectuals, artists and writers, whose *raison d'être* was contempt and derision of established faith.' Rob gazed at the largest of the megaliths, then added, 'But the Hellfires still had no conclusive proof that religion was false or "wrong". It was only when Jerusalem Whaley, of the Irish Hellfires, returned from his trip to Israel that the true story of Gobekli became known. In Jerusalem he was given the so-called Black Book, by a Yezidic priest. We do not know why. We do know the book was actually a box: the box you have now, containing the bizarre skull, and a map. The skull was not human. It was a hybrid. The map showed a graveyard near Gobekli Tepe, the graveyard of the evil gods: the Valley of the Slaughter. The priest explained to Whaley the significance of each.'

Kiribali frowned. 'And this significance was?'

'Jerusalem Whaley had, therefore, learned the truth about the descent of Man, and the genesis of religion. He had proved that religion was a charade, a folk memory, a relived nightmare. But he had also discovered something else: that an evil trait has infiltrated itself into the human bloodline, and that this trait gifts its carriers with great talent, intelligence and charisma. It makes them leaders. Yet leaders tend to sadism and cruelty because of this same gene cluster. Jerusalem Whaley only had to look at his own bloodline for proof, especially his brutal father, descended in turn from Oliver Cromwell. In other words, Whaley had discovered an *appalling* fact: that the fate of man is to be led by the cruel, because sadism and cruelty are linked to the genes that make men intelligent and charismatic leaders. The genes of the Northmen.'

Kiribali went to speak; but Rob stalled him with a gesture; he had nearly finished. 'Shattered by this revelation, Jerusalem Whaley hid the evidence: the skull and the map; the Black Book that Christine and I found in Ireland. And then he retired to the Isle of Man, broken and frightened. He was convinced that the world could not bear the truth – not just that all the Abrahamic religions were based on a falsity, an amalgam of remembered terrors and sacrificial urges – but that all political systems, aristocratic, feudal, oligarchic or even democratic, are bound to produce leaders predisposed to violence. Men who like to kill and to sacrifice. Men who will send thousands over a trench. Men who will fly a plane into a tower of innocents. Men who will clusterbomb a helpless desert village.'

Kiribali regarded him, grimly.

'And so the Hellfires disbanded, and the matter was suppressed. But one family preserved the terrible truth discovered by Jerusalem Whaley.'

'The Cloncurrys.'

'Exactly. The descendants of Jerusalem and Burnchapel Whaley. Rich, privileged and bloodthirsty, the Cloncurrys *carried the Gobekli gene*. They also passed down the knowledge once given to them by Tom Whaley. This knowledge was the deepest family secret, never to be revealed. If the knowledge was ever broadcast, elites across the world would be overthrown, and Islam and Judaism and Christianity likewise destroyed. It would be apocalyptic. The end of everything. The Cloncurrys' job, as they saw it, was therefore to ensure that this hideous truth remained suppressed.'

'And then poor Breitner came along.'

'Quite. After centuries of silence, the Cloncurrys learned that Gobekli was finally being dug up, by Franz Breitner. This was ominous. If the skull and the map were also found, and someone placed the pieces together, the truth would come out. The youngest scion of the family, Jamie Cloncurry, therefore recruited some rich kids, his acolytes, into a cultic gang with just this aim. To find and destroy the Black Book.

'But Jamie Cloncurry suffered another dynastic curse: he carried an intense version of the Gobekli gene cluster. Handsome and charismatic, a gifted leader, he was also psychotic. He believed it was his right to kill at will. Whenever he was thwarted in his quest for the skull and the map, the Gobekli gene revealed itself.'

There was a long, long silence.

At last Kiribali stood up. He shot the cuffs of his shirt, and adjusted his tie. 'Very good. I do so like stories.' He gazed directly at Rob. 'The best bits of the Bible and the Koran – those are the best stories. Don't you think? I have always believed that.'

Rob smiled.

Kiribali walked a few yards towards the megaliths, the polished toe-caps of his shoes gleaming in the moonlight. He looked back. 'There is an interesting coda, Robert . . . to all of this.'

'Yes.'

'Yes . . .' The detective's voice was sibilant in the quietness. 'I was talking to Detective Forrester.'

'The DCI.'

'Correct. And he told me something curious, about you and Cloncurry. You see, I rather pressed him for information.' The detective shrugged, in an unembarrassed way. 'You know how I am. And after some interrogation, Forrester admitted to me what he had found, in his research. On the internet.'

Rob gazed at Kiribali.

'Robert Luttrell. It's a fairly unusual name. Distinct. Is that not right?'

'It's Scotch-Irish, I think.'

'That's right. In fact,' said Kiribali, 'it is also found around Dublin. And it's that branch that mostly emigrated to America, to Utah. Where you come from.' Kiribali straightened his jacket. 'This is, therefore, the intriguing coda: it seems almost certain you are descended from them: from the Dublin Luttrells. And they were also members of the Hellfire Club. Your ancestors were related to the Cloncurrys.'

There was a significant pause. Then Rob said, 'I knew that already.'

'You did?'

'Yep.' Rob confessed. 'At least I guessed. And Cloncurry knew it too. That's why he kept hinting about family ties.'

'But that means you possibly carry the Gobekli gene? You do know that?'

'Of course,' Rob said. 'Although it is a gene cluster, even if I carry it at all. I am my mother's son as well as my father's.'

Kiribali nodded, keenly. 'Yes. Yes, yes. A man's mother is very important!'

'And even if I do carry some of those traits, it doesn't mean I am bound to my destiny. I would have to be in a certain situation, my environment would also play a part. The interaction is very complex.' He paused. 'I probably won't go into politics . . .'

The detective laughed, quietly. But then his expression darkened, once more.

'Robert. You say these terrible things happened . . . when we destroyed the environment. When we tore down the forests, to start farming—'

'Yes.'

'You say we were traumatised and scarred, is that correct? That we learned guilt and shame, and we turned to sacrifice and . . . savage religions.'

'I did.'

'Well.' He sighed, expressively, his face very white in the gloom. 'I'm just wondering. What will happen this time? We're doing it again? Aren't we? Destroying the world?'

Rob didn't know how to answer. Silence overcame them both.

At length, Kiribali smiled, and snapped his heels together, as if obeying an invisible commandant's orders. Then the policeman turned, and walked back to the car, perhaps sensing that Rob wanted to be alone.

Brushing the dust from his jeans, Rob stood, and strode down the familiar gravel path into the heart of the temple.

When he reached the floor of the excavations, he gazed about him, remembering the laughter he had experienced here at Gobekli, joking with the archaeologists. He had first met Christine here, too: the woman he now loved. But this was also where Breitner had died: and this was where the sacrificial terrors had begun. Ten thousand years ago.

The moon was rising, white and aloof. And there were the stones. Silent and imperious in the night. Rob walked between the megaliths. He leaned and touched the carvings: gently, almost warily, lost in a kind of awe, a reluctant but distinct respect. For these great and ancient stones, for this mysterious temple in Eden.

51

Rob and Christine wanted a small and simple wedding: on that they were agreed. The only question was where to have it. But when Christine heard that she had inherited Isobel's house in the Princes Islands, the dilemma was solved. 'And it's a way of honouring her memory: she'd approve, I know it.'

Isobel's beautiful garden was the obvious place. So they co-opted a beardy and bibulous Greek Orthodox priest, and hired some singers who were happy to be paid in beer, and even found a trio of very excellent bouzouki players. Close family and best friends were invited. Steve came over from London, with a smattering of Rob's colleagues; Sally brought a big present; Rob's mother was smiling and proud in her finest hat. And Kiribali attended in an extremely white suit.

The ceremony was sunlit and simple. Lizzie was a barefoot bridesmaid in her best summer dress. The priest stood on the terrace and intoned the magic spell. The sunshine filtered through the pines and the tamarisks, and the Bosphorus ferry hooted as it crossed the deep blue waters to Asia. And the singers sang and Rob kissed Christine and then it was done: they were married. Rob was wived, again.

There was a party afterwards. They all had lots of champagne in the garden, and Ezekiel chased a golden butterfly into the rosebushes.

Steve chatted with Christine, Christine's mum chatted with the priest, and everyone danced very badly to the bouzouki players. Kiribali quoted poetry and flirted with all the women, especially the older ones.

Halfway through the afternoon, Rob found himself standing next to Forrester, in the shade of the trees at the very edge of the lawns. Rob took the chance to thank the detective, at last: for turning a blind eye.

Forrester blushed, his champagne glass poised at his lips. 'How did you guess?'

'You're an astute guy, Mark. You let us just walk off with the Black Book. That's why you were arguing with Dooley, in Dublin. No?'

'Sorry?'

'You *knew* where we were going. You wanted to cut us some slack, and you persuaded Dooley to let us keep the box.'

Forrester sighed. 'I suppose I did. And yes I knew where you were heading. But I couldn't blame you, Rob. I'd have done the same, if . . . if a child of mine had been in danger. Taking the official route might have been disastrously slow.'

'Yet you rang Kiribali just in time. So I really mean it. Thanks for . . . keeping an eye on us.' Now Rob was struggling for words. A fleeting and terrible image of Cloncurry, white teeth bared, passed through his mind. 'I just dread to think,' he added, 'what would have happened if you hadn't got involved.'

Forrester knocked back some of his champagne, and nodded. 'How is she?'

'Lizzie? She's amazing. She seems to have, basically, forgotten it all. A little frightened of the dark. Think that was the hood.'

'But no other traumas?'

'No . . .' Rob shrugged. 'I don't think so.'

'The charm of being five years old,' said Forrester. 'Kids can bounce back. If they survive.'

The conversation dwindled. Rob looked at the dance party at the far end of Isobel's lawns. Kiribali was leaping up and down, clapping; doing a sort of impromptu Cossack dance.

Forrester nodded in Kiribali's direction. 'He's the man you should be thanking.'

'You mean the shooting?'

'I heard all about it. Incredible.'

'Apparently he was an Olympic marksman or something. Expert shot.'

'But it was crucial, yes?'

'Yes,' Rob agreed. 'Kiribali could see how far away Cloncurry was, and they couldn't reach us in time, because of the floods. So he took out his hunting rifle . . .'

The music was boisterous. The bouzouki players were really going for it. Rob drained the last of his champagne.

The two men walked back towards the wedding party. As they did, Lizzie came running over, laughing and singing. Rob leaned down and tenderly stroked his daughter's shining hair; the little girl giggled and reached for her father's hand.

Gazing at the father and the daughter, strolling hand in hand, smiling and alive, Forrester felt a stab of sharp emotion: the usual grief and regret. But his sense of loss was touched by something else, something much more surprising: the faint and fleeting shadow of happiness.

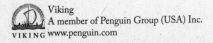

1

Simon Quinn was listening to a young man describe how he'd sliced off his own thumb.

'And that,' said the man, 'was the beginning of the end. I mean, cutting off your thumb, with a knife, that's not nothing, is it? That's serious shit. Cutting your own thumb off. Fucked my bowling.'

The urge to laugh was almost irrepressible; Simon repressed it. The worst thing you could do at a Narcotics Anonymous meeting was laugh at someone's terrible story. Just not done. People came here to share, to fess up, to achieve some catharsis by submitting their darkest fears and shames: and thereby to heal.

The young man finished his story: 'So that's when it, like, kicked in. I realized I had to do something, about the drugs and the pop. Thankyou.'

The room was silent for a moment. A middle-aged woman said a breathy *thankyou Jonny*, and everyone else murmured: *thankyou Jonny*.

They were nearly done. Six people had shared; pamphlets and keyrings had been distributed. This was a new group for Simon, and he liked it. Usually he went to evening NA meetings nearer his flat and his wife and son in Finchley Road, but today he'd had to come into Hampstead for business and *en route* he'd decided to catch a new meeting, try somewhere fresh; he was bored of the boozers at his usual meets, with their stories of guzzling lighter fuel. And so he'd rung the NA hotline and found this meeting he'd never been to before, and it turned out it was a regular lunchtime job – with interesting people who had good stories.

The pause was prolonged. Perhaps he should share his own story now? Give a little change?

He decided to tell the very first story. The big one.

'Hello, my name's Simon and I'm an addict.'

'Hello Simon . . .'

'Hi Simon.'

He leaned forward – and began:

'I was a drunk . . . for at least ten years. And I wasn't just an alcoholic I was . . . a polydrug abuser, as they say. I did absolutely everything. But I don't want to talk about that. I want to . . . explain how it started.'

The leader of the group, a fifty-something man with soft blue eyes, nodded gently.

'Whatever you want. Please go on.'

'Thankyou. Well. OK. I . . . grew up not far from here, in Belsize Park. My parents were pretty affluent – my father's an architect, my mother was a lecturer. My background is Irish but . . . I went to private school in Sussex. Hence the stupidly middle class English accent.'

The leader offered a polite smile. Listening attentively.

'And . . . I had an older brother. We were rather a happy family . . . At first . . . Then At eighteen I went off to university and while I was there I got this *frantic* phone call from my mother. She said, *your brother Tim has just lost it.* I asked her what she meant and she said, *he's just lost it.* And it was true. He'd suddenly come home from university – and he'd started talking absolutely mad stuff, talking equations and scientific formulas . . . and the maddest thing of all is that he was doing it in *German.*'

He gazed around the faces, gathered in this basement room. Then continued:

'So I shot home and it turned out my mother was right. Tim had gone mad. Genuinely cracked. He was doing a lot of skunk with his chums at Uni – maybe that was a catalyst – but I think he was schizophrenic anyway. Because that's when schizophrenia usually kicks in, between the age of eighteen and twenty-five. I didn't know that then of course.'

The middle-aged woman was sipping from a plastic cup of tea.

'Tim was a science student. Seriously bright – much brighter than me. I can barely say *bonjour* but he could speak four languages. As I say, he was doing a physics Phd, at Oxford, but he'd come home suddenly . . . without warning – and he was ranting, quoting scientific formulas in German. Doing it all night, walking up and down the landing. *Das Helium und das Hydrogen* blah blah blah. All through the night.

'My parents realized my brother had a pretty serious problem – and they took him to a doctor, and they prescribed Tim the usual drugs. The wretched little pills. Antipsychotics. And they worked for a while . . . But one night when I was home for Christmas I heard this *muttering* noise and . . . and it was this voice. Again. Yes. *Das Helium und das Hydrogen.* And I lay there wondering what to do. But then I heard this terrible scream and I rushed from my bedroom and my brother was in . . .' He closed and opened his eyes. 'My brother was there in my mother's bedroom and they were alone because my father was away . . . and . . . and my brother was *attacking* her, hacking at my mother, with a machete. A big knife. A *machete.* I don't know precisely what it was. But he was chopping away at her, our mother, so I jumped him and I held him down and there was blood everywhere, just everywhere – actually sprayed up the walls. I very nearly throttled him. Almost killed my own *brother.*'

Simon drew breath.

'The police came and they took him away and . . . my mother went to hospital and they stitched her up, but she lost the use of some fingers, some nerves were severed. But that was all, really, which was incredibly lucky. She could have died – but she was alright. And then we had this *terrible* dilemma as a family – should we press charges? My father and I said Yes, but my mother said No. She loved Tim more than the rest of us. She thought he could be treated. So we agreed with her, stupidly, crazily, we *agreed*. Then Tim came home and he seemed OK for a while, on the drugs, but then one night I heard it: *Das Helium und Das Hydrogen . . .*'

Simon could feel the sweat on his forehead; he hurried on with his story.

'Tim was muttering, again, in his room. And of course *that* was *that*. We called the police – and they came straight round. Then they put Tim in an asylum. And that's where he is now. Locked and bolted and shut in his box. He's been there ever since. He'll be there the rest of his life.'

As his conclusion approached, he experienced the usual relief. 'So that's when I started drinking – to forget, you know. Then sulphates and then pretty much *everything* . . . But I finally stopped the boozing six years ago and yes I did my course of NA antibiotics, my sixty meetings in sixty days! And I've been clean ever since.

'And I now have a wife and a son and I dearly love them. Miracles do happen. They really do. Of course I still don't know why my brother did what he did and what that means but . . . I look at it this way: maybe I haven't got his genes, maybe my boy will be alright. Who knows. One day at a time. And that's my story. And thanks very much for listening. *Thankyou*.'

A murmur of *thankyous* filled the warm fuggy space, like the responses of a congregation. The ensuing silence was a coda, the hour was nearly up. Everyone stood and hugged, and said the Serenity Prayer. And then the meeting was finished, and the addicts filed out, climbing up the creaky wooden stairs, out into the graveyard of Hampstead Church.

His mobile rang. Standing at the church gates, he clicked.

'Quinn! It's me.'

The phonescreen send Withheld, but Simon recognized the voice immediately.

It was Bob Sanderson. His colleague, his source, his man: a Detective Chief Inspector – at New Scotland Yard.

Simon said a bright *Hi.* He was always pleased to hear from Bob Sanderson, because the policeman regularly fed the journalist good stories: gossip on high profile robberies, scuttlebutt on alarming homicides. In return for the information, he made sure that DCI Sanderson was seen, in the resultant articles, in a flattering light: a smart copper who was solving crimes, a rising star in the Met. It was a nice arrangement.

'Good to hear your voice, DCI. I'm a bit broke.'

'You're always broke, Quinn.'

'It's called freelancing. What do you have?'

'Something nice maybe. Strange case in Primrose Hill.'

'Yes?'

'Oh yes indeed.'

'So . . . What is it? Where?'

The detective paused, then answered:

'Big old house. Murdered old lady.'

'Right.'

'You don't sound very enthusiastic.'

'Well.' Simon shrugged, inwardly, watching a bus turn left by the Tube, heading down to Belsize Park. 'Primrose Hill? I'm thinking . . . aggravated burglary, thieves after jewels . . . Not exactly unknown.'

'Ah, well that's where you're wrong.' The policeman chuckled, with a hint of seriousness. 'This isn't any fish and chip job, Quinn.'

'OK then. What makes it *strange?*'

'It's the method. Seems she was . . . knotted.'

'Knotted?'

'Apparently so. They tell me that's the proper word.' The policeman hesitated. Then he said, '*Knotted!* Perhaps you should come and have a look.'

2

Beyond the hospice window stretched the defeated beauty of the Arizona desert: with its vanquished sands, stricken creosotes, and blistered exposures of basalt. The green arms of the saguaro cacti reached up, imploring an implacable sun.

If you had to die, David Martinez thought, this was a fitting place to die, on the very outskirts of Phoenix, in the final exurb of the city, where the great Sonoran wastes began.

Granddad was murmuring in his bed. The morphine drip was way up high. He was barely lucid half the time – but then, granddad was barely lucid most of the time.

The grandson leaned over and dabbed some sweat from his grandfather's face with a tissue. He wondered, yet again, why he had come here, all the way from London, using up his precious holidays. The answer was the same as ever.

He *loved* his grandfather. He could remember the better times: he could remember granddad as a dark-haired, stocky, and cheerful man; holding David on his shoulders in the sun. In San Diego, by the sea, when they were still a family. A small family, but a family nonetheless.

And maybe that was another reason David had made it all the way here. Mum and dad had died in the car crash fifteen years ago. For fifteen years it had been just David in London, and granddad living out his days in distant Phoenix. Now it would just be David. That sobering fact needed proper acknowledgment: it needed proper goodbyes.

Granddad's face twitched as he slept.

For an hour David sat there, reading a book. Then his grandfather woke, and coughed, and stared.

The dying patient gazed with a puzzled expression at the window, at the blue square of desert sky, as if seeing this last view for the first time. Then granddad's eyes rested – on his visitor. David felt a stab of fear: would granddad look at him and say, *Who are you?* That had happened too often this week.

'David?'

He pulled his chair closer to the bed.

'Granddad . . .'

What followed wasn't much of a conversation, but it *was* a *conversation.* They talked about how his grandfather was feeling; they touched briefly on the hospice food. *Tacos, David, too many tacos.* David mentioned that his week of holiday was nearly up and he had to fly back to London in a day or two.

The old man nodded. A hawk was making spirals in the desert sky outside, the shadow of the bird flickered momentarily across the room.

'I'm sorry . . . I wasn't there for you David, when your mom . . . and your dad . . . y'know . . . when it happened.'

'Sorry?'

'You know. The . . . crash, what happened . . . I'm so damn sorry about all of it. I was stupid.'

'No. Come on granddad. Not this again.' David shook his head.

'Listen. David . . . please.' The old man winced. 'I gotta say something.'

David nodded, listening intently to his grandfather.

'I gotta say it. I could've . . . I could've done better, could've helped you more. But you were keen to stay in England, your mom's friends took you in, and that seemed best . . . you don't know how difficult it was. Coming to America. After the war. And . . . and your grandmother dying.'

He trailed into silence.

'Granddad?'

The old man looked at the afternoon sun, now slanting into the room.

'I got a question, David.'

'Yes. Sure. Please.'

'Have you ever wondered where you come from? Who you really are?'

David was used to his granddad asking him questions. That was part of their relationship, how they rubbed along: the older man asking the grandson about younger things. But this was a very different question – unexpected – yet also very acute. This wasn't any old question. This was *The Question.*

Who was he really? Where did he really come from?

David had always ascribed his sense of rootlessness to his chaotic upbringing, and his unusual background. Granddad was Spanish but moved to San Diego in 1946 with his wife. She had died giving birth to David's father; his father then met his mother, a nurse from England, working at Edwards Air Force Base in California.

So, for the first few years of David's life there had *maybe* been a certain sense of who he was – an American of Anglo-Hispanic parentage, a Californian – but the Latino surname and the dark Spanish looks still marked them out, as a family, as not *quite* your normal one hundred per cent Americans. After that they'd moved to Britain, and then to Germany and then Japan, and then back to Britain – with his father's career in the US Air Force.

By the end of this world tour, by the time he was ten or twelve, David hadn't felt American, British, Spanish, Californian – or anything much. And then his mum and dad had died in the crash – and the sense of being cut off, of being alone and anonymous and floating, had only worsened. *Alone in the world.*

Granddad repeated the query. 'So . . . David? Do you? Do you ever think about it? Where you come from?'

David lied and shrugged and said, *No, not really.* He didn't feel like getting in to all that, not right now.

But if not now, then when?

'OK. OK,' the old man stammered. 'OK, David. OK. And the new job? Job? You like that? What are you doing, I forget . . .'

Was granddad losing it again? David frowned, and said:

'Media lawyer. I'm a lawyer. It's OK.'

'Only OK?'

'Nah . . . I hate it.' David sighed at his own candour. 'I thought . . . at least reckoned it might be a bit glamorous. You know . . . pop stars and parties. But I just sit in a dismal office and call other lawyers. It's crap. And my boss is a tosser.'

'Ah . . . Ah . . . Ach . . .' It was a wrenching, old man's cough. Then granddad lay back and stared at the ceiling. 'Didn't you get a good college . . . college degree? Some kinda science, no?'

'Well . . . I did biochemistry, Granddad. In England. Not a lot of money in that. So I turned to law.'

Another hiatus. The light was bright in the room. At last his grandfather said:

'David. You need to know something.'

'What?'

'I lied.'

The silence was enveloping. David could hear a gurney rattling down a corridor.

'You *lied?* What does that mean?'

He scrutinized his grandfather's face. Was this the dementia, reasserting itself? He couldn't be sure, but the old man's face looked alert – as he elaborated.

'Fact I'm lying now son . . . I just . . . just can't . . . get past it, David. Too late to change. *A los cinco de la tarde*. I'm sorry. *Desolada*.'

This was perplexing. David watched the old man talk.

'OK I'm tired, David. I . . . I . . . I . . . Now I need to do this. Please look in there . . . Least I can do this. Please.'

'Sorry?'

'In the bag at the end . . . of my bed. KMart. Look see. Please!'

David got up smartly, and went to the assorted bags and luggage stored in the corner of the room, beyond the bed. Conspicuous in the rather forlorn pile was a scarlet KMart bag. He picked it up, and scoped inside: there was something papery and folded at the bottom. Maybe a map?

Maps had been one of David's passions as a child, maps and atlases. As he unfolded this one, in the desert light from the window, he realized he was holding a rather beautiful example.

It was distinctly old-fashioned road map, with dignified shading and elegant colouration. Soft grey undulations showed mountains and foothills, lakes and rivers were a poetic blue, green polygons indicated marshland besides the Atlantic. It was map of southern France and northern Spain.

He sat down and scrutinized the map more closely. The sheet had been marked very neatly with a blue pen: little blue asterisks dotted those grey ripples of mountains, between France and Spain. Another, singular blue star marked the top right corner of the map. Near Lyon.

He looked at his grandfather, questioningly.

'Bilbao,' said the old man, visibly tiring now. 'It's Bilbao . . . You need to go there.'

'What?'

'Fly to Bilbao, David. Go to Lesaka. And find Jose Garovillo.'

'Sorry?'

The old man made a final effort; his eyes were blurring over.

'. . . *Show him the map*. Then ask him about churches. Marked on the map. Churches.'

'Who's this guy? Why can't you just tell me?'

'It's been too long . . . too much guilt, I cannot, can't admit . . .' The old man's words were frail, and fading. 'And anyway . . . Even if I told you, you wouldn't believe me. No one would believe. Just the mad old man. You'd say I was mad, the crazy old man. So you need to find out for yourself, David. But be careful . . . Be careful . . .'

'Granddad?'

His grandfather turned away, staring at the ceiling. And then, with a horrible sense of inevitability, the old man's eyelids fluttered shut. Granddad had fallen back into his fitful and opiated sleep.

The morphine pump ticked over.

For a long while, David sat there, watching his grandfather breathe in and breathe out, quite unconscious. Then David got up and closed the blinds; the desert sun was almost gone anyway.

He looked down at the map sitting on the hospice chair; he had no idea what it signified: what connection his granddad had with 'Bilbao' or with 'churches'. Probably it was all some ragged dream, some youthful memory returning, between the lucidity and the dementia. Maybe it was nothing at all.

Yes. That was surely it. These were just the ramblings of a dying old man, the brain yielding to the flood of illogic as the final dissolution approached. Sadly, but truly, he was crazy.

David picked up the map and slid it into his pocket, then he leaned and touched his grandfather's hand, but the old man did not respond.

With a sigh, he walked out into the hot Phoenix summer night, and climbed into his rented Toyota, and he drove the urban freeway to his motel, where he watched soccer on a grainy Mexican satellite station with a lonely sixpack and a pizza.

His grandfather died early the following morning. A nurse rang David at the motel. He immediately called London and told his friends – he needed to hear some friendly voices. Then he called his office and extended his 'holiday' by a few days, on the grounds of bereavement.

Even then his boss in London sounded a little sniffy, as it was 'only'

David's grandfather. 'We are very busy David, so this is exceptionally tiresome. Do be quick.'

The service was in a soulless crematorium, in another exurb of Phoenix. Tempe. And David was the only real mourner in the building. Two nurses from the hospice showed up, and that was it. No-one else was invited. David already knew he had no other family in America – or anywhere for that matter – but having his relative loneliness underscored, like this, felt notably harsh – indeed cruel. But he had no choice in the matter. So David and the two nurses sat there, together and alone, and exposed.

The ceremony was equally austere: at his grandfather's request there were no readings, there was nothing – except for a CD of discordant and exotic guitar music, presumably chosen by his grandfather.

When the song was done, the coffin trundled abruptly into the flames. David felt the briskness like a punch. It was like the old man had been quick to get off stage, eager to flee this life – or keen to be relieved of some burden.

That afternoon David drove deep into the desert, seeking the most remote location, as if he could lose his sadness in the wasteland. Under an ominously stormy sky, he scattered the ashes between the prickly pears and the crucifixion thorns. He stood for a minute and watched the ashes disperse, then walked to his car. As he returned to the city, the first fat raindrops smacked the windscreen; by the time he reached his motel a real desert storm had kicked up – jagged arcs of lightning volting between the black and evil clouds.

His flight was looming. He began to pack. And then the motel phone trilled. His ex girlfriend maybe?

She'd been calling on and off the last couple of days: trying to elevate David's mood. Being a good friend.

David reached for the phone and answered.

'Uh-huh?'

It wasn't his ex. It was a breezy American accent.

'David Martinez? *Frank Antonescu . . .*'

'Uh . . . hello.'

'I'm your grandfather's lawyer! First of all, can I say – I'm so sorry to hear of your bereavement.'

'Thankyou. Uhm. Sorry. Uh . . . Granddad had a *lawyer*?' The voice confirmed: granddad had a lawyer. David shook his head in mild surprise. Through the motel room window he could see the desert rain pummelling the surface of the motel swimming pool.

'OK . . . Go on. Please.'

'Thankyou. There's something you oughta know. I'm handling your grandfather's estate.'

David laughed – out loud. His granddad had lived in a heavily mortgaged old bungalow in a tired suburb of Phoenix; he drove a twenty-year-old Chevy, and he had no serious possessions. *Estate?* Yeah, right.

But then David's laughter congealed, and he felt a pang of apprehension. Was *this* the reason for his grandfather's weird shame: was the old man bequeathing some insuperable *debt*?

'Mister Martinez. The estate comprises two million dollars, or thereabouts. In cash. In a Phoenix Bank savings account.' David swayed in the high wind of this revelation; he asked the lawyer to repeat the sum. The lawyer said it again, and now David experienced The Anger.

All this time! All this time his grandfather had been loaded, minted, a fucking *millionaire?* All the time, he, David, the orphaned grandson, had been struggling, fighting, working his way through University, just keeping a head above water – and all along the Beloved Grandfather had been sitting on *two million dollars?*

David asked the lawyer: how long had his grandfather possessed this money.

'Ever since he hired me. Twenty years minimum.'

'So . . . why the hell did he live in that crappy little house? With that car? Don't get it.'

'Damn straight,' said the lawyer. 'Trust me, Mister Martinez, I would tell him to use it, spend it on himself, or give it you of course. Never would. At least he got a good rate of interest.' A sad chuckle. 'If you ever do find out where the money came from, please let me know. Always puzzled me.'

'So what do I do now?'

'Come by the office tomorrow. Sign a few documents. The money is yours.'

'Just like that?'

'Just like that.' A pause. 'However . . . Mister Martinez. You should know there is one codicil, one clause to the will.'

'And that is?'

'It says –' The lawyer sighed. 'Well . . . it's a little eccentric. It asks that first you have to utilize some of the cash to . . . do something. You have to go to the Basque Country. And find a man called Jose Garovillo in a town called Lesaka. I think that's in Spain. The Basque Country I mean.' The lawyer hesitated. 'So . . . I guess the best way to do it is this: when you reach Spain you just let me know and I'll wire the cash into your account. After that it's all yours.'

'But why does he – did he – want me to find this guy?'

'Search me. But that's the stipulation.'

David watched the rain through the window, as it turned to drizzle.

'OK . . . I'll drive by tomorrow morning.'

'Good. See you at nine. And once again, my sympathies on your loss.'

David dropped the phone and checked the clock: working out time differences. It was too late for him to call England and tell anyone the bizarre and amazing news; it was too late for him to ring his boss and tell him to go choke on his stupid job.

Instead he went to the little table and picked up the map. He unfolded the soft, sadly faded paper and scrutinized the tiny blue asterisks. The stars had been firmly and neatly handwritten next to placenames. Striking placenames. *Arizkun. Elizondo. Zugarramurdi.* Why were these places marked out? What did this have to do with churches? Why did his grandfather even own this map?

And how come his impoverished grandfather had *two million dollars that he never touched?*

He needed to look for flights to Bilbao.